Praise for Peter Robinson

'It's neither the setting nor even the characters that makes Robinson's work so satisfying, but the plotting of Swiss-watch precision'
Independent

'[Peter Robinson deserves a place] near, perhaps even at the top of, the British crime writers' league'
The Times

'Classic Robinson: labyrinthine plot merged with deft characterisation'
Observer

'Gut-wrenching plotting, alongside heart-wrenching portraits of the characters who populate his world, not to mention the top-notch police procedure'
Jeffery Deaver

'Robinson has a way of undercutting the genre's familiarity. With a deceptively unspectacular language he sets about the process of unsettling the reader' *Independent*

'Peter Robinson is good at producing ingenious mysteries, and this one does not disappoint'
Daily Telegraph on BAD BOY

'Most admirers of Robinson will find themselves utterly involved in this haunting, textured mystery . . . If Robinson is to turn out one-off novels as assured as this perhaps we wouldn't mind too much if Alan Banks was to retire and take up beekeeping in Sussex'
Barry Forshaw, *Daily Express* on BEFORE THE POISON

PETER ROBINSON

No Cure for Love

HODDER

First published in Canada in 1995 by Penguin Canada

First published in Great Britain in 2015 by Hodder & Stoughton
An Hachette UK company

This paperback edition published 2016
1

A CIP catalogue record for this title is available from the British Library

A format paperback ISBN 978 1 473 62682 9
B format paperback ISBN 978 1 473 61097 2
Ebook ISBN 978 1 473 61093 4

Typeset in Plantin Light by Hewer Text UK Ltd, Edinburgh

Printed and bound by CPI Group (UK) Ltd, Croydon, CR0 4YY

Hodder & Stoughton policy is to use papers that are natural, renewable
and recyclable products and made from wood grown in sustainable
forests. The logging and manufacturing processes are expected to
conform to the environmental regulations of the country of origin.

Hodder & Stoughton Ltd
Carmelite House
50 Victoria Embankment
London EC4Y 0DZ

www.hodder.co.uk

For Sheila

Foreword

by Michael Connelly

Authenticity. I think it is the most important aspect of both writing and reading. As a writer, you want your characters, your places, your dialogue, your message to crackle with authenticity. As a reader you want the story in front of you to be so real that you are nodding your head in agreement as you read without even realizing it. You are submerged in a world that might be wholly alien to you but it nevertheless holds true to you. You think this is how it is. This is true because you are there.

So it is no surprise then that the most important aspect of writing is one of the most difficult. Getting it right. And this may be sacrilege to say, but research is not the answer. Fifty words of authentic description can't do what one word of telling detail does. One line of dialogue is completely undone if it suffers from what I call the writer-behind-the-words syndrome, the malady that occurs while reading when you see the writer at work behind the prose.

So it is no wonder that writers tend to stay in their comfort zones. That is, the places they know, the accents they're used to, the slang they need no interpreter for, the world they have written about before. I'll raise my hand right here and admit I am one of them. I can't say that I have strayed too far from the groove that I have been in for a long time. I talk about it, yes. Talk about the big challenge almost every time it is time to start a new book. And then . . . you get where I'm going.

The reason I bring all of this up is that the 'Big Challenge' is out there for all of us but only a few of us meet it. In this book, you witness it happen. Peter Robinson is an

Englishman by birth and a Canadian by home, and this is a terrific Los Angeles novel by any measure. Before reading it, I remember asking myself *Why did he do it?* After I finished reading it the question was *How did he do it?*

I first read this novel almost twenty years ago. I was impressed with it then but I am even more impressed with it now after a second reading. Because now I know better what a feat this was to pull off. Back then I said to myself this guy Robinson really did his research. Now I know that research is the easiest part. It takes an author with amazing empathy, a snare-trap ear for dialogue and a clear eye for the telling detail to make something like this work. And *No Cure for Love* works.

But on top of that – getting away from who wrote it and from where – it is that rare book that entertains, enthralls and also teaches. Somehow this story from back then has something to say about right now. In a world that increasingly is fascinated with fame and all media spirals into celebrity-centricity, it is always good to step back and take a look at the dark side of all of that. From that angle this novel transcends its time and place and becomes important. How does it do that? You guessed it. Authenticity.

Michael Connelly
Los Angeles, 2015

And most of all would I flee from the cruel madness of love,
The honey of poison-flowers and all the measureless ill.

– Tennyson, *Maud, IV, x.*

Part One

Part One

I

My Darling Little Star,

Thank God I have found You again. When I lost you I entered the darkness. Lost in the dark silent Room with only the Hum of my Machines and my Memories and Images of you.

I told myself you could not have known what I feel for you. Love strikes me Dumb. I see all that now. Thank you for giving me another chance, thank you for seeking me out. This time there will be no mistaking my Love. This time I will prove myself to you again and again until you feel the Power of my Love and come to me. I won't let you go this time.

*You think you do not know who I am, but you do. **They** took you away and Seduced you and stole you from me, just as the others did before. **They** have tried to blot out your Memory of me. And I failed you, Sally. Yes, I did. But everything is clear now. The months I spent Lost and Wandering in the dark Room have made everything bright as Day, the Visions I bore witness to have made my Purpose clear, they have revealed our Destiny. Now I watch you on the Screen and I know you are speaking only to me.*

As I labor to prove myself to you, you will remember me and you will come to me. Then, my love, will we lie together and I will bite your Nipples till the Blood and Milk flow down my chin. We will hack and eat away the Corrupting Flesh, the Rank Pollution of Tissue and Sinew, and go in Moonlight shedding our Skin and spilling our Blood on the Sand through the

*Mirrors of the Sea where all is Peace and Silence and no one
can harm us or tear us apart ever again Forever and Forever.*

*Be Strong, my Love. I have much to Plan and Execute before
we can be together as Fate intends. My mind Boils and Seethes
with the Burden, the Weight and the Glory of it. All for you. Let
me prove I am more than equal to the Task.*

With all the love in my bursting heart,

M.

Sarah Broughton's hand shook as she let the letter drop on the glass-topped table. She wiped her palm on the side of her jeans.

It was the third letter in two weeks, and by far the most detailed. The others had merely hinted that she should begin to prepare herself for a special event. This was also the first one to contain anything even remotely sexual.

Sarah walked over to the sliding glass doors. Beyond the deck and the narrow strip of lawn, the rocky promontory on which her house stood dropped twenty feet. Below, fine white sand sloped down to the Pacific Ocean, darkening where the breakers pounded the shoreline not more than fifty yards out.

Sarah stood and watched a wave swell until its rounded peak turned translucent green then burst into a crest of foam that rushed horizontally along its length until everything churned into a roiling white mass. Sometimes she thought she could stand and watch the waves for ever. The roar was deafening, and through the open door she could smell salt and seaweed and something dead, that odour of primordial decay that always seemed to linger around the edges of the sea.

Though the temperature was in the mid-sixties, Sarah shivered and hugged herself. Her nerves weren't that good to begin with, hadn't been for over a year, and now she felt defiled, violated and scared. But even as she trembled, she found herself probing the feeling, storing it for later use. If she ever had to play a victim again, this memory could be useful.

She walked back to the table, picked up the letter and made to rip it up like the others, but she stopped herself in time. No. She would show this one to Stuart. No more procrastination.

It was close to eleven in the morning, and she was due to have lunch with him in a couple of hours. She would show him the letter then. Stuart would know what to do.

She looked at the envelope again. It was postmarked Pasadena, dated 14 December, which was Friday, four days ago, and addressed to Sarah Broughton at the beach house address on the Coast Highway.

So how had 'M,' whoever he was, found out her address and phone number? Like most people in the movie and TV business, Sarah guarded her privacy well. Or thought she did.

He could have found out from the article in *TV Guide* that mentioned she lived in Malibu. Which wasn't quite true. Strictly speaking, the house was in Pacific Palisades, close to the Los Angeles city limits, but that probably didn't sound quite as glamorous to Josephine Q. Public, Ottumwa, Iowa, who liked to read about actors and actresses in *TV Guide*.

All in all, Sarah supposed, the secrecy was probably something of an illusion. When it came down to it, no address was that hard to come by in Hollywood. Everything was for sale.

Stop worrying, she told herself, folding the letter and putting it back in its envelope. There are millions of perverts out there drooling over actors and rock stars, and this is probably just one of them. A harmless one, more likely than not.

She imagined some overweight, pimply nerd with Coke-bottle glasses, dandruff and halitosis masturbating in a candlelit room with nude pictures of her plastered all over the walls. Somehow, it wasn't a comforting image.

Sarah slipped the letter in her purse and decided to take a walk on the beach. She slid open the door, walked down the wooden steps from the deck to lawn, then down the stairs carved in the rock. At the bottom stood a gate made of six-foot-high metal railings, painted black, all with very sharp points. It didn't offer much security, though, Sarah realized. Anybody who really wanted to could climb up the rocks beside it easily enough.

On the beach, she slipped off her sandals and wiggled her toes in the sand. Though the sun was only a white ball through the haze, its brightness made Sarah squint and reach in her purse for her sunglasses.

There was hardly anyone around. For Sarah, the mid-sixties was warm enough for sunbathing, but it was chilly to the natives. Also, while this area of the beach wasn't exactly private property, access was difficult because of the solid wall of houses, flanked on both sides by low-rise office buildings.

Out towards the horizon, water and sky merged in a white glare. A light ocean breeze ruffled Sarah's cap of short blonde hair. It would soon dispel the sea-mist. She walked with her hands in her pockets, eyes scanning the beach for interesting shells and pebbles.

To the north, the mountains were almost lost in the haze, and to the south she could just about make out the Santa Monica Pier with its restaurants and amusement palaces. Funnily enough, it reminded Sarah of childhood holidays in Blackpool, staying at Mrs Fairclough's boarding-house. Of course, it was rarely over sixty degrees in Blackpool – more often than not it was about fifty and raining – but her mum and dad would always splurge on one good variety show at the pier theatre, and it was there that her love of show business had begun. And just look at her now. Top of the world, Ma. Well, getting there, anyway. Such a long journey, such a long, long way from Blackpool to Hollywood.

As usual, thinking of her mum and dad brought her other problem to mind: the family she had put off dealing with for too long. She hadn't been home in two years now. Her mother was dead, had been since long before the rift, but there were still Paula, her dad and the kids. Well, she would be facing them at Christmas.

And now, on top of everything else, the letters.

As she walked along the edge of the beach, Sarah felt uneasy. Not for the first time these past couple of weeks did she keep looking over her shoulder. And whenever she did notice anyone walking towards her, she felt herself tense, get ready to run.

There was something else as well. Earlier that morning, when she was coming back from her run, she had seen something flash in the sun, way up on the crest of the hills above the Coast Highway. Of course, there were a lot of houses up there, and there could be any number of explanations – windows opening, even car windshields glinting in the light – but she had felt as if someone were looking down on her through binoculars.

Now she thought she saw something flash again, further up the beach this time. But she was being silly. It could be someone's glasses, a ring, anything at all. Maybe just a birdwatcher.

She told herself not to be so paranoid, but she couldn't shake the feeling. There was something else that bothered her, too. This time, in the letter, he had called her Sally.

2

She should have left for work hours ago, but he hadn't seen her go. Usually a cab or that grey-haired man in the Cadillac picked her up to take her to the studio around eight-thirty. Not today. She had to be still in the house. He hadn't seen her leave, and he knew he couldn't have missed her; he had been in the area for four hours, since before dawn, watching her house just like he had every day for the past two weeks, first up in the hills, now down on the beach.

As usual that Tuesday morning, he had found his safe, secluded spot in the hills before dawn and watched her run. His powerful Zeiss binoculars silhouetted her moving image against the slowly brightening sea. Every morning she ran at least a mile up the beach and back as the sun came up. She was always alone, the only one out at that time.

As he had lain high above her, though he could sense the city throbbing and buzzing behind him, hardly a soul stirred nearby. He could see the lights of ships twinkling out at sea, the head-lights of cars on the Coast Highway, already pale in the light of the rising sun as they arced around the long curve between Topanga and Santa Monica.

She timed herself against the sunrise, as if following and emulating its natural rhythms, in tune with it, like the dawn goddess. Or so it seemed to him. Every day now the sun rose a little later, but it was always just hidden behind the eastern hills when she started out and balanced on top of them like a huge fireball when she got back.

He watched the tide, too, how it ebbed and flowed. She always ran right along the water line. He had seen the spent waves foam and sparkle around her feet as if she were the very rebirth of Venus.

Suddenly, here she came again. Walking out of the gate onto the beach. Not to run this time, but just walking, looking contemplative. His heart expanded so much he thought it would explode in his chest. She was thinking about him. He knew it. She must have received his latest letter and read it. Now she was walking alone on the beach thinking about him.

He lay on a rock about a quarter of a mile further west, on the Topanga State Beach. It was eleven in the morning now and there were a few people around, some brave surfers and couples walking hand in hand. They didn't bother him, though. He knew he just looked like someone lying on a rock watching the seabirds. Plenty of other people did that. It didn't look strange at all.

In fact, living here, you would have to think very hard to find anything that really did seem weird, he thought. His kind of city. The place where he had finally become what he had been from the start but had only vaguely sensed before; where he had recognized himself at last; the place where he had both lost and found his soulmate, his life's companion.

He pulled her into focus through the lenses. The binoculars were so strong that he could fill them with her head and shoulders. She wasn't silhouetted now, and he could see her downcast eyes, see her chewing softly on her lower lip, that slightly crooked tooth overlapping at the front, the only blemish on a perfect face. Well, that could easily be altered.

He could almost hear her thoughts, how she was racking her brains to remember who he was, who it was loved her so much, so she could come to him. He felt her calling out to him. But no, not yet. There was still much to do before they could truly be together. For a moment, he felt guilty for torturing her so, but it passed. After all, wasn't anticipation one of the sweetest parts of conquest? And he had yet to conquer her.

While he didn't know what would happen after the consum-
mation – when he thought of that, everything turned red – he
knew that he would continue to feel this exquisite blending of
aching and longing, of joy and desolation, while he courted her
from a distance. And he knew that she could feel it too.

There was also something special, something subtly erotic
about watching her through the binoculars. To the naked eye, she
was nothing but a dot in the distance, but when he raised the
lenses, there she was, right in front of him, in his face, her thoughts
clear for him to read in her almost-perfect features. And when she
made those little unconscious gestures, the things he loved her for
so much, like scratching the side of her nose with her pinky, and
he knew he was the only one in the world watching her, he felt
such pride and power in his possession that it was all he could do
to stop himself from jumping up and running into her arms.

But no. Not yet. For now, he must give himself up to the alter-
nate waves of ecstasy and terror that swept through him, made
him dizzy and wild, that whispered to him what he must do to
win her love. He must worship her from a distance. It was all too
new; he wasn't ready yet, and he didn't think she was either. Oh,
he loved her; Lord knew how much he loved her. But he had to
make her realize that she loved him, had to make her see that he
was the one. Soon, it would be soon . . .

As he lay there on his stomach watching her poke at small
shells and pebbles with her bare toes, her little nails painted pink,
his hands started to shake and he felt himself getting hard against
the rock.

3

They ate lunch at one of those Hollywood restaurants where six red-coated valets drag you out of your car and drive off with it if you so much as slow down out front. The first time it had happened, Sarah had seriously thought they were being carjacked, having read about such things in the papers, but Stuart had just laughed. He often laughed at her English ways. Stuart himself was Southern Californian all the way through.

Sarah recognized a couple of bit-part actors she had worked with on the series and said hello as she passed by. Most of the diners, however, were tanned, female shoppers taking a break from Rodeo Drive, the ultra-chic Melrose or La Brea.

Wherever she ate, Sarah tried to guess whether the waiters were aspiring actors or screenwriters. This one, who introduced himself as Mark, was tall, with dark good looks, a muscled body and sleek black hair tied in a ponytail. Definitely an aspiring actor. Rarely had Sarah known writers to look as good as that.

Stuart looked at the tables crammed close together in the small patio area. 'Fuck,' he complained, 'these things must multiply overnight. And I thought this place was supposed to be so crowded nobody comes here any more.'

Sarah raised her eyebrows.

'Yogi Berra,' Stuart explained.

'What?'

'Yogi Berra. You know, the baseball guy. Known for his redundancies and *non sequiturs*.'

Sarah shook her head. Mark scraped her chair back over the terracotta and beckoned her to sit. Sunlight filtered through the trellises, where a parkful of greenery climbed and entwined, occasionally offering a white or red blossom to the close observer. Mark explained the specials, then handed them menus, handwritten on laminated fuchsia cards about four feet by two.

'"It ain't over till it's over,"' Stuart tried. '"It's *déjà vu* all over again."'

'Oh, yes. I've heard that before.' Sarah thought she should mollify him a little.

Stuart beamed. 'See. Yogi Berra. He said that.'

Sarah laughed. Stuart Kleigman was about fifty years old and twenty pounds overweight, tanned, wore black-rimmed glasses and had sparse silver-grey hair swept back to reveal a pronounced widow's peak.

Dressed very conservatively for Hollywood, in an expensive lightweight grey suit and cheap maroon-and-ivory striped tie, he always stood out among the Hollywood crowd, with their silk shirts buttoned up to the top, their T-shirts, jeans and running shoes. Stuart's shoes were handmade in Italy, and the black leather was so highly polished that you could see your face in them. He reminded Sarah of a bank manager from one of those fifties American comedies that ran day and night in syndication: *I Love Lucy* or *The Beverly Hillbillies*.

Stuart was head of casting at the studio, but he had also become her friend, and he meant more to her than anyone else in the country; he had believed in her, given her a chance at fame and fortune, without demanding anything in return. But it was more than that; he had given her back her self-respect and her confidence. Well, some of it, anyway.

She turned back to the menu. California cuisine. It never failed to amaze her. Back in Yorkshire, where she had been born and raised, the standard fare was fish and chips – fries, as they were called here – with a side order of mushy peas and maybe, for the truly adventurous, a dollop of curry sauce on the chips. A salad usually consisted of one limp, translucent lettuce leaf with a thin slice of greenish yellow tomato squatting on top of it, and there was generally a bottle of salad cream nearby, too, if you really wanted it.

Now, though, here she was in Hollywood trying to decide between a Swiss chard and leek frittata or Belgian endive and dandelion greens with Cabernet vinaigrette. Salad dressings alone must be a growth industry in California, she thought. If only her mother could see her now. Or her father. She could just picture him scanning the menu with a scowl on his face and finally commenting, 'There's nowt edible here,' most likely within the hearing of the chef.

Finally, she decided on the endive and dandelion with a glass of Evian water. Stuart went for rosemary chicken strips and fettucini with sun-dried tomato and garlic cream, but then he always did overeat. That was why he was twenty pounds overweight.

'Going to Jack's birthday party tonight?' Stuart asked after Mark had disappeared with their order.

Sarah sighed. 'Wouldn't miss it for the world.'

'That's my girl. I'll pick you up at eight. So where's this letter you were telling me about on the way here?'

Sarah opened her purse, took out the letter and handed it to him. 'It's probably nothing, really,' she said. 'I just . . .'

Stuart pushed his glasses up on the bridge of his nose and frowned as he read.

'Hmm,' he said, putting it back in the envelope. 'I've seen worse. I'd say the real mystery is why you haven't had anything like this before now.'

'What do you mean?'

Stuart waved the envelope. 'This kind of thing. It's all over the place in this business. Occupational hazard. Everybody gets them. Fuck's sake, Sarah, you're a beautiful woman. You're in the public eye. Hardly surprising some fucking wacko has decided he's in love with you, excuse my French.'

'But what should I do?' Sarah asked. 'Should I go to the police?'

'I can't see that they could do very much.'

'It's the third,' Sarah admitted.

Stuart raised his eyebrows. 'Even so. I don't think it's anything to worry about. Believe me, I've seen dozens of these things, much worse than this. These guys are usually so sick all they can do is write letters. If he ever met you face to face he'd probably crap his pants if he didn't come in his shorts first.'

'Stuart, you're disgusting.'

'I know. But you still love me, don't you, sweetheart?'

'I've heard of cases where they turn violent,' Sarah said. 'Rebecca Shaeffer. Didn't she get shot by someone who wrote letters to her? And what about that man who shot Reagan to impress Jodie Foster?'

'Hey, look, kid, we're talking about serious wackos there. This guy, he's just . . . You've only got to read the letter.'

'What do you mean?'

'Well, he's even fairly literate, for a start. Most of the guys who write these things don't know how to spell or put a sentence together. What's with this "Little Star" business, anyway? Someone been listening to Little Anthony and the Imperials?'

Sarah shrugged. 'I don't know.' But even as she spoke, a faint, distant bell rang deep in the darkest part of her memory, sounding a warning.

'Sure it doesn't mean anything to you?'

'No. I don't think so.'

'And he calls you Sally, too.'

'Yes. But he could have got that from the *TV Guide* interview. Or maybe *Entertainment Tonight*.'

'I guess so. That was a great feature on *ET*, by the way. Should up your profile a few notches.'

They kept quiet as Mark delivered their food. It looked very pretty – nicely colour-coordinated – and it tasted good, too.

'I just don't want you to worry, sweetheart, that's all,' said Stuart.

'It *is* a little scary,' Sarah admitted. 'I've had fan letters before, back home, and some of them were a bit racy, maybe, but . . . I mean, he says he knows me.'

'In his dreams.'

'I think someone's been watching me through binoculars, too. I've seen them glint in the sun.'

'You don't know that for sure. Same way you can't really believe him when he says he knows you from somewhere. Sarah, these guys live in a fantasy world. They watch you on television once and think they've known you for ever. They read about you in a fan magazine, find out your favourite colour, foods and zodiac sign and they think they know your most intimate secrets.'

Sarah shrugged. 'I know. But even so . . .'

'Look, when are you going back home?'

'Thursday.'

'How's your father doing, by the way?'

Sarah stirred her food with her fork and shook her head. 'Not so well.'

'I'm sorry to hear that. But listen to my point. In a couple of days you'll be gone, miles away in England. Right?'

Sarah nodded.

'How long?'

'Nearly a fortnight.'

'A "fortnight"?'

Sarah smiled. 'Two weeks.' She was getting used to having to explain herself to Americans.

'Okay. So by the time you get back, your Romeo will have probably found someone new to pester.'

'You think so?'

'I guarantee it. Look, if you want, I can arrange with the post office to have your mail sent through me or the studio, get it vetted. A lot of people do that.'

'Maybe that's a good idea,' Sarah said.

'Consider it done.'

Mark appeared again out of nowhere and asked if their meals were all right. Given the attention they were getting, Sarah suspected he had recognized Stuart as a casting director. They told him things were fine and he faded back into the greenery. Sarah hadn't been aware of the conversations around her, but now she heard low voices, the occasional burst of laughter, drinks rattling on a tray.

Stuart spread his hands. 'You're welcome to come stay with Karen and me till you leave, if you want.'

'No. Thanks, Stuart, but I'll be okay.'

Stuart picked up the letter. 'Can I keep this? There's a guy I'd like to show it to, just to get his opinion. Like I said, it's nothing, but maybe he can put you a bit more at ease.'

'A policeman?'

'Uh-huh. He can at least have a look at the letter, reassure you there's nothing to worry about. It's his job. He deals with shit like this all the time. He's an expert.'

'Okay,' said Sarah.

Mark came back and asked them about dessert. Sarah only wanted a decaf cappuccino, but Stuart went for the pink gingered pear compote with cassis, which was duly delivered.

'Now,' he said when Mark had vanished again. 'Are you sure it's a good idea to do this Nora in this . . . what is it?'

'*A Doll's House*. Ibsen.'

'Right. Are you sure it's a good idea to do this thing on Broadway?'

'I should be so lucky. Jane Fonda played her in a movie.'

'That's right,' Stuart said. 'That's right, she did. Now I recall.' He paused, ate a spoonful of compote, then fixed her with a serious gaze and said, 'But, Sarah, sweetheart, think about it. Do you really want to end up making exercise videos and marrying a millionaire tycoon?'

'Well, I suppose there are worse things in life,' she said, laughing. But her laughter had a brittle, nervous edge.

4

'So what do you think?' Maria asked, looking at her watch.

Arvo shrugged. 'Give him fifteen, twenty minutes, then we're out of here.'

It was almost three o'clock in the afternoon. Detectives Arvo Hughes and Maria Hernandez, from the Threat Management Unit of the LAPD, had been sitting in a diner near Sunset and Vine for almost two hours waiting for Sandi Gaines's self-styled boyfriend, Chuck, to turn up.

Last week, Sandi, who worked as a waitress in the diner, had been referred to the TMU by Hollywood Division. A guy called Chuck, whom she had dated casually once or twice and then ditched, had been pestering her, phoning and making threats and racist insults. He had also walked into the diner the last two Tuesdays, just after the lunchtime rush, and acted weirdly, threatening to kill her and himself if she didn't give him another chance.

On both occasions, Sandi had been able to persuade him to leave without much trouble, but she was shaken and worried. So Arvo and Maria were here to talk to him. The detectives on the TMU usually worked alone, except on interventions like this. Arvo didn't expect any trouble, and rarely got any, but you had to be careful. The simple obsessionals – the ones you had *known* and been emotionally involved with – were by far the most dangerous kind of stalkers.

The diner was an old-style bar and grill, with a lot of brass around the bar and booths separated by dark wood panels.

The tablecloths were starched white linen, the benches plush red leather, and paintings of coastal scenes hung on the burgundy walls.

The owners had made a couple of seasonal concessions, including a fold-out Santa Claus on the wall, a few streamers on the ceiling, fluttering in the draught from the air conditioner, and red and green napkins on the tables.

A shabby Christmas tree, about three feet high, stood in the corner near the entrance to the men's room. One or two gift-wrapped packages had been placed underneath it, presents from staff members to one another, most likely. Or empty boxes. It wouldn't do to leave your Christmas presents lying around in open view in a place like this.

'So tell me about Nyreen while we're waiting,' Maria said. 'You never did tell me how you met.'

Arvo laughed. 'On a stake-out. Can you believe it?'

'Like this one?'

'No. No, this was a Hollywood job.' He looked around. 'I mean celebrity Hollywood, not like this place. This soap star, he'd been getting weird letters from a female fan for about a year. She'd send him locks of her hair, toenail clippings, you know the routine. Once she even sent him a used tampon.'

Maria wrinkled her nose.

'Anyway, she approached him a few times at public events and eventually he found her lurking around his neighbourhood, going through his trash, that sort of thing. We're not talking Beverly Hills security here, you understand. The guy wasn't *that* big. I think he lived in West LA, if I remember correctly. Anyway, when he got a temporary restraining order against her, she sent him a death threat, said she'd carry it out where all his friends could see. So what does he do? He holds this big birthday bash at The Bistro, and we're there running interference in case she turns up.'

'Did she?'

Arvo shook his head. 'Nope. While we were soaking up the Parisian ambience and stuffing ourselves with gravlax and swordfish, she was hanging herself in Orange County with the cord from her bathrobe. A neighbour found her two days later.'

Maria shook her head. Her mass of shiny black curls bounced around her shoulders. She had a dark complexion, with warm hazel eyes where humour and sadness mingled, a small, straight nose and full lips that looked as if they were shaped for long, lingering kisses.

Arvo could make out the outline of her white bra under the cotton blouse, cupping her full breasts, and though he couldn't see at the moment, he knew that her small waist swelled gently into hips that looked sensational in tight jeans. So sensational, in fact, that he thought she should be doing ads. Maybe she should audition, get an agent. Lots of cops moonlighted.

Arvo pulled himself up short. Only in LA from Detroit three years himself and already starting to think like a native. Scary.

Some of the guys said Maria was gay, but Arvo suspected that was because they had made their pitches and struck out. She was funny and smart as well as being a great-looking woman, and a lot of men felt threatened by that. Born into a large, poor immigrant family – her father was a cab-driver in San Diego – she had worked her way through school as a waitress and got a degree in psychology. Now, at the age of twenty-nine, she was a valuable member of the TMU. Nobody talked down to Maria Hernandez and got away with it.

Sandi came by and topped up their coffees. From where Arvo sat, he could see the door. He always liked to sit with his back to a wall and his eyes on the door. Sandi said she'd give him the nod when Chuck walked in. It was ten after three now, and the crowd had thinned out since lunch. Apart from one group of five celebrating someone's birthday at the table near the window, the place was empty.

Arvo looked at his watch. 'Is he likely to come this late?' he asked.

Sandi nodded. 'Says where he works they sometimes have late lunches.'

'But he didn't say *where* he worked?'

Sandi shook her head. 'Nope. Just said he worked in movies, that's all, the lying creep.'

Jesus, Arvo thought, looking at the statuesque Sandi in her micro-skirt and white silk blouse, with her model-school posture and chocolate-coloured, beauty-clinic skin, does *everyone* around here want to get in the movies?

'I just hope you catch the bastard trying something that'll land his ass in jail and out of my face, that's all,' Sandi said, turning away.

It was an unfortunate turn of phrase, Arvo thought. He looked at Maria, who raised her eyes and smiled. 'What about when you met Nyreen?' she asked. 'You didn't get to that.'

Arvo sighed. 'Ah, Nyreen. Well, she was at that party I was telling you about. She worked in public relations for the studio.' He held his hands out, palms up. 'What can I say? I fell for her right there and then. Love at first sight. She was blonde and beautiful. She seemed bright and she had a great body. She was also full of life and vitality, and she laughed a lot. Two weeks later we were married, and nine months later it was over.'

'Two weeks?'

'Well . . . yeah.'

'I didn't know that. So you really waited till you'd got to know each other first, right?'

'Okay. No need to rub it in.'

'What I don't understand is how an intelligent guy like you could fall for a bimbo like Nyreen. I'm sorry, Arvo, but I mean it.'

Arvo shook his head. 'Whatever Nyreen might be, she's not

a bimbo. But how did it happen?' He shrugged. 'Hormones, I guess. Lapse of judgement. I don't know. If we could explain things like that, I suppose life would be a hell of a lot easier.'

Maria laughed and touched him lightly on the arm. 'And maybe a lot more boring, too,' she added.

Arvo looked out past the neon Coors sign in the window, where the sun flashed on the windshields of the passing cars. The air-conditioner hummed and the atmosphere in the diner felt cool and clammy. He didn't want to think or talk about Nyreen any more. Talking about her just made his guts knot up and his chest constrict. Made him feel stupid, too.

'Anyway,' Maria went on, maybe sensing Arvo's mood shift, 'it just goes to show you, doesn't it?'

'Goes to show what?'

'You never can tell what might happen on a stake-out.'

Her eyes flashed with humour as she spoke, but she held Arvo's gaze long enough to make him a little hot under the collar. Maybe the three-month hormonal freeze was coming to an end.

Before he could respond, the door opened and a young man in his mid-twenties walked in. Good-looking, in an Iowa farm-boy sort of way, he was about six-two, slim build, with hair the colour of wheatfields in August, and he was wearing a navy blue suit that had seen better days. He also looked as if he had been drinking. His face was flushed, his eyes a little wild, and his brow was oily with sweat.

Sandi, in the middle of the floor with a tray full of mixed drinks for the birthday party, looked at Arvo and nodded vigorously. Arvo started to edge his way out of the booth.

Because they hadn't been able to pinpoint where Chuck lived or worked, the idea was to get him out of the bar with a minimum of fuss and have a good talk, point out the error of his ways. Sometimes it worked with the simple obsessionals. But the best laid plans of mice and men . . .

Chuck glanced around nervously, saw Sandi and walked right over to her. While Arvo was still stuck between the table and the bench, Chuck pulled a gun from the inside pocket of his suit and pointed it at her head. It looked like a .38 revolver.

Sandi screamed and dropped the tray. Glasses shattered and booze splashed everywhere. The mingled smells of gin and bourbon filled the air. Everything became very quiet for maybe a couple of seconds while everyone in the place took in what was happening. Then the bar staff ducked down behind the counter, and the people in the birthday group screamed and dived under the tables.

Shit, thought Arvo. Whatever the rule book or the training courses said about situations like this didn't seem to count when they really happened. All you could do was keep talking, keep calm and try not to get yourself killed.

Arvo slid out of the booth and walked very slowly over to Sandi. He knew that Maria was behind him, still sitting, covering him. If anything went wrong, he hoped she was a good shot. He prayed he wouldn't have to find out.

Chuck flicked his eyes sideways at Arvo and licked his lips. 'Stay there,' he said. 'You stay right there or I'll blow her brains out. I mean it.' He had the gun pointing at the side of Sandi's head.

Sandi whimpered and shook. Arvo stood still and held his hands up. 'Okay,' he said. 'I'll stay here. I'm not moving. But we've got to talk, Chuck.'

'What about? Who the fuck are you anyway? You her new boyfriend?'

'No, Chuck. I'm not her boyfriend.' Arvo told him who he was. As he spoke, he felt himself shift into what he called *no time*. He'd been there twice before: once during a hostage-taking in Detroit, and again during a domestic intervention, similar to this one, in Van Nuys. The first time, he had successfully talked the hostage-taker down; the second time, the

ex-husband's gun had jammed. It was *no time* because you
had no time to do anything but talk. It was *no time* because
time seemed suspended. And it was *no time* because that might
be all the time you had left.

'A cop?' Chuck scowled at Sandi. 'Bitch. I might have
known.'

Arvo had to keep his attention, get his focus away from
Sandi and calm him down. 'Look, Chuck,' he said, hands
spread in the open, 'why don't you put the gun away and we
can talk?'

'What about?'

'Your problems. Whatever you want. Just put the gun down.'

Chuck laughed harshly. The gun wavered in his hand but
remained pointed in the general direction of Sandi Gaines's
head. 'You want to talk about *my* problems. Man, that's a
laugh. The minute I put this gun away you'll have me on the
floor and be beating the shit out of me like I was Rodney
King.'

'That's not true,' Arvo said softly, 'and I think you know it.
You're smarter than that. Put the gun down, Chuck.'

Chuck licked his lips again. Again, his gun hand wavered,
but he didn't put the weapon down. He didn't want to fire it,
Arvo could tell, but that didn't mean he wouldn't.

'Ask *her* what my problems are,' Chuck said, glaring at
Sandi. 'Ask *her* why I'm here in this state, all to pieces. I can't
sleep because of her. I lie awake thinking about her all night.
How much I want her. How much I love her. The black bitch.
Black witch. She's put a spell on me. What's wrong, Sandi?
White man's meat not good enough for you, huh?'

He pushed the gun closer until the barrel was touching
Sandi's temple. She flinched. Sweat prickled on Arvo's brow.

'Chuck,' he said as calmly as he could, 'this isn't helping
matters at all. You don't want to hurt anyone. I know that. You
know that. But accidents happen. Give me the gun and we'll

sit down and talk like rational human beings, okay?' He held out his hand.

Chuck looked at the hand, then ignored it. 'Rational?' he echoed. 'She didn't behave like a rational human being, did she? She never even gave me a chance. What is it, Sandi? They really do have bigger cocks, your own kind? That it? This not big enough for you?'

He fumbled at his fly with his free hand.

'There's no need for this, Chuck,' said Arvo. 'Come on, give me the gun. You're making everyone nervous.'

'Let 'em sweat. I get no sleep because of this bitch. I get headaches. Here. This not good enough for you?' His dick hung limply out the front of his pants. 'Why don't you kiss it, bitch! Why don't you go on your knees and kiss it.'

'Oh, God. Don't kill me. Please!' Sandi wailed.

Chuck was crying now, passing his peak like a roller coaster on its way back home. Arvo figured if he could get through the next few seconds there might be a chance that they would all get out of the place alive.

'Come on, Chuck,' he said, holding out his hand. 'We can talk about this. I know we can. You're an intelligent man. You don't want to hurt anyone. Give me the gun, Chuck.'

Chuck looked directly at Arvo for the first time, his face slick with sweat, tears flowing down his cheeks. Arvo held eye contact for what seemed like hours, aware only of the sound of the streamers fluttering in the draught, but at the end of that time, he knew he had him. The man was a habitual loser, just desperate, trying a little harder than usual to succeed at something, at *anything*.

'Ah, what the fuck,' he said finally, shoulders slumping. 'It's only a replica anyway.' He handed the gun to Arvo, put his dick away and zipped up his fly.

Arvo felt like smashing his stupid face in. Instead, he gritted his teeth and patted Chuck down. Though he was sure the man would hardly use a replica when he had a real gun in his pocket, it was best to be safe and follow routine procedure. He didn't bother with cuffs. That could wait until a patrol car arrived. Chuck wasn't going anywhere right now. He looked like a man who wanted to talk.

Sandi dashed off to the washroom, hand over her mouth. Slowly, the members of the birthday party started peeking from under the table and getting to their feet, all a little sheepish now it was all over. Pretty soon, Arvo thought, they'd be indignant. They'd start asking for their money back, replacements for the drinks that got spilled, maybe even threaten a lawsuit. He'd seen it happen before. Then they'd embellish what had happened for their friends, be the centre of attention at parties.

The bar staff stood up and dusted themselves off. One of them poured himself a stiff shot of Scotch. Arvo nodded to Maria, who went to call Hollywood Division, then led Chuck by the elbow to one of the booths and jammed him in the corner.

Chuck wiped his face with a napkin. The tissue was so thin that it shredded and pieces stuck in little clumps on his cheeks and chin, like the bits of paper you put over shaving nicks.

'I'm glad it's over,' he said. 'You know that? I'm glad it's over. I feel such relief. I haven't slept for two weeks thinking about her. You know that? You know what that does to your mind? I loved that woman. Do you believe it? Loved her. She treated me like dirt. I couldn't kill no one, man.'

'Calm down, Chuck,' Arvo said. 'You only dated her a couple of times, isn't that right?'

'So? What does it matter how many times I dated her? Don't you believe in love at first sight?'

Arvo sighed and wondered if he should give an honest answer. If truth be told, he'd lost a fair bit of sleep over Nyreen, too. Before he could say anything, though, Sandi stormed over to the booth and stood over them, hands on her hips. 'Now look what you've done, you piece of white trash. A whole tray. You're gonna have to pay for them drinks.'

Chuck fell silent for a moment, mouth open, then he started laughing through his tears. Arvo almost felt like laughing with him.

Sandi just stood there, eyes flashing, and Chuck looked at Arvo. 'Isn't she unbelievable? Isn't she magnificent?' Then he turned back to Sandi, adoration clear in his eyes. 'How about bringing me a drink, honey? Make it a Martini. Very dry. With a twist.' He glanced at Arvo again. 'And maybe one for my friend, here, too.'

Arvo shook his head. One of those days. Then he heard the welcome sound of a police siren.

5

Sarah stood on Jack's deck and looked at the lights of the other houses across Laurel Canyon. Some of them had Christmas displays, chains of green, red, yellow and blue winking on and off in the night. Someone had even put up a tall Christmas tree outlined in lights about halfway up the hillside. It was a clear evening, and cold enough that Sarah needed to wear a sweater over her blouse. The stars shone thick and bright above, and car lights meandered along the canyon road way below. She could smell woodsmoke in the air.

Standing so high up the canyon side, Sarah felt suspended in space. Behind her, the party was in full swing. People were laughing, dancing, drinking. Janis was belting out 'Get It While You Can' into the night air. But Sarah was taking a moment's breather from the crowd.

Her peace was soon broken. Guests came out onto the deck and stopped to tell her how much they loved the show, how 'great' she was, or how 'great' she looked, the way people did in Hollywood, as if it were the only thing in the universe that mattered.

In return, Sarah smiled and made small talk as best she could, sipping on the same glass of rum and Coke that Jack had poured her when she arrived. The ice had melted by now, and the Coke had lost most of its fizz. Between conversations, she would glance around nervously now and then to make sure Stuart, her escape route, was still nearby.

The sweet, acrid smell of marijuana drifted through the air.

Two young actors who played uniformed cops on the show stood near the door snorting coke through a rolled-up dollar bill. Or it could have been a twenty. Apart from the numbers, American money all looked the same to Sarah. She turned away from the actors; the scene brought back too many memories, all of them bad.

Music blasted out of Jack's megawatt stereo system in the main room. Janis gave way to the Rolling Stones doing 'Angie.' Sarah studied the lights of the houses across the canyon again and wondered if *M* were watching. Was she on stage tonight?

Inside the house, people danced wildly, tossing frantic shadows over the stark white walls. Sometimes the shadows and the dancers didn't seem to connect, as if so much wildness disconnected them the way a retina might be detached from the back of the eye. Sarah looked for Jack, hoping he would manage to get away from the throng for a minute.

Jack Marillo was her co-star in *Good Cop, Bad Cop*, the biggest early-season hit the network had had for years, such a success that it was even being shown in the UK already.

People said the main reason for the show's success was the chemistry between Sarah's controlled, repressed and icy blonde homicide detective, Anita O'Rourke, and her spontaneous, rule-bending, bed-hopping partner Tony Lucillo, played by Jack. Why was it, Sarah wondered, that female TV cops always had names that started with an 'O' and male cops had names that ended with one?

Sarah's character was tough and competent, with a hint of vulnerability, an occasional hairline crack in the professional carapace. She was the one who always kept her cool when Lucillo shouted, gesticulated and went into his tantrums, but she also shed a tear or two in private after discovering the raped and murdered corpse of a twelve-year-old street kid.

Stuart said the audience liked the characters because they kept people in suspense about whether they'd end up in the sack together. They had filmed a kiss for the Christmas special – a chaste one, but with definite possibilities – then the network would be showing reruns for a couple of weeks to keep the viewers on tenterhooks.

Stuart also said the male viewers loved Sarah because, although she seemed a bit aloof and prim, very Brit, they just *knew* she was a screamer between the sheets. All that repressed passion. Strictly footprints on the ceiling.

Sarah took all the praise with a pinch of salt, and she took Stuart's crude comment as a compliment. That, to her, was what acting was all about. Being someone different. She was by nature shy and quiet; her shyness was a personal prison she could only escape through acting. She could only be truly alive and real on stage or in front of the cameras.

Being reserved, Sarah didn't like parties very much, either, but she understood the importance of attending them, especially in Hollywood. It wasn't just a matter of being seen at the right places. Certainly that was important, as Sarah was still only an up-and-coming star, rather than a fully fledged one. But she was also relatively new to America, and she wanted to make friends; she wanted to be liked. It was especially difficult being English. People were inclined to think you were stuck-up and stand-offish just because of your accent.

So she showed up when she was invited, mingled and said the right things. She never really made any close friends that way, but at least she collected more faces to smile at when she dined at Spago's, which she usually tried to avoid because it was too noisy there to hear yourself think.

Sarah turned to the sliding door and smiled to see Jack coming towards her with a bottle of beer in his hand. She liked Jack. Of all the people she'd met in Los Angeles – Stuart aside – he was the closest she had to a friend.

Handsome in a TV star sort of way, Jack was tall and slim, not exactly muscular, but in good athletic shape, with a dark complexion and a great head of shiny black hair. Sarah liked him because he was straightforward – no games, no bullshit – full of mischief and energy, and he had a sense of humour. Jack could act, too, not like some of the people in the show, who had walked right out of toothpaste commercials and used-car lots.

Sometimes they went out together to restaurants, plays and concerts. There had been one or two media attempts at rumours of romance, of course, but even the greenest of entertainment reporters hadn't been able to maintain that fiction for long, reverting instead to the cliché of the beautiful star's lonely life, her Garbo-esque love of solitude and privacy.

Sarah knew that Jack was gay, and that the one marriage he had tried, to appear hetero, had been a dismal failure. If the gossip columnists also knew, they weren't saying anything. Hollywood could be very funny about things like that, even today.

'Playing wallflower again?' Jack asked, standing next to her. They turned to face the canyon and he draped his arm over her shoulder in a brotherly fashion. The solid wooden fence they leaned against was all that stood between the two of them and a long plunge into the dark.

'Oh, shut up, Jack,' Sarah said, thumping his arm. 'You're such a party animal, you ought to be ashamed of yourself.'

Jack feigned a frown. 'Not for much longer. In case you hadn't noticed, it's my birthday. I'm getting old.'

'Thirty-seven's not old.'

'Easy to say that when you're only thirty-four.'

'How did you know that?'

Jack winked. 'Same way I know your real name's Sally Bolton. No problem if you flirt a bit with one of the secretaries.'

'Swine.' Sarah nudged him in the ribs, but a chill went through her when he mentioned knowing her real name.

'Oh, I love it when you talk dirty to me,' Jack joked. 'Especially with that plummy London accent.'

'Plummy?' Sarah countered, switching to the broad Yorkshire she'd lost after years playing other people, other voices. 'Ee bah gum, lad, tha mun't call us plummy.'

Jack laughed.

'Is that true?' Sarah asked him. 'About the secretary?'

'No. You told me yourself in the fall. Don't you remember?'

'So I did. It's just . . .'

'What is it? Is something wrong?'

Sarah shrugged. 'No. Well, not really.'

He took his arm away, grasped her shoulders and turned her to face him. 'Come on, Sarah,' he said in his TV voice. 'It's *me*, Tony Lucillo, your partner.'

Sarah slipped out of his grasp and turned to face the canyon. 'Oh, it's nothing,' she said. 'It was just you saying how easy it was to find out things about me. You know, personal details. I got some weird letters, that's all.' She turned to face him and touched his arm. 'Please don't say anything. I'd hate it if everyone knew about them.' The music stopped. Sarah heard police sirens in the distance.

'We all get weird letters. I got one from my ex-wife's lawyer just the other day. She wants more money. Stop being so goddamn British. What was it, threatening, dirty?'

'Neither, really. But . . . well, a bit of both, maybe.' Sarah turned back to the canyon and told him about it.

'Ooh,' said a voice behind them when she'd finished. 'That *is* creepy.' Sarah and Jack turned around and saw Lisa Curtis. Lisa looked as gorgeous as ever in a low-cut, strapless black dress, which contrasted with her creamy skin, and her thick, glossy chestnut hair falling in extravagant curls and waves over her shoulders. 'Sorry,' she said, 'but I couldn't help overhearing.'

'Oh, it's you, Lisa,' Sarah said. 'That's all right. Just don't go

broadcasting it around, okay? I could do without the attention. It's nothing really.'

Lisa, who played the police dispatcher in the show, pointed
to her impressive chest. '*Moi*? Broadcast? But I'm the soul of
discretion, Sarah, you ought to know that.'

'Right.' Sarah laughed. 'Aren't you cold, dressed like that?'
she asked.

'Goose-bumps are in. Anyway, I think they're fascinating.'

'What? Goose-bumps?'

'No, dummy. Your letters.'

Jack excused himself to attend to his guests and said he'd be
back later. Lisa cornered Sarah by the edge of the deck. The
music started again; this time it was Kiri Te Kanawa singing
an aria Sarah recognized from *Tosca*. Jack sure had catholic
tastes, and this was clearly the Italian in him coming out. Te
Kanawa's strong, clear voice rang out over the canyon.

'Something like that happened to a friend of mine,' Lisa
went on. 'Well, a friend of a friend, really. I mean, I never actually *met* her. She dated this guy, like, a few times, and he got
too serious, too possessive, so she dumped him. Time to move
on, right? Like, get a life. Anyway, this is the kind of guy who
won't take no for an answer. He starts sending her letters
every day. Like, really graphic ones about the things they used
to do together in bed and how he would love her for all eternity and couldn't bear being away from her body. That kind of
thing. Real yukky. Then next it's phone calls, flowers, the
whole deal.

'She tries to tell him she's not interested, right, but it's like
he isn't even hearing her. He says he knows she still loves him
and she knows it, too, deep down. She's just like fighting it
because her feelings are so overwhelming and so powerful
they frighten her. Can you believe it? This asshole tells her if
she looks deep inside herself she'll find the truth and the courage to act on it. Well, she tells him the only thing that frightens

her is his behaviour, but he just laughs and tells her not to be a silly girl, like one day she'll wake up and know it's true.'

Sarah sipped her warm rum and Coke and nodded in all the right places. That was one thing about a conversation with Lisa; it wasn't too demanding, if you had plenty of patience. Laughter spilled from inside the house, glasses tinkled and Kiri sang on about how she lived for art, her warm soprano soaring in the clear night air.

'Next he starts hanging around outside the bank where she works,' Lisa went on. 'She was an assistant manager. I mean, she's one bright lady. And the guy was a stockbroker or something. We're not talking lowlifes here. Anyway, finally she gets really freaked. She starts to believe it really *is* her fault, that she must be encouraging him in some way, giving him signals. Like, *maybe she really did want him*.' Lisa put her index finger to her temple, turned it a hundred and eighty degrees and back, and mimicked the *Twilight Zone* theme.

'What happened?' Sarah asked.

'He goes too far is what. Just when she's starting to feel like it might be easier to give in than keep on dealing with him. I mean, he's got her so messed up she's even starting to feel flattered by the attention. This guy would neglect his job and hang around outside the bank all day just to catch a glimpse of her. I mean, just a glimpse. She wouldn't even talk to the sucker. He keeps telling her he loves her, buys her diamonds and stuff and she won't give him the time of day.'

'But how did he go too far?' Sarah asked, fascinated despite herself. 'What did he do?'

'I guess he didn't feel he was getting anywhere. Like, she never answered his calls or his letters. She always returned his presents. She'd even cross the street to avoid him and make sure there was someone with her when she went out on her lunch-break. Well, one time she'd been to lunch with this guy, you know, from the bank, a few times, and he comes out from work one day and finds his tyres slashed. It doesn't take a rocket scientist to figure out who did it, right?'

'What did your friend do?'

'She confronted him with it next time he phoned.'

'And did he admit it?'

'Sure he did. Tells her it's just a friendly warning. That she belongs to *him*. Then he starts talking about how if he can't have her alive they can be together in death. That, like, brought her to her senses again. What a loser. I mean, the guy's almost got there after months of presents and stuff, then he blows it. Anyway, she's all freaked now and he's like getting *really* mad.'

'Did she go to the police?'

'Not at first. She just warned him, like that was it. No more. *Nada*. Goodbye. That's all she wrote.'

'And?'

'And one day while she's at work he, like, breaks into her house. You know what he does?'

Sarah shook her head.

'He steals a pair of shoes, that's all.'

'Shoes?'

'Uh-huh. Navy pumps. Is that weird, or what? But wait for it. Not only does he steal a pair of her shoes. The next time he phones, do you know what he tells her?'

'What?'

'He tells her he's had the fucking shoes bronzed, that's all. *Bronzed!*'

'I don't believe it.'

'Cross my heart.'

'What happened next?'

'She calls the cops. What she should've done right from the start, you ask me. They slap a restraining order on him. Like, he isn't supposed to go within two miles of her or something. This is a while ago. I hear we've got better laws now.'

'Did he obey the order?'

'Dream on. Two days later he breaks into her house again. This time while she's there. First he shoots her in the head, then he takes her clothes off. Then he gets undressed, puts his arm around her and shoots himself in the head. The cops find them huddled naked and dead together on the sofa like some modern-day Romeo and Juliet. Isn't that just *so* bizarre?'

Sarah shivered. Even the sweater wasn't warm enough to keep out the chill of Lisa's story. Kiri finished and Jack started with the sixties music again. This one Sarah recognized; it was Led Zeppelin doing 'Whole Lotta Love.'

'Anyway, don't worry about the letter, honey,' Lisa said, resting her hand lightly on Sarah's arm. 'I mean, this was different. The guy *knew* her. They'd dated. It wasn't just like, you know, some pervert writing out of the blue. That happens all the time. See you later, sugar, I just *have* to go and dance to this song.'

And Lisa dashed off inside the house. Sarah finished her rum and Coke and chatted with a few other guests, her mind hardly on it at all, then looked for Stuart to take her home.

Not being able to drive was a hell of a drawback in Los Angeles, she had found, but the idea of getting behind the wheel of a car – especially on the freeways – terrified her even more than the inconvenience of calling cabs or relying on friends.

She wasn't 'big' enough yet to merit a limo and driver from the network, so Stuart would often give her a ride to the studio. He lived in Brentwood, which, while it was practically in the opposite direction, wasn't very far away. If Stuart couldn't make it, she would call a cab.

The show's producer wanted Sarah to learn how to drive – at least enough to look comfortable behind the wheel of a police cruiser on TV. Stuart had taken her out in the desert a couple of times for lessons, and she'd learned the basics, like how to turn on the ignition and put it in 'Drive,' which was the gas pedal and which was the brake, but that was as far as she had got. The roads out there had been empty; she couldn't imagine herself ever driving in traffic.

Led Zeppelin rocked on. The bass and drums were so loud that Sarah worried the vibrations would shake the house loose and send it careening down the hillside the way mudslides often did in the canyons.

The whole setting was ridiculous anyway: a house propped up on stilts near the top of a steep slope. How could Jack live up here, perched so precariously? Sarah didn't think she could.

Still, it seemed that no matter where one lived in Los Angeles, there was danger from the forces of nature. Impermanence was a fact of life that insinuated itself into people's psyches in odd ways. Sarah had often thought that explained some of the general craziness of the place. Nothing's permanent, so don't get hung up on anything.

Since she had been living in LA, there had been fires, heavy rains and a major earthquake, and she had heard people say that the four seasons in Southern California are called flood, fire, earthquake and riot. Yet here she was, standing on the deck of a stilt-house high on a canyon side probably within spitting distance of the San Andreas fault. Crazy.

Talk about floating on air. It was bad enough *feeling* as if she were forever wobbling on stilts, constantly feeling that some-day someone would come and pinch her and say, 'It's all been a mistake, love, you're not really a star, you're just a snotty-nosed little girl from Yorkshire and all this has just been an illusion, now it's back to the meat-packaging factory where you belong.'

Bad enough *feeling* it, let alone living it. Suddenly she felt an attack of vertigo coming on; she had to get back to solid ground. Brilliant, our Sal, she thought, catching Stuart's eye across the deck, now Los Angeles is a metaphor for your insecurities.

Before she left, she looked again at the Christmas lights across the canyon and shivered. 'This was different,' Lisa had said of her friend. 'The guy *knew* her.' Then she turned and looked at the party crowd. Could it be someone close to her, someone who *knew* her, someone who knew her real name and her address, like Jack and Stuart? Then she tried to dismiss the idea from her mind as ridiculous. Jack and Stuart were the only real friends she had here. They weren't perverts. They couldn't be.

6

'What are the chances of an ordinary person becoming the target of the kind of person you've been talking about? Someone like me, for instance.'

Arvo scanned the sea of faces for his questioner and noticed that she was a good-looking redhead in a green silk blouse. She had a southern accent. Arvo straightened his tie, the one with the Salvador Dali melting watch design.

Tall and tanned, with the physique of a long-distance runner rather than a sprinter, and smartly dressed in a lightweight wool suit, Arvo was generally thought attractive by women.

He was thirty-five years old, had thick brown hair, perhaps a shade too long over the collar, and a boyish smile enhanced rather than hindered by slightly crooked teeth. He also had good bone structure, including high cheekbones and a strong jaw, which he had inherited, along with his unusual first name, from his Estonian mother.

His brown, expressive eyes always gave the impression of being interested in whatever people were saying to him, but if you looked closely you could see a diamond glint of toughness at their centre. They were eyes that had seen violent death and faced danger; they were cop's eyes.

Arvo didn't know what he had acquired from his Welsh father, except perhaps his crooked teeth and his public-speaking abilities. The Welsh, his father had told him, had a tradition of great oratory.

That was no doubt why the lieutenant had chosen him to

speak on 'Assessing Erotomaniacs and Love Obsessionals' to a National Law Enforcement Convention in the Pasadena Hilton that morning.

The LAPD Threat Management Unit was the only such department in the country. As the unit could only operate within the Los Angeles city limits, its members always seemed to be advising out-of-town police departments, acting as consultants to the FBI, the Secret Service or the CIA, and giving talks like this. Arvo had even appeared on a PBS TV special, where he had been so nervous all he remembered now was how hot the studio lights had been.

'It's a subtle difference,' Arvo answered carefully. 'In most cases, both erotomaniacs and love obsessionals target unattainable objects, almost always people they have never met. Senators, congressmen, movie stars and suchlike. Erotomaniacs generally believe that the person they have chosen is in love with them. For the love obsessionals, though, that doesn't matter. They're in love with whoever they've chosen and they believe that that person will probably come to love them in time, if they do the right things. The danger to ordinary individuals is far more likely to come from what we call "simple obsessionals": that is, someone they know, someone they have been intimately involved with and spurned. A past lover, for example.'

The redhead thanked him. He could tell by the way her eyes smiled along with her mouth when she looked at him that if he stayed around after the talk she would approach him with another question, that he would ask her out to dinner and she would only hesitate as much as good taste demanded before saying yes, and that at the end of the evening they might end up in bed together, probably in her hotel room.

Knew it, but didn't want it. If he wanted to go to bed with anyone, it was with Maria. But that situation was fraught with complications: they worked for the same department; they were friends; they were both on the rebound. Plenty of reasons not to.

Instead of hanging around, he ducked out fast onto Los Robles. It was clear and seventy-five degrees in Pasadena, and the San Gabriel Mountains rimmed the northern horizon like a jagged dark-green chalkboard streaked with white doodles. He put on his shades. The traffic on the Pasadena Freeway was as light as it ever got at eleven o'clock in the morning.

Arvo tuned in to FM 93.1, an oldies station, and listened to The Association, Quicksilver Messenger Service and Strawberry Alarm Clock. Downtown, he exited the freeway at Hill, drove through the colourful Chinatown strip, then turned east on Temple. A group of press people with microphones and cameras stood interviewing someone outside the Criminal Courts Building. Arvo turned south on Spring.

The Threat Management Unit, part of the Detective Support Division, was located at 419 Spring Street, the south-west corner of Spring and Fourth, in the heart of shabby downtown Los Angeles. Across the street was the run-down façade of the old Pacific Grand Hotel – which now looked like the kind of place even a hooker might avoid taking her client – and a liquor store barricaded with mesh and metal grilles against the street people and aggressive panhandlers who infested the area.

Arvo took the elevator to the fourth floor, turned left and walked along the flecked carpet. The unit was located at the far end of a largely empty open-plan office. The desks faced one another, each with a teal blue divider coming up to about shoulder height when the person was sitting, so the detectives could see one another over the tops. The lieutenant had his own desk at the far end.

'Well, if it ain't *Pro*-fess-or Hughes,' said Eric Mettering when Arvo walked up to his hutch. There were only eight detectives on the Unit at the moment, and most of them were out. Eric had hung his jacket over the back of his chair. His top button was open and his tie loose. He ran his hand over his shiny bald head. 'How'd it go?' he asked.

'Fine,' said Arvo. 'Had them hanging on my every word. Anything new?'

'Nope. Pretty quiet morning, so far. Apart from the phone's been ringing most of the time.' He pointed to Arvo's desk. 'One for you. Called twice.'

Arvo checked the message. It was from Stuart Kleigman, asking him to call back. Arvo knew Stuart, had worked with him before, and knew he wasn't the kind of guy to cry wolf.

Stuart answered on the third ring. 'Arvo,' he said. 'Good of you to call. Can you come over to the studio?'

'Problem?'

'Weird letters.'

'Hold on.' Arvo covered the mouthpiece. 'Where's Maria?' he asked Eric. He wanted to talk to her about the paperwork on the Sandi Gaines case.

'Out in Devonshire talking to some guy who's scared shit-less his ex-wife's gonna do a Bobbit number on him.'

'When d'she leave?'

Eric looked at his watch. 'About half an hour ago.'

Devonshire. The Valley. It was just after noon now, so that meant she wouldn't be back for a while. Hell, the paperwork could wait. He took his hand off the mouthpiece. 'Stu?'

'Yeah. Look, Arvo, I can come over to Spring Street if it's a problem for you.'

'No problem. I'll be there soon as I can.'

'Great. Thanks. See you soon.'

Arvo told Eric where he was going, then he left the building and got into his car again. The engine was still warm after his drive back from Pasadena.

The security guard at the studio gate eyeballed his ID and waved him through. Arvo parked in the visitors' lot and walked over to the long, narrow office building. He checked in at reception and went up to Stuart's second-floor office.

The door was ajar. Arvo tapped lightly and went in. He had already heard the TV set from the corridor and remembered it from his last visit. He wondered if Stuart always had it turned on while he was working. Right now it was showing a *Flintstones* rerun. *Yabba-dabba-doo.*

'Coffee?' Stuart offered.

'Sure.'

'Sit down.' Stuart picked up the phone and ordered.

'Can you turn the TV down?' Arvo asked.

'What? Oh, sure.' Stuart pressed the mute button. Arvo could still see Barney Rubble from the corner of his eye.

'You get used to it,' Stuart said. 'Can't think without it on these days. And at least it's a kind of constant noise, covers up the racket outside.' He pointed to the window. Arvo had heard some shouting, so he went over and looked out.

Opposite Stuart's window was a street that the studio had constructed for a movie set so long ago no one could remember its title. But the street remained. It looked like thirties New York to Arvo – definitely an eastern city, anyway. It came complete with grimy tenements, fire escapes out front, black metal railings, fading ads for Pears soap and Dr Graves high on the end-of-block walls, and even something that looked like a New York subway exit in the middle of the sidewalk. There were basement shops and restaurants, too, all of them empty.

One corner shop, down some steps with black railings at each side, had been given signs proclaiming it as a video rental centre, and that was where the cameras, actors and studio technicians were milling around filming a scene. All around it, scaffolding had been erected to accommodate the various lights and camera angles. A couple of TV cop cars were parked outside at sharp angles, and some of the actors were wearing Kevlar vests.

The coffee arrived. After Stuart's secretary had poured, Arvo sat down and asked, 'What can I do for you this time?' He had helped a couple of Stuart's clients in the past couple of years, and he liked the man. Stuart Kleigman was one of the old guard, a gentleman in a business populated largely by sharks and cut-throats, and he had still managed to hold on to a good reputation. His easygoing exterior, Arvo guessed, must cover a mind like a steel trap and guts of seasoned leather.

Stuart handed over the letter and polished the lenses of his glasses. 'It's the third,' he said.

Arvo picked up the envelope carefully and sniffed it first. You never knew. He had come across any number of enclosures in his time, from that used tampon the soap star had received to human excrement, dried oregano and even a half-eaten tuna salad sandwich.

Nothing this time. Just a plain, clean paper smell. He took out the letter and examined the printed typeface, then he ran his finger carefully over the front and back of the single page. No indentations. Which probably meant a laser printer, most likely, or an inkjet. Very clean and impersonal.

Arvo read the letter, then he put it down on the desk. He had seen hundreds of these things, and in most cases there was nothing to worry about; the suspect was unlikely to harm the victim, no matter how vile and terrifying his threats and fantasies looked on paper. In most cases, writing letters was about all they could manage.

In most cases.

But there was always the exception, the possibility. Victims had been hurt, even killed by people who started off writing letters. While Arvo couldn't *predict* the level of danger, he could *assess* it statistically. But to do that he needed more than one letter. He needed a pattern of obsessive behaviour he could analyze and compare to the profiles already on file.

'Well?' asked Stuart. 'You think there's anything to worry about?'

'What happened to the other two?'

'She destroyed them.'

'Did the subject sign a name on any of them?'

'She didn't say.'

It was odd that the writer didn't identify himself with anything other than the initial, *M*. Usually people who wrote letters like that wanted their victims to know who they were. This one seemed to want her to guess who he was, if the contents of the letter were to be believed. A big if.

'Any phone calls?'

'Nope.'

'What about visits? Home or studio?'

Stuart shook his head. 'Not that we know of.'

'Has anyone been stalking her?'

'No. I mean, she did say she felt there might have been someone watching her from a distance. Through binoculars.' He shrugged. 'Just a feeling, though.'

'Could it be someone she's dumped lately getting revenge, trying to scare her?' Arvo asked.

Stuart leaned forward and rested his hands on the desk. 'Arvo, Sarah hasn't been seeing anyone lately. In fact she hasn't been seeing anyone all the time I've known her, which is nearly a whole year.'

'You sure?'

'I'm sure.'

'Anything like this ever happen to her before?'

'Not that I know of. And she would've told me.'

'Who's "Little Star"?'

'She doesn't know.' Stuart shrugged. 'Must be his pet name for her or something. Don't they do things like that?'

'They?'

'The fucking perverts that write this garbage.'

'Does the initial *M* mean anything to her?'

'She says not.'

'And?'

'And I believe her.'

'What about "Sally"?'

'It's her real name.'

'Interesting,' said Arvo. 'I'd like to talk to her.'

Stuart rubbed his chin. 'Well, that'll be difficult,' he said. 'She's going back home for Christmas. England. Leaving tomorrow evening.'

'I mean now. Is she around?'

'She's on the set. Working.'

'Maybe she can take a short break.' Arvo picked up the phone and held it out.

Stuart hesitated a moment, then sighed and took the receiver. 'It's sound stage eighteen,' he said, after a brief conversation. 'They'll be breaking for lunch in about twenty minutes, if you can hold on.'

Arvo nodded and squinted at the envelope again. 'Who is she, anyway, this Sarah Broughton?' he asked.

Stuart flopped back in his chair. 'Jesus Christ, Arvo! Sarah's only one of the fastest-rising stars of one of the most success-ful television cop shows the networks have had in years, that's all. She's maybe not exactly a household name, but she will be by the end of the season, and you can quote me on that.'

Arvo smiled. 'I don't watch much television. And I sure as hell don't watch cop shows. Movies and books, sure, but TV . . .'

Stuart waved his hand. 'Your choice. I just can't believe it, that's all. You live in LA and you don't watch much television. You might as well be on Mars. It's like living in a fucking whorehouse and being celibate, for Christ's sake.'

That hit close to home; for the three months since Nyreen had gone, Arvo *had* been celibate. Now, he wasn't quite sure whether it was due to choice or circumstance. 'Believe it, Stu,' he said. 'I've got better things to do with my time.'

'Like what?'

'Read. Think. Watch real movies. Try to recapture some of that lost childlike wonder. Try to make life easier for the Sarah Broughtons of this world.'

'Uh? Right. Sure.'

'So,' Arvo said. 'Tell me about her.'

All of a sudden a voice came over a loudspeaker from outside: 'Come on out!' it yelled. 'We've got the place surrounded. You can't get away. Give yourself up now!'

Stuart looked at Arvo and shrugged. 'See what I mean? Believe me, it's better with the TV set turned on.'

Arvo rolled his eyes and gestured towards the window. 'Are they serious?' he said. 'That kind of talk went out with the rubber hosepipe. Who've you got for technical adviser on this one? A rookie?'

'Why? Looking for a little extra work?'

'Not me. Go on. Sarah Broughton.'

'Right.' Stuart went over to his filing cabinet, slid out an eight-by-ten glossy and passed it over. Arvo looked at the black-and-white photograph. It showed the head and shoulders of a strikingly beautiful woman. Though she looked composed and capable, there was also a hint of vulnerability about her, the eyes especially.

She had short blonde hair with ragged bangs over a heart-shaped face; sensual lips with little dimples at each side; a small, slightly retroussé nose; and large, almond-shaped eyes. Arvo couldn't tell from the black-and-white photograph, but he guessed they were blue. He found himself wanting to know exactly what shade of blue.

Stuart leaned back and linked his hands behind his head. His belly hung over his black leather belt and Arvo noticed that one of the buttons on his white shirt was undone, giving a glimpse of pale pudgy flesh. 'Sarah Broughton,' he began. 'Her real name's Sally Bolton. She's a Brit. Comes from Yorkshire or some place like that. Got an accent, anyway.'

'What kind of person is she?' Arvo asked.

'Well, she's a sweet kid, really. She's very private, bit of a recluse in some ways. She's taken a few hard knocks in her time and she's still a little fragile. But she's got guts. And she's a hard worker – an incredibly hard worker – not to mention one hell of an actress. She started with rep over in England, then she went to the Royal Academy in London. Did a stint with the National Theatre – Larry Olivier's people – acted in Shakespeare, Pinter, that kind of stuff. A few artsy British films. All flops. She appeared in a couple of *Masterpiece Theatre* and *Mystery* series, and then she dropped out of sight for a while. Now she plays Detective Anita O'Rourke in *Good Cop, Bad Cop.*'

'Lousy title.'

'I know. It wasn't my idea.'

'Does she live alone?'

'Yes.'

'Where?'

'Beach house in Pacific Palisades.'

Arvo whistled. 'You must be joking.'

'Nah,' said Stuart. 'She's got a great deal. Place belongs to this eccentric old broad, used to be in movies. Probably silents, at that. Must be ninety if she's a day. She had the place built in the thirties and now she spends most of her time in the British Virgin Islands guarding her bank accounts, but she doesn't want to sell. So she rents. Through me. Real cheap.'

Arvo raised his eyebrows. 'Let me know if Ms Broughton decides to move.'

Stuart laughed. 'Back of the line, pal. I let Sarah have it ahead of a few people because I like her. You don't get to say that often about people in this business.'

'Is she scared?'

Stuart frowned. 'Not so much *scared*,' he said. 'A little rattled, maybe. Like I said, she might be a bit fragile, but deep down she's tough, and she can be stubborn when she gets her heels dug in. I just don't want her any more upset than she is. She's got a lot of things to concentrate on right now and this kind of shit she doesn't need.'

'Who does?' said Arvo. 'She own a gun?'

'No. Do you think she should—'

Arvo held his hand up. 'No, I don't. Definitely not. I'm asking because if she did get jumpy, and if she did have a gun around, someone could get hurt. That's all. Are you sure?'

'I'm sure. She hates the fucking things. Doesn't even like handling the TV gun, for Chrissake, and that's loaded with blanks. Now me, I've got a gun and I know how to use it.'

Almost on cue, the gunfire started up outside. Arvo guessed that the guy in the video shop just didn't want to come out with his hands up. At least he *hoped* the gunfire was part of the show. He still felt shaky from yesterday's confrontation with Chuck. There's nothing like talking to a guy holding a .38 for concentrating a man's thoughts, even if it does turn out to be a replica.

'Any idea who the letter-writer might be?' he asked.

'No.'

'Do you think *she* does?'

Stuart hesitated.

'Do you?' Arvo asked again.

Again, Stuart hesitated.

Arvo pushed the letter across the desk. 'Look, Stu,' he said, 'you asked me to come here for a reason. You've seen letters like this before. What is it about this one that's got you so rattled?'

'It's just . . . You know, I told Sarah there was nothing to get her panties in a knot about, tried to stop her worrying. Like I said, she doesn't need that right now. But . . . I don't know . . . I think there's more to it. I think it really might be someone she knew once but can't remember. Someone really weird who's come back to claim her.'

'What makes you think that?'

Stuart shrugged. 'Just the way she reacted when I asked her about it, that's all. Hell, it's mostly just a gut reaction on my part. I'm probably imagining things. But he does say in the letter that he's known her before.'

'Oh, come on, Stu. That means diddly. That's a common fantasy in this type of letter. You can't take the content of these things at face value. There's how many million viewers out there? All with the hots for pretty Miss Sarah Broughton. Those are the kinds of dreams you sell, Stu. That's the business you're in. What's the odds that there's more than a few of them out there two tacos short of a combination platter?'

Stuart pushed his glasses back over the bridge of his slightly hooked nose. 'Can you help, Arvo? Can you tell me how dangerous this guy's likely to be?'

'We don't even know it's a guy, for a start.'

'Shit. Are you telling me you get stalking dykes?'

'Sure we do. It's an equal opportunities business. No discrimination allowed.'

'So what are you going to do?'

'Leave it with me. I don't think there's any real danger yet. The highest probability of approach comes from people who have sent between ten and fourteen letters over a long period. But I'll have a closer look at it.'

'Thanks, Arvo.'

'No problem.' Arvo looked at his watch. 'Can we go over and talk to her now?'

7

Arvo and Stuart walked along the perimeter road of the studio lot. As they neared the commissary, a group of people came out and walked towards them. One of them, a small, wizened elderly man, smiled and said hello. He looked familiar, and Arvo felt he should recognize him, but he couldn't put a name to the face.

Stuart was smiling. 'Know who that was?'

Arvo shook his head.

'Mel Brooks.'

Of course. It was obvious when someone told you.

They crossed the road to the sound stages, huge, white hangar-like buildings laid out in a grid system over several blocks. There were twenty of them altogether, and in the boom days they might have all been in use. Now, though, many of them stood empty and silent. It was easy to spot the ones that were being used because they had trailers outside for the actors.

As they walked between the stages, technicians and office workers passed to and fro, some of them using little golf-carts to get around.

'Here we are,' Stuart said, pointing to the hangar ahead.

Outside the sound-stage door, the caterers had set up barbecues of plump chicken breasts, shrimp and bay scallops on skewers, T-bone steaks, salmon and swordfish. Arvo smelled the sauces and marinades before he even saw the barbecue and realized he had forgotten to eat lunch. Maybe later. If he was lucky.

They went inside and Stuart led Arvo over to the set. 'You might as well stay here,' he said. 'I'll go find her.'

Arvo looked around. He was in a fake police precinct, which looked as if it had been built in about 1930 and not cleaned or redecorated since. The puce plaster walls were cracked and stained, the wooden desks scratched. The glass in one of the windows was broken and the paintwork around it was chipped and grimy. It looked derelict now, but under the 50,000-watt lights it would look only as grungy as people expected a precinct house to look.

Outside the window was a night view of skyscrapers across the street, a painted or computer-generated backdrop about ten feet high, which would look real on camera. The duty rosters and wanted posters pinned to the corkboards looked real enough, too, though the paper seemed yellow and dry.

A couple of minutes later, Stuart walked back in with Sarah Broughton. She was wearing what Arvo took to be her TV uniform, a simple grey suit over a white blouse, and carrying a black purse. Smaller than he had expected, about five-four, she was even more beautiful than her photograph, though he got the sense that she was still at least partly in her character and trying to look rather more prim and severe than she would normally. Her eyes were a deep, disturbing cobalt blue. The colour and depth of a cold ocean a man could easily lose himself in.

'Sarah Broughton, Arvo Hughes,' Stuart introduced them. They shook hands; hers was cool and limp. Then they sat in the rickety chairs, Stuart leaning back against a desk. The irony of a real detective interviewing a TV detective in a fake precinct house wasn't lost on Arvo.

Sarah sat erect at the edge of her chair, legs crossed, hands linked just below her right knee. Her right leg was moving slightly back and forth, as if in time to some unheard music.

'Were all three letters addressed the same way?' Arvo asked.

'Yes.'

'What did the first two say?'

'I'm sorry, I don't recall the exact wording. They were short, much shorter than the third. I think he just said how happy he was to find me again after so long and he promised not to let me go this time. He said he would write again soon, that he had a lot to think about.'

'Were there any sexual references?'

'No. Not in the first two.'

'Any threats?'

'No.'

'I understand you think someone's been watching you?'

'Maybe. But it's just a feeling. I mean, I haven't actually seen anyone.'

'Where?'

'In the hills across the highway. And further up the beach. I thought I saw binoculars flash a couple of times, but I was already jumpy. It could have been anything, anyone.'

'Does the name "Little Star" mean anything to you?'

She hesitated. Her leg started moving more quickly, as if the tempo had increased. 'No,' she said. 'I mean, I don't remember.'

'What don't you remember?'

'Anyone calling me "Little Star."'

'But it *is* familiar to you, isn't it? You *think* it comes from somewhere, means something, don't you?'

Her jaw muscles seemed to tighten and her leg moved faster. 'I don't remember.'

'Okay. What about *M*?'

She shrugged. 'It could be anyone couldn't it? I have a friend called Miriam. I know a Michael and a—What are you doing?'

'Writing the names down. I'll get the full details from you later. I'll have to check them out.'

'But surely that's not necessary?'

'It *could* be someone close to you.'

'But he . . . he's crazy. I don't know anyone like that.'

'He could appear quite normal. Let me do my job, Ms Broughton. Just give me the names and addresses. Everyone you know with the initial "M." First name, middle or last.' He smiled. 'I'm not going to haul people in for questioning, you know. I can be discreet.'

Sarah's eyes flashed briefly, then she said, 'Very well.' She took an address book from her purse and gave him the information.

Arvo went on. 'In the letter, he – let's assume it's a *he* for now – he refers to you as Sally. Stu told me that's your real name, Sally Bolton.'

'That's right.'

'Why did you change it?'

'The studio thought it sounded too . . . I don't know . . . too lower-class. I'll never be able to fathom what goes on in the minds of these sales and marketing people. Sarah Broughton just sounded more California Brit to them. More classy.' She flashed a nervous smile. One upper front tooth overlapped the other, and Arvo thought it looked sexy as hell.

'How long have you been living here?' he asked.

'About fifteen months. Since a year last September, to be exact.'

'Before that?'

She shrugged. 'I lived in London. I travelled . . .'

'And you came over here to work on this series?'

'No. That came later.'

'How much later?'

She looked at Stuart. 'Let me see,' she said. 'They started casting last January.'

'Did you apply?'

'No. I was staying with an old friend from England, Ellie

Huysman. She used to be Stuart's assistant here. When the part came up, she thought of me.'

'When did you change your name?'

'March.'

'Any idea who might be sending the letters?'

'Not the slightest.'

'Ex-boyfriends?'

She reddened a little but kept her composure. 'There haven't been very many.'

'Who was the last?'

'It's of no relevance. He's dead.'

'How did he die? When?'

Sarah paused for a moment. Arvo noticed a tic at the left side of her jaw. 'I told you it's irrelevant, but if you must know, he died of a drug overdose. Late last year.'

'Were you with him at the time?'

'No, we'd split up.'

'What about the one before that?'

'The only serious one was Justin. Justin Mercer. I lived with him for five years in London, but that was a long time ago.'

'How long?'

'Ten years. He was older. An actor. I was new in the business. It started as an affair, then he left his wife ...' She shrugged. 'I can't very well see Justin pursuing me this way. He dumped me for a younger model just after my thirtieth birthday.'

'I didn't see his address in your book. Mercer does begin with an "M." Have you still got it?'

'No. We haven't stayed in touch. You should be able to find out easily enough, though. He's quite famous.'

'He still lives in England?'

'As far as I know, he does.'

'What about while you've been here, in Los Angeles.'

She shook her head. 'There's been no one.'

'Anyone who might *like* to have been?'

That small smile came to her lips again, just revealing the overlapping teeth. 'Probably a few,' she said. 'But nobody who's been really troublesome.'

'What about dates, casual affairs?'

'You mean one-night stands?'

'If you like.'

'I don't go in for that sort of thing.'

One of the director's assistants walked in and said something about getting the show on the road again. Technicians started ambling among the snaking cables at the edges of the phony precinct house.

'Okay,' Arvo said to him. 'Almost finished.' Then he turned to Sarah again. She sat down slowly. 'Are you sure you can't think of *anyone* who might be doing this?'

'No, I can't. I'm sorry.'

'Well, think about it, will you? And think about "Little Star." You might remember something important. If the writer *did* know you, it could help us find him.'

'I'll try. Is that all?'

'For now.' Arvo stood up and handed her his card. 'And get in touch immediately if anything else happens, okay?'

She nodded.

'I understand you're leaving the country tomorrow?'

'Yes.'

'Between now and then, I suggest you take extra security measures, just in case. Make sure everything's locked up properly, avoid walking around alone, that sort of thing. Common sense stuff.'

'I will,' she said.

Outside the sound-stage, Stuart picked up two skewers from the barbecue and offered Arvo one. He accepted. The shrimp was delicious, marinated in some sort of Thai sauce, spicy and sweet at the same time.

'What do you think?' Stuart asked as they walked back to the administration block.

'I don't know,' said Arvo. 'But I think you're right. I got the feeling that she's either holding something back or she really can't remember. Either way, "Little Star" means *something* to her.'

'Why would she hold anything back?'

'That's one of the things that puzzles me. But if she's not holding back, then why can't she remember? Whatever the reason, it's worth opening a file.' He popped the last shrimp in his mouth, said goodbye to Stuart and headed for his car.

8

The Boulevard was a kaleidoscope of broken colour, shards of green, orange, red and blue neon fragmenting through his windshield as he cruised, looking for the right place.

*He stopped at a red light. His chest felt tight and his breath was coming in sharp, rapid gasps. Hanging from the rear-view mirror was his talisman, a small framed icon of Sarah/Sally. She was naked from the waist up, her small breasts firm and rounded, thrust forward like the figurehead of a ship. And **she was smiling at him**.*

The light changed and the car behind him honked its horn. A wave of anger swept through him and for a moment he felt like ... but no. He knew he had to keep control; he mustn't give in to blind rage. This was for Sally.

Slowly, he edged down the throbbing Boulevard. From store windows, mannequins followed him with their gaze; crowds wandered from bar to bar, oblivious to him. But that would soon change.

*Finally, he found the stretch he had been looking for. A place where the pickings would be easy. It didn't matter who the victim was, only **what**. Like a cat, he thought. Does a cat really care which bird it captures? Doesn't one pigeon look just like another?*

He pulled over and parked by the curb, engine still ticking over, and wound down the window.

Maybe it was okay to be a little nervous. It gave him an edge; it honed his vision. The lights had never looked so sharp; they felt like knifepoints piercing his eyeballs. He knew that he would never see anything as clearly as what he was to do tonight. And it was all for her. He gazed proudly at his icon.

A figure separated itself from a small group standing outside a minimart and strutted towards him. He held his breath and gripped the wheel tightly. His pigeon.

9

Sarah woke with a start at four-fifteen in the morning. At first she felt confused, not sure what had woken her. For a while she just lay there, hardly daring to breathe, frightened that there was someone in the house. But it was probably just a siren or a squeal of brakes on the Coast Highway. As the policeman had suggested, she had locked up everything securely, including the outside gate to the beach. She lay still and listened for ten minutes. Nothing. All she could hear was the ceaseless rolling of the waves and her own heart beating too loud and too fast.

When she was certain she could hear no one else in the house, she got out of bed and walked over to the sliding glass doors that led to the second-level deck. She left the light off, just in case there was anyone watching her, and slid the doors open slowly and quietly. If *he* was out there somewhere, she didn't want him to know that she had heard him.

But she could see nothing out there, either, only the ocean rippling and rolling under its pale blanket of moonlight. She thought she saw something further up the beach, the sudden movement of a flashlight, perhaps, but it was gone before she could be certain.

She wondered if she should phone the police, but decided they would think she was getting paranoid. After all, she had only received three weird letters. As Stuart said, there was nothing special about that in Hollywood.

Still a little nervous, she knew she wouldn't be able to get back to sleep. She was also thirsty from the red wine she'd had with Jack at dinner that night, and Italian food always gave her heartburn. First, she padded to the bathroom, where she drank a large glass of water and took a couple of Maalox tablets. Then she went downstairs to the kitchen and put water and ground beans in the coffee-maker.

She would have to watch the drinking, she admonished herself, feeling the weight of a mild headache as she moved. For over a year now she had hardly touched a drop; even at Jack's party she had held on to one rum and Coke for the entire evening. But last night at dinner, she had drunk four glasses of red wine and laughed too loudly. Bad signs.

It was her habit most mornings to get up around dawn. First she would make coffee, then, while it was brewing, she would go for a run. It was too early yet, though. She liked to wait until she could sense the first light before she set off.

She put on her tracksuit, drank coffee, ate toast, did a little housework and read J.B. Priestley's *The Good Companions* for a while. It was the third time she had read the book, and it always made her feel homesick. Then, when she felt the light growing outside, she stood up and stretched. After her warm-up exercises, she set off. Originally a chore, the morning run had soon become compulsion, and now it was a pleasure.

She liked to run in the damp sand by the shore and feel the foam wet her feet. As she ran, she would watch the sun coming up behind the mountains, the light growing in the water, and breathe the ozone that the crashing surf seemed to exhale into the atmosphere.

This morning, as she ran, her reading of *The Good Companions* made her start thinking about her own childhood and how she began playing parts to escape the grime and the coal dust, the suffocating aura of defeat, poverty and broken dreams all around her. She remembered the time she organized a couple of her friends and, with sheets borrowed from the washing-line, they improvised the story of Ruth among the alien corn that they had learned in Sunday school the previous week.

Sarah's mother had been livid. Not only had her daughter been participating in the trivialization of a Bible story, she had also dirtied freshly washed sheets. In her mother's mind, Methodism and theatre weren't as close as cleanliness and godliness.

Sarah hadn't run more than a quarter of a mile when she noticed something about a hundred yards ahead of her in the sand. It was an odd, humped shape she couldn't quite make out. Probably driftwood.

It had been an odd relationship, she thought, the one she had had with her mother. Alice Bolton's religion had been deeply enough ingrained to make her theologically opposed to most forms of human artistic endeavour, even if they were dedicated to the praise of God, yet she had been proud of her daughter. More so than her father. If only—

Sarah stopped dead in her tracks as another childhood memory thudded into her mind with the force of a hammer blow.

Let's bury Daddy in the sand.

It was a game they used to play on seaside holidays in Blackpool, on the rare warm days. She and her older sister, Paula, would dig a hole in the sand and Daddy would lie down in it, then they would cover him with sand and pat it down. In the end, only his head would be showing. He would stay there for a while, then all of a sudden he would jump up and chase them, as they giggled and screamed, into the cold, grey Irish Sea.

The figure that lay in front of her now hadn't been quite so well buried. The hands and forearms stuck out, as did the feet. The face was above the surface, but it was covered with a light dusting of sand, as if blown there by the breeze, and she couldn't make out the features. She couldn't even tell if it was a man or a woman.

Sarah stood and stared, hands on her knees, panting for breath. She didn't know what to do. In panic, she looked around but there was no one in sight. There never was at this time. Only the gulls screeching and squealing overhead in the pale morning light. Was the person dead? She thought so. Should she run back to the house and phone an ambulance? Maybe she should make sure first?

Gingerly, she leaned forward and grasped one of the hands. She braced herself for the weight, but as soon as she exerted the slightest pressure, she fell back on the sand.

Then she saw it. In her hand, she held a human arm, severed just above the elbow, where she could see the dark, clotted blood and tissue matted with sand. She dropped it and got to her feet. Blood roared and waves pounded in her ears.

Just before she turned away to run back to the house, she saw something else, something that made her blood freeze.

The image looked as if it had been drawn in the sand with a sharp stick. It showed a heart pierced by an arrow, like the ones teenage lovers used to carve into trees or chalk on walls. Inside the heart was her name: Sally.

Sarah put her hand to her mouth and staggered back a few paces before turning to run back to the house.

Part Two

10

Judging by the expressions of delight and surprise when the captain announced that it was a clear and sunny day in Manchester, with a temperature of fifty degrees, Californians had just as many illusions about the English weather as the Brits had about theirs. Either that or global warming was messing everything up. No one took off their jackets, though; fifty was still too cold for an Angeleno in December.

As Sarah had a British passport, she avoided the long queue at immigration. Her one large suitcase, packed with Christmas presents, arrived quickly at the carousel, and though one of the officers gave her a second glance when she walked through the 'Nothing to Declare' exit, it wasn't because he thought she was smuggling something in.

The airport was noisy with the clamour of waiting relatives. Sarah's plane had arrived at the same time as a Jamaican flight, which explained the colourful costumes and the steel band. Here to greet a visiting dignitary or a sports team, she guessed.

She stood by the barrier holding on to her pushcart and scanned the crowd for Paula. There she was, waving both arms in the air behind a group of Indian women in colourful saris.

Sarah pushed forward, muttering excuse-mes as she went. The arrivals concourse was so crowded that it was impossible to get through without bumping into people. She almost ran over a small child and earned a dirty look for catching an elderly woman a glancing blow on the shin before she reached Paula. They hugged briefly, then Paula pushed Sarah back to arm's-length and examined her.

'Let's have a look at you, then, our Sal.'

The broad Yorkshire accent came as a shock to Sarah, though she didn't know why it should. She had spoken that way herself once, but now it sounded awkward and primitive to her, the mark of a certain class. She felt embarrassed for thinking such thoughts and cursed the English class system for always leaving its mark, no matter what you achieved. Had she been born to the upper classes and bred for success, Sarah thought bitterly, she wouldn't always be so consumed by self-doubt and lack of confidence, wouldn't always feel the bubble was about to burst.

'Well,' said Paula, 'I must say it's a big improvement on the last time.'

'What is?'

'Don't you remember? The make-up, the frizzy hair, the leather?'

Sarah laughed. 'Oh. Yes, of course.' She didn't remember, though, which was hardly surprising given the condition she had been in during her last visit home. That was before California, before the U.S. tour with Gary and his band, but it wasn't before the drugs and the drinking; though she hadn't recognized it immediately, the craziness had already begun. She didn't remember *anything* very clearly about that period of her life. Nor did she wish to.

This time she was wearing stonewashed jeans and a red sweatshirt, carrying her quilted down coat of many colours over her arm, and her blonde hair was trimmed neat and short. She also wore no make-up, a real treat after having the stuff plastered on every day at the studio.

'Mind you,' Paula went on. 'You could do with putting a bit of meat on your bones. Have you been slimming and going to one of them health club places like they do in Hollywood?'

Sarah laughed. 'I run every morning on the beach, but that's about all.' *In fact, only yesterday morning I stumbled across a dismembered body,* she almost added, but stopped herself in time. No point getting into *that* with Paula. 'Anyway,' she said, 'it's illegal to sell fatty foods in California.'

'Is it?'

'Only kidding. Though sometimes you'd think so.'

'Well, you looked a bit better padded last time I saw you on television. How long ago did you make that programme?'

'Not long. Television puts at least ten pounds on you, didn't you know that?'

'How would I? I've never been on telly. *I'm* not the star in the family.'

'I just thought people knew, that's all,' Sarah said. 'Anyway, I hope I don't look that fat on the series.'

'I didn't say *fat* did I? Just a bit better padded.'

'Well, thanks.'

'Don't mention it. Anyway, I suppose you look healthy enough,' Paula went on. 'Though for the life of me, I can't see where you're hiding your tan.'

'Which way?'

Paula pointed and Sarah started pushing the cart through the throng. 'I don't tan well,' she said. 'I never did. You know that. The sun just burns me.' Besides, she might have added, the studio prefers my 'porcelain' complexion; they say it goes with the plummy Brit accent.

'Well, pardon me for mentioning it.'

Sarah laughed. Same old Paula, prickly as a cactus, quick to take offence when none was intended.

Finally, they arrived at the car park and found the red Nissan.

'Unless you've learned to drive since you were last here, love,' Paula said, 'I'd try the other side.'

Sarah blushed. 'Sorry.' She'd gone automatically to the driver's side. She got in the correct side and fastened her seat belt. 'How was the drive over?' she asked.

Paula lit a cigarette and breathed a sigh of relief. 'Not bad. Roadworks near Barton bridge and an accident just past Huddersfield, but other than that . . .' She negotiated her way out of the car park, refusing Sarah's offer of money to pay the man in the booth, and headed for the motorway. 'It's a bloody maze round here,' she muttered.

The car felt cramped and tinny to Sarah after Stuart's gigantic hunk of Detroit steel. She wriggled around in the seat to get comfortable, but still the roof was too near to her head and the windshield too close to her face. Cars made her more nervous than planes, which was one reason why she had never learned to drive. The smoke made her cough.

'All right?' Paula cast her a sideways glance.

'Yes, fine.'

'I'll open the window if you want.'

'No, it's all right.'

'Really. I don't mind. It's no trouble.'

'Well, maybe just an inch or so.'

Paula opened the window a crack and pretended to shiver. The draught blew the smoke right into Sarah's face.

'Shit!' Paula missed a turning and went around the round-about again. Sarah thought of the little roundabout in Venice, one of the few she had seen in the United States. She felt a momentary pang of homesickness for her beach house. It was the only place where she had felt truly at home in years, perhaps because it was where she had started putting her life back together after Gary.

But thinking of the house also brought to mind a fleeting image of the severed arm and the heart in the sand. Then she remembered the letter she had slipped in her luggage, unopened. She had found it when she dropped by the house with Stuart to pack – at the last minute, as usual – before going to the airport.

She looked out of the window and saw a local diesel train rattling along beside a canal. Two boys stood on the stone banks leaning over the water with fishing nets. She doubted they had much hope of catching anything there in December, mild as it was. A yellow sign showing a man digging with a shovel appeared by the side of the road, then another. Soon the motorway was reduced to two lanes and they were crawling along between a silver Peugeot and a juggernaut from Barcelona. But there were no men digging with shovels.

Only when they had left the Manchester conurbation behind did Paula seem to relax at all. She still sat hunched forward in her seat, though, gripping the steering-wheel so hard her knuckles were white and squinting at the road and the cars ahead as if they were some sort of malevolent entities bent on her destruction. She doesn't like driving, Sarah realized. It must run in the family. Her father and mother, she remembered, had never owned or driven a car in their lives.

Soon the Pennines loomed ahead, furry green hillsides made eerie by mist swirling on their lower slopes.

There was still plenty of traffic on the motorway as it passed through the grimy urban sprawl round Rochdale and Oldham, but the cars thinned out as it climbed a long, slow hill and cut a swath through the Pennines.

All around, sheep grazed and becks and streams trickled through deep clefts in the dark green hillsides, flashing in the winter sun. They passed lonely barns, hamlets, small stone bridges, a reservoir. At one point the motorway got so high up that Sarah's ears went funny like they did on the plane. She yawned.

Paula glanced sideways again. 'Tired? You're quite a hit over here, you know. There'll be plenty of people in the village wanting your autograph. Just thought I'd warn you. You probably get enough of that over there.' She jerked her head back, indicating the Atlantic.

'Not really,' Sarah said. 'Hardly at all, in fact.' In the first flush of her television success, Sarah had worried about people recognizing her and approaching her in public places. She dreaded living the kind of life Elvis Presley had, for example, imprisoned in Graceland, having to hire a whole movie-theatre just to see a film, or an entire fairground to go on one ride, always surrounded by bodyguards.

But after a while, she had learned a very interesting thing: people tended not to recognize her unless she went out of her way to be noticed. As herself, she could walk along the street, shop in the Beverly Center, or browse along Rodeo Drive, and nobody came up demanding autographs.

On the other hand, if she dressed more like Anita O'Rourke, then people spotted her immediately. Most of the time she went around in jeans, a T-shirt and a Dodgers cap. Even the detective she talked to at the beach hadn't recognized her at first.

Again, she thought of the letters and the body in the sand. She remembered the touch of the hand, cold and stiff like a broken marble statue, and then the dark blood clotted with sand. There *had* been a body, she couldn't deny that, but it had nothing to do with her. When she went back there with the police, the heart had gone. She had been under so much stress she must have started seeing things, she told herself.

'Have you seen the show?' she asked Paula, snapping herself out of the reverie.

'Oh, aye,' said Paula. 'We seem to get nothing but American stuff these days. The kids like it. Not that I think they under-stand it, mind you, but they know it's their Auntie Sal. It's not bad.'

'And Dad?'

In the silence that followed, Sarah looked at her sister's

profile and saw the lips pressed tight together, the dry, raw skin of her cheeks. Paula had never been the beauty – always just a little too shapeless, her features just a little too pinched and sharp, hair too coarse and oily – but the years had also been unkind to her.

Though she was only thirty-six, Paula looked in her mid-forties, at least, Sarah thought, with deeply ingrained lines around her eyes and the corners of her thin lips, and a permanent aura of weariness and suspicion. She could do something about herself if she tried – wore more suitable clothes, went to a good hairdresser and chose the right make-up, for example. Her eyes were still beautiful. A lighter blue than Sarah's, they could light up a room when they weren't poisoned by distrust and bitterness, a sense of always being hard-done-to, as they usually were.

'He doesn't watch much telly,' Paula said finally. 'Only old films on video.'

'What does he do?'

'Reads the paper. Looks at his stamp albums. Stares into space a lot.'

'Does he get out much?'

Paula shot her a scathing glance. 'He's got bloody emphysema,' she said. 'He spends most of his time in a bleeding wheelchair with an oxygen tank strapped to the back. What do you expect?'

Sarah said nothing. She felt herself redden.

'Course,' Paula went on, 'it's the bloody pit that caused it, you know. Over thirty years down that pit, he was, then what do they do? Thatcher's lot closes it down and chucks him out on the dole, that's what. On the bloody scrapheap in his prime. A few years later he starts getting shortness of breath. And do you think there's any compensation? Is there hell-as-like.'

Sarah remembered that her father had smoked about sixty

unfiltered cigarettes a day as well as working down the coal mine, but she didn't see any point in mentioning that to Paula. She also had to get used to the idea that, while Paula might complain about not getting money she felt she was entitled to from the government, any offers of help from family or friends would be taken as charity and dismissed. It was fine for the state to pay out, but not for her sister to do so.

Sarah had been allowed to put down the deposit on the cottages and pay for the renovations when they were knocked into one, but Paula would struggle with the mortgage, with the help of Dad's pension and her earnings as a barmaid, and she even made it clear that she regarded the down payment as only a 'loan.' Stubborn northern pride, Sarah thought. But she knew she might not have got so far without it herself.

They edged away from the difficult subject of their father and Paula asked Sarah about life in Hollywood. Somehow, Sarah got the impression she didn't have much interest except for the occasional opportunity it gave her to put down the Americans and their ways.

To Paula, Sarah soon began to realize, Hollywood was, quite simply, a fantasy. It wasn't real; it didn't exist except on celluloid and in newsprint; its inhabitants were cartoon figures or cardboard cut-outs that just happened to look like handsome men and beautiful women. Their real-life exploits were scripted to titillate the masses.

Actually, Sarah thought with a smile, Paula wasn't far wrong, if only she knew it.

The sun had disappeared behind clouds now and rain was already starting to spatter the windscreen. Paula turned off the M62 south of Leeds and swung north-east towards the York bypass. It was too warm in the car now. Stifling. Sarah found herself fading in and out of sleep.

Rothwell, Swillington, Garforth. She saw them all through half-closed eyes. Run-down housing estates, burned-out cars on patches of wasteland, the odd small park with bare trees and empty flower-beds, lots of pubs, squat churches, schools with iron railings around the playgrounds, zebra crossings and Belisha beacons out front, the occasional strip of shops – newsagent's, mini-market, DIY, grocer's, turf accountant's – all in the inimitable mixture of dirty red-brick and dark mill-stone grit.

The road ran close to the house and shopfronts, separated only by a narrow flagstone pavement. Everything seemed so tiny, so scaled down. It all felt so close, pressing in. Stout old women in threadbare overcoats waited at pedestrian cross-ings, faces obscured by umbrellas.

Paula cursed the weather and lit another cigarette. Sarah opened her window another inch. The cool draught roused her a little. She could hear the hiss of the wheels along the wet road surface. The rain smelled fresh and sweet. A few drops moistened her cheek.

Paula glanced sideways. 'All right?'

'Mmm. Just a bit tired.'

'Forecast says we're in for a miserable Christmas,' Paula said with relish. 'Rain, rain and more rain. Maybe gale force winds, too. And hail. We won't be having a white Christmas this year. That's what they say. Course, they're not always right.'

Sarah closed her eyes and imagined fat snowflakes drifting into the sea and melting. Despite the freak conditions at Manchester, she had no illusions that the weather was going to be anything other than grim; she knew she would feel chilled to the bone day and night, no matter how many layers of clothing she wore or how high she managed to persuade Paula to turn up the central heating. After all, she had lived in England most of her life.

On the other hand, she really didn't care whether it rained or hailed – at least she knew it was going to be *cold*. That was all that counted. She couldn't get at all excited about the Christmas spirit in LA, especially with the unusual number of warm, sunny days they were getting this year. Even the few Christmas trees she had seen appeared to be wilting. She wondered what it must be like in Australia, when Christmas came in the middle of summer.

Sarah rolled the window up again when Paula finished her cigarette. As they headed over the bleak wilderness of the North York Moors, the rain driving almost horizontal and pouring so hard the windscreen wipers could hardly keep time, she slid sideways and rested her cheek against the cool glass. She closed her eyes and smiled to herself.

Paula was cursing a van churning up spray in front, but it didn't matter. Here, at least, were demons she could deal with, demons she knew. Family. It was hardly going to be a merry Christmas, but she might be able to rebuild a few bridges and, more important, while she was away all her problems back in Los Angeles would disappear. When she got back to the beach house, all would be as if it had never happened.

Or so it seemed as she sat with the cool glass against her cheek and the rhythmic swishing of the windscreen wipers lulling her to sleep for the first time since she had pulled that severed arm out of the bloody sand.

11

'You didn't ask me down here just to pick my brains about the college bowls, Arvo,' said Joe Westinghouse. 'What's on your mind?'

Joe and Arvo sat in a bar on Broadway – Joe's choice – a dim, quiet place for serious drinkers and adulterous couples. It was a vinyl and moulded-plastic kind of place, nothing special, but nobody bothered you if you wanted to drink and talk. Or just drink. Nobody came here to make deals; nobody talked on cellular phones or tapped away at notebook computers over cocktails; there wasn't even a pianist.

Soft elevator music permeated the smoky air like a whore's caress. The bartender had his back turned; he was polishing glasses and watching a small TV with the sound turned off. The Kings were playing the Maple Leafs in some weird time zone somewhere across the country. Arvo had a soft spot for the Leafs. Detroit was only a couple of hundred miles from Toronto, after all, and LA was a long way from both places. Still, when it came to baseball you could keep your Blue Jays, Dodgers and Angels; he was a Tigers fan all the way.

It was mid-afternoon. Apart from the bartender, the waitress, a few pairs of illicit lovers and a seasoned alcoholic at the bar knocking back the Martinis as if they were going out of style, Joe and Arvo were the only ones in the place.

Joe Westinghouse was a detective with Robbery-Homicide Division. He and Arvo had consulted on a case once before. They shared an interest in football and baseball and had been to games together now and then. Joe had been to UCLA on a football scholarship until he tore up his knee.

Joe was tall and broad-shouldered, his skin the colour and texture of well-tanned leather. His cropped black hair was sprinkled with grey at the temples, and his deadpan eyes occasionally twinkled with humour. Arvo thought he looked a bit like Dave Winfield, the baseball player. Also like a baseball player, Joe wore a lot of gold – watch-band, wrist chains, gold ear-stud, and probably even more under his white button-down shirt, where Arvo couldn't see.

Joe was working on a rye and ginger, and Arvo was drinking coffee. They had been playing catch-up on sports and department gossip for half an hour, bitching about the brass, but now it was time to get down to business.

'Okay. You're right,' said Arvo. 'It's about that body your guys found on the beach near Pacific Palisades a couple of days ago.'

Joe took another sip of rye and ginger. 'Uh-huh.'

'You know anything about the case?'

'Let's say I've got a passing interest.'

'Anything on it yet?'

Joe squinted at Arvo for a moment, swirling the ice in his drink, then seemed to decide to cut him a bit of slack. Must have been those great seats to the Dodgers' last game of the season, Arvo thought.

The waitress came by in her black fishnet tights and pink tube-top. 'Youse guys all want another?' she asked.

'Why not?' said Joe. 'He's paying.'

She smiled and went to fetch their drinks, wobbling on her high heels. Joe and Arvo watched her go. A body like hers took work, lots of it. Joe raised his eyebrows. They waited until she had set the fresh drink in front of Joe, refilled Arvo's coffee cup and tottered off again, then Joe said, 'Okay. Shoot. What do you want to know?'

'Have you ID'd him yet?'

Joe nodded. 'That was the easy part. Prints on file. Name's John Heimar, Caucasian male, just turned nineteen last October.'

'What's his background?'

'Exactly what you'd expect of a good-looking kid from the boondocks come to find fame and fortune in the city of sin.'

'He worked the streets?'

'Uh-huh. The Boulevard.'

Arvo nodded. He knew Joe meant the stretch of Santa Monica Boulevard that passed through West Hollywood, a big gay cruising area. A saccharine string arrangement of 'All My Loving' drifted across the room like a bad smell. Arvo winced and sipped his coffee. 'Where's he from?'

Joe rubbed his eyes then spoke in a monotone, as if he had heard it, seen it and said it all before. 'Grew up in Magic City, Idaho. Would you believe that? Middle-class parents, ordinary decent folks who didn't know what to do with a wayward kid. Pop runs the local hardware store and Mom teaches kinder-garten. Real *Leave It To Beaver* shit. It seems Magic City, Idaho, didn't have whatever magic it took to keep young Johnny around, 'cause he kept on running away since he was thirteen. New York once. Chicago twice. New Orleans. San Francisco. He wound up out here a couple of years ago. Lived on the streets ever since. Hollywood Division's had him in and out like they've got revolving doors. Nickel-and-dime stuff, mostly. Shoplifting, a little dealing. Nothing violent.'

'So what happened?'

Joe shrugged, tapped out a Winston and lit it. Arvo licked his lips. He'd given up smoking three years ago, when he moved out to LA to join the TMU, but he hadn't gotten rid of the craving yet. Cigarettes, he remembered, went especially well with coffee. With alcohol, too. And after dinner. Not to mention sex.

'You tell me,' Joe said, blowing the smoke out. 'Just plain bad luck, I guess.'

'Sex crime?'

'Looks like it.'

'How was he killed?'

'According to the coroner's office, somebody slit his throat from behind with a very sharp knife and stabbed him in the chest and neck. Then cut him up with some kind of saw or serrated blade. Arms. Legs. Head. Torso. Put him together again on the beach like a jigsaw puzzle and half buried him in sand.' He shook his head slowly.

'The throat?' said Arvo. 'That's pretty common in homosexual homicides, isn't it?'

'Uh-huh. Shrink says it's got something to do with the mouth and throat connection with oral sex.' Joe shrugged. 'I don't know about that. All I know is I've seen too much of it. You get it in a lot of high-octane emotional murders, too, mostly domestics. Seems when people see red they aim for the throat and chest with a knife. What the experts call the "overkill" element. Means the poor fucker's dead before the last fifty stab wounds.'

'Any fingerprints? Footprints?'

Joe shook his head. 'No physical evidence at all. Not yet.'

'Was Heimar killed on the beach?'

Joe tapped a column of ash into the glass tray. 'Nope. Not enough blood. He was just ... reassembled ... there. With about as much success as Humpty Dumpty.'

'Where he was killed, there'd be a lot of blood, right?'

'Yup. But so far we've got diddly. No suspects and no idea where it happened. Could've been some other beach, maybe the desert, up in the hills, or anywhere else out in the wilds. Could've been in some apartment for all we know. Or a house. A nice house somewhere in the 'burbs like Palos Verde or San Marina. People'd be surprised some of the things going on there behind locked doors out in the 'burbs. Gacey. Dahmer. Who the fuck knows anything any more?' Joe tossed back the rest of his rye and ginger and crunched the ice cubes. He waved for the waitress and she brought another. Arvo stuck with coffee.

'So what's your interest?' Joe asked finally.

'Sarah Broughton.'

Joe nodded. 'Right. She found the body. She wouldn't have been receiving any unwanted attention from warped members of the viewing audience lately, would she?'

Arvo smiled. 'You got it. Nasty letters.'

Joe cocked a finger at him and clicked his tongue. 'I'm not a hotshot detective with RHD for nothing, man.'

'There's nothing concrete,' Arvo said. 'It's just—'

'Too much of a coincidence?'

'That's right.'

'Do *you* think there's a connection?'

'No,' said Arvo. 'People who write weird letters are generally wimps. They'd be no more likely to commit murder than a nun would. But like you said, it's too much of a coincidence. I have to check it out.'

Joe nodded. 'Uh-huh. Never did trust those nuns,' he said. 'Anyway, a team of detectives canvassed the Boulevard strip, and all they could come up with is that a couple of other street kids saw John Heimar getting into a car about eight o'clock on the night he was killed. They figured he'd scored, of course. Needless to say, none of them was especially forthcoming.'

'Did they get the make?'

'Yeah. It's a blue-green-black Ford Chevy convertible sedan pick-up truck from Japan.'

Arvo laughed. 'Okay. Sorry I asked. You said earlier you thought it was a sex crime. Any other evidence yet, apart from the MO?'

'Some. The kid had been sodomized sometime before

death, but there's no telling when, or how willing he was. And there's no evidence at all to show that he was forced. Given the victim's line of business I'd say it's likely enough he'd been with at least a couple of other chickenhawks earlier that night, wouldn't you? On the other hand, you sometimes get cases where the john cuts off the guy's air supply from behind with some sort of ligature while he butt-fucks him. Supposed to be a real turn-on. Something like that could have happened, gone too far, then the john panicked and tried to cover up, make it look like a sex murder. The coroner's office found traces of semen from two different sources in the anus. Either he hadn't heard of AIDS or he liked to take risks. Or maybe the rubber had a hole in it.'

'Was he HIV positive?'

'Nope. They ran *that* test pretty quickly.'

Arvo took a sip of tepid coffee and pulled a face. 'What was the time of death?' he asked.

'Between about eleven that night and two in the morning. Wouldn't say any closer than that.'

'That's three hours after the kid was picked up.'

'Uh-huh.'

'Nobody saw him after he got into that unidentified car around eight?'

'Only the killer.'

'Any signs of torture?'

'Nope. Clean as a whistle. Under the sand, the kid was buck naked. Apart from the stab wounds and an old needle-mark or two, his body was in pretty good shape.'

'Are you running DNA tests on the semen?'

'Sure. Like I said, they got two different samples already. But you know as well as I do, Arvo, that shit takes time. Especially the way things are backed up right now. Thirty-eight homicides last weekend. *Thirty-eight.* Can you believe it? You can only push the coroner's office so hard. Those guys are up to their eyeballs in stiffs. Plus it takes so long for toxi-cology to get the test results from some of these things.'

Four businessmen came in, laughing and joking, fresh from the office by the looks of their clothes.

Joe looked at his watch. Just gone three. 'After-work crowd,' he said. 'They get in early on a Friday. Sometimes they get here so early they just sort of merge right in with the late-lunch crowd.'

Arvo laughed.

'I guess it's not often you get a homosexual killer writing love letters to a beautiful actress, is it?' Joe asked.

Arvo shrugged. 'Statistically speaking, no.'

'Fuck statistics.'

'Still no. Like I said, letter-writers don't usually do much more than write letters. I'm just poking around. All I'm look-ing for is some connection between Sarah Broughton and Heimar, and it doesn't look as if there is one.'

'If there is, I don't see it.'

'Me, neither. What's your theory?'

'Sex killer of some kind. Got to be. And he's so proud of his handiwork he wants people to admire it. Peacock mentality.'

'Pretty limited audience.'

Joe shrugged. 'Maybe.' Then he paused. 'These letters the actress has been getting. Anything there?'

Arvo shook his head. 'I've only seen one, and it's pretty low-level stuff. How did she react at the scene?'

'As you'd expect. I didn't get there till later, but according to the first officer she was pretty shaken up.'

'She a suspect?'

'Come on, Arvo, what do you take us for? She wouldn't be in England right now if she was, would she? When they'd got her calmed down, the detectives who caught the squeal had a good look around her place. No blood, nothing. Do you figure the stiff for her pen pal? He comes visiting and she kills him, then cuts him up, buries him under the sand and conveniently finds him on her morning run?'

Arvo shrugged. 'It was worth asking. Weirder things have happened.'

'True. But the answer's still no. She's clean.'

'Did she see anything?'

'Nope. Said she might have heard a sound or seen a light in the night, or she might have imagined it. It was later she found the stiff, when she was going for her regular morning run. She says she leaned forward and tugged the arm and . . . well, I don't have to spell it out for you, do I?'

Suddenly, Joe's eyes twinkled and he burst into laughter. It sounded like a braying horse. Some of the other drinkers looked over, smiling uneasily. 'Hey,' Joe said. 'What if the cameras had caught that, huh? TV star bends over to pull this guy up out of the sand and what happens? His fucking arm comes off, that's what, and she falls flat on her ass holding it out in front of her.'

Arvo visualized the scene, too, and couldn't help but laugh with Joe at the farcical absurdity of it. When they had calmed down, Joe knocked back the dregs of his drink and stood up. 'Got to go, old buddy,' he said. 'Or Mary will have my ass. Booked off early. It's little Sue's birthday party today and I promised I'd be there. Six. Can you believe it? Seems only last week she was crawling around on all fours and running through a six-pack of Huggies a day. Anyway, don't be a stranger.'

Arvo stood and shook hands. 'You, too,' he said. 'Any chance of a look at the crime-scene photos?'

Joe looked at his watch. 'Sure, I'll make a call and have copies sent over. And . . .' Joe paused and turned on his way out. 'Keep me informed.' He pointed a finger at Arvo and cocked it. 'I mean it.'

'Will do. And thanks.'

When Joe had gone, Arvo found he had no desire to stay in the bar any longer. The smoke had thickened since the after-work crowd had started to arrive, and some moron had arranged 'Suspicious Minds' for accordion and strings. Probably made a fortune out of it, too. Welcome to hell.

He had some leftover pizza and a couple of bottles of Sam Adams lager in the fridge at home, and the previous night he'd set his VCR to tape *I Married a Monster From Outer Space*. If he hadn't screwed up on the settings, it should be right there in the machine waiting for him. He'd seen it when he was a kid, but after Nyreen, the title took on a whole new perspective.

Arvo couldn't see any link between a homosexual murder and the letters Sarah Broughton had been receiving. Despite the publicity given to exceptions, the rule was that celebrity stalkers were rarely violent; on the other hand, male prostitution was certainly a high-risk profession, AIDS not being the only danger. It attracted more than its fair share of violent weirdos and thrill killers. So John Heimar's number had come up. As Joe said, that was just his bad luck.

But as he walked out onto Broadway, Arvo couldn't help but wonder. The body had been placed where *someone* would have the shock of finding it, that was for certain. The killer obviously had a theatrical flair and needed an audience, if only of one. What Arvo had to ask himself was why he had selected that particular stretch of beach, where Sarah Broughton went for her morning run.

12

Sarah lay half-asleep listening to the seagulls screaming and squawking outside her window. At first, she thought she was still in her own bedroom back at the beach house. Soon she would wake up and the bad dream would be over. When she opened her eyes, though, she felt a momentary panic. Everything was different.

This room was smaller, for a start, and a thin white radiator under the drawn curtains infused the air with what little warmth it possessed. The tip of Sarah's nose felt cold in a way it never had in Los Angeles. In the dim light, she could make out cream wallpaper patterned with poppies or red roses, matching the heavy duvet she pulled up to her chin. Her pillow smelled of lavender. Beyond the noise the gulls made, she could hear the sea pounding the wall.

Then she remembered: she was at the family cottage in Robin Hood's Bay. It stood at the bottom of the hill, on a row to the left of the main street, and looked out right over the North Sea. That was why her father had wanted it. In clement weather, Sarah knew, Arthur Bolton liked nothing better than to sit in his wheelchair at the bottom of the garden and look out to sea. She fancied that the open horizon somehow helped make up for the years he had spent in the dark, claustrophobic coalmines.

Everything seemed unfamiliar to Sarah because she had never slept in this room before. The last time she had visited, the two adjacent cottages had not yet been knocked into one and renovated. Though she couldn't remember the visit at all clearly, she had probably slept downstairs on the sofa-bed, stupefied with Quaaludes and cognac.

So far, she hadn't seen either her father or Cathy and Jason. They hadn't known what time Paula and Sarah would get back from the airport, so they had left a note saying they'd gone to visit a neighbour and wouldn't be long.

Sarah had felt so tired that Paula had packed her off to bed immediately with a cup of tea. It was still there on the bedside table, only half drunk. Sarah slid her hand out and touched it. Cold. She huddled under the duvet again and closed her eyes.

Even though she now knew where she was, Sarah still felt disoriented. Too restless to go back to sleep, she turned over and stretched, arching so her fingers scraped the wall above her. That felt better.

She pulled back the sheets and went to open the curtains. Outside, it was getting dark. The rain had stopped and the sky looked like a dirty dishrag slashed with charcoal. The slate-coloured sea sloshed heavily against the rough stone wall at the bottom of the garden. It was a sea view, all right, but light years away from the one she was used to, where bright sun bleached the vanishing point of water and sky.

Sarah turned the bedroom light on and took stock of her surroundings. Everything was fresh and clean, of course; that would be Paula's doing. There was even the old framed print of Atkinson Grimshaw's *Park Row, Leeds 1882* from the old house in Barnsley hanging on the wall opposite her bed. Paula knew Sarah had always loved it for its eerie moon and sky and the cobbles and tramlines all wet and shiny after rain. She must have put it there specially.

In the small bookcase beside the wardrobe were Sarah's old books. She hadn't looked at them for years and hadn't even known they had survived the move from Barnsley: childhood favourites like *Black Beauty* and *The Secret Garden;* Enid

Blyton, mostly the Famous Five and the Secret Seven; some girls'-school and nurse stories; and one or two Mills and Boon romances.

Then came the Romantic poetry of her early teens – Keats, Shelley, Byron – followed by the plays she had read first at home then studied later at university – collections by Shakespeare, Ibsen and Tennessee Williams, along with well-thumbed copies of *The Duchess of Malfi, Three Sisters* and *A Dream Play*.

Hanging from a hook at the back of the door was the red knitted Christmas stocking her mother had made, with her name, Sally, embroidered in white. Paula must have dug it out. Perhaps her family really did want her here for Christmas after all.

Everything was quiet downstairs. Either they were still out or Paula was hushing everyone up so Sarah could sleep. Time to unpack.

Sarah hefted her suitcase onto the bed and unfastened it. Clothes and presents spilled out, and there, stuck in among them all, was the letter. She hesitated, then reached out and picked it up. This one had no stamp; it had been delivered by hand.

Just then, she heard a door bang downstairs, followed by the clamour of children's voices. Jason called out her name. Paula told him to be quiet. Time to enter into family life again.

Sarah's heart leapt into her throat. She had never felt so nervous, even before going on stage for a first night. She looked at the letter again and dropped it back among the pile of clothes, half pleased that she had been interrupted before opening it. After all, she was in England now, thousands of miles away from her problems in LA.

She pulled on her jeans and sweatshirt, then opened the door and started down the worn stone stairs.

What she saw made her stop halfway.

Illuminated by the hall light, a man slumped in a wheelchair at the bottom of the stairs. Beside him, attached to the chair, stood a small tank, like the kind frogmen wear, from which a transparent tube ran to his nostrils. His shoulders sloped and his body looked emaciated under the thick woollen blanket. Bluish flesh sagged and wrinkled over hollow, bony cheeks and scared, bright, feverish eyes looked up at her. Even from halfway upstairs, she could hear the soft hiss of the oxygen and the struggle as he laboured for breath.

White-knuckled, she gripped the banister and took a faltering step forward. 'Hello, Father,' she said.

13

'I hear your actress found a body on the beach,' Maria said. 'Think there's anything in it?'

Arvo shook his head. 'I doubt it. Just unlucky, I guess. On the other hand . . .'

'What?'

'I don't like coincidences, that's all.'

'So what's she like?'

'Who?'

'You know. The actress. Sarah Broughton.'

'You watch that show?'

'Sure do.'

Arvo shook his head slowly. It was late Friday afternoon, and Maria was sitting opposite him. He hadn't seen her since the Sandi Gaines intervention. The only other team members in the office were Eric Mettering and Kelly Norris, one of the three females on the unit.

'Me, too,' Kelly called out from the far hutch. 'That Jack Marillo guy's got a great bod.'

Maria laughed. 'So tell me about her,' she insisted. 'What's she like? In the flesh?'

In the flesh, Arvo still thought that Maria herself was as desirable a woman as he had ever met, though he hadn't told her that, and just about the opposite physical type to Sarah Broughton.

They were different as day and night. Maria's sexuality was sensual and earthy, while Sarah Broughton's was more cerebral. While lovemaking with Maria would be joyous and uncomplicated, Arvo imagined, with Sarah it would mean searching for and freeing repressed emotions, finding ways through barriers and other defences. Maria's skin would be warm, would offer friction and texture to the touch, he thought, whereas Sarah's would be as smooth, and possibly as cold, as marble.

'What kind of question is that?' Arvo asked. '"What's she like?"'

'A pretty simple one, I'd've thought,' said Maria. 'Is she pretty?'

'Of course she's pretty. She's a TV actress.'

'They're not all pretty,' Maria countered. 'Especially the Brits. Some of them are downright plain and homely.'

'They've all got crooked teeth,' Kelly chimed in.

'Okay, so her teeth *are* a bit crooked,' Arvo said. 'So what? So are mine. Does it mean you can't be pretty if you've got crooked teeth?'

'You think you're pretty, Arvo?' Maria asked with a mischievous smile.

'That's not what I said. You're misinterpreting me. What I said was—'

'I know what you said. So you think *she's* pretty?'

'Sure she's pretty, in a cool sort of way.'

'What does that mean?'

'You know, she's blonde, pale complexion, has that accent.'

'You think she's frigid, is that it?'

'No, I didn't say that. Look—'

'So she's sexy as well as pretty?'

'I guess so.'

'Guess so? Come on, Arvo, you can do better than that.'

'Okay. Yeah. She's sexy. All right?'

'How sexy?'

'Just sexy.'

'No need to blush.'

'I'm not blushing.'

'Yes you are,' yelled Kelly.

'What about her personality?' Maria asked.

'General impressions?'

'Well you hardly know her intimately. Or do you?'

'She's an actress. You know actresses. She was partly in character. The cop she plays.'

'Anita O'Rourke,' Kelly chipped in again.

'That's the one.'

'So,' Maria went on, 'you're saying you didn't get a real good sense of her?'

'She's very reserved.'

'Sounds like a typical Brit.'

'I guess so,' he said. 'But I think she's scared, too.'

'Maybe she's got good reason to be. What's your sense of the guy who's writing the letters?'

Arvo thought for a moment, recalling the letter he had been studying earlier. 'He sees himself as her long-lost lover, now become her saviour, her rescuer, her knight in shining armour.'

'Rescuer from what?'

'From the evils of Hollywood. From *Them*.'

'The usual semi-literate diatribe?'

'Not really. This guy seems reasonably well educated. Not that that means a lot, I know. Bizarre forms of spelling and grammar hardly represent a greater threat than correct grammar – except to literacy. There are some unusual capitalizations – nouns like "Machines," "Power" and "Crazy."'

'Germans capitalize their nouns, don't they?' said Maria.

'Uh-huh. But this seems more like some sort of mental tic. It makes the concepts sound *Big*, and it goes with his gushing, flowery prose style.'

'What about the handwriting?' Kelly Norris asked. She had left her own hutch and was now standing beside Maria, interested, hand resting lightly on the divider. A tall, big-boned woman with a mass of curly grey hair and spots of colour high on her cheeks, Kelly had been the first woman on the team. She was wearing threadbare black cords and a baggy white cardigan over a red blouse. Kelly always did dress casually.

'It was done on a laser printer,' said Arvo. 'That means he either owns a computer set-up or he works in a place where he can get access to one.'

'Where did he send the letters?' Maria asked.

'Home address. She thought she kept it a pretty closely guarded secret.'

Kelly and Maria laughed. 'Her and everyone else.'

'Yeah. Well, maybe we can do a bit of checking around with the agencies and private detectives who sell that sort of information. See if anyone's bought Sarah Broughton's address recently.'

'Good luck,' said Maria. 'In my experience, those guys give you dick.'

'True enough. Still worth a shot.'

'Any occult stuff?' Kelly asked.

'No,' said Arvo. Often, the writers insisted that the victim should be initiated as a Dawn Goddess of the Order of the Golden Monkey Foreskins, or something. Arvo had seen plenty of those, and they always gave him the same feeling: somewhere between the creeps and the desire to laugh out loud.

'Apart from the romantic stuff,' he went on, 'there are a few disturbing references to hacking away the corrupt flesh. And a bit about biting through her nipple and luxuriating in the flow of blood and milk.'

'Sick-o,' said Kelly.

Maria put her finger in her mouth and mimicked barfing.

Even Eric looked up from the file he was working on and wrinkled his nose.

'The big three,' Arvo said. 'Sex, death and Mother. All in one sentence. All very mysterious.' But he stopped himself from reading too much into the images. After all, he wasn't a psychiatrist; he only had a degree in Communications, that catch-all for people who didn't really know what they wanted to do when they were between eighteen and twenty-one. And the TMU didn't demand special prerequisite training from its members, only that they be good detectives. Keen intuition, strong research abilities and general social skills were the essentials.

He shook his head. 'And Sarah Broughton's a puzzle, too. I think she knows more than she's telling.'

Maria raised her black eyebrows. 'Better watch yourself, Arvo,' she said. 'I've never known a man who wasn't a sucker for an enigmatic woman.' She nudged Kelly and they both laughed. Eric kept his head down, shiny bald pate towards them.

'Package for Detective Arvo Hughes!'

Arvo raised his hand and the patrolman walked right up to his hutch and handed over a thick manila envelope. He signed for it, stuck his thumb under the flap and ripped it open.

Crime-scene pictures spilled out over his messy desk. Jesus, he thought, as he looked at the stark black-and-white images and the garish colour Polaroids, someone had certainly done a number on John Heimar.

There were pictures of the general area and of the body half buried, *in situ*, with the bloody stump of an arm lying beside it, where, Arvo assumed, Sarah Broughton must have dropped it. Then there were photos of the various body parts as they were unearthed and pieced together on a canvas sheet on the beach. Photo after photo showed the reconstruction of a body: first the arm, then the arm and head, then an arm, a leg and the head, and so on.

There was very little blood; clearly most of it had been

spilled somewhere else and the rest had drained into the sand. The rough edges of flesh where the head and legs had been severed gaped like cuts of meat in a butcher's shop.

Arvo became aware of Maria's perfume and felt her warm breath on his neck as she came around and leaned over him. 'My God,' he heard her mutter. 'This is what your actress found?'

'Uh-huh.'

'The poor woman.'

But Arvo wasn't looking at the images of violent death any longer. Something in one of the early black-and-whites had caught his eye.

The photograph had been taken from the landward side of the body, and judging by the angle, the photographer had probably knelt to take it. The time must have been soon after sunrise, because the sun was shining over the hills in the east and casting fairly long shadows.

Just beyond the body, where the sand was getting wet from the tide, Arvo thought he could make out a faint indentation, as if something had been drawn there, then mostly washed away. He could only see it because of the sun's angle, and even then it was no more than an indistinct outline. It could have been merely a trick of the light and water, he thought, but it looked exactly like a heart shape.

14

As soon as Sarah got to the bottom of the stairs and bent to give her father a kiss on his rough cheek, Cathy and Jason dashed through from the front room and surrounded her, jumping up and down. She had hardly registered the sour smell of his breath before the kids had dragged her away to tell them all about the television series and what it was like living with all the stars in Hollywood. What were Arnold Schwarzenegger and Jean-Claude Van Damme *really* like?

After she had whetted their appetites with a few harmless exaggerations, magically transforming the humble beach house into something approaching the Hearst castle, she went to look for Paula and found her in the kitchen, warm in the heat of the gas oven.

'It's nowt special,' Paula said, by way of a warning. 'Just a chicken-and-leek casserole, boiled potatoes and a tin of peas. Not what you're used to over there, I expect.'

'It's fine, really,' said Sarah, smiling to herself. In a way it was a relief not to have to make her way politely through yet another shredded romaine and sweet onion salad with chèvre and roasted chestnuts, or duck and spinach ravioli with thymed tomatoes. 'Can I help?'

Paula gestured with a wooden spoon. 'You can peel those spuds, if you like.'

Put firmly in her place, Sarah began to peel the potatoes. 'Dad looks worse than I expected,' she said.

Paula gave a harsh laugh. 'Well, he's not getting any better, that's for certain. But there's good days and bad. Today's fair to middling.' She put down her wooden spoon and turned to face Sarah, tiredness and resignation showing in the lines around her eyes and the dark bags beneath them. 'It's the nights that are the worst,' she said. 'He has trouble breathing when he lies down sometimes. The doctor says it's normal, given his condition, but that doesn't help a lot, does it? The thing is, Sal, he gets so frightened when it happens. He thinks his time's come. His heart beats so fast and loud I'll swear they can almost hear it in the next street. And he gets confused, he doesn't know where he is or who I am. It passes, like, but it gets me worried. I hate to see him like that. And him such a vigorous man in his prime.'

She looked away, eyes burning, then shot Sarah a sly, side-ways glance before casting her eyes down. 'He calls me by your name sometimes, too, you know. "Sal," he says. "Sal, I've got to go now."' She sniffed and went back to stirring the sauce. 'Hurry up with those spuds, will you, or this bloody casserole will be well past its sell-by date.'

'It smells good,' said Sarah, flushed and tingling with what Paula had just told her. Her father had called *her* name – Sal – in his confusion. Perhaps he didn't hate her, after all. She ran cold water into the pan of peeled potatoes and put it on the ring.

'Thanks,' said Paula. 'You can set the table now, if you like.'

Sarah did so, and before long they all sat down to dinner. Cathy and Jason wanted to go in the front room and watch television while they ate from their laps, but Paula said no, they watched too much of the idiot-box as it was. She looked at Sarah when she said 'idiot-box' and Sarah didn't miss the dig. But that was Paula all over; she had given too much away in an unguarded moment, and now she had to go on the offensive.

The children sulked for about thirty seconds, then they

started humming the theme music of *Good Cop, Bad Cop*. Paula told them to shut up. Sarah laughed. Her father continued to pick at his food in silence, leaving most of it. Paula shot Sarah a long-suffering glance, as if to say, 'See, he's even off his food now. What am I to do? How can I cope with all this?'

It was hot in the dining room and Sarah felt a bead or two of sweat trickle down the groove of her spine. Had Paula turned up the heat for her benefit? It would be just like her to do that, and then complain about the bill. What little conversation they had over the meal was halting and banal, yet fraught with the tension of the unsaid, the unexpressed. She was beginning to feel like a character in a Pinter play.

As she ate, she began to think that there might be some kind of home or special clinic where her father could go and be well cared for. God knew, she could afford it. But she knew without asking that any such suggestion would be met with extreme resistance. Where she came from, you looked after your own.

After a Marks and Spencer's apple pie with custard, which Sarah declined, and some general chat about what a lousy summer it had been, Paula sent the children off to bed and announced that she had to go to work. Sarah did the washing-up alone, with only the sound of the wind whistling around the kitchen window for company.

When she had finished, she returned to the dining room and saw that her father was still in the same position at the table. He had one of his stamp albums open in front of him and was turning the stiff pages slowly.

Sarah could only stand in the doorway and gaze, held frozen by the emotion of a memory that leapt unbidden into her mind. She must have been five or six, at the cramped old pit house in Barnsley, and for the first time her father beckoned her over after tea to come look at his stamps. Even then he had spent hours at the table just looking at them, chain-smoking Woodbines and sometimes drinking a bottle of beer.

Sarah could remember the smells as if they were yesterday: the acrid cigarette smoke, the malt and hops of the beer, the lingering odour of dripping, bacon or kippers. And she had stood beside him – he with his arm loosely around her shoulders – and looked into what she could only describe as windows into bright new worlds. Small windows with serrated edges, or tiny screens onto which colourful images were projected. None of the stamps were very valuable, she thought, but the bright colours, the proud heads of monarchs, exotic birds, other animals and majestic ships and planes that decorated them enthralled her.

And now here he was, in a different, much larger house with any number of rooms to choose from, in the same position at the dinner table, poring over his collection. From where she stood, Sarah could see the flashes of colour.

In her mind, she could hear the memory of his voice as he told her the stories of the stamps, of how 'Suomi' meant Finland and 'Deutschland' meant Germany, who they had fought in the war, of how far away and how hot were the places like Gold Coast, British Guyana and Mauritius, and how the brightly coloured birds with the long feather tails, the macaws and birds of paradise, depicted on the stamps, really did live in those places. One day, she had vowed then, she would see them. Her eyes burned with tears as she watched him labouring to breathe over the images.

Her father looked up and frowned. 'What's up, lass?'

Sarah wiped her forearm over her eyes. 'Nothing,' she said. 'I'm fine.' She grasped the back of a chair and steadied herself. 'Still a bit tired. Must be the flight.'

'Like a drop of brandy?'

'No, no. I'm all right, really, Dad. Don't bother.' She rubbed her eyes again, this time with the backs of her hands.

He jerked his head. 'It's in that cabinet over there. I wouldn't mind one myself.'

When she was a child, there had always been 'medicinal' brandy in the house, and the one time Sarah had been given a drink, after the shock of falling off her bike and spraining her wrist, she had hated it. She had tried it since, however, and didn't mind the taste too much now.

She found the brandy and two glasses. She poured generous measures and put one in front of her father, then sat down with her own. He looked at his glass, smiled and said, 'Hand slipped, did it?' then took a sip.

An awkward silence followed. Sarah didn't know what to say. She didn't want to ask him about his emphysema – no more, she imagined, than he wanted to talk about it. Finally, her father broke the silence: 'Doing all right, then, are you, lass?'

'Yes.' Sarah cradled her glass in both hands and looked into the dark amber liquid. 'Yes, I'm doing fine.'

'Being ill like this . . .' He paused. 'It changes you. Puts things in perspective. Know what I mean?'

Sarah nodded. She didn't know what to say. Had he forgiven her?

'Aye,' he said. 'Well . . .' Then he shifted in his wheelchair, probably from embarrassment. As Sarah knew too well, he wasn't a man given to easy expression of his feelings. Well, no men were, really, but some were better than others.

'So what's Tinseltown like?' he asked.

'I . . . I don't really . . .' Sarah felt stuck for words. She had almost said she didn't live there, but of course she did. What on earth could she be thinking of? 'It's all right, I suppose,' she went on. 'It's warm most of the time. I miss the change of seasons. The snowdrops and daffodils in spring, the leaves changing and falling in autumn. I mean, I don't mind living there, but it's so . . .'

Lonely, she almost said, but she didn't want to expose herself, certainly not to her father. *Let's bury Daddy in the sand!* She shivered. Besides, isolation was what she wanted, wasn't it? Seclusion, no complications. And the beach house was where she had begun to find herself, begun the reconstruction of Sally Bolton. Instead, she simply said, 'Impermanent.'

'You're not planning on staying there?' her father asked.

Sarah shrugged. That wasn't what she meant at all, but she didn't think she could explain it to him.

'Do you still live by yourself?' he asked.

'Yes.'

'Isn't it dangerous? We see things on the news. Muggings, gangs, riots and fires and suchlike.'

Sarah shrugged. 'I suppose so. I'm working at the studio a lot. It's safe there. They've got very good security. And it's very quiet where I live. By the sea, like this.' Except for the maniac on the hill watching me through binoculars, she wanted to add. 'You should come and visit,' she said, not realizing until she had spoken that he probably couldn't travel very easily.

His lips formed a smile that his eyes didn't echo. 'I doubt I could survive that there smog,' he said.

Sarah laughed. 'Oh, come on. You'd probably be better off than the rest of us, what with your oxygen and all. Besides, it's not so bad these days. There's a lot of emission controls.'

He grinned, showing crooked black and yellow teeth. 'Aye, who knows? Maybe one day. I'd like to see all them stars on the pavement there before I die. Ronald Colman. Greta Garbo. Charlie Chaplin. Jimmy Stewart. I've always wanted to see those.'

Sarah was surprised. 'I'll take you,' she said. 'I'll show you them. I didn't even know you liked movies.'

He shrugged. 'Used to go to t'pictures a lot when I was a young lad. Before I met your mother and went down t'pit. Never had time for owt like that when you were a kid, though. I were always on some bloody awkward shift or another. That or sleeping.' He paused and took several deep breaths of oxygen before going on. 'And there weren't no videos and the like back then. It's a lot easier now. I can't get out and about much these days so I watch at home. Paula's a good lass, she goes and fetches them for me. Old ones mostly. Black-and-white. They're still the best. You can keep your sex and violence.' He looked directly at Sarah as he spoke, and she blushed and turned away, remembering the row they had after he'd seen her do a nude scene in a Channel Four film. The beginning of the end. 'Nay,' he went on, 'I hadn't time for t'pictures back then, had I? Your mother, though . . . now that were another matter.'

They fell silent for a moment, Sarah contemplating the times when her mother took *her* to the pictures. More stimulus for the budding actress. All kinds of memories came rushing back. She remembered the first film she had ever seen, when she was five or six – Walt Disney's *One Hundred and One Dalmatians* – and how scared she had been of Cruella De Ville.

When she next looked at her father, his eyes were closed and his chin rested on his chest. At first, she thought something terrible had happened to him, but she could still hear his struggle for breath and the slow hiss of oxygen.

Slowly, Sarah crept upstairs and picked up the envelope. She had been in two minds about it all evening: half afraid of opening it and morbidly curious about the contents. Now, while her father and the children slept, while Paula was at work, she opened it and slipped out the two pages. Then she read the words with mounting horror:

My Darling Little Star,

Oh my Love, if only everyone could see what I see. Patterns of the most delicate intricacy. Patterns of Spirit stripped of Flesh and Muscle. Sometimes I see Fountains of bright Blood gushing across a hundred television screens at once. Sometimes I hear you speak to me over the Electromagnetic Waves, telling me what I must do to prove my Love.

Don't you know who I am, my Little Star? You are the Detective now. Look into your past and find me. I am there, the dark Shape in the Shadows of your Memory. Find me, my love. Speak to me. Love me. Let me free you. Tell me you Know. I will rescue you. I will win you back from Them and we will look into each other's eyes over the candlelight and hold hands beyond the Flesh for centuries through the Mirrors of the Sea where none can live but us.

Tell me you accept my simple Offering. Now do you see how I can provide for you, how I can Honor you as no one else can? With your Love, there can be no Fear. With your Love, there will be no Limits.

But you must not think I enjoy causing pain. No, that is not it at all, that is not my purpose, surely you can see? The boy wanted Death. Every night he cruised the Boulevard looking for Death, for someone who would deliver him to his Destiny. The Boulevard of Death. I put him to sleep like a kind Anesthetist before I performed my Operation. My Knives were sharp. I spent hours sharpening them. I was gentle when I bent over him. He didn't feel a thing. Please believe me.

The disentanglement of Spirit from Flesh has a Scent and an Aura all of its own, my Love. One day I will show you, let you Smell and Taste it with me. We will disentangle our Spirits from our Gross Bodies and entwine for ever, cut away the wretched excess. I will bury my head between your Milk White Thighs and drink the Blood and Baptize myself with your Menses. Outside our Skins we will know Eternal Love.

*I must stop now. I am Weary and my Heart aches for you, my
Love. Darkness falls and more Visions await me.*

I am Yours, your Loving and Adoring Servant, unto all Eternity,
                                                              M.

Outside, Sarah could hear the waves crashing against the sea
wall and the wind gusting and moaning about the rooftops. A
shutter was banging somewhere. Inside, she was aware of the
loud beating of her heart. My God, she thought, he *did* do it.
She *had* seen the heart with her name in it drawn in the sand.
It wasn't an illusion. But *who* was he?

Down the street, the wind whipped a tile from someone's
roof and sent it smashing to the ground.

15

Arvo drove up the Coast Highway on Saturday morning with the top of his tan convertible open and the Allman Brothers singing 'Statesboro' Blues' on the radio. The ocean breeze ruffled his hair and forced its way deep into his lungs. He needed it to blow the cobwebs out of his mind and bring him back to life.

Last night had been a bad one, starting when he found that *I Married a Monster from Outer Space* had been delayed by a late-running hockey game, leaving him with only the first ten minutes of the movie.

As a substitute, he had dashed out and rented *Ilsa, Harem Keeper of the Oil Sheiks*, which was every bit as much of a turkey as the guy in the rental store had warned him.

He had woken just after four in the morning with a dry mouth and a pounding head, courtesy of the Scotch and Sam Adams chasers he had drunk after the leftover pizza. He hadn't been able to get back to sleep again, mostly for thinking about the Sarah Broughton case. He had arranged to meet Stuart Kleigman in Santa Monica for lunch, but first he wanted to take a look at the crime scene.

The backs of the houses that faced the Coast Highway were nondescript. Mostly, they were simple flat-roofed rectangular boxes of varying heights and widths, some beige or white stucco, some wood-frame. Some of them had high windows facing the road, but most presented a blank façade. Because the houses were close together, the narrow gaps between them had been closed with high chain-link fencing.

A hundred yards or so west of the houses was a white three-storey office building, with stairwells visible through the large plate-glass windows. Architecturally, it was nothing but a cube of white stone fitted with windows. The parking lot, with spaces reserved for ten cars, was empty, and Arvo pulled into the one marked 'Dr S.A. Pedersen.' You wouldn't catch a doctor or a dentist working on a Saturday if he could help it. Not as long as there were golf courses within driving distance.

He walked down the stone steps to the beach, the route Joe reckoned the killer must have carried John Heimar's body parts, probably in a plastic garbage bag.

At the bottom of the steps, Arvo stepped into the fine sand and looked around. Gulls skimmed the water's surface, looking for fish. The only people on the beach were two men walking a dog.

There were no signs left of the horror that had taken place here just a few days ago, nothing even to mark the spot where John Heimar's body parts had been buried. Since then, the tide had been in and out a few times and washed everything away. The crime-scene techs had had to work fast. Like King Canute, even the LAPD couldn't hold back the tide.

Set on a long promontory about twenty feet high, the houses had steps carved in the rock leading down to the beach. Each also had a high gate at beach level. Despite the difficult access, though, it wasn't a private beach, and such security as existed there – gates, wire – was pretty Mickey Mouse, in Arvo's opinion.

On the other hand, it wasn't a natural choice for dumping a body, and if the killer *really* wanted to show off his handiwork to the world at large, why not try Santa Monica, Venice or Redondo, further south? Maybe even have a good laugh when one of the bodybuilders on Muscle Beach pulled the severed arm loose? Plenty of people there, every day of the week.

Could Sarah Broughton have been the only audience he wanted? Arvo remembered the letter: *'I have much to Plan and Execute before we can be together as Fate intends. My mind Boils and Seethes with the Burden, the Weight and the Glory of it. All for you. Let me prove I am more than equal to the Task.'*

He shivered and returned to the car. In Santa Monica, he found a parking space in a side street and walked over the arched bridge onto the pier. Behind him, the white buildings along Ocean Avenue sparkled in the late December sun. To the north, across the bay, Arvo could just about make out the contours of the coastal hills behind where he had just been. Breakers crashed on the beach with a deep booming sound, churning up spume, and diamonds danced on the greenish-white ocean.

Just beyond the carousel, a Hispanic family stood busking: the father played guitar; the teenaged son sang in Spanish and looked as if he'd rather be just about anywhere else; the daughter danced as awkwardly as any spindly nine-year-old would; and the toddler stood with his mournful-looking mother by the upturned, white top hat, looking cute. Arvo grinned at him and flipped in a couple of quarters.

Stuart Kleigman was leaning against the chain-link fence past the Playland Arcade staring down the boardwalk towards Venice, where an endless stream of roller skaters glided back and forth.

At least Arvo thought it was Stuart. He was wearing light blue slacks and a shiny red blouson jacket, and when Arvo greeted him, he turned, revealing a blue-and-gold crest on the front of his jacket. Probably his bowling team, Arvo thought, unable to make out the lettering. The breeze blew a lock of Stuart's grey hair over his eyes and he pushed it back. Arvo had never seen him dressed so casually before.

Stuart raised an eyebrow and squinted out to sea. 'Probably five years since I've been here,' he said. 'You wouldn't think so, would you, Brentwood being so close, but it's true. Karen and I used to come here sometimes when we first got married, but that was ten years ago now. And we brought the kids here once or twice when they were little. Leora sure loved that carousel. Now the neighbourhood's gone downhill – you wouldn't catch me here after dark – and the developers have ruined the waterfront. You live around here?'

'Santa Monica, yes. Seafront, no.'

'Uh-huh. So what is it? Have there been any developments?'

'Yes and no.'

'What the fuck's that supposed to mean? Sounds like a lawyer's answer to me. Nothing's happened to Sarah, has it?'

'Not as far as I know. What I mean is, I'm not sure whether there have been any developments or not.'

'Look, let's go get something to eat, shall we?' Stuart rubbed his stomach. 'I'm starving. Then you can tell me all about it.'

They walked along the pier. Arvo caught glimpses of the sea through the gaps between the boards. It made him feel a little dizzy. They went into the English-style pub.

It was more of a wooden shack than a pub, really. A few of the tables were occupied by young couples and groups of young people taking a break from skating on the boardwalk; a couple of sullen teenagers were playing darts in the corner; and one group of obvious east-coast tourists looked around with sheepish smiles as their kids painted the tables and floors with food. They looked as if they were remembering how cute everyone thought it was when the kids made a mess like that in South Duxbury, Massachusetts, but starting to worry that maybe you could get shot for it in LA.

When the stoned-looking waiter wandered by, Arvo ordered a pint of Harp lager and a tuna melt, and Stuart asked for a Diet Coke, fries and a cheeseburger with the works.

'So what is it?' Stuart asked. 'This yes-and-no business?'

'It's about the body Sarah found on the beach.'

Stuart waved his hand in the air. 'Oh, that. Yeah. Some faggot kid from West Hollywood, right? Half a column inch in the *Los Angeles Times* and one pissy little item on the local news about how an actress who played a homicide cop on TV discovered a real dead body on her morning jog, that's all. Cute story. It was a joke to them. Filler on a slow news day. Soon as she was done with the cops I took her to Brentwood for the day and made sure nobody got near her. They lost interest soon enough. Especially after that dumb kid from the new NBC sitcom ran his fucking Porsche off the Coast Highway Thursday night.'

Their drinks arrived. Arvo took a long swig of Harp to slake his thirst. It was good. Cold, clean and hoppy.

Stuart pointed to his Diet Coke and made a face. 'Doctor's orders,' he said. 'Can you believe it? Fifty years old and not a day's hospitalization in my life, and I'm supposed to go on a fucking diet.'

'Hey, Stuart, you want to live for ever like everyone else in this town, then you better follow your doctor's orders.'

'Fucking doctors. What do they know?'

The food arrived. Stuart started burying his burger under relish, pickles, hot peppers and ketchup, which he then liberally poured over his fries. Arvo looked away and tucked into his tuna melt. So much for Stuart's doctor's orders, he thought, looking at the mess of fat, cholesterol and red meat on the plate.

Stuart bit into his burger. Yellow mustard and green relish oozed out the sides and dribbled down the corners of his mouth. He wiped it with a napkin.

'Did Sarah jog along that part of the beach every morning?' Arvo asked.

'Sure. I mean, I think so. She said she did, and I had no

reason to think otherwise. She loved her morning run. I can't say I was ever around there that early, myself.'

'Same time, same place?'

'Yeah. That was her routine. I mean, you live somewhere nice like that, why go somewhere else to work out? Know what I mean?'

Arvo nodded. 'Have there been any new letters?'

'Not that I know of.' Stuart frowned. 'Look, Arvo, I don't like what I'm hearing, if I'm hearing your tone right. Is there something I'm missing, something I ought to know?' He pushed the basket of fries towards Arvo, who waved it away.

'No, thanks.' Arvo took another sip of Harp and shook his head. 'I wish I knew. I'm sorry, Stu. I'm not trying to hide anything. I'm just looking around for some way to get a handle on this.'

'Yeah, I can see that. The letters and the stiff. You think there's a connection. I'm not that fucking stupid. What I don't see is how or why.'

Arvo told him about the heart.

Stuart frowned and shook his head. 'A heart usually symbolizes love, right? You're saying the stiff was planted there for Sarah to find. Like an offering, a gift?'

'I'm saying it could have been.'

Stuart put the remains of his hamburger down. 'Jesus H. Christ. And you said there was nothing to worry about.'

'I said there was probably nothing to fear *yet*, that we didn't have enough to go on. We're dealing in statistical probabilities, Stu, not certainties. If new information comes in, the whole pattern changes. If he's suffering from schizophrenia or some personality disorder that involves delusions or hallucinations, then the normal rules don't apply any more.'

'But why would anyone want to do a thing like that? Crazy or not. Plant a body for someone to find?'

Arvo finished his Harp. 'No reason that would make sense

to you or me,' he said. 'But people often have their own logic: attention, exhibitionism, vindictiveness, need for approval.'

'A psycho. You're talking about a fucking psycho, aren't you? Silence of the fucking lambs, that's what it is.'

'I told you, I don't know. But I want to look into it. If it's some stranger living out a fantasy, we've got a problem, but if there really *is* a connection, and it's someone from her past, then maybe we can find him before she comes back. It's worth a shot, isn't it?'

Stuart ran his hand through his hair. 'Okay. Sure. Look, do you think she's in any danger in England?'

Arvo shrugged. 'I doubt it. Stalkers *have* been known to travel great distances after their prey. One guy even went so far as to go to Australia looking for Olivia Newton-John. But things like that cost a lot of money, take a lot of planning. And if all she's got so far is three letters, he's still in the early stages. You might give her a call and suggest she take care, but I don't really think there's anything to worry about. After all, we don't even know for certain that there is a link between Sarah and the body. It's just a theory I'm working on.'

Stuart nodded. 'So where do we go from here?'

'To start with, I need to know as much as you can tell me about Sarah Broughton.'

Stuart slapped down enough cash to cover the bill. 'Okay,' he said. 'But let's walk. This fucking cheeseburger's giving me indigestion.'

They walked into the hazy sunshine. Stuart screwed up his eyes against the light, and Arvo put his sunglasses on. Outside on the pier, a puppeteer had set up his show, spinning a grinning marionette through a gruelling break-dance to loud rap music. Quite a crowd had gathered around. Stuart clapped his hands over his ears and hurried ahead.

They crossed the walkway to Ocean and turned left towards Palisades Park, a stretch of grass and trees right between Ocean and the cliffs above the Coast Highway. Christmas decorations hung across the street. The music began to fade into the distance. Joggers lumbered by, dripping sweat, grunting with shin-splints and gasping for breath. Couples walked hand in hand. Homeless people slept against the boughs of the palms and sheltered under the smaller shrubs by the path. Many of them were wrapped in heavy overcoats, despite the heat, and some clutched plastic bags full of meagre possessions.

'Truth is,' Stuart said, 'now I come to think of it, I hardly know a thing about Sarah except what I've told you.'

'You don't know anything about her past?'

'A scrap or two, at best. Nothing interesting.'

'She said her last boyfriend was dead. Know who he was?'

'Gary Knox. The rock singer. Have you heard of him?'

Arvo whistled. He had heard of Gary Knox but hadn't known about his association with Sarah. It seemed an odd combination. Knox was hardly Sarah's type, from all Arvo had seen and heard.

Gary Knox had found rock-legend immortality when he walked out of a Hollywood hot-spot after his US tour last summer and dropped dead right on the sidewalk. Drug overdose. Arvo remembered reading the endless obits and eulogies in the press, many of the writers obviously trying hard to find a kind word to say about the obnoxious, egomaniacal junkie Knox had apparently been towards the end. Well, now he was part of that eternal junkie jam session in the sky, him and Jimi Hendrix, Janis Joplin, Jim Morrison, Elvis, Kurt Cobain and the rest. At least he was beyond doing anybody harm now.

'How long were they together?' Arvo asked.

'I don't know. She came over here from London on the tour with him last year. I think that started in the spring, playing outdoor stadiums all across the country. Apparently they'd split up before he died. That's all I know.'

'Why did they split up?'

Stuart shrugged. 'She didn't say. Just walked out on him.'

'I don't remember hearing anything about them being an item. Wasn't there a lot of publicity surrounding their relationship?'

'Not particularly. I mean, she wasn't well known then. You'd have had to cast a pretty fucking wide net around here to find anyone who'd heard of Sally Bolton. You think everyone sits down and tunes in to PBS?'

'I guess not.'

'You bet your ass not. As far as most people are concerned it's strictly *Beavis and Butt-head*, *The Simpsons* and *Married with Children*. You can forget your fucking *Middlemarches* and your endless P.D. James adaptations. Your average television viewer ain't got the attention span for shit like that. And she looked different then.' Stuart laughed. 'Boy did she ever look different. I've seen pictures. You know, the frizzy hair, green and orange, and the weird make-up, black lipstick, skin-tight leather pants, bare midriff. Fucking earrings as long as your arm. She even had a tattoo of a butterfly on her left shoulder. Still got it, I guess.' He laughed again. 'She sure wasn't the Sally Bolton who came to my office that day with Ellie.'

'Sarah mentioned Ellie, too,' Arvo said. 'Said she was the one who brought the two of you together. That right?'

'Right. Ellie Huysman. She and Sarah went to drama school together in London, then Ellie decided she didn't have either the talent or the stamina for acting, so she came over here and went into the business side. Eventually got into casting and ended up working for me. Small world, huh?' Stuart laughed. 'I think after a couple of years she wished she'd stuck with acting. Would've been a lot fucking easier.'

'And you met Sarah through Ellie?'

'That's right. I was meeting with her one day about this new cop show the network was coming up with and she mentioned she thought Sarah would be perfect. They were looking for something different but the same, as usual on TV, if you get my meaning, and there's always a pretty good market for the right kind of Brit women. You know, Amanda Donohoe, Emma Thompson, Helena Bonham Carter and the rest. So I ordered some videos of Sarah's work from PBS, and I saw what Ellie meant.'

'Is Ellie Huysman still around?' Arvo asked.

'Moved to Canada late last year, just after she introduced me to Sally. Said she couldn't stand living in LA one more minute. Not that I blame her, some days. I mean, we got a few problems here, right? But I ask you, fucking Canada? Anyway, she lives in Toronto now. She's still in the business. Apparently they make movies up there in the snow, too.'

'You got her number?'

'Sure.' Stuart pulled a small address book from his pocket and gave Arvo a number with a 416 area code. 'She'll be able to tell you a lot more than I can about Sarah,' he said. 'Like I said, they're old friends. Go way back.'

'What does Karen think about your relationship with Sarah?'

Stuart narrowed his eyes. 'I know what you're getting at, Arvo,' he said, 'but forget it, there's nothing like that between us at all. Never was. Sarah's special. It's like she's family.'

'Karen goes along with this?'

'Karen adores her.'

That satisfied Arvo for the moment. He had met Karen a year ago at a party Stuart had thrown. She was a strong-willed, intelligent woman about twenty years younger than Stuart, and she had given up a promising acting career for her husband and family. She and Sarah would be about the same age, Arvo calculated, around thirty-four. If Karen accepted Sarah, that was a good enough character reference for him.

They leaned on the railing and looked out over the ruffled ocean. A smell of fresh-brewed coffee drifted over from a waterfront café and mingled with ozone on the light breeze. Perfect, Arvo thought. Just enough glare to make you put on your shades. Warm, but not so you'd start sweating. There was one more possibility he had to pursue with Stuart.

'Right now Sarah's hot property, isn't she?' he asked.

'Up and coming. This series is really putting her on the map. And real quick. We've got movies lined up. Real movies. Maybe Merchant-Ivory. You know, all those English country houses and big lawns in the mist and rain. The real thing, not just Hollywood made-for-TV crapola, though there'll be some of those, too. Bread-and-butter shit.'

'Can you think of any reason why someone might want to sabotage her career before it's even got off the ground?'

'What?'

'You heard me. I'm saying maybe somebody's playing games with her, trying to freak her.'

'Oh, come on, Arvo. That's crazy.'

'No crazier than any other possibility. No matter what you read in papers or see on the screen, there aren't psychopaths lurking around every street corner. But maybe there *is* someone who hates Sarah Broughton so much he wants to pull the plug on her career.'

'Like that cheerleader thing, where the girl's mother tried to have the competitor's mother killed just to put the kid off her stride?'

'Could be. She must have beaten people out to get the part.'

'Sure, but . . . No, no, I can't see it.'

'If Sarah's a little fragile to start with, you can see how someone might think that sending her crazy letters like that could send her over the edge.'

'Not to mention finding a dismembered body practically right in front of her house?'

'That too.'

Stuart rubbed his chin. 'You're saying that the letters, the love stuff, might just be a way for someone to get at her? That whoever is doing it is crazy in some other way from the way he makes it seem?'

Arvo laughed. 'You could put it like that. Sometimes crazy people are clever enough to pretend to be crazy in a different way. People read about stalkers in the newspapers all the time. They're probably easy enough to imitate. We've had at least five false-victim cases. Maybe this is just the other side of the coin, a false-obsessive case. Do you know anything about Sarah's private life that might help me pin someone down?'

'Far as I can tell, her private life is very private these days, and that means as in *by herself* private. I know it might seem crazy to you, her being a beautiful Hollywood celebrity and all, but she's kept to herself that way ever since I've known her. No drugs, no wild orgies, no tabloid headlines. This woman is squeaky clean. Christ, she hardly even fucking drinks.'

Stuart paused. Arvo looked out to sea and saw a large oil-tanker drifting across the horizon. From an open window across the street, he could hear Nat King Cole singing about chestnuts roasting on an open fire.

'She buries herself in her work,' Stuart went on. 'I'm telling you, this lady is *different*. Has to be or this town would've chewed her up and spit her out by now. She's not impressed by us. She's just not your typical asshole star. When she's not working, she just wants solitude, peace and quiet.'

Arvo looked around. 'Hell of a place to come for that.'

Stuart scratched the side of his neck. 'Fuck, don't I know it. But for Chrissake, Arvo, the last guy she was in love with OD'd outside a nightclub. That's gotta have some effect on a person's psyche. Maybe work helps keep her mind off things she'd rather not think about. I don't know. I'm no shrink. But these letters and now this murder . . . Maybe you're right. If he keeps this up, it might just send her over the edge. Tough or not, there's only so much a person can take.'

'I'm looking for a name, anything, just somewhere to start,' said Arvo. 'You know as well as I do that these guys usually haven't met their victims. They watch them on TV or at the movies and think they're getting personal messages over the airwaves. Then they start stalking them, find out where they live, get hold of their addresses and phone numbers. It's not difficult. You can buy them along with the map to the stars' houses on Sunset Boulevard. But if our man really *does* know Sarah Broughton, whether he's a true stalker or just someone out for revenge or sabotage, that could give us an edge.'

Stuart gave a little shiver. 'Yeah, I know.'

'So back to my question. Do you know of anyone she associates with who gives you any cause for concern? Friend? Colleague?'

Stuart chewed his lower lip as he thought. 'Shit, Arvo,' he said finally. 'Like I told you, this town is so full of loony tunes I wouldn't know where to start. And I'm just talking about people I've seen around, you know. People on the show.'

'Other actors?'

'Yeah. And some of the crew. They've got a cameraman I swear's the fucking image of Charlie Manson, but everyone tells me he's a harmless whale-hugging vegan, not to mention one of the best damn cameramen in the business.' Stuart shrugged. 'I guess I can't really answer your question.'

'Can you get me a list of all the people she works with and comes in contact with at the studio?'

'Sure I can.'

'At least that's a start. Have you heard of this Justin Mercer, that old boyfriend she mentioned?'

'I know the name. Why?'

'You've got plenty of contacts in the business, so maybe you can find out where he is these days.'

'I guess I could do that.'

'What about Jack Marillo, the co-star?'

'They're pretty good friends.'

'Just friends?'

'That's right.' Stuart lowered his voice. 'Just between you and me, Jack's queer as a duck. Nice guy, though.' He looked at his watch. 'Sorry Arvo, but I gotta go now. Karen's expecting me. Got people coming. Fucking holidays, huh?'

Arvo nodded. He had almost forgotten it was 22 December. He made a few notes in a tiny, spider-trail hand that no one could read but himself, then moved away from the railing.

'Thanks for coming,' he said. 'I don't know where we're going with this, but I'll stay in touch.'

'No problem.' Stuart shook hands and walked down to the nearest cross-light.

As Arvo walked towards his car, a bum detached himself from the greenery and stuck his hand out. Arvo gave him a buck.

'Merry Christmas,' said the bum.

16

On Saturday morning, Sarah walked halfway to Whitby and back along the beach. She had spent much of last night unable to sleep, thinking about the letter. It so obviously admitted to the murder that she couldn't simply overlook it. She knew she would have to do something soon. Like a bad tooth or a lump in your breast, you could ignore it for a while, but it wouldn't go away. She had been good at procrastinating in her life. Too damn good.

The problem was that she didn't know whether she should phone the detectives in Los Angeles and tell them everything now or let it wait till she got back.

Finally, distance helped her decide on the latter. What good would it do anyway? She didn't know *who* the letter-writer was. Besides, surely now that he had murdered someone, the police would have forensic evidence to go on? By the time she got back, they probably wouldn't need her. She would hang on to the letter, of course, and give it to them later – it might be useful as evidence – but beyond that, she didn't see how she could help.

Also, if she phoned, they might send the local bobby round to put her on the next plane back to LA, and she would miss Christmas with her family. Just when she felt she was making some progress.

A bitter wind blew off the North Sea. Bundled up in a shirt and sweater under her down jacket, a woolly hat, mittens and earmuffs, Sarah didn't feel too cold. The sky was as grey as used dishwater, but now and then the clouds would break for a moment and a shaft of sunlight would shoot through and dance on the pewter sea, reminding her of the calm after a storm.

Behind her, the whitewashed, red-tiled cottages seemed piled on top of one another like children's playing-bricks, huddled together in crooked, cobbled alleys higgledy-piggledy fashion. The village straggled down a steep hill to the sea in much the same way as the ones on the Greek islands that Sarah had visited with Gary. A small church perched on top of the cliffs, and even though it wasn't Sunday, Sarah could hear children's voices singing 'Away in a Manger.'

She had forgotten how unusual the geology was around the bay. There wasn't much sand, only the curved layers of dark, barnacle-encrusted rock, which looked like a slice through an enormous onion, or a giant scalloped seashell embedded in the shore. The grooves showed where the waves had eroded the older rocks more quickly than the bands of limestone and ironstone between them. It was a great place for fossil hunters, and it also created numerous rock-pools where Sarah stopped to watch tiny crabs scuttle beneath the pellucid water.

Out to sea, Sarah could see a ship with white sails flapping in the wind. She shivered, imagining what it would be like out on the North Sea today in a sailboat. She pulled her jacket more snugly round her neck and carried on walking. The wind whistled around her earmuffs.

When she arrived back at the harbour, she walked up the ramp to the street. It was just after noon. Instead of returning to the cottage, she decided to call at the pub where Paula worked and give her sister a surprise.

There weren't many people in the public bar, but when Sarah walked in, what conversation there was stopped at once. Even the clack of dominoes ceased. The only sound came from a radio playing an old pop song somewhere in the back. Sarah recognized it: Susan Maugham singing 'Bobby's Girl.'

At first, the reaction she got reminded her of the opening scene of *An American Werewolf in London,* where the young tourists get lost in the Yorkshire Dales and go into an isolated pub to ask their way. She could see the grizzled, sea-leathered, wind-reddened faces trying to place her. She smiled and said hello to everyone, then walked towards the bar.

Paula came through from the lounge and said, 'Sal! So you've finally decided to grace us with your presence, after all?'

'I thought I'd drop by for a quick one, yes,' said Sarah, taking off her mittens and rubbing her hands. 'It's cold out there.'

'Not half as cold as it will be in a day or two, lass,' said one of the drinkers behind her. Then they all laughed.

'This is my sister, Sally,' Paula said to all and sundry. 'You know, the famous actress. Calls herself Sarah Broughton now.' She tilted her head, put a finger to the tip of her nose and turned it up.

They all nodded shyly and said how d'you do, then went back to their dominoes and muffled conversations. Sarah doubted if any of them watched her show on television. Besides, she was getting sick of this *star* business Paula kept going on about. She wasn't a star; she was a supporting actress on a network drama.

Still, she supposed that in a village like Robin Hood's Bay, she would have to accept that she was a star.

She unzipped her jacket and sat on a stool at the bar. It was a long time since she had been in a real English pub, and she took in the rows of unfamiliar bottles, the mirrors and brass rails. There were plenty of imitations in Los Angeles, but nothing quite like the real thing, with its bags of pork scratchings and roast salted peanuts, its upside-down bottles in the racks with optics attached, stone-flagged floor and roaring fire in the hearth.

'What'll you have?' Paula asked. 'Whatever it is, the first one's on the house.'

'Thank you. I'll have a whisky, please.'

'Good idea,' said Paula 'Summat to warm the cockles of your heart.'

Paula handed her the glass and Sarah sipped. It burned all the way down her throat and spread a warm glow in her stomach.

She hadn't been paying attention to the radio, but at that moment, Gary Knox came on singing 'Blue Eyes, Black Heart,' his biggest commercial success and his least favourite song.

Sarah turned pale and almost dropped her glass.

When Paula realized what had happened, she went into the back. A few seconds later the song stopped and another station came on: an innocuous Whitney Houston number, this time.

'You didn't have to do that,' Sarah said quietly to Paula when she came back. 'But thank you.'

'Think nowt of it. Maybe one day you'll tell me about him?'

Sarah managed a weak smile. 'Maybe one day, yes.' She had heard only a snatch of the song, of Gary's distinctive voice – like honeyed gravel, a poetic reviewer had once written – but it was enough to bring his image back to her mind's eye.

Tall, thin, stooped, dark-haired and hollow-cheeked, with a lock of hair constantly falling over his right eye and a distant, crooked smile, he had always looked the way she imagined one of the Romantic poets might look after he had been up all night grappling with a particularly recalcitrant sonnet and a bottle of laudanum. Young Coleridge, perhaps, with feverish opium eyes and mussed-up hair, and that distracted look, as if he were hearing and seeing things no one else could. And, like many a Romantic poet, Gary had died young.

She had tried to imagine Gary's death many times, how he had faced it. Many of his songs were about death; it was a subject he had thought intensely about since adolescence. She had recognized a kind of death-wish in much of his drug use and recklessness, a sort of cocking one's hat against the grim reaper and saying, come on, catch me if you can.

As far as Sarah had heard, Gary had simply dropped dead on La Brea after leaving a nightclub with a group of friends. The autopsy had revealed a lethal mixture of cocaine, ecstasy, heroin, LSD, alcohol and barbiturates. His heart had, quite literally, just stopped beating. Had he had time in the moment of his death to savour the experience that had fascinated him so much in his life? Sarah didn't know, and never would.

Their life together was still something of a blur. Of course, she remembered the early days: the party where they met in Camden Town, and how they walked the quiet London streets all night talking; the sunny idyll on the Greek island of Santorini, all vivid blues and whites, when Gary was writing the songs for what was to be his last album; the frustrations of studio work; the tour.

It was crazy from the start. Pushed by the record company to promote the new album when he was still exhausted from its creation and production, Gary set out for a mammoth US and Canadian tour with the band. Sarah went along for the ride.

And what a ride it was.

She could only remember patches of the chaos: backstage arguments, smelly tour buses, short, gut-churning air hops. New York, Boston, Philadelphia, Pittsburgh, Montreal, Toronto, Chicago. The names sped by and meant nothing; she saw nothing but hotel rooms and concert halls. Half the time she didn't even know whether she was in the USA or Canada.

Gary was too sick from drugs to perform in Omaha, and he collapsed on stage in Dallas. The fans loved it. After only a couple of days' rest, the band hit the West Coast and life became a non-stop party tinged with mayhem and madness. Vancouver, Seattle, Portland, San Francisco, Los Angeles, San Diego, picking up groupies and hangers-on all the way like a snowball picked up snow going down a hill. The further south they got, the more Sarah's memory started to fail her.

Somewhere along the line, Gary had changed. He was pushing himself at an insane pace, drunk and stoned or coked-out all the time, almost as if he were running headlong to embrace death. There were no rules; nothing was sacred; everything was permitted. Total derangement of the senses. Well, Sarah had read Rimbaud, too, and look what happened to him.

At first she wanted to know why, what was wrong, but he wouldn't talk to her about anything. They didn't even make love. When he was capable, he suggested threesomes with poxy groupies or all-out gang-bangs with the whole band. When she refused, he ridiculed her. Maybe she didn't always refuse; she couldn't remember. But something had driven her over the edge; something had given her the courage or fear to walk out and salvage what little self-respect she could.

But until then, hurt and humiliated day after day, she had snorted coke to get up, though it no longer made her feel good, and she took booze and 'ludes to get her to sleep. Ecstasy in between. She liked the downers best. 'Ludes or nembies, it didn't really matter.

After a couple of bad LSD trips, one of them a terrifying nightmare in Tijuana, where she was almost raped by a half-crazed local pimp, whom Gary's entourage had adopted for the night, she stopped taking hallucinogens altogether. Life had become hallucinatory enough without them. Everything was crumbling, falling apart, until that one day when she just walked out. She felt that she had run so far and so fast with Gary she had left herself behind.

The weeks after she left marked the lowest point in her life: her 'illness,' the Great Depression. She couldn't remember details or events, the number of times she had just wanted to die, except that Ellie had taken her to the clinic and saved her life. But she could still feel the shadow of the emotion, the sense of utter worthlessness; she could still hear the echo of the voices that berated her, told her she was an evil slut, a trollop, a tart. And, from time to time, she still felt the impulse towards suicide. The darkness was still there inside her, and sometimes it beckoned.

'Penny for them.'

'What? Oh, sorry, Paula, I was miles away. I think I'll have another whisky, please. A double.'

'You want to be careful, you know.'

'Don't worry, I'm not turning to the bottle. As a matter of fact, I hardly drink at all back in Los Angeles. I just can't get used to this English cold.'

'You grew up with it, same as me.'

Sarah laughed. 'Yes, but it's amazing how quickly you get soft.'

Paula snorted and poured her a drink.

Sarah paid, then Paula wandered off to serve someone else. The place had started to fill up, Sarah noticed, and one or two people looked at her as if they knew who she was. It wasn't as if, with her red nose, woolly hat and raw cheeks, she resembled Anita O'Rourke, but probably because she was a stranger in the village and Paula had told them all her famous sister was coming. The actress.

When she met Gary, she remembered, she had been at a

loose end because she felt her acting career in England was going nowhere. She was either underdressed in Channel Four art-house erotica or overdressed in BBC costume dramas. There seemed no place for her in a British series. If the Americans put too much of a premium on bland good looks, then the English went too far the other way – crooked teeth and bad skin.

Just before she met Gary, her father had seen one of the Channel Four films. He stopped talking to her for a month and after that, things had never been the same.

She knew her father had always preferred Paula, anyway. Paula did all the right things. Paula got married (even if it didn't work out). Paula had children. Paula didn't make dirty films. Paula was the sensible one, the practical one, the down-to-earth, salt-of-the-earth lass who didn't have ideas above her station.

Paula hadn't traded the accent God gave her for fame and fortune in a heathen land. Paula hadn't tossed aside all the moral values she had been brought up to believe in. Paula hadn't changed the name her parents had christened her with.

Too late to do anything about that now. Sarah finished her whisky. It was time to go back to the cottage.

'Catch you later,' she said to Paula, who was busy serving a man in a fisherman's jersey, then she zipped up her jacket, put on her mittens and left. As she walked out, she was struck by the thought that the tour was by far the most logical place to start looking for her tormentor, if only she could remember more about it. After all, just about everyone had been crazy back then.

17

Arvo spent most of Sunday at home sprawled on the floral-pattern sofa in the living-room watching *Tunes of Glory* for the thousandth time and putting his notes on the Sarah Broughton case in order.

He lived in a tiny, detached Spanish Colonial Revival bungalow hidden away on a residential street in the southern part of Santa Monica, near the college. Apart from one or two new low-rise apartment buildings in the modern, cubist style, most of the houses on the street were older, like his. They were similar in design, all white or beige stucco with low-pitched red tile roofs, but each was just a little different from its neighbour. Some had shutters, for example, while others had metal grille-work around the windows. Arvo's had both.

A short path wound through a postage-stamp garden crammed with small palms, ferns, jacaranda and bougainvillaea, so overgrown that you had to push the fronds aside with your hands as you walked to the portico. Sometimes it felt like walking a jungle path, but the shrubbery provided excellent shade and kept the place cool in summer.

Inside, the living room was immediately to the left, the kitchen and dining area to the right. A short hallway, with closet space for coats and shoes, led to the hexagonal hub, off which doors led to the three small bedrooms and the bathroom. The floors were of unglazed tiles, the colour of terracotta, and there were little art deco touches over the tops of the doorways and windows: a zigzag here and a chevron there.

The living room was where Arvo spent most of his time. Nyreen had had very particular ideas about art, and after she left with all her contemporary prints, he put up two large, framed movie posters on the walls, one for *Casablanca* and one for *The Big Sleep*.

There were two large built-in bookcases in the room, flanking the shuttered windows: one was filled with an eclectic mix of books, from movie history to theatre, urban planning and hard-boiled detective fiction; and the other housed his video collection, from *Citizen Kane* to *Hollywood Chainsaw Hookers*.

He had found the down payment for the house from the money he inherited on the death of his parents, and bought it as soon as he knew he had the job on the TMU. The mortgage stretched his resources almost to the limit, but he hoped to hang on to the place if he could, even if he never got to eat out again.

A good house in a pleasant neighbourhood was hard to get in LA, real-estate prices being what they were, and apartment living didn't appeal to him. He had done it in the past and found he quickly tired of smelling someone else's cooking, or listening to someone else's music, domestic arguments and sexual gymnastics.

When he had finished note-taking, the movie was over, the pot of coffee was empty, and he had sheets of paper spread out all over the floor and armchairs. But he was still no better off than when he started. The list of names Stuart Kleigman had faxed him gave him thirteen people with the initial *M* in either their first, middle or last names.

In addition, Stuart had found out very quickly through the movie-industry grapevine that Justin Mercer, Sarah Broughton's ex-lover, had been working on a movie in a London studio for the past two months. Which let *him* off the hook.

Arvo stuck some leftover chili in the microwave for dinner, tossed a quick salad and opened a bottle of Sam Adams lager.

While the chili reheated, he dialled Ellie Huysman's Toronto number again. There was a three-hour time difference, so it would be about nine-thirty in the evening there. He had tried three or four times during the day but got neither an answer nor a machine he could leave a message on. This time, as he was about to hang up after the tenth ring, he heard a breathless voice in his ear.

'Yes?'

'Is this Ms Ellie Huysman?'

'Yes, yes it is. Who's calling? Oh, damn – Magwitch! – hang on a minute, will you? *Mag*witch!' She put the phone down on a hard surface.

Arvo heard what he thought were a dog's paws scrabbling over a wood floor.

'I told you not to do that. Darling, could you . . .'

Arvo heard a man's voice, but didn't catch what he said, then Ellie Huysman picked up the phone again. 'Sorry about that. The dog. We just got back from the carol service and he seems rather more than pleased to see us. Can you hang on a minute?'

Before Arvo could answer, she had put the phone down again. He heard more voices, laughter, a door opening and closing, then she picked up the phone again. 'Hello? Are you still there? I'm sorry about that. What can I do for you? Who are you anyway?'

Arvo introduced himself.

'What's it about?' she asked. 'Hang on again, will you, I want to take this in the living room, on the sofa. I've been sitting on a hard pew all night and my bum feels like pressed cardboard.'

Arvo kept his patience as she set the receiver down once again on the hard surface. A few seconds later, she picked up the other extension and called for someone to replace the hall phone. That done, she said, 'That's better. Now I can sit down, kick my shoes off and have that stiff G and T, which I've been dying for all evening. Now then, Detective Hughes of the LAPD, what's it all about? I'm curious.'

'Sarah Broughton.'

'Sal? Nothing's happened to her, has it?'

Arvo had already debated what to tell her and decided there was no point holding back. She wasn't a suspect; she was a friend of Sarah's; and she lived in another country. 'She's been getting some disturbing letters,' he said, 'and the writer seems to indicate that he knows her, that she should know him. Normally, we wouldn't take a lot of notice of claims like that, but . . .'

'But what, Detective?'

'Well, she discovered a body on the beach near her house the other day, just before she left for England. She didn't know the victim, and there's probably no connection, but even so—'

'It's a coincidence you don't like? I don't like it, either. Poor Sal.'

'Are the two of you still close?'

'Ye-es, I'd say we are. Maybe not as close as we've been at some points in our lives – distance is a problem – but still firm friends. Look, if I can help you in any way, I will, but shouldn't I verify your identity? I mean, you could be any Tom, Dick or Harry, couldn't you? You could even be the person who's been writing these letters. Why don't you give me your police switchboard number and I'll ring you back?'

A light breeze fluttered through the window and brushed Arvo's cheek. He could hear the leaves and fronds rustling in the dark garden. Beyond that was the constant hum of cars on the freeway. He took a swig of Sam Adams. 'I'm calling from home,' he said. 'I could give you my badge number, and you could call the duty officer downtown and verify it.'

'But I still won't know it's really you, will I? I've never met you. You could have killed this Hughes fellow and stolen his badge.'

Arvo laughed. 'Good point. Maybe you could call Stuart Kleigman, or even Sarah Broughton and ask one of them to describe my voice?'

'Oh, sod it,' she said. 'This is getting far too bloody complicated. I'll take my chances you're who you say you are. What is it you want to know?'

The microwave beeped to tell Arvo his chili was ready. He ignored it. 'Stuart Kleigman says he knows nothing about Sarah's private life, or about her life before she met him,' he said.

'That doesn't surprise me. Sal always was a bit cagey when it came to confiding in people. Comes from getting burned once too often.'

'Well, the letters are local, at least the one I saw was postmarked Pasadena, so we're thinking it might be someone she's met since she's been in California, or at least in the United States. When would that be?'

'She came over to the States in . . . let me see . . . May last year, to New York first, where the tour started. As far as I know, she hasn't left the country since. Until now, of course. She arrived in Los Angeles last autumn, early September, just after the Labour Day weekend.'

'Do you know of anyone who might be doing this?'

'Not offhand I don't. Just a mo.' Arvo heard a lighter click and the satisfied sigh of someone blowing out smoke after a long time without. 'Ah, that's better,' she said. 'If one can't indulge one's vices after a carol service, when can one? But the answer's no. Sal kept very much to herself when she came round to my place.'

'Where were you living then?'

'Redondo Beach. Plenty of loonies there.'

Arvo laughed. 'Was there anyone trying to date her while she was with you? Anyone pestering her at all?'

'No.'

'Are you certain?'

'Trust me. Yes.'

'Stuart told me that before she came to you she'd been going out with Gary Knox.'

'That's right. The creep. If you ask me, that's what did it.'

'Did what?'

She paused. Arvo heard her inhale and blow out smoke again. Ice tinkled in her glass. 'I suppose I *did* sort of decide to trust you, didn't I?'

'I think you did, yes.'

'And Sal could be in danger when she gets back?'

'It's a possibility. If we don't get somewhere quick.'

'All right. The tour's what caused the breakdown, that's what.'

'Sarah had a mental breakdown?'

'Mental, physical, you name it. I think the technical term is "Major Depressive Episode."'

'After she came to stay with you?'

'I can't be that exact about the timing, but I got the impression she was probably right in the middle of it when she arrived on my doorstep. She was in a hell of a state, anyway. Had nothing but the clothes on her back. I even had to pay the cab driver, and she'd come all the way from Anaheim. Not that I minded.'

'What happened?'

'Oh, I held her, calmed her down, gave her some hot chocolate, put her to bed. She didn't say a word. But she was sobbing and trembling all the time. Her teeth were chattering. Her eyes were out of focus.'

'Drugs?'

'Yes, I'd say so.'

'Did anyone from the tour ever come looking for her?'

'If they did, they didn't find her.'

'Was there anybody around with the initial, *M*?'

'Not that I recall. Is that his initial?'

'We think so.'

'No. I'm sorry I can't be more help. But Sarah really didn't see anyone for a long time.'

'How long did she stay with you?'

'On and off for a few months.'

'Where was she during the "off" times?'

He heard Ellie suck in a lungful of smoke. Bogie and Ingrid Bergman were staring at him from the wall. 'The first few days,' Ellie said, 'she was uncommunicative, cried a lot, went off her food, didn't seem interested in anything. When she did talk, it was just to say how worthless she was and how I should forget about her. Then, when she'd been there just over a week, one night I heard a noise and found her in the bathroom washing a handful of Nembutals down with a bottle of Courvoisier. I stuck my fingers down her throat and made her puke it all up. Luckily she'd just started and the capsules hadn't even dissolved. The next morning I drove her out to a clinic I knew, a place that had helped another good friend of mine. Very discreet.'

'What clinic?'

'It's called the Shelley Clinic. No kidding. Like the poet. Out on 33 a few miles north of Ojai. Dr Fermor.'

'And they helped?'

'You've seen her now, haven't you?'

'Yes.'

'Well, if you'd seen her that night, you'd know they've worked a bloody miracle.'

Arvo let that sink in, then said goodbye to Ellie Huysman, making sure she would be available if he needed more information. As he walked into the kitchen to get his chili, he found himself thinking about what Ellie had said.

It certainly seemed as if someone or something had messed

up Sarah's mind, and it made him wonder if what was messing her up now was in some way connected: the tour, drugs, a dead rock star. Or was it someone even *closer* to home? Or a random stalker, some nut who had seen her on television and fallen in love with her? All possibilities. Too many damn possibilities, that was the problem.

Arvo carried his chili through to the living room, opened another bottle of Sam Adams and scanned the bookcase for a movie to watch. *In a Lonely Place* – Bogey and Gloria Grahame – that would suit his mood just fine.

18

He gazed lovingly at the small, blurred photo of Sally at LAX, leaving for England, above the brief article in the Los Angeles Times. *Then he reread the text:*

Actress Sarah Broughton, who plays Detective Anita O'Rourke in the hit series *Good Cop, Bad Cop*, boarded a flight today for England, where she is to spend Christmas with her family in the coastal village of Robin Hood's Bay. Sources say Ms Broughton, 34, was still shaken by an incident that occurred earlier that day. It seems that real life imitated art just a bit too closely for comfort when she discovered a dismembered corpse partially buried in the sand near her beach home. What would Anita O'Rourke have done?

What indeed? He wondered where Robin Hood's Bay was. He would have to look it up in an atlas and try to imagine her there. It was a bay, at least, which meant it must be on the sea, so for the moment he could picture her the way he had watched her in Pacific Palisades.

He sighed and put the newspaper down. Well, just because she was far from him physically, it didn't mean she wasn't still with him. He gazed around his room and her image stared back at him from every square inch of wall-space: close-ups, head and shoulders, full body, nudes, evening dress, casual clothes, stills from movies and TV, you name it.

Wrapped in a warm cocoon of Sally, he could function

*properly, see things clearly. The only thing he didn't know was
what would happen after the consummation. He could only visu-
alize two main possibilities, depending on the circumstances.*

*If all went well, they would end up living in a nice house by
the sea in a nice neighbourhood. Not in Los Angeles, but somewhere quieter and smaller, somewhere less vivid. Maybe even
Robin Hood's Bay, if it was as quaint as it sounded. He would
like to meet her family.*

*If that happened, he thought they should start a family as
quickly as possibly and have maybe six children. Or fewer if she
thought that was too many; he didn't want to turn her into a baby
factory against her will. He would work from home so he would
never have to leave her, and she could devote all her time to the
house and children. They would be together all day, every day.*

*Of course, they would have people over for dinner – he didn't
know who; he didn't know anyone he wanted to invite, and it
certainly wouldn't be anyone from her present lifestyle – and they
would talk and drink wine in the candlelight. He would hold
hands with her secretly under the table.*

*In bed they would lie together naked and . . . But when he
thought of the act itself he started to feel excited, confused and
angry; waves of red surged in front of his eyeballs. It was the same
way he felt when he watched the video: so disturbed and violent
that he sometimes bruised his penis and made it sore when he
masturbated. Well, that part of their relationship would take care
of itself when the time came.*

*If things didn't go their way, though – and he could at least
admit that might happen, as they had many rich and powerful
enemies – then it might be necessary to forgo the earthly paradise
and head straight for the heaven beyond the flesh.*

*Sometimes that seemed like the best idea, anyway. He was sure
there was no comparison between the world of the flesh and that
of pure spirit. But when you pit the known against the unknown,
usually the known has an edge. That was something for him to*

*work on: learn to love the unknown more. Faith, that was what
he needed. Faith was the key. And courage.*

For now, though, he had his images of her, and he would create
more while she was away. With his computer, he could do
anything he wanted to photographs or video images. He could
play God with the arrangement of body parts and even put
different heads and bodies together.

He had experimented with several permutations: putting
Sally's head on the body of a porn image, for example, so that she
smiled at him with her legs wide open, one hand holding herself
and a finger inside her vagina. The bottom part wasn't Sally, of
course. Though she had appeared nude in some films – he had
videos of them all – she had never done anything remotely as
pornographic as that. She wouldn't. He knew that. At heart, she
was a decent, wholesome girl. But this was a part of his power;
his ability to play God with images. And God had a sense of
humour, too. Once he had put Sally's head between the legs of the
porn photo and it looked funny smiling at him from where the
model's pussy should be.

But his crowning glory was the footage he had rearranged
from an erotic video and several photographs of himself and
Sally. As he ran it now and watched, he felt that familiar surge of
excitement and anger. It was a simple scene: a man and woman
in a bedroom. The man lay on his back, erect and ready, and the
woman lowered herself onto him, taking his penis in her hand
and guiding it into her. Then she began to rock back and forth,
gently at first, and then more wildly.

The woman had Sally's face; the man had his.

It was still rather primitive, of course. Their faces were both
grafted from photographs, so their expressions didn't change.
Throughout the whole five minutes or so, she retained her sweet
smile and he looked far too serious.

You could also see a faint line where the heads had been joined
to the bodies, as if someone had slit their throats.

Their heads looked a little fuzzy, and the skin tones were slightly different. Though he had added a soundtrack of moans, cries and grunts from another porn video, they weren't well enough synchronized. The whole thing sounded dubbed. Which is exactly what it was.

But the more he concentrated, the more he was able to forget the imperfections and lose himself in her smile, her body, her cries, her love. Sometimes he felt a little guilty about what he was doing with the images and all, just a little naughty. But it was all he had of her flesh while they were being kept apart. He knew she would understand and forgive him. Besides, she was his, after all, wasn't she?

And the best thing of all was that, afterwards, she talked to him, told him her most intimate secrets. And, more important still, if he listened very closely, she told him what he had to do to win her love. She was telling him to do something right now. It wasn't clear exactly **what** *yet, but it would be soon.*

19

Early on Christmas Eve, Arvo went out to a watering-hole on Wilshire with Maria, Kelly Norris, Mike Glover and Larry Matsuoka from the unit.

As they wedged themselves into the only semicircular booth left, Arvo couldn't help but smile at the bizarre twist the Sandi Gaines case had taken that day. After everything that had happened, Sandi had come by the office that morning saying she didn't want to press charges; she was willing to give Chuck a second chance; maybe she'd been wrong about him.

But Chucky was facing charges, all right. Plenty of them. Arvo had suggested counselling for Sandi. A relationship like theirs could only end in violence, and it was a good idea to try to save the department more work down the line. A good idea, but almost impossible. In the centuries-old war between reason and passion, who ever listened to reason?

Green and red streamers hung across the ceiling and walls, a small Christmas tree covered with lights and tinsel stood near the door and Elvis was singing 'Blue Christmas' on the jukebox. It took nearly ten minutes to get a round of drinks.

Arvo found himself crushed next to Maria, a very enjoyable sensation. Her thigh pressed against his, and sometimes when she moved he could feel the warmth and softness of her breast against his arm.

'What do you make of it?' he asked her about Sandi Gaines. The bar was so crowded and noisy he had to lean close to her ear to be heard. Close enough to smell her musky perfume.

Maria took a sip from a tall frosted glass full of coloured liquid and chunks of fruit topped with an umbrella and shook her head. The bartender called it a Santa Special because it was mostly green, white and red. 'I think she's crazy,' she said with a slight shrug. 'But half the world's crazy and the other half's working on it. I don't know.'

'She said he made her feel wanted.'

'I suppose if a guy walked in a restaurant and threatened to blow my head off he'd make me feel wanted, too,' said Maria.

Arvo laughed. 'She said she hadn't realized he was such a man, hadn't thought he had it in him.'

Maria rolled her eyes. 'Give me a break, Arvo.'

'Haven't you ever felt that way? Liked a guy because he felt so passionately about you he'd do something like that?'

'Nope.'

'How about someone who was willing to get violent because of you, like fight for you?'

Maria thought for a moment, then said, 'It's not the same. Chuck didn't fight for Sandi, he didn't defend her honour or anything, he threatened her. He's a creep, and if she gets off on being scared, that's her problem.' She took another sip of her drink.

'Ms Sensitivity,' he said.

Maria grinned. 'There was this guy in ninth grade once,' she went on, putting the glass down. 'See, there was this asshole kept razzing me, calling me "wetback," "spic," "hot chili pepper" and other real original shit like that. Only one guy stood up for me. Patrick O'Reilly, that was his name.' She smiled at the memory. 'Knocked two of the asshole's front teeth right down his throat and got himself suspended for it.'

'You admired him for doing that?'

'Sure did. We even dated for a while. You know, I once asked him why he did it, him being an Anglo and me a Mexican and all that. Only time I ever saw him get upset. He said he wasn't

Anglo, he was Irish, and his grandparents, or his great-grandparents, whatever, came over here after the potato famine. He told me hundreds of thousands of his people died in that famine and he was damned if he was going to stand by and watch someone made to suffer just because she came from another country for a better life, especially from a poor country.'

'What happened to him?'

'I don't know. We lost touch.'

Just then, Mike Glover caught Maria's attention and Arvo found himself leaning over the table trying to carry on a conversation about the prospects for the Rosebowl with Larry and Kelly. The din in the bar made it difficult. One particularly noisy group kept popping champagne corks and squealing with delight every time they sprayed half a bottle all over themselves. Elvis's 'Why Can't Every Day Be Like Christmas?' gave way to John Lennon singing 'Happy Xmas (War Is Over).'

For a moment, Arvo drifted away from the conversation, thinking about John Lennon, shot by the kind of person the TMU was trying to get some insight into. December 8, 1980. Arvo had been barely out his teens himself back then, but he had cried for John Lennon, listened to all those oldies they played on the radio all day: 'In My Life,' 'Working Class Hero,' 'Mother.' Just a fucked-up working-class kid from Liverpool, or so Arvo's Welsh father said, but a hell of a talent.

That December day in Detroit was wet, grey and chilling to the bone. Arvo remembered passing an empty playground where one of the swings was rocking gently back and forth in the wind, as if occupied by a ghost. He had his Walkman on and the radio station was playing 'Jealous Guy.' It made Arvo feel inexplicably sad, that empty swing rocking back and forth on the grey day after John Lennon got shot. If Arvo had known then that one day he would be working on a special unit . . .

'Arvo?'

'Oh, sorry. What?'

It was Maria again, slipping on her herringbone jacket. 'I've got to go now,' she said. 'Long drive ahead.'

'Okay. Drive carefully and have a great time.' He knew she was going to spend Christmas with her family in San Diego.

She smiled, then leaned over suddenly and gave him a quick kiss on the lips. He could taste grapefruit juice, orange, salt, tequila and something else, maybe Maria herself. From the corner of his eye, he saw Kelly Norris raise her eyebrows. Maria gave his arm a squeeze and said, 'Merry Christmas. Take care of yourself, Arvo,' then she turned to the group at large and waved. 'Have a good one!' And before they knew it, she was gone.

'So what do you think?' Larry asked.

'What do I think about what?'

'Michigan. The Rosebowl. You got a bet on?'

'Oh . . . right . . .'

Arvo chatted for as long as it took to drink a second beer then headed out himself, once again thanking Mike Glover for inviting him to Christmas dinner but pleading a prior engagement. A white lie.

As he drove home bumper to bumper in the constellation of lights along the Santa Monica Freeway, he could still taste Maria's kiss, smell her perfume, and the memory of it stirred his loins. He turned off the freeway at Cloverfield and pulled up in the street outside his house around seven o'clock.

In his mailbox he found a card and small package post-marked Palo Alto. Inside, he first checked the answering machine for messages – none – then he kicked off his shoes and took off his gun and nylon holster. After pouring himself a stiff Scotch, he flipped on the television news, then he sat down, put his feet up and opened the card.

It showed a Breughel village scene. Tiny figures lost in the whiteness. Not a mention of Christmas. Typical Nyreen. Very politically correct when it came to religious sensitivity. So much so that she didn't have any religion at all. The greeting read, 'Sorry I've screwed things up. You know I'll love you for ever.' Arvo ripped up the card and put it in the garbage.

Just as he was on his way to the fridge to see if there was anything for dinner, his beeper went off. That could only mean work. He checked the number, saw it was Parker Center and went to the phone.

Joe Westinghouse picked it up at the other end on the third ring. 'Arvo,' he said. 'Merry Christmas. We put a rush on the John Heimar toxicology. Only way to get it done before the holiday. I just got the results back and I thought you might like to know that the kid had enough barbiturates in his system to kill half the state of California.'

'Come again?'

'I'm not just talking recreational drugs here, Arvo. Far too much for that. The kid was poisoned before he was chopped up.'

20

On Christmas Day, a cold wind buffeted Robin Hood's Bay, smashing the sea in a frenzy of foam hard against the old stone wall and churning the dawn sky into a shifting pattern of ashes. Everyone woke early, and in no time, it seemed, Cathy and Jason were dashing down to open their presents and the day had begun.

Jason loved his Mighty Ducks jacket, and Cathy was ecstatic over the sweatshirt with Bugs Bunny, Daffy Duck, Sylvester the Cat, Tweety Pie and other Warner Brothers cartoon characters on the front.

The Rodeo Drive blouse left Paula almost speechless (only *almost:* what she actually said was, 'You shouldn't have. When will I ever get a chance to wear something like this?').

Sarah's father thanked her for the watch, but she felt she had misjudged there. She noticed him fiddling unconsciously with the gold band all day, as if it were too tight. She had been cautious enough to avoid buying him something too ostentatiously expensive, like a Rolex, but it still seemed she was wrong. Perhaps it reminded him, too, of how quickly his time was ticking away? Sarah thought it might be a good idea at least to replace the band with a simple leather strap.

Most of the presents Sarah received consisted of some form of warm clothing – a scarf, gloves, a pullover – as if her family had expected her to come over from sunny California in a T-shirt and shorts. Paula had bought her a nice pair of earrings, though: hand-crafted silver inlaid with what looked like lapis lazuli.

While the children played with their toys and filled themselves with chocolates, Sarah helped Paula stuff the turkey and prepare the dressings.

They ate at three o'clock, and after dinner the children, who could contain themselves no longer, dashed off to show their American presents to their friends in the village. Arthur Bolton fell asleep in his wheelchair, wheezing and snoring, and Sarah and Paula shared the washing-up.

Most of the evening they sat around and watched television, sipping port and sherry until it was time for the children to go to bed. Arthur Bolton followed soon after.

'Let's have another drink,' Sarah suggested when she and Paula were alone. 'It's been a long time since we last got tiddly together.'

A fire blazed in the hearth. It was only lava rocks heated by gas, but it looked and felt like a real fire, and it made Sarah remember the coal fire they used to have all winter when she was a child. With her father working at the pit, they got a coal allowance.

'I don't know,' Paula said. 'I shouldn't. There'll still be so much to do tomorrow.'

'Come on. It's Christmas.'

'We can't all live your easygoing lifestyle, you know. The kids will be needing me just as much tomorrow as they did today. Then there's Dad to look after. And work.'

'Come on, let your hair down.'

Paula chewed her lip for a moment, then said. 'All right, you've twisted my arm. Maybe just one. A little one, mind you.'

'Why don't you try your new blouse on?'

'Don't be daft.'

'Go on. I want to see if it fits.'

'I can't. I'll feel silly.'

'No you won't. You'll look gorgeous. Go on, Paula, do it for me.'

'Well, I suppose it'll go with my suit.' Muttering to herself, Paula disappeared upstairs and came down wearing the blouse. It was Thai silk, handmade, and a very delicate coral colour. Paula wore it under a dull, off-the-peg cream suit. But that was Paula all over: Rodeo Drive blouse and C & A suit.

'There you are,' said Sarah. 'You look great.'

Paula fingered the high collar. 'It *is* nice . . .'

'But?'

'Well, I can hardly wear it to work, can I?'

'I should hope not. It wasn't meant for work. Don't worry, there'll be occasions. I just wanted to buy you something a bit frivolous, that's all.'

Paula gave a long-suffering sigh. 'It's all very well for some. We can't all afford to be frivolous, though. Some of us have responsibilities.'

'Oh, Paula, give it a rest.' Sarah felt squiffy enough to defy her big sister. She dug out the medicinal brandy and poured them each a healthy measure. 'To family reunions,' she said, raising her glass.

Paula snorted.

Sarah slammed her glass down, breaking the stem and spilling brandy all over the coffee table. 'What the hell's wrong with you?' she demanded. 'You don't give a bloody inch, do you? Can't you see I'm trying? I'm trying very hard. Do you hate me so much?'

'What do you mean?' said Paula, already wiping at the spill with a napkin. 'Of course I don't hate you. Whatever gave you that idea?'

'Oh, leave it alone,' said Sarah, grasping Paula's arm. Paula shook herself free and carried on mopping up. A spot of brandy stained the hem of her suit. Sarah got another glass from the cabinet and filled it close to the brim. 'All the time I've been here you've done nothing but whine and moan,' she said. 'I'm getting sick of it. If your life's so bloody awful, do something about it.' The moment she had spoken, Sarah regretted the words, and her harsh tone, but it was already too late.

'What do you mean "do something about it"?' Paula shot back, colour flashing to her cheeks. 'As easy as that, is it? What do you suggest I do? Pack in my job? Dump the kids? And what about Dad? Do I just let him die? Maybe you don't realize it, but *someone's* got to look after this family, and it bloody well isn't you.'

'You ungrateful bitch. I've offered you all the help I can and you just throw it all back in my face.'

'Help? That's a good one. Money, that's what you've offered. That's all. Money. You can't buy everything with money, you know.'

'If you weren't so damn stubborn and proud you'd realize you can do a lot with money.'

'Like send Dad to a home?'

'Well let's face it, that'd be one less burden for you, wouldn't it?'

Paula shook her head. 'A *burden*? You just don't bloody understand, do you, Sal? Has all this high living turned your head so much you don't even understand your family any more? Has America done this to you? You didn't used to be so heartless.'

Sarah ran her hand over her hair. 'I'm sorry,' she said. 'I didn't mean it. You just made me so angry.'

'I wouldn't mind,' Paula went on, 'if you weren't so obviously Dad's favourite, no matter—'

'What did you say?'

'You heard.'

Sarah was suddenly conscious of the wind screaming

outside, like some outcast creature in despair trying to get in. 'But that's ridiculous,' she said. 'He hates me. Maybe not hates, but . . . Oh, he tolerates me, for appearance's sake. After all, I *am* family. He's polite. But he's never forgiven me for not being what he wanted me to be, for that bloody sex scene, for Gary, the drugs, for moving to LA—'

'You stupid cow, can't you see it? He adores you. It doesn't matter how many times you've embarrassed him or let him down, he still thinks the sun shines out of your arse.'

'But—'

'No, let me finish.' Paula sat forward and rested her hands on her knees. 'It's about time you heard a few home truths, little Miss High and Mighty. I'm not saying he puts no value on me, of course he does. I think he respects me. He certainly appreciates how I take care of him. He's grateful. But he *loves* you. Can't you see the difference?'

Sarah shook her head. 'No.'

'Then you're a fool. When you made those dirty films and then took off with that drug addict Gary Knox, you broke Dad's heart. He thought he'd lost you for ever. He's a proud man and he's used to being obeyed, so of course he cut you off. What would you expect of him? But I know what he really felt. Remember, I've lived with him all this time, heard him calling me by your name when he's half asleep and afraid of dying, seen him looking at the phone, willing it to ring, waiting for the postman. I've seen the pride, the way his face lights up when he sees you walk on the screen.'

'But you said he didn't watch the series. He said—'

'Of course he watches it. Every bloody Tuesday without fail. And if anything ever comes up to stop him, I have to tape it for him. Oh, Sal, I might have done all the right things in my life, even if they didn't all work out. And there's the kids, too, of course. Dad adores the kids. But you're the one he loves most. You're the one who took on the world and won. You're the one who broke away. You're the one with all the guts, the one who doesn't give a damn what people think. You're the star, the shining light. You're the one he's so bloody proud of he could burst.' She shook her head. Her face was flushed and her eyes were glittering with tears. 'Don't you ever try to convince me he doesn't prefer you, because I *know* he does. He always has done. And that's something I've just had to learn to live with.'

Suddenly, some of the old memories made sense to Sarah. *Let's bury Daddy in the sand,* bedtime stories and, she remembered, he *had* taken her to the pictures when she was a little girl. She remembered him falling asleep during *Fantasia* at the Lyceum, and the woman next to them nudging him and telling him to stop snoring. He must have just finished a twelve-hour shift down the pit. Maybe Paula was right. But Sarah still couldn't believe it. Struck dumb, she reached for the brandy bottle and poured another drink.

Paula held out her glass. 'I think I need another one, too. He'll go spare when he sees that broken glass.'

'Oh, bugger the glass. I could buy him a hundred sets of Waterford crystal if he wanted.'

'Haven't I got through to you? That's not what he wants. Look at where he comes from, the kind of man he is. He's happy with meat and two veg, a bottle of beer, a night or two a week out at the club and a roof over his head. He doesn't want your money, or what it can buy. He wants your love. Have you forgotten how to give it? Is that what fame does to people?'

'Perhaps I have.' Sarah took a large pull on the brandy. It was a cheap make, she noticed, and it burned all the way down. Her hand was shaking. 'I'm sorry,' she said. 'This is all such a shock. I didn't know . . .'

'Of course you bloody didn't. You've been far too busy with your career to spare a thought for family. Truth be told, you've always been a bit too selfish, our Sal.'

'It's not that. Oh, it's true I've been working hard, maybe too much. But I've been ill, too. I fell to pieces, Paula. I came unstuck out there, thousands of miles from home. And there was no one to help me, no one I could turn to. I nearly died. I mean I nearly killed myself. I *wanted* to die.'

Paula stared at her. 'What? Over that worthless Gary Knox?'

'Partly. Maybe. But it wasn't just that, it was everything. And he wasn't worthless, Paula. He wasn't always worthless. He changed, that's all. People do, you know.'

'I heard about what happened to him. Dad said it served him right.'

'Oh, I'd left him by then. But I lost it, Paula. Listen to what I'm saying. I just . . . lost it. Ever since then I've hidden myself in my work, buried my head in the sand. I've been too ashamed to come home and face you all.' She felt the tears burning in her eyes, felt the pent-up emotion ripping itself loose from her heart. 'Why don't you come back with me?' she said. 'You. Dad. Jason and Cathy. A new life.'

Paula laughed. 'Don't be daft. We couldn't possibly. First off, there's school for the kids, and Dad . . . well . . .'

Sarah looked directly at her. 'I mean it,' she said. 'You can do it if you make an effort. Come over and stay with me, Paula. I'm lonely. I'm so lonely.' And she let the tears come. Her head fell to rest on Paula's shoulder, which hardened with resistance at first, then yielded. First, Paula put an arm around her, then Sarah felt her sister's hand stroking her hair, just like she had all those years ago. 'Somebody's trying to destroy me, Paula,' she sobbed. 'Somebody's trying to drive me insane.'

21

All day the insects crawled over his exposed flesh: face, wrists, ankles. Some of them were biting him, too, drawing blood, but he didn't mind. It was only their nature.

The rain came and went. He squatted in the trees at the back of the house. When you stay still for so long, he noticed, your mind moves into a very strange space indeed. Perceptions are heightened. Especially touch, smell and hearing.

He could smell not only every individual leaf of the eucalyptus and pine trees but any number of other, small wild flowers and shrubs in the vicinity. He could smell the dirt and earth-mould beneath him, still damp after rain, and he was even aware of the changing smells of his own skin as the chemical balances inside him altered minute by minute.

It was as if the whole spectrum of electromagnetic radiation beyond the puny strip occupied by visible light had suddenly opened its secrets to him. He could smell the light slowly changing to darkness, too: like saffron and cinnamon to coal dust and ashes. He liked it.

And he could feel every tiny insect footprint on his flesh, could hear every antenna brushing against the hairs on his wrist where the thin cotton gloves ended. He could feel the stingers, or whatever they used, slowly pricking into his skin, sucking his blood for incubation, or injecting inflammatory chemicals, and he could smell his blood as it flowed out.

But there was no pain. The things he experienced were all part of a vast continuum of sensation in which everything could be sensed, but in which nothing felt either good or bad.

He imagined this was what the Zen Buddhists meant when they talked about mindlessness and detachment.

He didn't even daydream to pass the time. Nothing but pure sensation registered in his mind. He was so exactly focused on the here and now that there was no place for memory, doubt, fear or fantasy. Deep down, he knew why he was here, knew what he had to do and who he was doing it for. He didn't have to think about it any more; it had become a part of his nature.

So all he had to do was wait, crouched in the woods with the insects getting in his hair and crawling down the back of his shirt collar, up his pant legs. Making tiny whistling, sucking and screaming sounds as they drew his blood.

He heard a car in the distance and instinctively his hand tightened on the hammer he held. It was the only movement he had made in six hours, apart from blinking.

22

It rained on Christmas Day in Santa Monica. All day. A slow, steady drizzle, at times indistinguishable from the fog.

Arvo woke late, showered, brewed a pot of fresh coffee and tuned the radio to FM 93.1. He knew every oldie almost by heart. As he half listened, he thought about what Joe Westinghouse had told him the previous evening. In some ways, it came close to confirming what he had suspected: that the Heimar murder might have been carried out for Sarah Broughton's benefit.

Before the toxicology results, it had still been possible to believe that Heimar had simply picked up the wrong john and become the victim of a possible homophobic killer. Prostitutes, both male and female, made easy victims because they were often estranged from their families and lived far from where they grew up. They had no community beyond their own kind. If they disappeared, nobody noticed, and if another prostitute did notice, the odds were that he wasn't going to call the cops.

But now Arvo knew that the Heimar kid had been given so much pentobarbitol that he had been in a coma *before* his throat was cut, *before* his neck and chest were stabbed and slashed repeatedly, *before* his body was cut into pieces, then it looked less like an impassioned sex killing and more like a cold, deliberately planned murder.

Joe had also checked with the coroner's office about how the drug might have been administered. There were no fresh needle-marks, so intravenous injection was out, and it was unlikely that Heimar had been given it in a drink. Pentobarbitol tastes lousy and he would surely have noticed it, unless he had been almost paralytically drunk, which he wasn't.

Most likely, Joe had thought at first, the kid had been offered the pills by his killer and had simply taken them himself, for fun, or to dull the pain of what he was doing, the way a lot of street kids do.

But the forensic pathologist who carried out the autopsy found traces of barbituric acid in Heimar's anus and a high concentration of the drug in his rectal tissue. Which meant that Heimar or his killer had shoved the pills up his ass, probably as a prelude or a coda to anal sex. After all, straw behind the ears or not, John Heimar was a genuine, dyed-in-the-wool LA male prostitute.

Arvo tried to push the depressing thoughts aside. There was nothing more he could do until tomorrow, after the holiday, when life got back to normal. Besides, he still couldn't be certain it wasn't a potential serial killer making his first tentative foray into murder and dismemberment. But if he took everything into account – the watcher with binoculars; the letters, with their promise of 'proof'; the placing of the body and timing to coincide with Sarah Broughton's regular morning run; the coldly premeditated abduction and murder of an easy victim – then it seemed more likely there was a connection.

All morning, he had been eyeing the small package on the table by the window: his Christmas present from Nyreen. He couldn't decide whether to open it or throw it out.

Finally, he opened it. Under all the padding and tissue lay a small, delicate glass bowl with a rose etched on the side. Nyreen was into glass-blowing these days, and it was probably something she had made. What its purpose was, Arvo had no idea. But trust Nyreen to send him something she'd blown. He put the bowl on the mantelpiece and tried to ignore it.

He hadn't put up a tree this year – there seemed no point – and the few cards he had received stood on the tile mantelpiece – some from old friends in Detroit, one from his brother, Michael, in New York, one from his grandparents in Wales. His maternal grandparents had died when he was very young, before he had a chance to get to know them. When he was a boy, his mother once told him they had been murdered by Stalin after the war, but he hadn't known what that really meant until much later.

By noon, Arvo felt restless. He drove down to Ocean, found a parking spot without any trouble and walked along the clifftop by the palisades, with his collar turned up and his hands shoved deep in his pockets. The rain and mist felt like cool silk brushing against his face. The Christmas lights strung across Wilshire, where it ended at Ocean, looked eerie, hanging there disembodied, blurred and smudged by the wet grey light.

All the horizons were lost in misty rain. From the top of the cliffs, he could hear the waves as they crashed on the shore below, and could just about make out the sloshing grey mass of the ocean. Gulls swooped in and out of the fog, squawking and squabbling, seemingly oblivious to both the weather and the birth of Christ. Even the traffic on the Coast Highway, way down at the bottom of the sheer cliffs, was quiet today.

A bundle of rags stirred at the base of a palm tree and a grubby hand shot out, accompanied by a mumbled request for money. Arvo gave him a buck. Sometimes he seemed to hand over half his salary to bums. Why, he didn't know.

As he crossed the road to get back to his car, a police cruiser slowed to a halt beside him. He realized that, apart from the bums, he was the only person on the street. Everyone else was at home with the family eating turkey and watching *It's a Wonderful Life* or *A Christmas Carol,* and the only places open were video stores and minimarts.

'What's your destination, sir?' asked the young officer on the passenger side.

Arvo flipped his shield. 'Just walking.'

'Sorry, sir,' the officer said. 'Routine. Merry Christmas.'

His partner nodded and drove off.

'Merry Christmas,' Arvo said after the car. He supposed he did look suspicious out there alone with the bums on the street. Bums were vulnerable, like prostitutes. Sometimes people killed them for pleasure, the way people killed boys like John Heimar. The two cops – poor bastards pulling the Christmas Day shift – were only doing their jobs.

Arvo remembered pulling Christmas shifts as a uniform cop in Detroit. Christmas Eve was pretty bad, a lot of domestic violence and shit like that. But some of the real stuff that took longer to build up exploded on Christmas Day, usually in the afternoon.

Nobody who hasn't done it can ever understand the feeling you get driving to work around dawn, seeing the Christmas lights all lit up on the porches and watching the bedroom lights flick on inside the houses and apartments as you drive by, maybe remembering the anticipation you used to feel when you were a kid, the excitement that this was the day you'd been waiting for, the day you were going to get that mountain bike you'd been longing for all year, or that new Sega Genesis game everyone else at school seemed to have but you. But this year, you aren't going to be part of it at all.

And that was the *best* part of the day.

So you'd arrive feeling a little nostalgic, maybe, and the early part of the shift you'd be bored to tears, just wishing you were at home with your family like everyone else. By afternoon, though, things started to change. The calls started coming in, and by the time your shift was over you never wanted to work a holiday again.

The first one might be a dangler, been hanging there in the

middle of the living room since he woke up and found himself all alone on Christmas Day and accepted at last that there really was no future for him. By the time you get there, his neck is two feet long and his shoes are full of shit.

Because holidays like Christmas are when really bad things happen. On Christmas Day, the husband who has been feeling depressed over being laid off for a couple of months has too much to drink, decides he doesn't like the tie his wife bought him and shoots his children, his wife and then himself. And who cleans up? The cops and the ambulance guys.

On Christmas Day, the wife who has been holding back her feelings about her husband's affair ever since she found out about it in November has too many glasses of wine with the turkey, which she spent all morning preparing, and when he says he just *has* to go out for a while after dinner, she feels the edge of the carving knife and looks at his throat.

On holidays like Christmas, people get together, drink too much and kill one another. Or they get depressed all alone and they kill themselves. Either way, it makes a busy time for the emergency services. You want a good argument against the family, Arvo thought, then you should spend a Christmas Eve in the police station or in the emergency ward of your local hospital.

Arvo had no sooner got home than the phone rang. His chest tightened when he heard Nyreen's voice. 'Merry Christmas, honey,' she said. 'How did you like the present?'

'It's fine,' said Arvo. 'You made it yourself?'

'Uh-huh.'

'Look, I'm sorry I didn't send you—'

'Hey, it's okay. No problem. The pleasure's in the giving, right? Arvo, I'm not stupid. I realize I've hurt you and you're probably still pissed at me and all, but you know I still care a lot about you. I hope we can be friends?'

'I don't know if that's possible, Nyreen.'

'Well, okay, maybe not right now. I understand that. Maybe it'll take time. But what I'm saying, honey, is don't cut me out of your life completely. Things just didn't work out for you and me, but I still love you, you know. Okay?'

'I don't know. I need some time.'

'Are you okay?'

'Sure. I'm fine.'

'Are you enjoying Christmas?'

'Yeah. Look, I've got to go. You know Mike Glover? He and his wife invited me over for dinner.' He had been invited, but he wasn't going. The last thing he wanted on Christmas Day was someone else's family being solicitous about his well-being.

'Great. Have a good time. And give Mike and Rosie my love. Oh, and before I forget, Arvo, I've got some real good news.'

'What's that?'

'I'm pregnant. Isn't it a *rush?* Vern is absolutely *thrilled.* So am I, of course. Aren't you just a teeny-weeny bit happy for me?'

'Sure I'm happy for you, Nyreen. I wish you all the best. Gotta run now.'

Arvo hung up with a lump in his throat. Pregnant. Now *there* was a surprise. When he and Nyreen had discussed children, she had made it quite clear that she didn't want any, not for a few years at least. Arvo had gone along with her, though he had wanted to start a family sooner. She said she needed time to pursue her career in public relations, which she had now given up to go live with Vern in Palo Alto and blow glass. Life. Go figure.

Now, all of a sudden, she was pregnant and just thrilled to pieces about it. Well, that little bit of news had just shunted Nyreen at least another million miles away from Arvo. Now she was having Vern's child, she was less his problem than she had ever been. At least that was his view. Somehow, he had a feeling that she would see things differently. She always did. Maybe she'd want him to be godfather. And that would probably be after she'd claimed half the house.

Arvo realized he was hungry. So okay, he told himself, getting up and stretching, the hell with Nyreen. Stop feeling sorry for yourself and get Christmas on the road.

In the four years after his parents' death, Arvo had got into the habit of spending Christmas alone. In fact, now he thought about it, he and Nyreen had only been together for one Christmas.

As he had spent two of his three Christmases in Los Angeles alone, so far, returning to the familiar ritual for his fourth gave him a degree of comfort. He wasn't a Christian, and the drop or two of Jewish blood he had inherited from his mother's side hadn't galvanized him into any sort of Judaic interests or beliefs, but the season nevertheless had a certain something; it demanded some sort of recognition, if only a brief genuflection in the general direction of the twin gods, Mammon and Glutton. It was also a time that tended to encourage introspection.

First he went to the fridge and took out the smoked salmon and selection of imported cheeses, cold cuts and pâtés he had bought a couple of days ago at the farmers' market on Fairfax – some Caerphilly, to remind him of his Welsh roots, old Cheddar and cambozola because he liked them.

Then there was that Welsh delicacy, a can of laver bread, made from seaweed and absolutely delicious with a couple of rashers of Canadian bacon. Finally, he would nibble on a couple of the Welsh cakes his Granny Hughes had sent him, as she did every Christmas, without fail. If he were still hungry at supper time, there was a microwavable turkey dinner in the freezer.

When he had set up his tray, he popped the cork on a bottle

of Schramsberg Californian 'champagne' and poured himself a glass. Then he went over to his CD collection and put on Richard Burton reading Dylan Thomas's 'A Child's Christmas in Wales.'

By the time he had got through the third glass of champagne and most of the smoked salmon, his mind began drifting. He thought first, as he always did at Christmas, of his parents and the family Christmases in Detroit, all the houses in the street decked with coloured lights, the presents under the tree, turkey with sage-and-onion stuffing and cranberry sauce, shovelling the piles of snow from the driveway. Well, maybe *that* wasn't such a romantic image.

He thought of his grandfather in Amlwch, how at eighty-five he still got around with the help of a knobbly walking-stick and never missed a lunchtime session at the pub, and how his wife, at eighty-two, would bawl him out if he was late back.

He thought about Maria down in San Diego with her family. The thought of her brought back the memory of her perfume, of her warm breast against his arm, and it made him feel horny.

Then he thought of Nyreen and how last year, only a couple of weeks after they had got married, they had gone to the Christmas boat parade down in Marina del Rey.

Bundled up in a green wool sweater against the cool evening, Nyreen had clung onto his arm and jumped up and down like a child, pointing at the procession of boats bobbing by with their illuminated reindeers, angels and fake blue-lit icicles hanging from their bows. Arvo had thought it was tacky, but he was happy to see her so excited and alive. He remembered how passionately they had made love that night. Now she was pregnant in Palo Alto, living with Vern.

By the time Arvo was on his fourth glass of bubbly and his second Welsh cake, Richard Burton was bringing the story to a close. When it was over, Arvo wasn't sure whether the tears that came to his eyes stemmed from nostalgia for his father's homeland or from drunken self-pity. He rubbed them away with the backs of his hands and finished the bottle.

In the evening, he watched a double bill of two of his favourite sci-fi videos: *Them!* and *The Creeping Flesh*. He stumbled to bed sometime around midnight without having got around to the frozen turkey.

It wasn't until eight o'clock the next morning that his beeper went off, shocking him out of a chaotic dream about a giant ant with Nyreen's face trying to explain to him how ants procreated. He woke into a real jackhammer of a headache. When he dialled the unfamiliar number and spoke his name into the receiver, his voice was hoarse with dehydration.

'Arvo, it's Joe. Joe Westinghouse. Sorry if this seems to be getting to be a habit, but it looks like there's been another one.'

Still fuzzy from sleep and alcohol, Arvo mumbled, 'Another what?'

'Another murder.'

Well what was so odd about that? Arvo thought numbly. Day after Christmas in LA. Any day in LA. Bound to be plenty of other murders. And Joe did work Robbery-Homicide.

'Maybe you'd like to come and have a look?' Joe suggested. 'I think this one will interest you.'

'Just a minute,' Arvo croaked, reaching for the pencil and paper he always kept on his bedside table. 'Give me the address. I'll be there as soon as I can.'

23

At eight-thirty in the morning the day after Christmas, there was plenty of traffic on the San Diego Freeway as the shoppers headed for the post-Christmas sales at the huge malls out in the Valley. Arvo turned off at Sunset and drove with the top of his convertible open. He needed a little air to blow a few of the cobwebs out of his brain.

No matter how many times he had passed through Bel Air and Beverly Hills, he had never ceased to marvel at the incredibly opulent bad taste that juxtaposed Elizabethan stately homes with Spanish haciendas, fairy-tale castles and French chateaux, all tucked away at the end of long driveways behind walls and elaborate metal gates, all surrounded by immaculately kept lawns. Well, you never did stop marvelling, did you, if you were from Detroit? It made Grosse Point look like the projects.

Still, there was something morbidly fascinating about it all, the way there often is with such overt bad taste. To gild the lily, some of the large houses were strung with gaudy displays of Christmas lights, and there were even a couple of oversized Christmas trees among the topiary, hung with tinsel and baubles. Probably imported from Norway or somewhere.

It was a perfect morning. The whole city had a fresh look and a clean, crisp smell, as it often did after rain. Sometimes, if only for a few hours, it seemed as if a day's rain could wash all the poison from the air and rinse away years of grease and grime from the streets.

The early sun shone piercingly bright on the white stone of the protecting estate walls, and a few high white clouds floated serenely across the pale blue sky. In the far distance, way beyond the Hollywood Hills, stood the San Gabriel range, greenish-brown slopes scattered with chaparral and sagebrush. High up, near the jagged peaks, rough white striations stood out in relief, where snow had settled in the gullies and fissures.

After three glasses of water and four extra-strength Tylenol, Arvo was feeling a little more human, but he still experienced waves of dizziness and nausea and his heart seemed to be labouring to circulate the sluggish blood through his body. The bright light hurt, even through dark glasses. He didn't bother turning the radio on; he knew the way a hangover distorted his sense of hearing so much that even the organized harmony of a Mozart quartet would sound like a series of random sounds scraped by chainsaws on iron railings.

He drove up Laurel Canyon to the turn-off road Joe had mentioned, then turned left up the hillside and looked for the hand-painted sign.

Three police cruisers had pulled off the road to block the drive, lights flashing in the bright sun. Arvo parked his car by the roadside and flipped his shield. One of the officers raised the yellow crime-scene tape to let him through and made a note of the time and Arvo's name on a clipboard.

The short driveway led to the backyard of a small timber A-frame, the front of which, held up by stilts sunk in concrete in the hillside, looked out over the canyon. Trees shaded the whole area and cast eerie, slow-moving shadows over the earth as the breeze stirred their heavy limbs. The air smelled of freshly cut grass, eucalyptus and pine trees. Even though it was early on a December morning, the temperature was in the mid-sixties. Raindrops still clung to the leaves like dew.

Someone had fixed a crime-scene card to the door, which meant that Joe had probably established a 'double crime scene.' It made sense in a case like this, which was probably going to attract a few dignitaries and high-ranking police officers, not to mention high-fliers from the DA's office.

What you did was you set up two crime-scene areas, one starting at the driveway and the second at the door to the house itself. The second, inside the house, of course, was the *primary* crime scene, the most important area to seal off, and Joe would now be responsible for who did and who didn't get in there.

When the brass arrived, they would get the opportunity to breach at least one police line; they would be allowed through the driveway as far as the back of the house. That served two purposes: first, it would gratify their sense of importance; second, it would keep them out of the way of the *real* crime scene and avoid further contamination. So the brass saved face and the crime scene remained as intact as possible. Everyone gained.

Over by the trees, a young man wearing grey shorts and a red T-shirt sat on a tree stump beside a gas barbecue with his legs planted wide apart and his head in his hands, crying. A lock of straight blond hair had slid down and hung almost to his knees. A female patrol officer stood beside him.

Joe Westinghouse stood talking to another detective outside the back door. Joe was smoking, tapping his ash carefully into the yellow Sucrets tin he always carried with him to crime scenes. Jim Sung, from the coroner's office, stood beside them with his scuffed black bag, waiting to go in. Jim nodded as Arvo approached. He looked as calm and bored as he always did, slowly chewing away at a piece of gum.

The three of them wore blue LAPD jumpsuits and disposable gloves to avoid contaminating the crime scene, or, in some cases, to avoid being contaminated by it. AIDS was a constant threat if there was a stranger's blood splashed around the scene.

Arvo took his jumpsuit out of the trunk, slipped it on over his Tigers sweatshirt and jeans and walked over. He could feel the tension between Joe and the other man as he approached them.

'This is Detective Heffer, Hollywood Division,' said Joe. 'He caught the squeal.'

Arvo nodded at Heffer, who had a pale, almost albino, complexion and an unusual combination of thin face and lips and a pug nose, revealing almost circular nostrils. His cold grey eyes were flecked with yellow, and his sparse hair was the colour of bleached straw. Like Jim Sung, he was also chewing gum, and occasionally he paused to blow a bubble. He gave no acknowledgment of Arvo's greeting, nor did his eyes betray any emotion.

Arvo knew Heffer, or at least knew of him. Word was he had applied for the TMU and been turned down. As a result, he had a hard-on for the department and didn't hesitate to let it show.

Joe pointed towards the blond man in the shorts. 'His name's Jaimie Kincaid. Victim's boyfriend. He phoned in at seven thirty-nine this morning and Officer Laski over there with him was first officer on the scene. You can get the details later. I suggest we go inside and have a look first.'

'Okay,' said Arvo.

'You ever been at a homicide scene before, Hughes?' asked Heffer. He had a squeaky voice that grated on Arvo's nerves.

'Once or twice.'

'Uh-huh, it's just that I figured you real *élite* star-fuckers down at—'

'Heffer. Shut the fuck up,' Joe cut in.

'Yes, *sir*,' Heffer said, and turned sullen.

The four of them went inside.

The back door led directly into a modern kitchen with fitted blond wood cupboards and shelves. Rustic copperware hung from hooks on the wall, and a large laminated chart showed the varieties of herbs and spices. The kitchen smelled of tomatoes, garlic and basil, and Arvo got the impression that the person who had lived there was quite the gourmet cook. A wooden rack held a set of kitchen knives; the biggest one was missing.

Even though he was wearing gloves, Arvo kept his hands in his pockets to avoid the temptation of touching something. He was also careful to step around the blood and mud smears on the ceramic tile floor.

Like Sarah Broughton's place at the beach, the stilt-house was small but laid out in a design that made the best of its space and emphasized the view. At the front, sliding glass doors led to a large timber deck and looked out over the canyon.

The downstairs area consisted of one split-level room, the back, and higher, section fitted with a black matte dining table and matching chairs, the front with an off-white three-piece suite. The interior walls and floors were made of bleached pine. Contemporary paintings hung on the walls: the kinds of squiggles and seemingly random blocks of colour that Arvo had never been able to work up much enthusiasm for.

A black-iron spiral staircase led upstairs, where there was one large bedroom, two smaller ones, a bathroom and closet space.

In the master bedroom, the naked body lay face up, spread-eagled on the king-size bed, hands and feet bound to the brass rails, a halo of blood around his head on the pillow. His clothes were neatly folded over the chair beside the bed, the missing kitchen knife resting on top of his white shirt, smearing it dark red. Face down on the bedside table lay a paperback copy of *Lonesome Dove*, about half read, along with a sachet of white powder.

In life, Jack Marillo had been a six-foot, slim, vital, healthy, handsome, Italian male. In death, he looked pale and blood-less, nothing but an empty shell. His lifeless eyes were ringed with dark circles, like a raccoon's, as if he had applied thick kohl or gone too many nights without sleep. They stared at a knothole in the ceiling. Though the body hadn't started to decompose, the stench of blood and death in such a warm, enclosed space was almost overwhelming.

All around him, on the walls, on the rugs, on the bedsheets, Jack's blood had been spilled. It had splattered over the abstract paintings, Arvo noticed, making hardly any differ-ence at all to the quality of the art. Real Jackson Pollock stuff. On the sheepskin rugs that littered the floor, it resembled ink blots, and on the bedclothes around the body, it looked as if someone had emptied a couple of buckets of sludge.

Joe and Heffer hung back in the doorway. They had clearly been in the room earlier, where Joe would have pulled out his pocket Instamatic and taken a few photos before the 'experts' arrived and messed up the scene. Nothing would have been touched yet, nothing moved. Jim Sung, who had seen every-thing you could imagine and more, looked around, sniffed, made a few notes, then went over to the body.

From where Arvo stood, the cause of death looked obvious enough, though he knew from experience not to jump to conclusions. Around Jack Marillo's throat and chest were numerous stab wounds, at least one of them nicking the carotid artery just beside his jaw. That was the source of the fountain of blood that had sprayed over some of the paintings.

In addition to the stab wounds and the halo of blood on the pillow, there was one very odd and disturbing thing about the body. In the soft flesh of the upper abdomen, just below the lowest stab wound, someone had carved the crude shape of a heart with an arrow piercing it. It measured about three or four inches across at its widest point, Arvo guessed. Whoever cut it had also tried to carve something inside, maybe a name or some words, but it had turned out to be illegible, at least to the naked eye.

Jim Sung touched the skin, then he felt the jaws and neck.

'Okay to turn him over?' he asked.

'Just a minute,' said Joe. He took a penknife from his pocket and cut the cords that tied Marillo to the bed rails. He did this in a very special and methodical way to preserve them as evidence. First, he cut the cord between the rail and the hand, or foot, then he cut off the rest of the cord that was tied and knotted around the rail, making sure he didn't cut through the knot itself. As he went, he tied the pieces together with string, which Jim Sung supplied from the depths of his bag, so that they could retain their original form for the experts. Sometimes, you could tell a lot from knots. He left the cords around Marillo's wrists for the coroner.

When the body had been freed, the first thing Jim Sung did was turn him on one side to check post-mortem lividity.

'Uh-huh,' he nodded. 'Looks like the dirty deed was done up here, all right.'

Arvo could see that for himself. What blood hadn't sprayed out into the room had collected down Marillo's back, showing as a slight purple discolouration of the skin. It wasn't as marked as that he had seen on other bodies. Because Marillo had lost so much blood when he was killed, there hadn't been all that much left to sink to his back after death.

Jim Sung pressed the discolouration with his finger. It didn't change. 'See?' he said. 'No blanching.'

Arvo saw. Blanching of post-mortem lividity occurred in only the early stages, before the blood had clotted.

Jim Sung inserted a rectal thermometer and turned to face the others as he held it in place. 'I can't tell you exactly how long he's been dead,' he said, 'but I'd say from all the signs it's somewhere between eight and ten hours.'

Joe looked at his watch and nodded. 'That makes it around midnight, one in the morning. Late last night, anyway.'

Jim Sung checked the temperature and made some calculations. 'Uh-huh,' he said. 'Body temperature bears that out.' He turned back to the body and began examining it, making notes, muttering to himself as he worked. 'This should interest you guys,' he said, pointing to the back of the head.

Arvo had noticed blood on the pillow, and now he could see the reason for it. At the back of Jack Marillo's skull was a roughly circular depression, cracked bone matted with hair, blood and brain tissue.

'Looks like some sort of hammer wound,' Joe said.

'What about the black eyes?' Arvo asked.

'You often get that effect with a blow to the back of the head,' Jim Sung explained. 'Look, there isn't a lot more I can do here,' he said, moving away. 'Might as well get the specialists in, then call the meat wagon. You guys want to stay in here and talk or go outside and smell the flowers, a nice day like this?'

Arvo looked around the room. At the foot of the bed was a large TV and VCR set up on top of a couple of shelves of tapes. He glanced at the titles and found a mix of Hollywood classics and gay soft porn.

'Well?' said Sung.

'Have you checked out the bathroom?' Arvo asked.

Joe nodded. 'Looks like someone took a shower there recently, but it's impossible to say when. Judging from the time it takes my own shower to dry out, I'd say maybe last night. There's what looks like traces of blood on the bottom of the tub, too.'

'Makes sense,' said Arvo. 'There must have been one hell of a lot of it spraying around.'

Joe nodded and led the way out. After the death room, it was a relief, Arvo felt, to smell the pine and the fresh-cut grass again, and especially the eucalyptus after rain. Sparrows and starlings twittered in the trees. He took a long, deep breath. The sun still shone in a blue sky, laced with wisps of white cloud like milk spills, but the city already seemed a little dirtier now than it had an hour ago.

As soon as they stood in the backyard again, Joe reached for his cigarettes. Arvo felt his own craving rise as Joe lit up. He gritted his teeth and waited for the urge to pass.

The blond man on the tree stump had stopped crying and was staring down at his linked hands on his lap.

'Want to tell us what happened, Mr Kincaid?' said Joe.

The man looked up. His eyes were red from crying; the lock of hair still covered one side of his face. He had Nordic features, high cheekbones and ice-blue eyes, their effect enhanced by a touch of smudged blue eyeshadow, and he looked both miserable and frightened. Hardly surprising, Arvo thought, given the circumstances.

'Must I?' he said. 'I've already given my statement to Detective Heffer.'

'Come on, Jaimie,' coaxed Joe. 'You'll feel better if you tell me, too.' They went over to the picnic table, where Arvo, Joe and Kincaid sat down. Heffer remained standing, hovering over them, hands in his pockets, with the beginnings of a sneer twisting at his lips.

When they had sat, Kincaid squinted at Joe. 'What do you mean, I'll feel better? For what?'

'What was it, Jaimie, a lovers' quarrel?'

'Now wait a minute—'

'No, *you* wait a minute, Jaimie.' Joe spoke quietly, but his voice carried authority. 'Tell me if I'm wrong. You and Jack get a little high and get into a bondage situation, right? Things get way out of hand, maybe Jack says something, or maybe the coke's rotted your frontal lobes, so you go get the kitchen knife and you kill him. When you see what you've done, you take a shower and call the cops. Is that how it went down?'

Jaimie paled. 'No.'

'Then tell me, Jaimie. I want to help you.'

'Look, will you just fucking listen to me.'

'No need to swear, Jaimie. Stay calm. Of course I'll listen.'

'How can I stay calm when you're practically accusing me of murder? Jesus Christ.' He put his head in his hands again and moaned.

Joe just sat and watched, tapping ash into his little Sucrets tin. 'Take your time, Jaimie,' he said. 'No hurry.'

Jaimie took a deep breath and ran his hand over his hair, pushing the errant lock back in place. 'Right. Okay. You're listening?'

'I'm listening.'

'Jack's my friend, right, and we were going away together for a few days this morning.'

'Where?'

'Jack has a cabin up in the Sierras. Mammoth.'

'That your car?' Joe pointed to a red Honda Civic parked next to a silver Porsche.

Kincaid nodded. 'Uh-huh. And the Porsche is Jack's. I came to pick Jack up and I . . . I . . .'

'You did what, Jaimie?'

'He didn't answer the door.'

'The door was closed?'

'Yes.'

'Was it locked?'

'No. I mean, it opened when I turned the handle. Then I saw the mud and blood on the floor.'

'You knew it was blood?'

'That's what it looked like to me.'

'What do you do, Jaimie? What's your occupation?'

'I'm an interior decorator.'

Arvo heard Heffer suppress a chuckle, turning it into a cough and putting his hand over his mouth. Kincaid caught it too and glared up at him. Heffer shook his head and wandered up the driveway.

'Seen a lot of blood in your line of work, have you?' Joe went on, ignoring the brief interruption.

'Well, no, but . . .'

'It could have been ketchup, couldn't it? Or paint?'

'It was blood. I . . . I just. I could *feel* there was something wrong.'

'Feel? You a psychic?'

'No. Jack and I are close. I just had a feeling, that's all. A bad feeling.'

'What did you do next?'

'I called his name. He didn't answer.'

'Was he expecting you?'

'Yes. I told you. We were going to Mammoth. I told him I'd pick him up at seven-thirty. It's a five- or six-hour drive and we wanted to get there for lunchtime.'

'You two didn't live together, then?'

'No.' He blushed a little. 'We wanted to keep our relationship as discreet as possible. Because of Jack's career.'

'Where do you live?'

'I've got an apartment in West Hollywood.'

'You didn't spend Christmas together?'

'No. We were both with our families.'

'And your family lives where?'

'Irvine.'

'And Jack's?'

'The Valley. Northridge.'

Arvo knew they could find the full address easily enough. Someone would have to break the news to Jack Marillo's folks.

'Do you know if Jack was planning to come home last night?'

'He said he'd probably come home, yes. Get a good night's sleep before the trip.'

'And you arranged to pick him up here at seven-thirty?'

'Yes.'

'Why couldn't he drive to Mammoth himself?'

'We didn't think there was any point taking both cars. Besides, we wanted to spend time together, travel together.'

'Why not take his Porsche? It's a hell of a lot smoother ride than a Honda Civic.'

Kincaid shrugged. 'We were going to. But I was going to drive. Jack didn't like driving long distances. He broke his foot badly in a basketball game when he was at college and it still aches when he drives.'

'Okay. So you got no answer when you called his name. What did you do next?'

'Well, it wasn't like him, but I thought he might have overslept. You know, he'd been working very hard on the series. Anyway, I—'

'Just a minute,' Joe cut in. 'Let me get this clear. When you went in the house, you thought you saw blood mixed with mud on the kitchen floor and you had a real bad feeling. Then you thought maybe Jack had overslept. Which is it, Jaimie?'

'Look, you're confusing me. I mean, maybe it was later I thought it was blood. When I came back down. I don't know. But I didn't know Jack was *dead*. I mean, why would I even *think* something like that?'

Joe shrugged. 'You tell me, Jaimie.'

'Well, I didn't. That's what I'm telling you.'

'Okay. So what did you do?'

'I went upstairs and I saw the body. My God.' He shook his head slowly from side to side. 'I couldn't believe it.' Tears gathered again in his eyes.

'And then?'

'Then I ran back down to the kitchen and called the police.'

'The kitchen?'

'I was running out of the house. I wanted to get out. The

kitchen's at the back. When I got to there I knew I had to call the cops, so I did. I wasn't thinking clearly.'

'You called from the kitchen phone?'

'Yes. The red one on the wall.'

'Did you touch anything else?'

'No.'

'You sure you didn't touch the body, to check if he was dead?'

'You've seen the body,' Jaimie said. 'It was obvious even to me that Jack was dead. I . . .'

'Yes?'

'I wanted to cover him up. He looked so *exposed* lying there like that.'

'But you didn't.'

'No. I've seen enough cop shows to know not to mess with a crime scene.'

Joe winked at Arvo. 'Well, at least we've got something to thank television for. But you *did* use the kitchen phone?'

'I had to. I don't have a car phone and I knew I had to call the cops. Think how it would have looked if I'd gone off look-ing for a payphone and someone else had found the body. Besides, I had to stay there. I just had to. Sort of keep watch over him. It was very quiet. Only the birds.'

'You stayed outside?'

'Yes. I didn't want to go back in.'

'Did you remove anything from the scene?'

'No.'

'Did you use the bathroom at all?'

'No.'

'Sure you weren't sick? It'd be only natural, Jaimie.'

'No. I wasn't sick.'

'Weren't you scared?'

'Of what?'

'The killer might have been still in the house, or maybe somewhere nearby. Didn't that frighten you?'

Kincaid looked puzzled, then he turned pale again. 'It never entered my mind. I mean, I was upset. I called the cops. I never even imagined there might still be any danger there. Christ, if I had . . .'

'What?'

'I don't know. I might just have got the hell out of there.'

'You see, that bothers me. I think most people would be a little nervous, Jaimie. Unless, of course, they knew they didn't have anything to be frightened of.'

'You're doing it again.'

'What am I doing?'

'Accusing me. I'm telling you, I would never have hurt Jack. Never. Not in a million years. I . . . I . . .'

'You what?'

'I loved him.'

'You know what's behind most murders, Jaimie, when you get right down to it?'

'What?'

'Love.' Joe called over one of the uniformed officers. 'Take Mr Kincaid downtown,' he said, then he turned back to Jaimie and smiled. 'We'll talk some more in a little while.'

Jaimie was still pale. 'Am I under arrest?'

'Not yet.'

'Jaimie,' Arvo asked. 'Did you know Sarah Broughton?'

'Sarah? Of course.'

'Were you friends?'

'I wouldn't say exactly *friends*, but we knew each other. The three of us would have dinner sometimes. Why? You can't think—'

'How long have you known her?'

'Only since she started working with Jack. Look, Jack and I weren't exactly out of the closet, like I said. We tried to keep our relationship as private as we could. Sarah was one of the few who knew. I like her. She didn't judge.'

'Have you ever written her any letters?'

He frowned. 'No. Why should I have?'

'You know anyone who might have done this?' Joe asked.

Jaimie shook his head.

'Did Jack play the field? Did he like to pick up strangers, that sort of thing?'

'Absolutely not,' said Jaimie. 'Jack was faithful. I'd stake my life on it. He wasn't into that sort of sexual promiscuity. Me neither. We're not all like that, you know.'

Joe nodded. The uniformed officer took Jaimie by the elbow and led him up the driveway. Joe crooked his finger at Officer Laski, the first officer on the scene. She was a little overweight, Arvo noticed, and she was perspiring in the heat of the morning.

'What time did you arrive here?' Joe asked.

'Seven fifty-seven, sir.'

'What did you do?'

'I went into the house and checked that the victim was deceased. Then I secured the scene and called it in to Division. They sent Detective Heffer first, then you came just after him.'

'Was Mr Kincaid here the whole time?'

'Yes, sir. He was here when we arrived, waiting for us at the end of the driveway, then he stayed outside with my partner, Officer Clark, while I checked the scene.'

'Did you notice if there were any signs of forced entry?'

'There weren't. No broken glass, nothing.'

'Were any of the lights on?'

'Just the light on the stairwell.'

'Did you turn on the bedroom light?'

'No, sir. I used my flashlight.'

'Did you open any of the blinds or shutters?'

'No. They were already open.'

'Did you call in over the police radio?'

'No, sir. I used a landline, the kitchen extension. Mr Kincaid told me he had already used it, so I didn't think I would be destroying any evidence. I know the media listen in to the police band, and that something like this would get their attention.'

'Good thinking.'

'Thank you, sir.'

'Okay,' said Joe. 'That's it for now. Carry on.'

'Yes, sir.'

Officer Laski walked away, gun bouncing against her well-padded hip, rubbing her forearm across her brow. Heffer came back down the driveway and joined Joe and Arvo by the table.

'Mind if I ask a question first?' he said.

Joe raised an eyebrow. 'Go ahead.'

Heffer flicked a glance towards Arvo. 'What's the TMU doing here? Why isn't he out babysitting starlets?'

'You demonstrate a remarkable ignorance—' Arvo began, through clenched teeth, but Joe held up his hand and quieted him.

'Wait a minute, wait a minute,' he said. 'You got a point to make, Detective Heffer?'

Heffer shrugged. 'Just want to know what's missing here, that's all.' He jerked his thumb back towards the house. 'Has lover boy in there been getting threats or something?'

'Not as far as we know,' Joe said. 'And as long as I know why Detective Hughes is here, that's fine for the moment, okay?'

'You're the boss.'

'You got that right. Now, have you got any ideas?'

Heffer shrugged. 'It's as clear-cut a faggot murder as I've ever seen,' he said. 'And we do get a few of them in Hollywood, you know.'

'Oh?' said Joe. 'Care to tell us what happened?'

'Guy's coming home from Mom and Pop's, maybe been at

the old vino, and he feels, you know, the urge, a little frisky. So he cruises the Boulevard until he finds what he wants. It's all out there, man, Christmas or no Christmas. Figures he'll give himself a real Christmas present. Maybe a hot date with one of Santa's elves. He brings the kid back here, they snort a few lines of prime coke and wham, lights out.'

'Why?' Joe asked.

'Come on, man, these people don't need motives. You know that. It's a fucking sport to them.'

'I mean why would a male prostitute kill a john? Only motive I can think of is money. And in case you didn't notice it, Marillo's wallet was still in the back pocket of his pants with a couple of hundred dollars cash in it, not to mention the credit cards. And from the blood and the scuff-marks, it looks as if Marillo was hit on the head from behind in the kitchen, soon as he got in the house, maybe even while he was opening the door, then carried up to the bedroom and killed there later. Like I said, why?'

Heffer shrugged. 'Kid musta flipped out. Or maybe lover boy over there found them together. He's waiting and he sees Marillo come back with some kid from the Boulevard. Loses it. Who knows? Point is,' he went on, 'those throat and chest wounds are classic faggot style. And the heart with the arrow, the cords around the bed rails. Ritual shit.' He narrowed his eyes and looked at Arvo. '*Has* Marillo been getting threats?'

Arvo said nothing.

Heffer popped another bubble and shrugged. 'Okay, so you don't want to tell me. Fine. I get the feeling it's not gonna be my case anyway. In fact, I get the feeling you real important boys from downtown want this one. Am I right? And I also get the impression that there's a lot you're not telling me. Am I right again? Well, excuse me for just being a fucking drone from Hollywood station. I'll just go back home to bed, shall I, if that's all right with you?'

'Why don't you do just that,' Joe said, staring him in the eye.

Heffer held eye contact for a moment, then broke it, muttered, 'Assholes,' turned on his heel and took off.

'Oh, thwarted ambition,' mused Arvo after him.

'More like that cat's fast running out of lives,' said Joe. 'The way I hear it, the department doesn't know where to put him next. What's your theory?'

'Kincaid didn't do it,' Arvo said. 'Unless he's behind it all, which I doubt.'

'Behind all what?'

'The letters, the Heimar murder.'

'More speculation?'

'Partly, but the connections are getting stronger. Listen, Joe . . .' And Arvo told him about the faint outline of the heart he thought he had seen in the Heimar crime-scene photograph.

'Why didn't you tell me this before?' Joe asked.

'Because I thought I might be seeing things. Forcing connections where they didn't really exist. Then I did a lot of thinking after you told me about the pentobarbitol. Look for yourself. It *could* be some sort of optical illusion caused by the light and wet sand. There's no report of anyone noticing it at the scene.'

'Tide was coming in fast. Now what do you think, now you've seen Marillo's body?'

'I think that whoever's been writing letters to Sarah Broughton abducted and killed John Heimar, buried him on the beach for her to find and drew a heart in the sand beside the body to let her know he'd done it for her.'

'So why didn't she say anything about the heart in her statement?'

Arvo shrugged. 'Maybe she didn't see it. Maybe it had all but washed away by the time *she* got there. You really have to look for it, with the light just right. Or maybe she's keeping it back. I don't know.'

'Go on.'

'I also think the same person waited for Jack Marillo in the trees behind the house here, hit him on the back of the head with some sort of hammer as he was fiddling with the key in the door, carried or dragged him upstairs, butchered him and carved the heart on his stomach.'

'Why didn't he cut the body in pieces this time?'

'I don't know. Could be something spooked him. Or maybe he didn't need to this time. Maybe he'd already proved that point with Heimar.'

Joe lit another cigarette and thought for a moment, then said, 'I'd accept Heffer's theory a lot easier if everything had happened up in the bedroom, using a weapon at hand. In my experience that kind of spontaneous violence usually happens after something triggers it, and that something usually happens in bed. If Marillo did pick up a kid on the Boulevard, he sure picked himself a real winner. How many hookers you see carrying hammers, Arvo, male or female? Maybe blades, but not hammers.'

'Right.'

'But Kincaid did admit that Marillo said he was coming back to the house last night. How could the killer have known he wouldn't be away for days, especially at this time of year? It doesn't look like this happened just by chance.'

Arvo shrugged. 'He must have waited. If we're dealing with the kind of killer I think we are, it wouldn't mean anything to him, having to wait hours, maybe even days. He's obsessed, Joe, fixated, completely focused on what he feels he has to do to gain Sarah Broughton's love. And remember, she's thousands of miles away.'

Joe sighed and ran his hand over his cropped salt-and-pepper hair. 'So you think we've got a psycho on our hands?'

'Looks that way.'

'Okay, Arvo, forget Heffer, he's history. You're working with me on this. I'll clear it with your lieutenant, all right?'

'Fine by me.'

Joe looked at his watch. Sun glinted on the gold band. 'Pretty soon we'll have the brass and media here. It'll be a fucking circus, believe me. Television homicide cop victim of homicide? They'll lap it up. Especially if there's a gay angle. *Macho* homicide cop victim of *homosexual* killing. Tailor-made.'

'What do you want from me?'

'I'm going to look into Marillo's background and I'm at least going to consider that he picked up some kid who went ape-shit and killed him. I'm also going to run Kincaid's balls through the wringer. I don't think he did it, either, for what that's worth, but I have to do it. It's still the most likely scenario. And I want to see that letter.'

'No problem.'

'And as soon as Sarah Broughton steps off that plane at LAX, I want her in my office.'

'Let me talk to her first. You said it yourself, she's not a suspect – if anything, she's a victim – and a homicide cop might scare her off. Let's face it, Marillo's murder isn't going to help her nerves any. They were close friends. Leave it to me, Joe. I'm used to talking to people like Sarah Broughton. It's my job.'

Joe grinned. 'You think a big, black, mean ugly motherfucker like me might scare the pretty white lady right out of her wits, huh?'

'Joe, I never said you were mean.'

Joe laughed. 'Okay. You talk to her first. But don't go too easy on her. Remember, if what you say is right, she hasn't come clean with us yet. Anything else?'

'There's a couple of leads I'm following up. I was going to talk to Jack Marillo, so you might find a message from me still on his machine when you get around to checking it out.'

Joe frowned. 'Did you tell anyone?'

'What?'

'That you were going to talk to Marillo.'

'Oh, come on Joe, you can't be thinking he was killed to stop him talking to me?'

'Got to consider *every* possibility at this point.'

'Okay. No, I didn't tell anyone. Stuart Kleigman suggested I talk to Jack. As far as I know, he's the only one who knew outside the department. And he'd be a fool to suggest I talk to someone then go kill him before I get the chance.'

'A fool or a very clever man covering his ass.'

Arvo shook his head. 'Stu? Honestly, Joe, I can't see him doing this.'

'You got to cultivate a more suspicious nature, Arvo.'

'Even so.'

'Okay,' Joe said. 'Let's work it this way. You follow your leads and I'll coordinate the homicide investigations, see if I can find anything in common between Marillo and the stiff on the beach – forensics, witnesses, that kind of thing. After all, Marillo was gay, and Heimar *was* a male hooker. We shouldn't have any trouble getting extra staff to help on this one. And you and me will have regular meetings. Okay?'

'Okay.'

Arvo walked back down the driveway to his car and set off down the canyon, a million bits of information spinning around in his mind. At least he had forgotten his hangover.

On the narrow, winding trail, he had to pull over right to the trees to let the convoy past. The road wasn't made to handle the kind of two-way traffic it was getting this morning.

The crime-scene specialists led the procession in their van, followed by a couple of local TV station vans. In one of them, Arvo noticed a well-known anchor putting the finishing touches to her red-blonde mane. He also recognized a couple of newspaper reporters following in their own cars. So word had got out already, despite Officer Laski's discretion. Heffer? Arvo wouldn't have been surprised.

As he watched the vans and cars pass, he heard helicopters overhead. They liked to cover every angle, the television people; if they couldn't get to the crime scene from the ground, then they'd damn well show bird's-eye footage. All they needed now was the ride of the fucking Valkyries.

After the reporters came Stuart Kleigman, looking ashen behind the wheel of his maroon Caddy, and behind him came Assistant Chief Summers.

When their cars were parallel, the AC glanced at Arvo and frowned. It was either recognition or puzzlement, Arvo thought, as the road cleared and he drove on. He wondered if it mattered which and decided it didn't. Either way, the more people who saw a member of the TMU on the fringes of a celebrity homicide case, the more likely was the kind of media circus that Joe Westinghouse had mentioned.

If Arvo hadn't realized before, he knew now that the single letter in the file back at headquarters was a time bomb waiting to go off in his face if he didn't start making progress fast.

He knew that his original assessment of the danger level posed by the letter had been correct. He also knew that he had done the right thing in arranging to meet Joe Westinghouse to discuss the beach murder case. At least now Joe could cover him in the interim, could verify that they were pursuing the possibility of a link between the letter and the homicides.

But he also knew that all the statistics in the world can't protect you from the random element, the unpredictable, the one that just doesn't fit. Call him the psycho, as Joe had, or the serial killer, whatever you want, but know that he will take all you think you know, believe and understand, and turn it inside out right in front of your eyes before ripping it to shreds.

Part Three

24

Sarah's heart sank when she walked out of customs and immigration into the waiting phalanx of reporters and cameras at the Tom Bradley Terminal of LAX. More than ten hours in the air, though, she realized, allowed plenty of time for someone to leak the details of her arrival. They would have been expecting her anyway. If she hadn't been a star before, she probably was now. Celebrities and murder. How Hollywood loved that combination.

Even though she knew it would be getting dark outside, she wore sunglasses and kept her head down all the way to the car. Stuart and an airport security guard did their best to steer her through, but the crowd jostled and harassed them all the way to the automatic doors, shoving mini-cassette recorders in her face, flashing cameras at her, yelling questions.

'What was your reaction to the news of your co-star's murder, Miss Broughton?'

'Miss Broughton, had you any idea your co-star was homosexual?'

'Miss Broughton, what are the plans for the future of the show?'

'Is there any truth in the rumour that Richard Romano is being considered to take Jack Marillo's place in the series?'

As soon as they left the air-conditioned airport environment for the LA evening, still pursued by reporters brandishing microphones, Sarah felt that familiar balminess in the air, the mild warmth caressing her cheeks.

The arrivals area outside the terminal was the usual chaos

of cars, limos and shuttles zipping along the half-dozen or so lanes, piles of luggage and confused tourists looking for the van stops. The air was acrid with exhaust fumes. As she ducked into the passenger seat of Stuart's waiting Caddy, Sarah noticed the tatty airport palm trees by the concrete walls of the parking structure across the lanes of traffic. So they hadn't been smoked out of existence yet.

When the porter had finished packing Sarah's luggage in the trunk, Stuart tipped him and edged the Caddy into the lanes of traffic. A car pulled out behind them, but Sarah didn't pay it any special attention.

She took off her dark glasses and looked at Stuart's profile. 'I can't believe it,' she said. 'Jack . . . who would want to harm Jack?'

Stuart kept his eyes on the road. 'I know, sweetie,' he said. 'I know.'

'What happened?'

'The cops don't really know anything yet.'

'All you told me on the phone was that Jack had been killed and the police thought it was either Jaimie or some sort of homophobic maniac. I can't believe it was Jaimie.'

'Arvo doesn't think it was, either.'

'Then it was some maniac?'

'Well, there's a theory it might have been someone Jack picked up on the Boulevard or—'

'Oh, come on, Stuart. You know as well as I do that Jack wasn't like that.'

'Yeah . . . well.' Stuart scratched the side of his nose. He seemed a little sheepish, cagey.

Sarah paused a moment, then said, 'Did the detective suggest that there was any connection with the letters, the body I found on the beach?'

'Look,' Stuart admitted, 'I didn't really want to go into it over the phone, but yes, Arvo says it's all too much of a coincidence. I mean, he thinks someone could be out to bring down the show, some fucking crazy.'

'There *couldn't* be any connection,' Sarah murmured. But she knew there had to be. 'Does he have any evidence?'

Stuart shook his head. 'Not that he's told me about. He just seems very sure of it.'

Stuart negotiated the airport maze, a small city in itself, and took Lincoln. It was early evening, just getting dark, and a pale full moon shone low in the indigo sky. Opposite, the western horizon glowed deep vermilion. When Stuart turned on the radio, The Doors came on singing 'LA Woman.' Sarah asked him if he would change the station and he did, finally settling on a Mozart wind quintet.

As they rounded a curve in the road, just for a second they were at such an angle that the fanned leaves of one of the tall distant palms stood silhouetted against the full moon like a decal. That was so Southern California, Sarah thought, nestling deeper in the seat as the moment passed. Picture-postcard stuff. Beautiful but theatrical. And ephemeral.

Sarah closed her eyes and took slow, deep breaths. It was Thursday, 27 December, two days after Jack Marillo's body had been discovered mutilated on the bed of his Laurel Canyon home. Stuart had phoned Sarah in England on Boxing Day, and she had managed to get a flight out of Heathrow the following day. She had left London close to three o'clock, and now it was just after five in LA.

That morning, after a miserable, sleepless night, she had received another letter. Mailed in Los Angeles and sent express delivery, it was addressed simply to Sally Bolton, Robin Hood's Bay, England.

It was a Christmas card.

The picture on the front showed a typical garish manger scene with bright, blurry stars and the vague figures of the three wise men in the distance.

In addition to the heart with her name inside, the message read, 'Merry Christmas. *I miss you and I'm thinking of you always. I know we are One in Spirit. Maybe one day soon we will have a Baby to love like Little Baby Jesus.*'

On top of the news of Jack's murder, the card had made Sarah physically sick. Now she carried it in her purse next to the letter. She knew the police would be pleased to have his actual handwriting.

Sarah listened as Stuart told her exactly what he had discovered. So far, no drugs had been found in Jack's system, despite the three grams of cocaine the police had found on his bedside table. And that was entirely consistent with the scenario they had constructed: Jack had just arrived home from Christmas dinner at his parents' house in the Valley, which he had left at eleven o'clock that evening, and someone – either his lover, Jaimie Kincaid, or a stranger – had been waiting for him. He hadn't had a chance. As far as the police knew, there was nothing of any value missing, so robbery was ruled out as a motive. They were still in the dark.

Jack dead? Sarah could hardly believe it. More than that, she had a terrible feeling that it was *her* fault. She had refused to face reality. Not only had she told no one about the heart drawn on the beach except Paula, whom she had sworn to secrecy, but she had even denied to herself that she really had seen it. She had almost convinced herself, too, until she read the letter she had carried with her to Robin Hood's Bay.

If the same person had killed Jack, an idea she was still resisting, then she was at least partly culpable. If she hadn't been such a bloody fool and denied to herself the existence of the heart, if she had acted immediately when she got the letter that referred to it, then Jack might still be alive. Paula was right; Sarah was selfish, and she had put her own Christmas plans above someone's life.

Maybe she couldn't blame herself for taking the letter to

England and not reading it sooner, but that wasn't the point. The minute she *had* read it, she should have phoned Arvo Hughes. Maybe he would have arranged for her to fax it or have it couriered to him immediately. And maybe it would have led him to the killer *before* he got to Jack. What could she say to the detective now? How could she even face him?

The car hit a bump and jolted her. 'What?' she said.

'I didn't say anything,' Stuart answered. 'I think you must have been dreaming.'

'I'm sorry,' said Sarah, rubbing her eyes. 'I'm *so* tired.' She realized she had been dozing and looked at her watch. 'It's after one in the morning for me, you know.' When she looked up, she caught a glimpse of a car in the side-view mirror and thought she had seen it pull out behind them at the airport. She could have been mistaken. It was dark, and she couldn't tell one car from another most of the time. Even if it was following them, it was probably a reporter too impatient to wait for tomorrow's scheduled press conference at the studio. Or maybe even some sort of bodyguard, a police escort. She mustn't let her paranoia run away with her. Next thing she'd be suspecting Stuart.

Stuart dipped under the Ocean Avenue tunnel, where Highway 1 hit the coast again after its inland detour from Long Beach. Sunset colours writhed on the ocean's ruffled surface like oil slicks. On the hillside, oil pumps jogged rhythmically back and forth like giant insects. The car was still behind them.

They didn't talk much for the last couple of miles. Sarah settled deep in the comfortable seat staring out of the window through half-open eyes, gnawing at her lip and wondering what the hell she would say when the detective interviewed her. Which he would surely want to do before long.

She knew she should just tell him everything, but she felt so foolish and so damn *guilty* over what had happened to Jack that she didn't know if she could. She was tired and scared; and when she got scared she got all hard-shelled and defensive. At least she hoped she would get some time to rest first, take stock and prepare herself, like she did for a stage role.

Occasionally, she glanced back through the mirror and became convinced that the same car had been following them all the way from the airport.

When Stuart put his left blinker on to turn towards the house, Sarah noticed that the car behind them did exactly the same. That was too much of a coincidence. She panicked.

'Don't stop, Stuart,' she said. 'Please. I think he's after us. Just keep going.'

But Stuart turned off the highway towards the parking area.

'Stuart!' Sarah repeated. 'Please!' Why was he ignoring her?

Stuart didn't reply until he had come to a complete stop, and by then the other car was pulling up behind them.

'Calm down, honey, it's okay,' he said. 'It's only Arvo. He wants to talk to you, and he won't wait. I agree with him. Things have gone too far. And there's no way you should come back here alone.'

Sarah nodded. Her spirits sank. She should have known. Now she wouldn't get any chance to bolster her defences before the questioning began.

25

Arvo pulled up on the dirt shoulder behind Stuart's Caddy. He took the keys from a tired and edgy-looking Sarah, opened the door and punched in the alarm system code that she had given him.

The door opened into a long hallway with a welcome mat and a closet full of jackets and shoes. It was stuffy inside the house, consistent with a place that had been shut up for a week.

Slowly, gun in hand, Arvo headed down the corridor, flicking on light switches as he went. The kitchen was first on the right, the bathroom next. The entire left side was taken up by the walled-off garage space, which he guessed Sarah Broughton never used. A connecting door, locked and bolted, led from the hall.

Next he went into the living room. The drapes were closed. A red light flashed on the telephone answering machine.

He opened the drapes and the sliding glass doors to let the sea breeze in, then flipped on the outside light. Steps from the wooden deck led to a short platform of rock that dropped about twenty feet almost sheer to the beach. Arvo glanced down into the dark where a narrow stairway had been cut into the rock. Moonlight illuminated the tall gate at the bottom with sharp iron railings. It was closed.

Next, he went upstairs, where he found three bedrooms and a second bathroom, all neat and tidy, all empty. The two smaller bedrooms were over the garage, and the largest,

Sarah's he assumed, was at the front, over the living room. It, too, had sliding glass doors and an open balcony facing the ocean. The carpet, duvet-cover and wallpaper, he noticed, were in blended shades and swirls of green and blue, reflecting the imagery of the sea. He found the colour scheme a little cold but couldn't deny it seemed to suit her.

Stuart and Sarah carried the baggage into the hallway, Stuart huffing and puffing, then they came through to the living room. Sarah dimmed the light and turned on a shaded table-lamp.

Her movements, Arvo noticed, were all fluid and unself-conscious, full of grace, despite her evident weariness, and her actions immediately transformed the ordinary room from a place of possible threat and menace into a safe and comfortable place to be.

She was the kind of person who created atmosphere rather than simply responded to it, Arvo felt. Probably an actress's skill, and one to watch out for. She seemed much more natural in her bearing now than she had the first time he met her, on the set of *Good Cop, Bad Cop*.

The room reflected in the half-open glass doors, centred around the dim, warm glow of the lamp. Arvo could hear the ocean and he could see, beyond his reflection, the white line of foam as the waves crested and broke.

The room had a waxed parquet floor, except where a Turkish carpet of intricate design covered the tiles in front of the rough stone fireplace. The wallpaper was a neutral off-white shade and Sarah's taste in art, Arvo noticed, favoured Native American prints, bold and austere in the weak light, and Canadian Inuit sculptures. He approved. He didn't collect art, couldn't afford to, but if he did, that was the kind of thing he would be looking for.

There were some framed Hockney prints of bright California scenes, which he also liked, and some Georgia

O'Keeffes – flowers in close-up, skulls in the desert. Arvo wasn't too sure how he felt about those. At least he assumed they were prints, like the Hockneys; surely even a TV actress as popular as Sarah Broughton couldn't be rich enough to buy genuine Georgia O'Keeffes?

The sparse furniture was modern in design, the Scandinavian kind, in either black or white. Facing the fireplace, a three-piece suite, upholstered in black leather, ranged in a semicircle around a low glass coffee-table.

Sarah said she was just going upstairs to change and asked if they wanted coffee, apologizing because she only had instant.

Stuart and Arvo nodded.

'I want to talk to Sarah alone,' Arvo said to Stuart when she'd gone out of earshot.

'Why?'

'Because she's confused, she's got a lot of defences and I don't want her inhibited by anyone else's presence, and I certainly don't want anyone else interrupting the interview, answering her questions for her.'

'I'll keep quiet. I promise. I'll—'

'You won't be here, Stu. Period. It's not a request. Look, I know you're concerned, but go for a drive or something. I'd say she should count herself lucky we didn't take her straight down to Parker Center and let Robbery-Homicide question her in a police interview room, the way Joe wanted it done.'

'Oh, come on, Arvo. This is fucking ridiculous.' Stuart was still red in the face from carrying the luggage. 'Sarah hasn't done anything. She's not a suspect.'

'That's not the point. The point is that it's my feeling she's been holding something back. This has gone beyond *possible* connections, Stuart. It's *real* now. I thought you realized that.'

Stuart shrugged and Sarah came back with a tray of coffee. She had changed into black jeans and a white chunky-knit

sweater, at least a size too big for her. Blue and green, black
and white; those were the colours she seemed to define herself
with, Arvo thought. Apart from the paintings, there wasn't a
hint of red, yellow or orange in the place.

'What do you take in it?' she asked Arvo. 'I'm afraid I've
only got Coffee-mate.'

'Black's just fine with me,' said Arvo. 'Stu won't be staying.'

A look of alarm crossed her face. 'Not staying? I . . . I . . .
don't understand. Why?'

'It's okay, honey,' said Stuart, getting up and touching her
arm. 'Don't worry about it. Arvo here's good people. Why
don't I just go out and pick you up a few groceries, huh?
Maybe some milk, eggs, bread . . . you know. Some real coffee
beans. Hey, it's not everyone gets a big Hollywood casting
director to do their shopping, is it?'

He patted Sarah's shoulder and she managed a smile. Then
he left. Arvo sat in one of the black leather armchairs and Sarah
took the sofa. She put her coffee cup on the low glass table.

'You didn't have to send him away like that, you know,' she
said as they listened to the Caddy start up and drive off.

In the pause that followed, Arvo got his first long look at
Sarah Broughton. At the studio, she had been playing the lady
cop, Anita O'Rourke.

Even after a long flight and without make-up, she was
certainly a beautiful woman. Her heart-shaped face caught
his attention most of all. Her skin was pale and flawless, what
he would call an alabaster complexion, which was certainly
different from most of the tanned denizens of Hollywood he
came into contact with. Her blue eyes matched her lapis lazuli
earrings, and though they looked capable of expressing many
emotions, at the moment they showed mostly anxiety and
weariness – enough to warn him that this might be a difficult
interview ahead – and they had bags under them.

Beyond all the external features, though, was the

unmistakable gleam of intelligence and, Arvo fancied, a strength of character born of suffering and deprivation. This was a woman who had been there, seen it, and come back changed. Was that an act? Arvo doubted it. Some things you just couldn't fake that easily.

She gave him a challenging, almost coquettish look. 'Do you like what you see, Detective Hughes?'

'I'm sorry,' said Arvo. 'I didn't mean to stare.'

She smiled. 'I'm used to it. Occupational hazard. Though I must admit I'm not at my best right now.'

For some reason, her response irritated him. Her smile looked far too self-satisfied; she was acting, toying with him. Before he could stop himself, he said, 'I suppose you think this is going to be just like the movies, don't you? Grunt cop falls in love with beautiful vulnerable actress.'

Her eyes turned to chips of ice. 'The last thing I need right now is for yet *another* creep to fall in love with me.'

'Sorry,' he said. 'Bad choice of words.'

She nodded. 'Indeed it was.' Very ice-queenly. 'Look, Detective, I'm really tired. If we can get this over with as soon as possible . . .' She pushed back the long sleeves of her sweater and picked up her coffee.

Arvo crossed his legs and leaned back in the armchair. It creaked as he moved. Christ, he hated the kind of furniture that made it sound like you farted every time you crossed your legs. 'I don't know how long it'll take,' he said. 'Depends on you, really. Maybe the caffeine will keep you awake.'

Sarah sipped her coffee and said nothing.

Arvo glanced over at the telephone answering machine, where the red light was still flashing. Three calls. 'You could start by playing back the messages,' he said.

Sarah got up and hit the play button. The first was a hang-up, the second a computerized sales call, and the third was a man's voice.

'I know you're not there, Sarah,' he said. 'I know you're in old Blighty. It's Christmas Eve and I've had a few drinks and I can't get it together to punch all those overseas buttons. Do they even have phones over there? Anyway, I just want it on record I *did* call to wish you a Merry Christmas. Maybe it'll give you a laugh listening to this when you get back. Am I slurring my words a lot? Hope you had a good one, sweetie. See you back at the sweat factory.'

The voice was vaguely familiar, but Arvo couldn't place it. Whoever it was, he certainly sounded drunk or stoned. He glanced at Sarah, and she looked at him through the tears that filmed her eyes. 'Jack,' she said. 'It was Jack. Just the kind of thing he'd do. Idiot.' She hit the stop button and wiped her eyes with the backs of her hands.

Jack Marillo, the day before he died. It was an eerie feeling. Arvo gave her a moment to sit down and compose herself, then he asked, 'Have you received any more letters?'

Sarah hesitated, then nodded.

'Will you show them to me?'

She reached for her purse and passed him the letter and card. He was aware of her watching him over the rim of her coffee cup as he read. Though he doubted that the specialists would find any prints or saliva traces – according to their report, whoever had mailed the first letter had used water and a sponge for the flap and stamp – he handled it carefully anyway.

'Interesting,' Arvo said, setting the card and letter down carefully on the table. 'When did you get the letter?'

'I picked it up on my way to the airport, when we came here to pack. I was running late. I didn't want to miss my plane.'

'No, I don't suppose you did. And I suppose you thought as soon as you were a few thousand miles away the police would get on with their jobs and clear up the mess for you before you came back? Right? Or maybe that it would all just magically go away?'

She chewed on her bottom lip.

'And the last thing you wanted to have to deal with when you got back was a situation even worse than the one before you went away, so you tried to convince yourself that none of it had really happened, didn't you? Denial.' He held up the letter. 'I don't suppose it occurred to you that this practically constitutes a confession to the John Heimar murder?'

'But I didn't see how it could help you,' Sarah protested. 'How I could help you. It doesn't tell you *who* did it, does it?'

'It's evidence,' Arvo said. 'That's the point. Have you thought any more about who could be doing this? About someone with the initial *M* and about what "Little Star" means?'

'I've thought about it, yes,' she said, 'but I still don't know who it could be.'

'Could it have anything to do with Gary Knox?'

She frowned. 'I don't understand. Gary's dead.'

'I know that. I mean before. The tour. It looks like we're dealing with an American, unless he's being very clever indeed. Look how he spells "honor" and "anesthetist." That means that if it is someone who knows you, then it's most likely either someone you're working with now, someone at the studio, maybe even on the show, or someone you came into contact with during the tour.'

Sarah seemed surprised. 'Who have you been talking to? Did Ellie tell you this?'

A light breeze fanned through the doors and ruffled Arvo's hair. The waves rolled and crashed on the shore. 'Does it matter? Why don't you just answer the question?'

'It could be. I don't remember a lot about it.'

'Drugs?'

Sarah said nothing.

'Look, can you just give me a name? Someone who might remember. I need some sort of lead here.'

She thought for a moment, then said, 'Stan Harvey. He wasn't part of it, but he promoted the tour here. I'd also met him in London once when he was on business. He was kind to me,' she added. 'Here, I mean. Funny, I should remember that.'

Arvo wrote the name down. 'And you spent some time in the Shelley Clinic, right?'

Sarah paused. 'Yes,' she whispered. 'Yes, I spent some time there.'

'Did you form any close relationships with any other patients in the clinic?'

'No. I was too . . . I was suffering from depression. I didn't really talk to anyone except Dr Fermor. I was very ill.' She put her hand to her forehead in what Arvo thought was a theatrical gesture. 'Please . . . I'm tired . . . what do you want from me?'

Arvo leaned forward. 'In a nutshell? I want you to tell me what you know. I think that the same person who's been writing you letters killed John Heimar. Then I think he killed Jack Marillo. And I think you know something you're not telling me. I'm not sure why, but I'd guess you're still trying to deny the connections to yourself, and you can't bear to admit any responsibility for Jack's murder. I'm not blaming you for that. Nobody wants to admit they're the victim of a love-obsessional, someone who has killed twice already. After all, you didn't ask for it, did you? You don't feel you've done anything to deserve it, do you? You just don't want to be involved in the mess. It'll spoil that neat, comfortable ordered life you've got going for you. But you are involved. The order is already spoiled. And that's not all. You're in danger, too, and I think you're scared. It's time to wake up, Sarah. Face the truth.'

Sarah put her coffee cup on the glass table, stood up and walked over to the sliding glass doors, her back to him. 'Why are you so certain that Jack's murder has anything to do with me?' she asked.

Arvo picked up the briefcase he had brought in with him, took out a black-and-white photograph and walked over to her.

'Is this scene familiar?' he asked, holding it out in front of her and pointing to the faint outline in the wet sand. 'Do you notice anything here?'

Sarah looked at the picture and shook her head, more in denial than to indicate no. She wrapped her arms around herself. The sleeves of her sweater were so long that they covered her hands, and she looked as if she were wearing a straitjacket. She was so tightly coiled in on herself that Arvo could feel the tension in the air around her.

'Sarah,' he said slowly. 'Does the symbol of a heart pierced by an arrow mean anything to you?'

He saw the blood drain from her already pale face, leaving her looking like a ghost, and he knew he'd hit the spot. Shock tactics, but he felt he had to play out this little game, run through the script, to get her where she wanted and needed to be.

'Why?' she asked.

'With maybe a name or something written inside?'

'A name?'

'We think it might be, yes.'

'What name?' she whispered.

'We can't read it.' This was the information about Jack Marillo's body that they had managed to keep out of the media. He was probably telling her too much, he knew, but he was running on instinct. He couldn't stop himself now if he tried.

'Why?' she asked again. 'Where did you find this thing?'

Arvo paused, then said, 'Someone carved it into Jack Marillo's stomach with a kitchen knife.'

A sound halfway between a gasp and a groan came from deep in her throat. She looked at Arvo with anger blazing in her eyes and started pounding on his face and chest with her fists until he got his arms around her and held her tightly. Then the violence subsided and she buried her head between his chest and shoulder, and her whole body shuddered with deep, convulsive sobs.

'You bastard,' he heard her repeat between sobs. 'You bastard.'

He didn't know who she meant – him or the killer.

26

When Sarah awoke the following morning, she felt as if she had taken a sleeping pill; her mouth was dry, eyes heavy, and her head felt muzzy, as if it were filled with warm cotton wool. For a while, she didn't know where she was. Then she realized she was home at the beach house again.

She lay on her back watching the play of green light on her ceiling and walls, listening to the waves, the gulls and the rumble of traffic on the Coast Highway. In the background, she could hear the gabble of a radio talk show coming from next door.

Slowly, she rolled out of bed, stretched and wandered downstairs to put the coffee on before she took a shower. She'd skip the run this morning. It would take a couple of days to get back into the routine. Maybe even longer.

She had finished grinding the coffee and was tapping it into the filter cone, when the man walked into the kitchen. At first she was aware only of a presence, like a shadow crossing her heart. Grasping a kitchen knife, she twirled round to face him.

It was the detective. He just stood there rubbing the sleep out of his eyes, tie askew, hair dishevelled, hand on his gun in its nylon holster at his waist.

And the next thing Sarah realized was that she was stark naked, as usual first thing in the morning. She always slept in the nude and came down naked to put on the coffee. There was no reason to worry about anyone seeing her because she

always closed the front drapes before she went to bed and
there were no windows at the back or sides of the house.

Though Sarah had never been concerned about appearing
nude in films, this time, in front of a stranger in her own home,
she felt vulnerable and shy about it. She especially didn't want
this man to see her naked. Too late for that.

She put the knife down, gave him a hard look and walked to
the door with as much dignity as she could muster. Dumbly,
he moved aside to let her through. They were so close that she
couldn't help but brush lightly against him as she went.
'Coffee's on,' she said over her shoulder, feeling her skin burn
with shame and embarrassment. She could feel him watching
her as she walked away.

In the shower, she began to remember how the previous
evening had ended, how she had sobbed uncontrollably and
he had comforted her in a perfectly gentlemanly way, held her
close, told her everything was going to be fine. She had been
crying as much for Jack as for anything else, and in a way it
had been a relief finally to let it all out.

Stuart had returned with the coffee and other groceries,
and the detective had asked him to leave. Then, she had told
him everything, just as she had told all to Paula on Christmas
Day.

Far from being angry with her, he had simply nodded,
made notes, asked more questions. Once he had broken
through the dam of her silence, he didn't criticize her for what
she had failed to do; he seemed to understand her denial.

When she went back downstairs, fully dressed this time in
jeans and a Hard Rock Cafe sweatshirt, she found Arvo sitting
on a stool at the kitchen island sipping coffee. She poured
herself a cup and sat opposite him. He still looked embarrassed. She felt irritated by his presence.

'Look,' he said, 'I'm sorry about walking in just now.'

She stared at him and shrugged. Was this the way it was

going to be until they caught the stalker? A man in her house. It wouldn't be Arvo, she knew that. But the police, or the network, would surely arrange to have someone watch over her. Scared as she was, the idea still upset her. She hadn't shared her space with anyone in a long time, and she didn't think she could stand it, whatever the circumstances.

'This is good,' he said, holding up the coffee.

'What are you doing here?' she asked. 'I don't remember asking you to stay.'

'You weren't in any shape to ask me anything.'

'You put me to bed?'

He smiled. 'Yes. But I didn't undress you, if that's what you mean. I just dropped you on the bed, that's all. Scout's honour.'

'So why are you still here? Couldn't you find the door or something?'

'Maybe *I* just got tired. Maybe *I*'d had too much to drink, too.'

'Policemen aren't supposed to drink on duty.'

'There's a lot of things policemen aren't supposed to do.'

'Had you?'

'What?'

'Had too much to drink.'

'No.'

'Then why did you stay? You already made it perfectly clear it's not your job to act as a bodyguard.'

Arvo sighed and ran his hand through his hair. 'It isn't. I just used my judgement. I didn't think it was safe for you to be here alone. It was late, too late to arrange for any other security, and you were tired and emotional. Last night, it just seemed easier for me to stay in the armchair, that's all. Besides, I'd nowhere better to go. If it's any consolation, I had a lousy night's sleep.'

Sarah couldn't stop the corners of her lips twitching in a brief smile. 'I slept like a log,' she said, then added softly, 'Thank you.'

'See, that didn't hurt did it?' Arvo said, then stretched and rubbed his eyes. 'Anything to eat?' He walked over to the fridge.

'You're staying for *breakfast*?'

'It's the least I can do. Ah-ha. Bacon, eggs. Perfect.'

Sarah rolled her eyes. 'It's obvious Stuart did the shopping. That man's diet . . .' She found some oranges in the basket on the bottom shelf and peeled one. 'At least he bought *some* fresh fruit.'

Arvo poured more coffee and fried up the bacon and eggs. Sarah turned her nose up when he offered her some, so he ate it all himself.

'Don't you have to be at work?' she asked.

'Trying to get rid of me already?'

'Just wondering.'

'I could ask the same.'

'I'm still on vacation. If . . . if Jack hadn't died I would still be in England.'

'You showbiz people get so many days off. Maybe I'm in the wrong business.'

'Try it,' she said.

Arvo finished his bacon and eggs and pushed the plate aside. Sarah picked it up and carried it to the sink. She was beginning to feel a little more comfortable around him, but she still hoped he would go soon. She hadn't even unpacked from her trip yet. Besides, a strange male presence infringing on her place of solitude and privacy disconcerted her. Apart from Stuart, Jack and Jaimie, she hadn't even had another man in the house.

'If you're ready,' Arvo said, 'I'll drive you over to the studio.'

'What?'

'You heard me.'

'But I'm not going anywhere. I'm staying here. I told you, I'm still on holiday.'

'Sarah—'

She slammed her coffee cup down. 'Don't you *Sarah* me! This is my home. You're the only one who's leaving. Right now.'

He didn't move.

'Did you hear me?'

'I heard.'

'If you don't go now I'll call the police.'

'I *am* the police.'

'Then I'll call your superior officer. You can't do this. It's *my* home.'

'My, you *are* grumpy in the morning, aren't you?' he said.

She tried to gauge his expression as he looked at her, but she couldn't fathom it. He was obviously giving her the same kind of stone-faced look he gave to the criminals he interrogated. After a brief staring match, though, he stood up, picked up his sport jacket and the plastic bag in which he had put the letter and card. Then he said, 'Whatever you say. An Englishman's home is his castle, right?'

'You're going?'

'Yes.'

'Well . . . what? . . . I mean . . . what do I . . . ?' She felt flustered by his sudden capitulation.

'What are you supposed to do?' He took a card out of his breast pocket, shrugged and dropped it on the island. 'Call me if you have any problems.'

'And that's it?'

He shrugged. 'The name of the game is cooperation, not coercion. The law helps those who help themselves. That means you have to be willing to help yourself if I'm going to help you at all. Obviously you're not. Good luck.'

'But aren't you going to send me a bodyguard or something? You can't just abandon me. There's someone out there been killing my friends.'

'Really? Give Stu a call. I'm sure the network will send somebody around, the lucky guy.'

Sarah glared at him for a moment, then ran her hand through her hair and sighed. 'Sit down. Please,' she said. 'I'm sorry. This is coming out all wrong. I'm just not used to having anyone around the place. Can't we work something out?'

Arvo held her eyes for a moment, then put his sport jacket on the back of a chair and sat down again. 'I thought we'd worked things out last night.'

She ruffled her hair and pulled a face. 'I know. I'm just confused. Scared. I don't know what to do.' She looked around. 'This is all I've got. I've always felt safe here, secure.'

'Not any more.'

'It hasn't really sunk in yet. I don't want to feel like a fugitive.'

'Can I have some more coffee?'

'Sure.' She poured him another cup.

'There are several options,' Arvo said. 'None of them perfect. If you stay here, you've got a choice of either one live-in bodyguard or two outside: one to guard the front and another to guard the back. Expensive, and the least safe. I talked to Stu briefly last night before he left and he thinks he can get the studio to increase the security around the lot, so you won't have to worry when you're at work, and maybe spring for a personal bodyguard for you—'

'But I—'

Arvo held up his hand. 'Hold on a minute. Let me finish. What Stu suggested is that you stay with him. Believe me, you're a lot safer with people around you. There'll still be a bodyguard around to keep an eye out for you, but he won't need to be under your feet all the time. Stu owns a gun, and I know he's qualified to use it. Maybe you don't know it, but he fought in Vietnam. He even won medals.'

'How long is this going to go on?' Sarah asked.

Arvo shook his head. 'I wish I knew. Naturally, if it goes on a long time we'll have to reconsider our tactics. There's always protective custody.'

'Jail?'

Arvo shrugged. 'Worst-case scenario. For the moment, will you just listen to me and let me take you to the studio? They'll give you some office space there. You can work on your scripts or something. Then you can go back with Stu tonight.'

'But won't it be dangerous for him, for Karen and the kids?'

'It's dangerous for everyone around you right now. Stu cares about you. He's willing to take the chance, and I think he's right. He's sending Karen and the kids off to her mother's in Santa Barbara for a few days. I told you, Stu knows how to handle himself. He's no fool. And there'll be someone else – a professional bodyguard – keeping an eye on the both of you.'

Sarah chewed on her lip and thought for a moment, looking around the kitchen. 'You worked all this out between you while I was away, did you?'

Arvo nodded. 'After Jack's murder, yes.'

'All right,' she said finally. 'It doesn't seem like I've got much option. It's just as well I didn't unpack, isn't it? Can you give me a few minutes to throw some clean clothes together?'

'Sure.'

Outside, the first thing Arvo did was check the mailbox.

'It's been redir—' Sarah started to say. But she stopped when she saw him hold up a white envelope between his thumb and middle finger.

Sarah felt her chest tighten. 'He's been here,' she said. 'During the night, while we were here.'

'Looks like it.' Arvo put the letter in the plastic bag with the others. 'The last one was hand-delivered, too, remember. We'd better lock up and go,' he said.

Sarah was aware of herself nodding, even though all she still wanted in the world was a day alone at the beach house

relaxing, unpacking, phoning her family to thank them for
having her and to remind them she wanted them to visit her
soon.

She watched as Arvo locked the sliding glass doors and
pulled the drapes, then she picked up her windbreaker with
the show's logo emblazoned on the back and followed him out
to where the overnight bag sat by the door. She set the alarm
and they locked the door behind them.

Arvo's car was parked where he had left it on the dirt shoulder outside her back door. Something looked odd about it,
Sarah thought, then she saw how it rested flat on the ground.

'He's slashed the tires,' Arvo said. 'Jesus H. Christ! The
bastard. He's slashed the fucking tires!' He kicked the front
wheel then leaned forward and slapped his hands against the
hood, leaning forward like a guy being frisked by a cop.

Sarah touched his shoulder. 'Tell me the number,' she said.
'I'll phone and get help.'

27

Arvo stabbed at the elevator button again and swore under his breath. Parker Center elevators, he remembered, were always out of order. Finally, it stopped, discharged a couple of passengers and took him, groaning and shuddering as it went, up to the third floor.

Every time he went back to RHD, he became more and more thankful for the TMU's move to the relatively clean and spacious Spring Street headquarters. He hadn't noticed it so much when he worked at Parker Center, but Detective Headquarters was definitely run-down. If it wasn't quite as grungy as the make-believe precinct where Sarah Broughton filmed *Good Cop, Bad Cop*, it was pretty close.

The third floor was overcrowded, for a start; the air conditioning never worked, so you had to work with fans blowing your papers around all over the place; and there were so many earthquake cracks in the walls that nobody could remember which quakes had caused them.

As he walked into the corridor, he heard a radio playing from the secretaries' office: The Beach Boys, 'Help Me Rhonda.' For some reason, it made him think of Nyreen. California girl.

He opened the door to Robbery-Homicide and popped his head in. All the desks were pushed together in the centre of the room to make one long, rectangular island, around which the detectives sat facing one another. The room was hot and sweaty. Telephones rang constantly; papers littered the desks and filing cabinets flanked the walls and corners. Over them all, like some sort of guardian angel, a boar's head was mounted on the wall.

Fran Jenson was staring at her reflection in her compact mirror as she applied thick red lipstick. She looked up and winked at Arvo. Joe Westinghouse, two chairs down, saw him next and came over.

'Let's go grab something to eat,' said Joe. 'It's been a long day. I could do with a break. Besides, I need a smoke.'

'After all the trouble I had getting the elevator to come up here, *you* want to go out.'

Joe grinned. A gold filling twinkled. 'I'm buying.'

'You're on.'

It was easier getting down, and they soon walked out onto Los Angeles Street, office towers glistening in the sun. Downtown was the only really high-rise part of LA apart from Century City, with its bank towers vying with one another for tallest structure, so there were plenty of city workers out for cigarette breaks or late lunches. They didn't wander far, though; over on Main or down towards Sixth, the streets got grungy real quick.

Joe bought chili dogs and Cokes from a street vendor and he and Arvo sat on a low wall to eat. Arvo realized it was mid-afternoon and he hadn't eaten lunch yet. First, he showed Joe a photocopy of that morning's letter:

My Darling Little Star,

I hope you had a good Christmas at Home with your Folks. I think that Family must be important to you in a way it never has been to me. Or maybe it has been TOO important to me. Strange things have happened in my Family and one day you will know all about it. But we must make a new start with our own Kids and all. I hope that your Family will be my Family too one day soon.

Though you were far away in Body, I felt that we were together in Spirit. I surround myself with your Image. I stand against my wall and I project your Image onto my Skin. I feel the warmth of the Light brush over me and I think it is you gently caressing me. But you were so far from my Arms and I saw you kiss him. I watched him put his Arms around you. I couldn't bear it. You know what I can do, you have seen the Fruits of my Labors. All for you. For Love of you. Now you're just a little bit freer than you were before Christmas. One of the Ties that binds you to Them has been cut. Accept my offering in the spirit of love and devotion with which it was intended. I will come for you soon then we will both be free to breathe beyond the Mirrors of the Sea for ever.

Love, M.

Joe frowned and handed the letter back. 'Weird,' he said. 'Know what he means?'

'At first I didn't,' said Arvo, folding the letter and putting it back in his pocket, 'but this morning I checked the *Good Cop, Bad Cop* tapes for the time Sarah Broughton was away in England. There was a show on Christmas Eve where the Jack Marillo character kissed Sarah. It was just a friendly kiss, really – you know, a peck on the cheek. She was upset about a kid she was trying to help who got shot in a drive-by, so he gave her a hug and a kiss. I think that might have been what set him off.'

'What else did you find out from the actress?'

Arvo took a bite of his chili dog and told Joe about the heart drawn in the sand by John Heimar's body. He also handed him a copy of the Christmas card and letter Sarah had found the morning she left for England.

'Shit,' said Joe after he'd read the other letter. 'Two letters, two hearts, two confessions. Wouldn't stand up in court, but it's good enough for me. Why didn't she tell us this before?'

Arvo shrugged. 'Scared. Thought it would all just go away.'

'She's been withholding evidence.'

'True. But she's also been playing denial. She didn't want to believe it was happening. Couldn't believe it. Wouldn't admit it to herself. Not until Marillo's murder.'

'And now?'

'Oh, now she knows. Now she feels guilty. Thinks she might have been able to save him if she'd acted sooner.'

'Some hope.' Joe paused to take a mouthful of chili dog, then said, 'Why are you defending her all of a sudden?'

'I'm not. I talked to her, that's all. I think she's scared enough to tell the truth.'

'Sure she's not working that old Hollywood charm on you?'

An image of Sarah Broughton's nakedness flashed through Arvo's memory again: particularly the butterfly tattoo on her left shoulder, a beautiful, professional job done in red, blue and green, about three inches across. Somehow, seeing that tattoo had changed her again in his eyes; it added yet another dimension to what was already an enigma. But charm?

'Fuck you,' he said.

Joe laughed. 'Yeah. Methinks this gentleman doth protest too much. But I'd rather be me than you when the Chief finds out.' He took another bite of his hot dog. Chili sauce dribbled from the corner of his mouth and onto his jacket. He swore and dabbed at it with a napkin.

'What do you mean?'

'We've got the links we were after now,' Joe said. 'The heart. Both scenes. The letters. There'll be no sitting on this. Just wait till the media get hold of it.'

'Christ, you're right,' said Arvo. 'Any rookie reporter should be able to put two and two together.'

'True,' said Joe. 'But it's my bet they'll be busting their asses on the gay angle, if you'll forgive the pun. And look on the bright side, man. This is a *major* case now.'

'That doesn't seem a particularly bright side to me,' Arvo said. 'What it means is we've got a major *political* case. We've got the Chief and the DA's office falling all over one another to get an arrest on this. We won't even be able to take a crap without somebody looking over our shoulders to make sure we're doing it right.'

'What I'm saying is we've got unlimited resources now. Manpower. We've got people looking into every nook and cranny of Marillo's and Heimar's lives, see if they intersected anywhere, plus we get a rush on all forensic evidence. It ain't all bad.'

Arvo was silent for a moment. Maybe Joe was right. Anything they wanted, they'd just have to ask. But Arvo was right, too; whatever they did, they'd have to do it under scrutiny. 'This guy's smart, Joe,' he said. 'He might be crazy, but he's smart. He's not going to be easy to stop unless he starts getting careless. He's very patient and very careful. Whoever planted Heimar's body must have watched Sarah Broughton for days or weeks to get the timing just right. He had to know how far the tide would be in or out, what time she would pass the spot where he left the body. If he drew that heart for her to see, he didn't want it washed away before she got there.'

'He probably waited a long time outside Marillo's house, too,' said Joe. 'There's no way he could have known where Marillo was, or even if he was coming back that night. Shit, it was Christmas Day. Normal people spend it with their families or close friends.'

Sure, Arvo thought, remembering his own solo Christmas celebration. 'I don't think Christmas means a hell of a lot to the guy we're looking for,' he said. 'You read the letter. He's very confused about family.'

'I guess so, if he could spend all Christmas Day hiding in the woods waiting for Marillo.'

Arvo nodded. 'He's a loner. Fits the profile. He's also either very brave or very foolish. He put that letter I just showed you in the mailbox at Sarah's beach house last night.'

'She was *there*?'

'Yeah. From the airport. I told Stu it seemed like the best environment to talk to her, where she'd feel most comfortable, be most likely to open up.'

'What about protection?'

'I was there, too.'

Joe raised an eyebrow and his eyes twinkled with humour. 'All night?'

'Don't say a word, Joe,' Arvo told him. 'Not a word.'

'Who, me?'

'Nothing happened.'

'Sure it didn't, Arvo.'

'The bastard slashed my tires.'

'Jealous?'

'That would be my guess.'

'Then *you'd* better be careful.'

'That thought had occurred to me. Anything else on the Marillo killing?'

Joe threw away his chili-dog wrapper and lit a cigarette. 'Found some footprints in the ground back of the house – cheap Korean sneakers – but that's all. Mostly dead ends, nothing but dead ends. And believe me, we've been pushing it. There's plenty of pressure from above.' He pointed with his thumb towards the sixth floor of Parker Center, where the Chief had his office.

'What about Jaimie Kincaid?'

'Kid's clean. And, believe me, we went at him hard. The DA's office really liked him for it at first. Pretty young faggot, lovers' quarrel. So we really put him through it. He stuck to his story. We got a search warrant and went through his place, gave it the works. Nada. No physical evidence whatsoever connecting him to the murder. Given that Marillo bled like a stuck pig, it would've been hard to get rid of every last drop. Footprints aren't his, either.'

'So you've let him go?'

'Yup.'

'I told you he didn't do it.'

'Yeah, yeah. I know. You?'

Arvo took a sip of Coke. 'I talked to Sarah's shrink, Dr Fermor, on the phone. Seems Sarah was pretty much in isolation while she was out at the Shelley Clinic, and she didn't form any relationships at all, even at a distance. I also phoned Stan Harvey, who promoted the Gary Knox tour in LA. He put me on to a guy called Carl Buxton down in Orange County. I'm going to see him in a couple of days, when he gets back from Mexico. This guy was the drummer on the tour. He should have some firsthand knowledge of what went on.'

'What makes you think that'll help?'

'Well, if the killer really does know Sarah from somewhere, from what I've heard that tour might have attracted more than a few crazy hangers-on. I want to see if Buxton remembers anyone in particular. Sarah disappeared from public view for over a year after she split with Knox, then she resurfaced, with a new name, as the star in a major network series. The timing makes sense, Joe. It also gives him a year to brood over his lost love.'

'But wouldn't she remember someone like that?'

'Not necessarily. Dr Fermor also told me that Sarah's illness might cause some memory loss. If that period of her life is really as hazy as it seems, then the illness might explain why she doesn't remember. Some sort of retrograde amnesia. When I first talked to her, I was sure that "Little Star" meant something. Maybe the truth is that she can't remember exactly *what* it means, or who said it. Maybe it was someone on the periphery. A guy like this wouldn't need much to set him off. Maybe she smiled at him once.'

'I guess. But what's he after, Arvo? That's what I don't get. Is he just trying to scare her?'

'Scare her? No, I don't think so. Not the way he sees it. Mostly, he's trying to impress her.'

'What? By killing people in front of her, dropping them at her feet? I've worked homicide a few years now, and I thought I'd seen pretty much everything, but this scenario . . .' He shook his head.

Arvo finished his chili dog, dropped the wrapper in a garbage bin and took a long swig of Coke to cool the heat in his mouth. 'Like a cat does,' he said. 'Ever noticed that, Joe? We had a cat when I was a kid. Called him Watson. My father's idea. He was a criminology prof. Anyway, he got run over when I was about twelve – Watson, not my father. But the point is, I remember him once getting on the roof, killing a pigeon and bringing it in his mouth through the bedroom window and dropping it on the floor in front of me looking for approval. My pa yelled at him and threw the pigeon out in the garbage, but goddammit if he didn't come back with another half an hour later. And another after that. No matter what we said. And what I remember especially is that look on his face: "See what I've done for you? Isn't it wonderful? Love me for it."'

'You saying this guy's the same? But surely he must know how much he is scaring her, whether he means to or not?'

'He's out to impress her, he's looking for approval, but he's tuned in so close to his own frequency that he doesn't hear her screaming at him to stop. It's like he's watching a different movie from the rest of us, Joe. To him, screams signify love, and murder gains respect.'

'Where is she now?'

'Sarah? She's at the studio. Then she's going to stay with Stu in Brentwood until this is all over. They'll have a bodyguard watching over them, and Stu's no slouch. Also, I want to put the beach house under surveillance, though I think he's smart enough not to show up there again.'

Joe dropped his cigarette butt on the sidewalk and ground it out with his heel. 'Is *she* in serious danger,' he asked, 'or is it just the people around her?'

'You read the letters, Joe. That weird stuff about the mirrors of the sea, cutting away the flesh and all. Now he's jealous as hell, too, going out of control. Love, approval, jealousy, murder – they're all mixed up together for him. And he says he's coming for her soon. The gloves are off now. I sure as hell hope she doesn't have to face him alone.'

28

The black stretch-limo left Stuart's Brentwood home at ten in the morning on December 31. Karen, Leora and Ben had come back from Santa Barbara for the day, and they sat in the car along with Stuart and Sarah.

The three days Sarah had spent at Stuart's house had been uneventful. Every evening Arvo phoned to make sure everything was okay. Sarah was getting used to his concern, but she still resented his intrusion into her life, the way he seemed to have taken control out of her hands, and she still felt annoyed that he had seen her naked.

As it turned out, Jack's murder meant that there was a lot of work to do at the studio, retaking scenes, rethinking plot lines and so on. At least work took Sarah's mind off her problems part of the time. Pity it was so bloody depressing on the set without Jack.

So it had been a simple routine: drive to the studio, work, drive back to Brentwood, read or watch TV, then sleep. Every time they went back to the house, the bodyguard, Zak, drove on ahead to check the place out. He was close to them even now, on the way to the funeral. The saving grace was that his presence was so unobtrusive Sarah hadn't even *seen* him yet.

The day was warm and hazy inland. As they drove through Sepulveda Pass on the freeway, cool and comfortable in the luxury car, Sarah glanced through the separating glass and the windshield and saw the San Fernando Valley spread out below them, its neat little blocks of grid-work streets stretching as far as the distant mountains, all shimmering under a thin veneer of amber smog.

She remembered what a powerful sight it had been the first time she saw it, which must have been that evening Jack took her for Thanksgiving dinner at his folks' house in Northridge. She had never had any reason to go to the Valley before that; she didn't know anyone who lived there. It was night-time then, and all she could see were the lights spread out across the broad, flat valley-bottom as far as the eye could see. It was like seeing the city from a plane coming in to land.

Closer to home, Jack had shown her the earthquake damage, too: a three-storey apartment building collapsed to two; a Bullock's store with the entire roof caved in; house after house fenced off, waiting for demolition. Jack's parents had been lucky; all they lost was their chimney and a few roof tiles.

After heavy traffic on the Simi Valley Freeway, the limo finally pulled up at the cemetery at ten to eleven, ten minutes before the service was set to begin.

It was a small funeral, only immediate family members, a few personal friends, like Jaimie, and colleagues from the show, such as Sarah, Stuart and Lisa, who turned a few heads in a black gown cut just an inch or so too low for the occasion.

Network security and Jack's family had done a great job of keeping the media at bay. There was a reporter from the *Los Angeles Times*, but that was about all. No TV cameras. Arvo Hughes was there, Sarah noticed as she followed Stuart into the cool chapel, and his presence felt like an intrusion into the privacy of her grief.

The service was brief. Jack's parents had never been particularly religious, and though Jack himself had flirted briefly with the Catholicism his Italian background suggested, it hadn't really taken hold. How could it, Sarah thought, with such a medieval attitude towards gays?

A non-denominational minister said something about the frailty of the flesh and how we must always be ready to face God because we never know when He will call us to His bosom. He made Jack's murder sound like more of a blessing, a joyous occasion, than a tragedy.

Then Jack's older brother, Denny, gave the eulogy. They hadn't been close, Sarah knew, and generally when they met they argued. But the eulogy moved her to tears because it didn't skirt the family problems; it confronted them head-on.

The brothers had fallen out partly because Denny couldn't handle Jack's being gay. This was his younger brother, his reasoning went, and he was supposed to keep up the family tradition of handsome, macho Italian maleness. Instead he'd become a goddamn sissy and shamed his family.

Jack's parents, Sarah knew, usually avoided the issue altogether, pushing the question of Jack's sexuality right to the backs of their minds. After all, they had a lot to be proud of. Jack had done well for them in so many ways and Denny was still only a glorified used-car dealer. So what if they were BMWs; they were still used cars.

In his eulogy, Denny spoke of their arguments, of the torment he suffered because *he* thought his brother wasn't normal, about how he worried about Jack getting AIDS. But he also said he wished he'd sloughed off his prejudice and taken the time to get to know his brother better. And that Jack had been there for him when he needed it, no questions asked. When it came right down to it, maybe they were too much alike ever to get along easily. The circumstances were different, but what Denny said made Sarah think of the way she and Paula related, or failed to relate.

Dabbing her eyes, Sarah followed the others outside, still in a daze after seeing the coffin wheeled away. It was hot and humid outside the air-conditioned chapel. Sarah felt the beads of sweat gather around her brow and temples, and a tiny rivulet tickled as it coursed down the groove of her spine.

After she had given her commiserations to the Marillos, she felt someone touch her elbow and turned to see Arvo Hughes standing beside her. Sarah flinched at his touch. She wasn't ready for him again right now. Not here. Not in this state. She had revealed too much of herself to him already. He must think she did nothing but break down and cry.

'What are you doing here?' she asked rather more sharply than she intended. 'You didn't know Jack. Are you expecting his murderer to turn up and gloat, or something?'

'Maybe,' he said. 'But that usually only happens in your line of work. Believe it or not, the cases I work aren't just numbers to me.' He nodded towards the chapel. 'I never met him, but he seemed like a decent guy.'

'He was.'

'And in case you're beating yourself over the head about it, I still don't think there was a hell of a lot you could have done to prevent what happened. Joe Westinghouse agrees.'

'He does? Well, isn't that wonderful. Thank you both very much. I feel so much better now.'

'Christ, you're pricklier than a porcupine. There's no need to be sarcastic. What I'm saying is, letters or no letters, there's no way we could have predicted this would have happened. No way. And even if we could have, do you think we could have found a way of protecting everyone you knew? No. So don't go blaming yourself. What could you do, anyway? Has *M* given you any choice about when and who he kills? All we've got is twenty-twenty hindsight.'

'Well it's a pity you policemen don't have a lot better vision than that, isn't it? Have you ever thought about that? Maybe if you were doing your jobs instead of . . . instead of . . . Oh!' She pushed him aside and walked away in tears. She felt embarrassed and phony doing it – like she was playing the prima donna or something – but she knew she would only have felt worse if she had stayed.

'What you doing here? We did not invite you.'

Sarah heard the raised voice and turned. Oh no. It was Jack's mother, and she was waving her fist at Jaimie Kincaid.

'You no-good pervert,' she went on, her voice getting louder. 'You kill my Jack. Is *your* fault my Jack's dead. You hear me? Police should have keep you locked up. You go away now. I call police.'

She saw Jaimie walk off, slump-shouldered. Jack's father put his arm around his wife to calm her down. Denny went after Jaimie. Sarah hoped, after the eulogy, that he would have a few kind words to say rather than simply repeat what Mrs Marillo had said, punctuated by blows.

Christ, Sarah thought, is everyone looking for someone to blame? The detective was right; she did still blame herself, especially after he had told her about the heart carved into Jack's body. She knew that, logically, he had been right today, too. Even if she had told the police everything right from the start, it still wouldn't have saved Jack. She also felt guilty for suspecting Stuart, even for one fleeting moment. Since she had overcome her reservations and gone to Brentwood, he had been nothing but solicitous and steadfast.

But the truly frightening thing was that there was an evil force out there, and she was beginning to wonder if anyone could stop it before it reached its intended destination: Sarah herself.

29

Waiting. Waiting. Waiting. Sometimes life seemed to consist of nothing but waiting. He remembered those hours in the woods at the back of the canyon house, so focused and unmoving he had felt himself become an animal, operating only on instinct, out of appetite and necessity.

He had crept so stealthily across the dirt that his prey hadn't heard a sound before the hammer came down with a sharp crack on the back of his head and he pitched forward onto the kitchen floor. It had been perfect.

And it had been perfect because he had waited so long. Anticipation heightened awareness; it honed all his senses to razor-edge sharpness, and brought into play some he didn't even know he had.

Afterwards, he decided that luck was a sense, too, not just some random deal of the cards; if you got into the right state of mind, you could use luck the way you would use sight or smell. Courage, too, perhaps, and maybe even silence.

Now he was sitting in his car on a street in Santa Monica, waiting again. The light was on in the house; he could see it through the slats in the shutters. It was New Year's Eve, and a block north someone was holding a loud party. But his quarry seemed to be alone. At least the house was quiet, and he had seen no one go in during the hour he had been waiting there.

He knew this one had to be next, but he also knew he had to think it out clearly. For a start, he didn't have a gun, and his

*quarry did. Somehow guns didn't fit with the kind of hunt he
had set himself. He knew where to get one easily enough, but they
were too distant, too abstract. You pointed and pulled the trigger
and someone far away fell down dead.*

*With guns, there was no real contact, no sense of flesh yielding
to hammer or the knife. And that was what he liked about killing.
The sound the hammer made, for example, when it fractured the
skull, or the way flesh resisted cutting far more than he had
thought it would, then how the fat, muscle and sinew under the
skin seem to peel back in layers as you cut, presenting colours you
had never imagined inside the human body. Maybe he should
have been a surgeon.*

*But not having a gun was definitely causing a problem here.
He needed total surprise on his side. And tactics.*

*And it wasn't as if there was any choice in the matter of who it
had to be. This person had spent the night at Sally's, keeping her
prisoner, and people must be made to see that they shouldn't do
things like that.*

*He was certain nothing had happened. In fact, it never even
entered his mind for a moment that she would be unfaithful to
him or that she had been anything other than an unwilling
captive. But someone had been in the house, keeping him away,
and all night he had suffered headaches and stomach pains. She
must see that was not good. These people would only exert a bad
influence on her, and she was so impressionable.*

*First, he had presented her with a random offering; now he was
working on real obstacles, on cutting them all out of her life so she
could come to him and they could live or die the way destiny
intended. It would be soon.*

*Then, suddenly, a car pulled up outside the house and someone
else went in. Two of them. One would have been difficult enough,
but two would be too much of a risk. Unless he could think of
something, maybe come up with a new sense.*

And so he kept on waiting. It was only ten o'clock. Plenty of time. If he remained still and focused his mind completely on the image of Sally hanging from his rear-view mirror, he knew that whatever he needed to do would become clear. And how to do it.

30

Shortly after ten o'clock on New Year's Eve, Arvo was thinking of going to bed. He was watching Roger Corman's *Attack of the Crab Monsters* on video, and it was no insult to the 1957 black-and-white B-movie that he couldn't seem to keep his eyes open.

It had been a rough two days, ending with Jack Marillo's funeral. He had checked the rest of the M's from the list Stuart had given him and come up with zero. One promising lead – a key grip called Kim Magellan who had once been arrested for stalking her ex-girlfriend – proved to be unconnected after Arvo had spent a couple of hours interviewing her.

He had also spent an uncomfortable afternoon closeted with the lieutenant and the Chief, laying out every bit of evidence and speculation in the Sarah Broughton case. While the pressure had been intense, the result was satisfactory. He and Joe were to coordinate the investigation, with plenty of resources at their disposal, and the department would try to keep the letters out of the media. Everyone agreed that excessive media attention would make it even more difficult to protect Sarah Broughton and the people around her.

It was only a matter of time, though, Arvo knew. They would find out. They always did. As the Chief had pointed out, there was already speculation about a member of the TMU being present at the Marillo crime scene. So far, however, the main theory seemed to be that Jack Marillo had been blackmailed or somehow harassed by a gay ex-lover.

Arvo sat with his feet up, shutters partly open, leaves rustling, traffic whooshing along the freeway, a cool breeze from the window about the only thing keeping him awake. It was the first time he had felt so completely relaxed in a while.

Then the doorbell rang.

By instinct, he picked up his nylon holster from the table beside him before he went to the door and grasped the handle of the gun. He wasn't expecting any visitors, and in LA it was almost unheard of that someone would simply drop by without phoning first. Even under normal circumstances, there were always plenty of people who wanted to do a cop harm, and some of them could even get hold of his address. And these were not normal circumstances.

Carefully, he opened the front door on its chain, and found Maria Hernandez standing there, a bottle of champagne in her hand.

'It's the real stuff,' she said, noticing him look at the bottle. 'At least that's what the guy in the liquor store said.'

'How did you know where I live?' was all Arvo could manage.

'Hey, I'm a very resourceful woman. I have a university education and I'm good with computers, too. Can I come in?'

Arvo stood aside and ushered her in. She was wearing a long black PVC raincoat against the evening chill and the earlier shower. Her black hair tumbled in waves over her shoulders.

'How did you know I'd be home?' Arvo asked.

'You told me, the other day. Remember? Said you hated New Year's parties and always stayed in alone watching a video. Aren't you pleased to see me?'

Arvo felt awkward. 'Of course. But, look, what . . . I mean is . . . you must have a party or something . . .?'

She fluttered her eyelashes and laughed. 'Pretty girl like me? Sure I do. But I didn't feel like going. Then I remembered what you said and I thought you might like some company. So here I am. Did I do wrong?'

Arvo felt himself grinning like an idiot. 'No. No, not at all.'

'Good.' She smiled and took her coat off. Underneath she wore a black-and-white polka dot dress. Polka dots, Christ. Arvo hadn't seen them for years. At least he didn't think he had. But what he knew about fashion wouldn't fill the back of a postage stamp.

The dress was cut low, showing a little dark, smooth cleavage, with two black straps over her shoulders. It flared out below her hips and ended about four inches above her knees. Her legs were bare and she wore a pair of black pumps. The way she moved, Arvo was beginning to think she was a little tipsy. Maybe she'd been to the party already.

'Come in.' He led her through to the living room and cleared the magazines off the sofa and chairs. Other than that, the place was reasonably clean and tidy, no dirty shirts, socks or boxer shorts hanging over chair backs.

'What *is* this?' Maria pointed to the television, where a giant crab crawled over the top of a sand dune.

'Oh, nothing.' Arvo picked up the remote and punched in the buttons to turn the TV and VCR off.

'Yes, it is. It's *Attack of the Crab Monsters*. You like fifties sci-fi movies?'

'Well, yeah,' said Arvo, feeling as if he'd been caught masturbating or something. 'Just sometimes, you know . . .'

'Why?'

'Well, I haven't really analyzed it much. I like lots of different kinds of movies, but I guess with these it's partly the simplicity, good against evil. And the evil's always something tangible . . . you know . . .'

'Like a giant crab?'

'Yeah. Or a monster from outer space. Or some mutation caused by atomic testing or something.'

'Not from inner space, like the stuff we deal with?'

'That's right. And maybe most important of all, it's just

pure fantasy, escapism, and the good guys usually win. You're not a fan, too, are you?'

'Me? Yuck, no. I saw it once on late-night TV when I was a teenager and it scared the shit out of me. I don't like scary movies, and I get scared even at the old ones, before they could do all the gory special effects. Even when you could see the strings.' She laughed. 'I like romantic comedies. Same pure fantasy, though.'

'Maybe you're right. Shall I get us some glasses?'

'Sure.'

Maria breezed over to the bookshelves that housed Arvo's video collection and started reading off titles. 'You've sure got eclectic taste,' she said. '*The Maltese Falcon, Doctor Zhivago, Killer Klowns from Outer Space, Bridge over the River Kwai, Bloodsucking Pharaohs in Pittsburgh.* Jesus Christ. Is there any order to all this?'

'Not really,' said Arvo, taking a couple of champagne flutes out of the cabinet. 'I just like movies. There aren't many that are perfect, like maybe *Citizen Kane* or *Chinatown*, but they all have *something* interesting in them – maybe good acting, some great dialogue, camerawork, whatever. Maybe just one good scene.' He shrugged and removed the wire from the neck of the bottle.

'Even *The Incredible 2-Headed Transplant*?'

'Has its moments.' Arvo grinned and eased out the cork. 'But I've got to admit, that one's a bit of a turkey. There's a similar movie with Ray Milland and Rosie Grier in it that's pretty funny, though. Ray Milland plays this racist and he ends up sharing a body with Rosie Grier's head. Weird.' The cork made a loud pop and champagne foamed around the mouth of the bottle but didn't spill over.

'I can see you've done this before,' Maria said.

'Uh-huh.' Arvo poured the champagne carefully into the flutes. 'My mother taught me.'

'Sounds like an interesting mother to have.'

'She was.'

'What did she do?'

'She was a chef.'

'What happened to your parents, Arvo? I know they're dead, but you never told me how. Auto accident? Plane crash? I mean, it's okay if you don't want to talk about it. I understand.'

Arvo was silent for a moment. It was true he had never told Maria or anyone else on the unit what had happened to his parents. Why, he didn't know. Now, it didn't seem to matter. Or maybe he wanted Maria to know. The only person in LA who had known was Nyreen, and she was gone now; he had no one else to share it with.

'No, it's okay,' he said. 'They were murdered.'

'Both of them?'

'Uh-huh.'

'How? Where?'

'Windsor, the Canadian side of the border, where my father taught university. Very ironic, seeing as we lived in Detroit, which is a pretty dangerous city.'

'What happened?'

'As far as anyone knows, they were on their way home from a faculty party, stopped at a red light on Wyandotte, when some kid came running out of a Mac's Milk store he'd just robbed, jumped in the car and told them to drive. The Ontario Provincial Police found my parents the next morning about ten miles out of town. Both of them had been robbed and shot in the back of the head.'

'My God. I . . . I don't know what to say, Arvo.'

'Well, maybe that's why I don't usually tell people. It embarrasses them. Anyway, it was over four years ago. I guess I'm as over it as I'll ever be by now.'

Maria shook her head. 'You don't ever get over something like that.'

'No. That's true. It does change you for ever.'

'Were they ever caught? The kids who did it.'

'Nope. Never. Anyway, I didn't want to stay in Detroit any more after that – nothing to stay for – so I put in for a transfer. When an opening on this unit came up, I took it like a shot. New life. New world. California, here I came. They were well-insured, and Dad had done pretty well on the stock market, so I inherited enough for the convertible and the down-payment on the house . . . And that's about it. Story of my life.'

'And then along came Nyreen,' said Maria.

'It never rains . . .'

Arvo put some Billie Holiday on the stereo. It was maybe more suited to bourbon and smoky bars than French champagne in a smoke-free living room, but what the hell. Maria held out her glass. 'Here's to next year,' she said. 'And may it be better than the last one.'

'Amen,' said Arvo and clinked glasses. They drank.

'Mmm,' said Maria. 'This *does* taste good.' She sat down on the sofa and Arvo sat in the armchair. 'Busy day?' she asked.

'Jack Marillo's funeral.'

'Was the actress there?'

'Uh-huh.'

'Have you fallen in love with her yet?'

Arvo remembered his exchange with Sarah Broughton at the funeral, then he remembered seeing her naked the other morning. He felt himself blush.

'Hey, I'm sorry,' Maria said. 'I didn't mean anything.'

Arvo laughed. 'No, it's fine. Really it is. And no, I'm not in love with her. I'm not sure I even like her, and she sure as hell doesn't seem to like me. She's scared, so at least she does what I say now, but as for liking . . .' He shrugged. 'I don't think she could ever like someone who's had to make her reveal so much of herself, give up so much of her privacy.'

'Hey. Can't win 'em all.'

'I'll drink to that.' For some reason, Arvo didn't want to tell Maria that he had spent the night at Sarah's place, albeit alone in an armchair. Or that he had seen her naked. It was crazy, they were colleagues, friends, they'd known each other ever since Maria came to work the unit only a few months after Arvo. Yet there were some things they never talked about.

Over the past three years, they had shared an occasional drink and a problem or two, patched up a few of one another's bruises, just the kind of things friends do without even knowing much about one another's taste, without even knowing exactly where one another lived, or so he had thought. There should be another category, Arvo had always thought, between friends and acquaintances, because that surely was where most people in his life belonged.

They had drifted apart when Arvo married Nyreen. Maria hadn't said anything about it, but then she hadn't needed to; her silence said it all. For a while, he had resented her for that, resented the idea that a friend should not be as happy as he was about his wedding, and their relationship had cooled. But that was when he had been head over heels in love with Nyreen.

Shortly after he began to realize what a mistake he had made in marrying Nyreen, he heard, through others, that Maria herself was breaking up with the guy she'd lived with for four years, an artist who lived in Venice. Arvo had always thought him a bit of an arrogant asshole on the rare occasions they had met socially. Burdened with his own problems, still pissed at Maria, he hadn't been there for her. So now there was a lot unsaid, a lot unresolved between them.

'More champagne?' he asked.

'Sure. You mind if I put the TV on? Regular network TV. I just like to watch the Times Square celebrations. It's a family tradition.'

'Sure.' Arvo flipped on the TV and found the right channel. 'My brother lives in New York.'

'Will he be there?'

'Michael? No, too afraid of getting mugged.'

Maria laughed and Arvo went to the fridge to get the champagne. He still felt awkward, on edge.

When he went back she was perched at the edge of the sofa watching people in tuxedos and evening gowns dance to a big band, with her hands folded in her lap. He handed her the glass, and when she took it she looked up to catch his eyes and the next thing he knew he was kissing her on the lips, gently at first, savouring their softness and the scent of champagne on her breath, and then harder, probing with his tongue, intoxicated by her response.

The kiss ended and she stood up close to him. She put her arms around him. 'That was nice,' she said. 'Why don't we go in the bedroom?'

'It's a mess.'

'Good, we'll make it even messier.'

'The champagne . . .?'

'We'll take it with us.'

'Maria—'

'Sshh.' She put her finger to his lips. 'We'll talk later. Right now, this is what *I* want to do, no strings, no explanations, and most of all no bullshit.'

Arvo took her hand and led her to the bedroom.

'It's not a mess,' she said. 'At least the bed's made.'

Arvo laughed. He left the door slightly ajar so they could make out outlines by the light from the other room. They could still hear the television, but he was in no mood to go back and turn it off. They put their champagne flutes on the bedside tables and sat together on the edge of the bed.

Maria turned her face up and Arvo kissed her again, this time running his hand over her bare shoulders, feeling one of the straps slip off. Maria kissed his neck, touching it with her soft warm tongue, and began unbuttoning his shirt. When she had finished, he stretched his arms back and she eased it off. Then she put her hands behind her back and unzipped her dress. The second strap slipped off her shoulder, and the material loosened and fell away from her skin. Arvo cupped one of her breasts in his hands and licked the hard nipple with his tongue. Maria moaned and put her hand at the back of his head, pulling him to her. Her breasts were as firm and smooth as he had imagined.

Soon they were naked and Maria urged him inside her. He felt her muscles tighten against his hardness as they began to move together, slowly at first, then faster.

As they came towards climax, he raised himself on his arms and looked down at her. She grasped the brass bed-rails with both hands and thrust her hips against him, breasts swaying with the rhythm, eyes closed, moisture glistening on her upper lip. Her lips were open but her white teeth were clenched tight.

When he felt he could hold on no longer, she sensed it and opened her eyes, then cried out, a shudder passing through her body. She took her hands from the rails and pulled Arvo onto her so his face was buried in her hair on the pillow. It smelled of apples and cinnamon and it muffled the sounds he made as he came and her nails dug into the skin of his back.

After, they both lay for a while sweating, getting their breath back, then they sat up in bed and reached for the champagne. They toasted in silence. The sound from the TV indicated that the old year was coming to a close.

'So, do you want to talk now?' Maria asked.

If truth be told, Arvo was far too content basking in the warm afterglow for talk, but he sensed that Maria needed the communication. 'Sure,' he said.

'If it's us working together and sleeping together that both-ers you,' Maria said, 'I can understand that.'

'You can?'

'That's why I said no strings, no explanations, no bullshit. I mean it, Arvo.'

'But we *do* work together.'

'It's not as if we're partners or anything.'

'But—'

'No, listen up a minute. I'm serious.' She turned on her side and propped her head on her hand. 'I came over because I wanted to,' Maria said. 'Sure it was a risk. Nobody likes rejection. But I wanted to go to bed with you. Have done for a while. And I thought you might feel the same way.'

'You saying you were only chasing me because of my body?'

'Asshole.' She gave him a playful thump on the shoulder. 'Let me finish, will you?'

'Okay.'

'What I don't want, Arvo, and what I don't think *you're* ready for yet, is a relationship. What we do need, I think, is a little friendly company just like this from time to time.'

'You mean this isn't a relationship?'

'You know what I mean. We've been friends a long time. I know we've had some ups and downs, but we've still been friends. Sometimes even the best of friends get horny for one another. Acting on that can sometimes ruin a friendship. But you and me, Arvo, we haven't got anyone else to hurt but ourselves. We're grown-ups. We can deal with it.'

'Wait a minute. Are you saying this is a one-night stand? A wham-bam-thank-you-sir.'

Maria laughed. 'No, that's not what I'm saying, butt-head. But what I *am* saying is let's not get hung up on it, okay? I don't want to live with you or marry you and have your children. I don't even want to date you. What I do want is for us to go to bed together like this now and then.'

'Can we negotiate maybe dinner once a month?'

'I'll think about it. But do you understand what I'm saying?'

'Yes, I think so.'

'And do you agree?'

'Uh-huh. In principle.'

'Shake on it?'

Arvo touched her hair. 'I think we can do better than that.' Maria laughed and slid down onto her side, moving closer to him. 'My, my, it *has* been a long time, hasn't it?' she said. 'Hey, listen.'

'What?'

'The countdown.'

And they listened to the crowd count the apple down three thousand miles away and three hours ago in New York City. But after the roaring and the whistling they weren't paying attention any more. It must have been about a quarter after twelve when the phone rang at a very awkward moment. Maria was closest to it at the time, and before Arvo could make a move, she had picked up the receiver.

'Yes?' she said. 'Yes, this is the Hughes residence . . . What? No, I'm sorry, I'm afraid he can't speak now. He's busy. His mouth is otherwise engaged. What? Sure. I'll tell him. And a Happy New Year to you, too, honey.'

'Why the hell did you do that?' said Arvo.

'Don't you want to know who it was?'

'It could have been the department.'

'No. They'd beep you. Especially on New Year's Eve.'

'Who was it, then?'

'Can't you guess?'

'Maria!'

'Okay, okay. It was your ex, that's who. Little Miss Surfing Bikini.'

'Nyreen?'

'Isn't it just the kind of thing she'd do, call you up to wish you a Happy New Year?'

'Well, I suppose so. What'd she say?'

Maria laughed. 'Not much when she heard *my* voice. She says to tell you you're a prick.'

Arvo frowned. 'Why would she do that?'

'You really don't get it, do you? Because she likes to control you, that's why. It's all right when she's running around with someone else and you're at home alone. But you're supposed to be suffering, longing for her, mourning the loss of the great love of your life, not having fun.'

'Is that right?'

'Yes. And there's something else.'

'What?'

'She's jealous.'

Arvo started to grin. 'Really?'

'Really.'

'Is there any more champagne?'

'Ah-ah, not yet, mister. You've got some unfinished business first.'

'I have? What? Oh, yes, I *have*.'

Afterwards, they finished the champagne, Arvo locked the house up and began to doze off, arm around Maria. He must have actually fallen asleep, because he felt like he'd been brought back from a long way off when he woke to feel Maria shaking him. He opened his eyes and saw the expression of absolute terror on her face.

'Arvo, there's a fire,' she said, shaking him. 'There's a fire somewhere in the house. I can smell it.'

Arvo couldn't smell anything, but he rubbed his eyes and got out of bed to check. There was nothing at the front of the house, but now he was beginning to smell smoke, too. The smoke detector started to screech, and when he went into the spare bedroom at the back, he saw the bright orange flames leaping up the walls.

31

Arvo took the Santa Ana Freeway all the way to Laguna Canyon. It wasn't a scenic ride, for the most part, but it was fast. He drove with the top of the convertible open and sang along with Neil Young's 'Cortez the Killer.'

It was 2 January, and Carl Buxton, ex-drummer of Gary Knox's band, The Heros, was back from Mexico. Arvo had asked if Buxton were willing to talk about the tour and about Gary Knox, and he had agreed. According to Stan Harvey, Buxton was about the only one of the band with any brain-cells left – enough, anyway, to get out of the rock scene after Gary died and start up a music-geared computer business.

Arvo got the impression that there had been a great deal of craziness around Gary Knox, and as Sarah Broughton had been a part of it for a while, it followed that here was the best place to start looking for her demon lover.

Whether Carl Buxton would remember any more than Sarah did was a moot point. What was the old saying? *If you remember the sixties you weren't there.* Well, it hadn't been the sixties, but rock 'n' roll was rock 'n' roll, and the drugs were much the same. Though the music press may have christened Gary the 'new Dylan,' Arvo had always thought he had more than a touch of Jim Morrison about him. Which meant madness and mayhem.

Everything depended on how observant Buxton was, or how curious he was about others and their problems. Arvo had met a few rock stars while he had been working with the

TMU, and he found them to be egocentric assholes, for the most part.

He glanced down at the map spread on the passenger seat. Just past Irvine, he took El Toro Road into Laguna Hills and wound down to the canyon.

Arvo remembered Laguna Canyon as a beautiful area, scattered with expensive homes, secluded by brush and trees. But he hadn't been there since the fires, and he wasn't prepared for the devastation he saw this time.

The steep, majestic hills that rose from the coast were reduced to brown scrub, with no vegetation left, and some areas had even been charred black by the intensity of the fires that had swept down into the canyons, fanned by the hot, dry Santa Ana winds. Here and there, twisted, blackened trees held up their gnarled branches like shaking fists against a bright blue sky.

Close to Buxton's house, Arvo stopped by a 'Restricted Access' area out of curiosity, left the car and wandered in, under the chain fence. It had once been a street of homes. Now all that remained were the foundations, the stone gateways and paths, brick fireplaces and chimneys. Walls, furniture and possessions had all been consumed by the fires.

Arvo walked up some steps through pink stucco gateposts to what was once the first floor of one house; now it was nothing more than a concrete foundation open to the elements. He wandered back into the barren garden; there, amid the blackened debris, a dead starling floated in a Jacuzzi full of stagnant water.

It could have been *his* house on New Year's Eve, he realized, if Maria hadn't had such an innate terror of fire that she had smelled it before it really took hold.

Arvo had gone out with the extinguisher and put out the fire easily enough, then found a bundle of charred rags by the back wall under the spare bedroom window. He had spent the rest of the night with the firefighters and arson investigators – discovering only what he knew already: that the fire had been deliberately set, and that it had started from a pile of gasoline-soaked rags. An amateur job, the fire department investigator said.

Some consolation.

Up in Laguna Canyon, Arvo noticed as he walked away, the real-estate agents had already put up signs on the burned-out properties. Soon, the ground would be cleared, new houses built, new vegetation planted, and the cycle would continue.

On one of those whims God is famous for, Carl Buxton's house had been spared. Hugging the ground not more than fifty yards away, across the street, it was a small English Tudor-style place with high-pitched gables, half-timbering, a tall chimney and casement windows of leaded glass. It reminded Arvo of illustrations he had seen in the fairy-tale books his father had kept from his childhood, more so because it was partially shrouded in shrubbery and trees.

He pulled up beside a white Mercedes convertible in the broad driveway. As he was admiring the car, the front door of the house – all oak and stained glass – opened and a tall, thin man in ice-blue jeans and a salmon-pink shirt walked out to greet him.

'Like it?' he asked, referring to the car with obvious pride in ownership.

Arvo nodded. 'Very much.'

'Had it shipped all the way from Deutschland. Cost a packet. Hi, I'm Carl Buxton.' He stuck his hand out and smiled. 'You must be the cop. Come in.'

Instead of the typical rock-star look Arvo had expected, Buxton had a baby face, pink lips, puckered like a cherub's in a Renaissance fresco, glaucous eyes and straight blond hair, with spiky bangs, just about covering his ears at the sides and reaching his shirt collar at the back. Arvo figured he must be in his late thirties, but he looked about twelve.

Arvo introduced himself.

'Arvo?' Buxton echoed. 'After the composer?'

Arvo shook his head. 'I don't know. What composer? It was my mother's choice. She was Estonian.'

'Yeah, man, like the composer. Arvo Pärt. Pronounced "Pert." Does really contemporary stuff, a bit of minimalism, some of that Gorecki-style religious music, a lot of solemn repetitions. Goes on a bit but I find it nice and relaxing sometimes. Man, I can't believe you've never heard of him.'

'Maybe the next time I feel like a bit of relaxation . . .'

But Buxton had already turned his back to lead the way. Arvo followed him through the house, getting quick impressions of a lot of dark wood panelling and antique furniture, and blurred glimpses of framed sixties rock posters on the walls: the Grateful Dead, Jefferson Airplane, Cream, Big Brother and the Holding Company. His favourite kind of music.

They ended up out back, where open french windows led out to a wooden deck that smelled of cedar. Music played softly upstairs: early Eagles, 'Take It Easy.' Bougainvillaea edged the neat lawn, tiny white flowers buried deep in the red bracts. Yellow, purple and pink plants Arvo couldn't name hung from the trelliswork that covered the patio and created a pleasant area of shade. Birds skittered and sang in the jacarandas. There were rose bushes, too: red, yellow and white.

'Nice,' said Arvo.

'Yeah. The gardener does a good job.' Buxton gestured towards a wicker chair. 'Take a pew.'

Arvo sat.

'Drink?'

'Iced tea?'

'No problemo.'

Buxton disappeared into the kitchen, leaving Arvo to inspect the oddly shaped cacti in pots arranged all around the deck.

'Interesting,' he said when Buxton returned with the drinks. 'I was expecting a woodland recording studio or something.'

Buxton smiled as he sat opposite Arvo and stretched out his long legs. He was drinking Old Milwaukee from a can. Arvo sipped his iced tea. It came complete with ice and a twist of lemon. 'Are you still in the business?' he asked.

'I do some studio work,' Buxton said. 'Just to keep my hand in. But it's more of a hobby, really.' He fiddled with a pack of Camel Lights and lit up. There were several butts already in the shell ashtray on the low wooden table. He blew smoke out through his nose. 'So, you want to know about that prick Gary Knox, do you?' he asked.

'I'd like your impressions of the tour and the people involved. We can start with Gary, if that's okay?'

'Fine with me, man. Gary snorted and swallowed everything he could get his hands on. I mean everything. Christ, he wasn't even that fussy. He'd shove it up his arse if he thought it would get him high.'

Arvo had a sudden and unpleasant memory of what had been done to John Heimar. 'How long had you known Knox?' he asked.

'I didn't know him, really. Jim Lasardi, the bass player, is an old mate of mine. We go way back. The last drummer quit before the tour to go into detox, and they were stuck for a replacement, so Jim gave me a call. I'd already semi-retired, but I needed the money.' He shrugged.

Arvo looked around. 'Not any more,' he said.

'No,' Buxton agreed. 'Not any more. But believe me, I earned every fucking cent.'

'So that last tour was the only one you did with Gary Knox?'

'Yes, thank God.'

Arvo took his notebook out of his pocket and rested it on his thigh. 'It's that tour I wanted to talk to you about, really,' he said. 'I've heard a few rumours that it was pretty wild. That true?'

Buxton put his feet up on the edge of the table, ankles crossed, and relaxed in the wicker chair. 'Wild is an understatement,' he said. 'But while you've got your notebook out, I'd like to make it clear that I never have, don't now, and didn't then, do any drugs other than the legal ones.'

Arvo grinned. 'Those being?'

Buxton held out the cigarette and can. 'Tobacco and alcohol, man. That's all. And I'm not even much of a drinker.'

'This isn't about drugs, Mr Buxton.'

'Carl, please. No? What is it about, then?'

'I'm sorry I can't give you any details right now, but you've got nothing to worry about. All I want is information.'

Arvo heard a sound behind him and turned to see a woman leaning against the door frame, one hip cocked. Her blonde hair was tied back in a ponytail, and she wore high cut-off denim shorts and a white shirt knotted under her jutting breasts. Her smooth, ridged belly was nicely tanned. Prime California girl, Arvo thought. The type they write songs about. Like Nyreen.

'Oh, sorry, honey,' she said to Buxton. 'I didn't realize you had company.'

'That's okay. This is Mr Hughes. He's come to talk about Gary Knox.'

'Oh.'

'I hadn't met Bella then,' Buxton explained. 'She never knew Gary.'

Bella didn't look as if she had even been born then, Arvo thought. But he knew he was being uncharitable; she was probably at least eighteen. She had a dreamy look in her eyes that Arvo was willing to bet wasn't caused by either alcohol or tobacco.

'You guys need anything?' she asked.

'No, love, we're fine right now,' said Buxton.

'Okay.' She waved her hands about a bit then chewed on a loose strand of hair. 'I'll just . . . you know . . . be . . . then . . .' She shrugged, turned and walked away with the kind of exaggerated rear motion a man rarely sees in this day and age. Only the flip-flopping of her sandals on the parquet floor spoiled the effect. Arvo noticed Buxton gazing proprietorially after her. He caught Arvo's eye and stubbed out his cigarette. 'My wife.'

'Very nice,' Arvo said. It seemed the proper response, like the one he had made to the Mercedes and the garden. 'How long have you been married?'

'About six months.' Buxton smiled. 'I suppose you could say we're still on our honeymoon.'

'Congratulations.' Again Arvo thought of Nyreen. Their honeymoon hadn't lasted that long. He hadn't heard from her since the New Year's Eve phone call Maria had answered. 'About the tour . . .?' he prompted.

Buxton shifted in his chair and recrossed his ankles. 'Oh, yeah, the tour. Well, it was certainly a marathon. I can't even remember how many gigs we did, but it seemed as if we had to play every hick town in the country. Mostly outdoor stadiums, festivals, that sort of thing. It was one hell of a hot summer, too. I mean, the whole thing was *gruelling,* man. Have you ever had to do anything like that? Spend so much time with the same group of people you practically end up going to the toilet to take a piss together? Well I'll tell you one thing: it soon makes you a hell of a lot less tolerant of your fellow man.'

'I heard it really creates strong bonds, too,' Arvo said. 'Like soldiers in the trenches, or the jungle.'

'Were you in Vietnam?'

Arvo shook his head. 'Nope. Too young.' And he *had* been

too young. Just. He often wondered what he would have done: gone to Vietnam, or headed for Canada. The latter would have been easy enough, seeing as they lived so near the border, and his father had plenty of colleagues at the university who took draft dodgers over in the trunks of their cars. His mother and father were against the war; they would have supported him if he had burned his draft card. What haunted him about it all now was that he would never know; he hadn't been put to the test, forced to make the choice.

'Well, quite frankly,' Buxton went on, 'let me tell you that bonding stuff's a right load of old cobblers, man. It's just a load of patriotic crap. All that being cooped up like that together for a long time does is show you what stupid wankers most people are when you get right down to it.'

'It does? That's an interesting point of view.' Arvo had a feeling that, to Carl Buxton, most of the world consisted of stupid wankers who didn't recognize or appreciate his genius. 'I haven't heard it put quite like that before,' Arvo went on. 'How many of you were there?'

Buxton crushed his empty beer can and dropped it on the table. 'Hard to say. It varied. There were four of us in the band, then there was Gary, the road crew, manager, assorted groupies and hangers on.' He shrugged.

'So it really was as crazy as people say?'

'Yeah. You've got to be really together to stay sane through a tour like that. I mean, I'm a professional musician. I've been on heavy-duty tours before – been there, man, and bought the T-shirt – and that one was tough even for me. It helps if you're fit, too, you know. A lot of people don't realize that. They think we're all just pill-popping, booze-swilling degenerates. I'll tell you something for free: Mick wouldn't still be up there performing the way he does at his age if he didn't work out, man. No way. Think about it.

'Anyway, I worked out whenever I got the chance. You

know, hotel gyms and pools, weight rooms. But there just wasn't enough time. Never is. Soundchecks. Rehearsals. Hassles. Too much junk food. Not enough sleep. Then there was all the stress of doing one show, two shows, a night. All the craziness around you. Egos. Tantrums.' He glanced towards the french doors and lowered his voice. 'And sometimes there's a groupie you want to spend the night with, you know. I'm only human. I mean, you just can't know what that's like, you can't possibly imagine it, if you haven't been there.' He shook his head slowly in recollection, then grinned. 'But that was all BB. Before Bella.'

'Gary was hanging out with Sarah Broughton, then, wasn't he? Can you tell me anything about her?'

'Sarah Broughton?' Buxton frowned. 'Oh, yeah, that's right. Threw me for a moment there, man. You mean Sally. Sally Bolton. At least that's what she called herself then. I see her on television sometimes. Some cop show. She a friend of yours?'

'No,' said Arvo. 'I'm a *real* cop.' And he smiled to take the sting out of it.

Buxton laughed. 'Right. Sorry. Reason I was asking is she was just as crazy as he was.' He looked over his shoulder again to make sure Bella wasn't around, and whispered, 'I fucked her myself once. And do you know what? I don't think she even remembered doing it. Pretty crazy, huh?'

Arvo nodded, wondering if there might be a good reason why getting fucked by Carl Buxton was so unmemorable. 'Pretty crazy,' he agreed. 'What was their relationship like?'

Buxton frowned. 'Hard to say. They were stoned most of the time. I mean, you can't really have a relationship if you're stoned all the time, can you? Your relationship's with the drugs then, not with another human being. Towards the end, though, they just seemed to kind of drift apart. Know what I mean?'

Arvo nodded. 'Was there someone else?'

Buxton laughed. It was a harsh, unpleasant sound,

something like a bark. 'There was always someone else for Gary, man. When he could get it up, that is.'

'What about Sar— Sally?'

'Nah. She was so spaced out by the time we hit the west coast anyone could just toss her on a mattress and fuck her like she was an inflatable doll or something, and she wouldn't know the difference. She would give you about as much response, too. It's funny, I watch her these days, you know, on television, and she looks like she's got class. I find it hard to believe it's the same person. She must have got her shit together, man. You've got to give her a lot of credit for that.'

Nice of you, you arrogant, self-serving little prick, thought Arvo.

'Yeah,' Buxton went on, 'it's kind of hard to pull yourself up by the bootstraps when you're that far down. I know, man. I've been there.' He pointed his thumb at his chest.

Arvo wasn't in the least bit interested in sifting through the dregs of Buxton's experience. 'So things degenerated as the tour progressed?' he said.

'You could say that.'

'Any idea why?'

Buxton lit another Camel and let the first lungful of smoke trickle out before speaking. 'Gary was a weird motherfucker to start with,' he announced finally. 'The drugs just made him weirder, more distant, more reckless. Have you ever seen that movie, *The Doors*?'

'Uh-huh.'

'It was like that. You know, walking on ledges of high build-ings waving his dick at the night and spouting poetry. Dylan Thomas. Walt Whitman. Allen Ginsberg.' He shook his head and took another drag on the cigarette. 'I don't know what his personal demons were, man, but they sure had him by the short-and-curlies by the time we got out to the coast.'

'How did Sally react to all this?'

'I've already told you, man. She was a fucking zombie by then. The tour mattress.'

'She didn't care that he had other women?'

Buxton waved his cigarette in the air. 'Women, men, it didn't matter to Gary then. Maybe even children and small, furry animals, too, who knows? By the time we got to LA, we'd picked up so many hangers-on it was like London Zoo.'

'What kind of people were they?'

'What kind of people were they? I'll tell you what kind of people they were. They were psychos, schizos, zombies, freaks, paranoids, pseuds, drunks, junkies, crazies of all descriptions. By the time we hit Fresno, we had two Napoleons and at least three Jesus Christs hanging around the fringes. Maybe I exaggerate a little, man, but you get my point? Gary attracted them. Shit, he even went out and picked them up off the streets and brought them back to the hotel and the concerts. Winos, street people. He was on a Jack Kerouac kick about the holiness of bums.'

'Why?'

'Who knows why? Because he was crazy himself and he felt right at home in their company. I don't know.'

Arvo was beginning to feel overwhelmed. He had suspected that things had been chaotic on the tour, but not this bad. 'Look, I'm kind of interested in the cast of characters,' he said. 'Could you describe some of them a bit for me? Maybe even give me a couple of names to follow up. Was there anyone in particular, anyone who really stands out in your memory, maybe as being a little creepy. Or someone who might even *appear* normal enough but still gave you an odd feeling?'

Buxton frowned for a moment, opened his mouth, closed it again, frowned, then leaned over and stubbed out his cigarette. 'Well,' he said, 'now that you mention it, you know, there *was* one guy in particular.' Arvo sipped his iced tea and watched a little Oregon junco with its hangman's hood and

dapper grey breast flitting between the branches of a jacaranda tree.

'This bloke was really strange,' Buxton went on. 'He gave
me the willies, man. I know I told you there was a lot of craziness around the tour, but most of it wasn't *serious* craziness. I
mean, a guy who thinks he's Jesus is crazy, sure, but he's also
pretty harmless. But the bloke I'm talking about was different.' Buxton shook his head slowly. 'Scary.'

A breeze ruffled the rose bushes. A starling hopped over the
lawn looking for crumbs. The music had stopped, and it was
quiet in the garden apart from the birds and the hiss of a
distant sprinkler. Occasionally Arvo heard a car passing or a
siren in the distance.

'Where did you meet this guy?' he asked.

'Frisco. We had three concerts there in four days. The
second night, a group of us went out on the town. I'd had a
couple of drinks in the hotel bar, the others had done a few
lines of coke, and we were in a mood for some fun. It was one
of those nights when everything seemed fine. One of the good
nights. Do you know what I mean?'

Arvo nodded. 'Go on.'

'We went to North Beach because Gary had this thing
about the Beats. Like I said, he used to quote poetry when he
was really flying. So he had this idea he had to go to City
Lights Bookstore and meet Lawrence Ferlinghetti. Apparently
this is the geezer who owns the place. He's a poet and he's
been around for years.

'As it turned out, this Ferlinghetti wasn't there – which is
probably just as well, because we were getting a few funny
looks by then – so we cruised some of the strip bars and
topless joints around Columbus and Broadway. We had a few
more drinks, then we ended up back in this bar called Vesuvio's,
where the Beats used to hang out, so Gary told us, right next
to the bookshop. Needless to say, Gary really liked it and

managed to calm down enough not to get us all thrown out. And then we met *him*.

'He was with a group of about three or four others. I can't remember all the details clearly because by this time I'd had a few beers myself. He's medium height, about five-eight, pretty muscular but nothing special – I mean, not like Schwarzenegger or anything – tattoos on his arms, likes to dress in black, and he has a dyed blond brush-cut and these really piercing light blue eyes.'

'Do you remember anything about the tattoos?'

'I don't know much about tattooing. It's just one of those things I never got into. But they looked quite intricate, you know, really professional. I think there was an eagle, or some kind of bird of prey, on one arm, and the other was a red flower, maybe a rose.'

'Any names on them?'

'No. Not that I recall.'

'What was his name?'

'Mitch.'

'His second name?'

'Dunno. It never came up.'

'Know where he lived?'

'No, but someone said he used to work in one of the North Beach strip-joints as a bouncer and he'd just got fired. I don't know which joint.'

'Okay. Go on with your story.'

'Anyway, he recognizes Gary and comes over, says he's a poet and a singer-songwriter and asks if he and his friends can join us. Gary says he can if he recites one of his poems. Like, that's the price of admission to our little clique. Typical fucking Gary. So he does. I don't know if it was any good or not, but Gary said he liked it and invited him and his group to join us. Mitch was with his brother, this other guy called Ivan, and a couple of girls. One thing led to another and we went back to the hotel. Gary fucked one of the girls and somehow they just didn't go away, they became part of the entourage.'

At this point, Bella appeared in the french windows looking bored silly. Her body seemed to be vibrating rhythmically, as if it had a motor inside. She was holding a long strand of hair, pulling it forward from the ponytail and sucking on it with one corner of her mouth. 'You guys need anything else?' she asked in a baby-doll voice.

Buxton glanced at Arvo and raised his eyebrows in question.

'Sure,' said Arvo. 'I'll have another iced tea, please.'

'And another beer for me, sweetheart,' Buxton said.

Now she had a purpose in life, Bella swayed back inside. Buxton gave Arvo a look as if to say, 'Women.' The fridge door rattled when it opened, then banged shut. Bella delivered the drinks and stood around for a moment, as if unsure what to do. Buxton patted her rear. 'Hop it for a while, love. Man talk.'

'Sure, honey.' She smiled and gave a little wave as she left. 'You won't be *too* long?'

'Course not, sweetie.'

Bella sashayed back through the french windows. Buxton pulled the tab on his beer, then Arvo asked what Mitch was like.

Buxton wiped foam from his lips. 'He was a cool customer,' he said. 'I mean cool in the sense of being cold. You got no real sense of warmth from him, no *feeling*. He was pretty quiet at first. You know, the kind who sits back and observes, tries to figure out all the angles. I got the impression that he was trying to learn how to behave in order to be accepted by us, to please Gary in particular. It was a spooky feeling, as if all his behaviour was planned. They say psychos are like that, don't they?'

'Can you give me an example?' Arvo asked.

'Let me think . . . Yeah . . . Like I don't think he had a sense of humour, but he figured out pretty sharpish that people wouldn't like him if he didn't, so he created one to order. If he laughed, you sensed that he wasn't really amused, that he just thought it was appropriate to laugh or people would think he was odd and wouldn't like him. Do you know what I mean? Never trust anyone without a sense of humour, man. That's my philosophy.'

'Absolutely. Can you tell me anything else about him?'

'He was really good at finding drugs. We hit a new town, he'd score whatever you wanted – whatever Gary wanted – in minutes, man. And he liked to play headgames.'

'What kind of headgames?'

'He liked to try and scare people, fuck with their minds. He had that *look,* for a start, with the eyes and all – you know, like Charlie Manson – and he also had an aura about him that made me feel someone had stepped on my grave every time he walked in the room. He carried a flick-knife, too. What do you guys over here call it? A switchblade, that's it. Not that I ever saw him use it except to clean his fingernails, mind you. But he made sure you knew he had it.

'Anyway, he was obsessive, man. If he got into something with you, he just wouldn't let go. If he got you to tell him something about your past, some little incident you were maybe ashamed of, he'd just keep digging and poking until he'd squeezed every detail out of you, every ounce of shame. He liked to humiliate people. Once he made eye contact, he wouldn't let go until he'd got what he wanted. We got to calling him Gary's pet pit-bull. A pit-bull of the mind. Once he got his teeth in your psyche . . .' Buxton gave a theatrical shudder.

'What about his friends, his brother?'

'They seemed normal enough, though God knows what they were doing hanging around with him. Ivan and Mitch's brother were both very quiet. I don't remember getting a word

out of either of them. The brother used to follow him around
like a pet dog. The girls liked to fuck a lot.' He lowered his
voice again. 'One of them gave great head. Candi, I think. The
other was called Aspen. I ask you, what kind of a name is that?
Who in their right mind would name their kid after a fucking
ski resort? Anyway, they were all, like, around, you know, but
Mitch was clearly the leader. He was the one people remembered.'

Rock music started playing from inside again. Louder, this
time, and a little more rebellious: Guns N'Roses. Buxton
didn't react to it at all. Arvo sipped some iced tea, then asked,
'What other kind of games did Mitch play?'

'He liked to tell elaborate lies. He used to talk about how he
wasted someone out in the desert once, or how he'd played in
a rock 'n' roll band, even made a record once. He even said
he'd seen the President coming out of a brothel in Reno. Lies.
Gary loved that sort of shit, lapped it up. You'd never think
such a miserable cynic as him could be so gullible, but he was.'

'Could any of the stories have been true?'

'I suppose it's possible, but I don't think so. Whenever you
asked him to elaborate, he got all vague about the details. You
know, like the record had been deleted and you couldn't find
a copy anywhere. That kind of bullshit. To be honest, man, I
didn't really care whether they were true or not. Mostly I just
tried to avoid being around him, but that wasn't always
possible.'

'Why not?'

'Because he was always *there,* always on the fringes. Because
Gary liked him.'

'He didn't scare Gary?'

'Not at all. But then Gary didn't always see things the way
normal people do, if you catch my drift. Nobody scared Gary.
He could fuck minds with the best of them.'

'Was Mitch ever violent in your presence?'

'Yeah. It could come on all of a sudden. Like, it would just erupt. He ended up being a sort of unofficial bodyguard for Gary and Sal. For all of us, really, whether we wanted him or not.'

'What sort of violent things did he do?'

Buxton thought for a moment. 'I saw him hit a few people, usually people who were being obnoxious or pushy. He generally did it very quickly, and they didn't get a chance to hit back. He was strong and he seemed to have a kind of quick reaction speed ... I don't know ... it's as if he'd studied unarmed combat or some of that martial arts stuff, or maybe been in the Marines.'

'Did he ever say anything about being in the armed forces?'

'Nope. And if you were too young for Vietnam, Mitch certainly was. I'd say he was about thirty, tops.'

He could still have been in the forces, Arvo thought, and if he had been, he might be easier to track down. True, there was no longer a draft, but anyone could sign up. There had certainly been more than enough wars since Vietnam. The Gulf, for example. On the other hand, you could learn martial arts just about anywhere these days. 'Are there any specific incidents you can tell me about?' he asked.

Buxton thought for a moment, then said, 'Yeah. Yeah, there was one time. And it tells you a lot about the guy, now I come to think about it. But why are you so interested in him? You haven't really told me what this is all about.'

'There's been some threats of violence, that's all, and we think it might be connected to someone who was on the tour.'

Buxton snorted. 'Well if it's threats of violence you're interested in, Mitch is your man. Who's he been threatening? Can't be Gary. He's dead.'

'I can't really say any more than that. Will you tell me about the incident?'

Buxton sulked for a moment, then sipped some beer, lit

another Camel and recrossed his legs, ankles resting on the table. 'Yeah. Okay. We were in this hotel bar in Santa Barbara, a few of us sitting around shooting the shit before a concert. Out of the blue, Mitch asks if anyone has a postage stamp and Jim – that's Jim Lasardi, the bass player I mentioned before – says, "Why, Mitch, do you want to write your autobiography?" It was just a meaningless sort of joke, really, because we don't know anything about the guy, right? Well, everyone laughs but Mitch. His face sort of twitches in a cold smile, which is definitely not sincere by any stretch of the imagination, and he changes the subject, or someone else does.

'Then Mitch gets all sulky. He says he doesn't want to go to the concert that night, so we go and play, and when we come back to the hotel after the show for a few drinks, all a bit wired, he's, like, still sitting there in the same chair in the bar. It's the only time I ever saw him close to being drunk. He must have drunk a whole bottle of bourbon and he was still in control.

'Anyway, he starts rabbiting on about all the things he's done in his life, like how he's worked down the mines, picked grapes with the wetbacks in Napa and Sonoma, written songs for a famous band whose name he can't remember, driven a cab in Frisco, published his poems, travelled around South America with nothing but a few dollars in his pocket . . . You get the message? He goes on and on and on, and nobody really knows why he's telling us all this, or even whether he's putting us on. But there's something in his tone that makes us keep quiet and listen till he's finished.

'Then he says something about people making a joke out of his life, belittling what he's done, and suddenly we all know what this is about. Uh-oh. This guy has been sitting brooding about Jim's stupid joke all night. *All fucking night.* Can you believe it? So Jim says something to ease the tension, like he didn't mean anything by it, but Mitch isn't hearing by now, and he just reaches over, really fast, pulls Jim by the collar and nuts him right on the bridge of the nose. Blood everywhere. Jim's nose is broken. Next thing, the hotel manager comes over and throws a fit and Mitch decks him as well. One punch to the side of the jaw and he's out.'

'What happened?'

'Gary smoothed things over.'

'And did Gary let him stay around after that?'

'Gary said he had a word with him and, to be fair, Mitch never did anything like that again. But things didn't feel the same any more. We all gave him an even wider berth. You have to understand, though, that Mitch would do anything for Gary. Anything. He loved the guy, hero-worshipped him. And Gary's ego was never so well stroked it couldn't do with a bit more.'

'What about Sally?'

'He was very protective about her. Very courteous. A real gentleman. Funny that, isn't it?'

'Did he ever come on to her?'

'Not that I know of. It wasn't like that. Everyone else treated her like a tart, but Mitch treated her like gold. He opened doors for her, that kind of shit. He even used to have pet nicknames for her.'

The hairs on the back of Arvo's neck prickled. 'Like what?'

'Oh, just cute stuff, you know. He'd call her "The Lady," for example. "The Lady's carriage awaits," he'd say when the limo arrived. Or "Princess." "Little Star." Names like that. Look, if Sally's been getting threats, they're not from Mitch. He worshipped the ground she walked on.'

But Arvo was no longer listening. He put his glass down and sat up.

'Do you know where he went after the tour ended?' he asked.

'Haven't a clue, man.'

'Mind if I use your phone?'

'No,' said Buxton, looking puzzled. 'Not at all. No, don't get up. Stay where you are. I'll get Bella to bring it out to you. Bella!'

32

Stuart and Sarah ate a hurried lunch at a table opposite Brentano's in the open plaza of the Century City Shopping Center. Sarah nibbled at a corned beef on rye she'd got from the deli and Stuart sucked at his Diet Coke and tucked into a Johnny Rocket burger with the works.

Sarah was still in her Anita O'Rourke costume from the morning's shooting – this time a navy-blue business suit over a pearl silk blouse – and one or two shoppers stared and whispered as they walked by, recognizing her.

It was almost three o'clock and the lunch hordes had gone by then. When she was filming, Sarah often didn't get a lunch break until two or three. Today, Stuart had taken pity on her and brought her here just to get her out of the gloomy studio atmosphere for an hour or so. At least that was what he told her. She knew Stuart well enough to know he had another agenda, too.

It had been a tough morning's filming, especially given the mood on the set over Jack's murder. The director wanted to do a few fill-in scenes and solo Anita scenes – the female cop at home feeding her cat, eating her breakfast and so on – basically just about anything he could get away with shooting without Jack.

The whole affair gave Sarah the feeling that the network was some sort of gigantic perpetual motion machine and, whatever happened, it must not be allowed to wind down. Sarah had found it difficult to concentrate and felt annoyed with herself because they had to do simple scenes over and over again. Usually she prided herself on her professionalism, but today she'd been like some kid fresh out of drama school. Worse, a high-school play.

Between mouthfuls, Stuart was telling her about the morning's meeting he had attended, but she found her attention wandering. Even in public, in broad daylight, she felt jumpy. She kept wondering if the dark figures she saw coming towards her out of the corners of her eyes meant to do her harm, if one of them might be *him*. It was hardly paranoia, she assured herself – someone really *was* after her – but somehow the thought didn't offer much comfort.

She had slept badly, hearing noises in the dark, worrying that the killer would find her there and kill Stuart like he had killed Jack. She even worried again for a moment that it might be Stuart and that he was lulling her into a false sense of security before the kill. Of course, that thought made her feel guilty.

'A penny for your thoughts?'

'Pardon? Oh, sorry, I was miles away. Forgive me?'

'Sure. Just try not to brood on it, huh? It won't do any good. Let the cops handle it. It's what they do.'

'I don't know. I can't seem to help but worry. But please go on. I promise I'll listen.'

'I was only talking about your future, that's all. And mine. Hell, maybe even the fucking network's future.'

Sarah smiled. 'Oh, so it's nothing very important then.'

'Right. Well, the main thing is they're not giving the show the ax just yet. We've got a few episodes in the can, and then there's reruns we can always throw in for a few weeks. Come February and March nobody notices anyway. Half the country's covered with snow and ice and shit like that. People watch anything just to avoid looking out their windows.'

'And Jack?'

'We've got to find a replacement. Sooner the better. You know the network. They want someone new in before the fucking ashes have settled in Jack's urn. Shit, I'm sorry, honey.' He ran his hand over his silvery hair. 'I can be an insensitive bastard sometimes. Maybe the pressure's getting to me. Anyway, they know that it'll take time if we want to get it right. And it's got to be right. That's why they've given me a week.'

'A week? To find a replacement for Jack?'

'Yup. Can you believe it? And you've got to help, too. You and Jack had a special kind of chemistry, and I don't think we should even try to duplicate that, but it's got to be someone you can work with. I mean, it has to be someone you have some sort of rapport with. You've got to meet some of the possibilities. Maybe dinner, cocktails, whatever. I'm sorry.'

Sarah nodded, pale. 'Don't worry. It's okay. And in the meantime? How do they explain Jack's absence?'

Stuart paused to glance around, then slurped some Diet Coke through a plastic straw, leaned forward and lowered his voice. 'Remember that scene you did when you both entered that suspect's apartment in the dark and someone fired a shot? The cliffhanger they were saving for later in the season?'

'Yes.'

'That's how Jack gets killed on screen.'

Sarah pushed her paper plate away. 'But that's sick.'

'No. That's network television, honey. I don't mean to sound hard here, but a lot of people have got a lot of money invested in *Good Cop, Bad Cop*. And it's not just this season, either. Sure, we could hobble through that, even without a replacement. But what about next year? The year after? We're talking about a high-rated show here. Real high. And the challenge is to keep pushing up the ratings without Jack. Sad as Jack's death is to them, it's not as sad as losing their jobs or their Bel Air homes. Not as sad as losing the beach house, either, or finding yourself out of work. Think about it.'

'You can't mean that. You know I'd give up the beach house if I thought it would bring Jack back.'

'That's exactly my point. Though I'm not sure that asshole Dean Conners would give up his new Saab, or that bimbo he's got stashed away down in Carlsbad, even if it would bring Jesus Christ back. What I mean is, *nothing's* going to bring Jack back, but the rest of us have to go on. The wheels continue to grind exceeding hard here. We don't just want a one-season wonder. You're either on the bus or you're off it, Sarah. Bottom line is we find someone you can work with real quick, or they can write you out, too, and start over. I'm sorry to be the guy putting the pressure on, especially with all the other shit that's going down right now. But it was either me or Ollie the Producer from Hell. I kind of volunteered.' He grinned.

Sarah smiled and patted his hand. 'Thanks, Stuart. I appreciate that. And I do understand what you're talking about. I'm not *that* naïve. It's just that to have him *murdered* on television the same as in real life doesn't seem right. It seems sort of cynical, sick, disrespectful.'

'I hear what you're saying, and you're probably right, but that's the way it's going to go down no matter what you or I think. Makes sense in a way. I mean, cops *do* get shot on the job.'

A young man in shorts and a UCLA sweatshirt approached the table and Sarah tensed, ready to run if he came up to her.

At first, it looked as if the kid was going to pass right by, then he made a sudden movement towards them. Before Sarah had even scraped her chair back, a figure seemed to appear from nowhere, grab the kid from behind and throw him to the ground. Shoppers and tourists scattered as if a bomb had been thrown among them. People at the cafés screamed and hid behind tables. Sarah and Stuart stood up and moved away.

The kid in the sweatshirt lay on his stomach, the other man

standing with one foot between his shoulder blades, holding a gun on him and talking on a radio handset. He was only medium height, but muscular, fit-looking, blond-haired.

'Hey, man!' the kid protested. 'You're hurting me. I only came to get her autograph, tell her how sorry I was about what happened to her partner. That ain't no crime, is it?'

'Shut up,' the other said, increasing the pressure on his foot so the kid screamed. 'Just shut the fuck up.'

Within moments, two security guards from the mall had arrived on the scene and the kid was being dragged away.

Stuart took Sarah's arm. She was shaking. 'Come on, honey,' he said. 'I'd better get you back to work.'

'What happened?' Sarah asked, in a daze, allowing Stuart to lead her towards the exit. 'Was that *him*?'

'Probably not. Like he said, just a kid after an autograph.'

'Who was the other man?'

'That was Zak, our bodyguard.'

'I'm glad he's on *our* side.' Sarah felt a little dizzy, and her heart was beating fast. 'I'm okay,' she said to Stuart, disengaging her arm. 'Just a bit shaken, that's all. If people keep treating my fans that way, I won't have any left before long.'

33

Not much more than an hour after Arvo left a balmy late afternoon in Orange County, he arrived in a chilly, foggy San Francisco. He picked up his gun from airport security and headed for the cab stand.

The area around the airport was clear enough, if you didn't count the dirty rags of cloud in the darkening sky, but fog loomed ahead over San Bruno Mountain as the cab sped along the Bayshore Freeway, past the still grey water around Candlestick Park, jutting out to the east.

Arvo had called the airport from Carl Buxton's house and found out the time of the earliest available flight. After that, he had phoned a hotel he knew near Chinatown and booked a room for the night.

He had left a message for Sarah Broughton at the studio, asking her if she could remember anything about a member of Gary Knox's entourage called Mitch, and leaving the name of his hotel. He had also let the lieutenant know where he was going and why, then he phoned Joe Westinghouse to see if Mitch's name rang any immediate bells with Robbery-Homicide. It didn't.

Around Union Square, it seemed to Arvo as if the fog really were some vast sea-wraith that had slid under Golden Gate Bridge and insinuated itself through streets, under doorways, smudging the neons and the streetlights, reducing the city to a few smears of blurred pastel on a grey canvas. It looked like a futuristic, *Blade Runner* kind of world; all it needed to

complete the picture was steam rising from soup-vendors'
pots and people standing around at open counters eating
noodles in the mist.

Arvo paid the cabby and checked into the hotel near the
Chinatown Arch on Grant Avenue. It was close enough to
North Beach. He hadn't bothered renting a car; he knew from
experience that wheels were more of a liability than a blessing
in San Francisco. If he got tired climbing the hills, he could
always hail a cab or jump on a cable car.

First, Arvo took a quick shower. He wished now that he had
taken the time to go home and at least pack a change of
clothes; he would stick out like a sore thumb in some of the
places he was likely to be visiting tonight. It could have been
worse, though, he decided, getting dressed. For his meeting
with Carl Buxton he had put on light khaki slacks, a tan
button-down shirt and his sport jacket. At least his appearance didn't scream COP.

When he walked out onto Grant Avenue, he wished he had
brought an overcoat, too, or at least a sweater. The fog seemed
to have cold, ghostly fingers that pried deep and soon found
every weak spot in every bone and muscle in his body.

Beyond the Chinatown Arch, the stores were open. Garish
displays of T-shirts, electronics, handicrafts and Oriental gifts
spilled out onto the sidewalk. Fog blurred the edges of the
neon characters over the stores. Tourists milled around asking
themselves if the no-name portable CD-player they bought
here at a giveaway price would really work when they got it
back to Buckeye, Sawpit or Bullhead City.

He heard the insistent clanging of a cable car as he
approached California. Then he saw it glide through the fog
across the intersection ahead of him like some special effect
from an Andrew Lloyd Webber musical. San Francisco could
get you like that sometimes.

Now and then Arvo fancied he caught a glimpse of

workshops through grimy basement windows, sweatshops where people pressed clothes in clouds of steam, or printed local newspapers and flyers. Though the bad old days were long gone, when the area was a poor, cramped ghetto riddled with opium dens, child prostitutes and disease, Chinatown could still seem like an overcrowded warren riddled with connecting passages and rooms beyond rooms, none of them empty.

Arvo turned right at Broadway, which pretty much marked the boundary between Chinatown and North Beach. Carl Buxton had said that Mitch used to be a bouncer in a North Beach strip-joint, so at Broadway and Columbus, Arvo started with the first place he saw. At the intersection, he could hear the regular two-tone droning of the foghorn from the Bay beyond the traffic noise.

Inside the bar, the smoke created the same effect as the fog outside. A top-heavy black woman on the stage moved to some bump-and-grind song Arvo didn't recognize. It hardly mattered, anyway, as her movements were out of sync and the meagre audience was more interested in the flesh she was about to display than anything else. Having no intention of staying in any of these places long enough to catch something, Arvo went straight to the bar to start asking questions.

He struck out in the first three places; staff turnover being what it was, he couldn't find anyone who had been in the job for more than six months. In the fourth place, he found a waitress who said she'd worked there for two years and thought she recognized his description of Mitch.

After twenty dollars had disappeared down the front of her lacy black panties, which was all she was wearing, he realized he'd been conned. He declined the blow-job, offered for only another twenty, and moved on. He supposed he should have been flattered by the price; he'd heard that the older you are, the more they charge, seeing as it takes you longer to get it up.

At the sixth place, thirsty from walking and talking and breathing so much second-hand smoke, he ordered a beer. What came from the tap would probably have failed any rigorous scientific test, but at least it was fizzy and cold. The bartender knew nothing of Mitch but suggested he ask Martha, the club's manager. As she happened to be talking to one of the waitresses only a few feet away, Arvo asked her if she would join him.

Martha was a squat, barrel-shaped woman in her early fifties. Her intelligent green eyes gave the impression that what she hadn't seen wasn't worth seeing. She had a dark mole beside her nose, with three hairs growing out of it, and a square chin under an almost lipless mouth, as thin and red as a razor slash. Her hair, which was cut short and layered, seemed a natural, healthy chestnut colour, though Arvo had been fooled before by the magical properties of chemicals. She wore a light-green cotton blouse tucked into the waist of a brown skirt that fell well below the modesty level.

Martha hoicked her hard, square butt onto a stool and looked ready to listen to yet another hard-luck story she didn't want to hear. On the stage, a flat-chested, anaemic dancer stumbled through the motions with her eyes half closed. Arvo thought he could see needle-marks on the insides of her thighs, but they might have been tiny moles, or a rash of some kind. Diaper rash, maybe, judging by how young she looked.

'Cop,' said Martha. A statement rather than a question.

Arvo nodded and pulled out his badge.

She scrutinized it. 'LAPD.'

'That's right.'

'Long way out of your jurisdiction, aren't you, sonny? I'll bet you don't even have any power up here.'

Arvo smiled. 'No more than any other citizen, ma'm.'

Martha looked him up and down. 'You've got the tan,' she

said, 'and the look, but you still don't seem one hundred per cent purebred La-La-Land asshole to me.'

'Maybe that's because I'm from Michigan.'

'That right?'

'Yeah. Detroit. Well, Birmingham, really. It's a sub—'

'I know where Birmingham is. Know *what* it is, too. Other side of the tracks.' She pointed to her formidable chest. 'Hamtramck. My daddy was a drunk and my mother was a saint. What do you want to know, Mr Arvo Hughes?'

Arvo smiled and shook the strong, dry hand she held out, then he told her what he knew about Mitch. 'Can you help?' he asked.

'Sure,' she said. 'I know Mitch. Mitchell Cameron. Haven't seen him for a while, but I know him sure enough. One of the meanest sons of bitches I ever had the misfortune to employ.'

Arvo took out his notebook. 'When was this?'

'About eighteen months ago. Sometime last summer, anyway.'

'What did he do?'

Martha paused for a moment and asked the bartender for a glass of milk. When she got it, she took a sip, made a sweeping gesture around the club and said, 'I don't know if you're familiar with this business at all, son, but the last thing you want is trouble. Sure, sometimes you get a customer cuts up a bit rough. When men get all excited they have a way of thinking with their dicks. And believe me, none of them are big enough to hold enough grey matter to understand a simple "No." So you need a bit of muscle around.' She laughed. 'Helps if they're eunuchs, of course, but hell, most of 'em have taken so many steroids they might as well be.'

Arvo laughed. 'How did Mitch fit in?'

'Well, Mitch was different. For a start, he wasn't so much muscular and threatening physically as he was mentally intimidating. He had killer's eyes and a scary presence. To put it simply, he scared the shit out of most people and never even had to lift a finger. Not that he couldn't if he wanted. That was the trouble.'

'He hurt someone?'

'Real bad. Damn nearly killed a guy. Not that it would've been any great loss, but like I said, the last thing we want in this business is the place swarming with cops.'

'What happened?'

Martha tossed back the last of her milk, saw Arvo looking puzzled and grinned. 'Stomach,' she said, patting her corseted midsection. 'Never has been quite what it should be. I blame it on too much borscht when I was a kid. Anyway, why drink the profits? What happened? The usual. Some drunken asshole gets a bit too fond of one of the dancers, and all of a sudden he's in love. A case of the spirit being willing but the flesh being weak, if you get my point.' She winked. 'Anyway, he's grabbed the girl and he's pulling her towards his lap when Mitch goes over. Instead of being Mr Diplomacy like he should and ushering the guy out with apologies and promises of good times to come, what does Mitch do? He breaks the guy's arm, is what. Just like that. Where the guy has his arm stretched out, dragging the girl, who's crying and pulling back, Mitch just puts the arm over his knee like it was a stick of firewood and snaps it. You could hear it crack over the music.'

Arvo shook his head in sympathy.

'And that was just for starters,' Martha went on. 'As if that wasn't enough he hits the guy flush in the face and breaks his nose. Blood all over the place. Then he starts banging the guy's head on the table.'

'What did you do?'

'Do? Well, luckily for us the guy was playing away from home – some asshole at a weedkiller convention or something – and he didn't want his wife and kids to know he'd been sniffing around strange pussy. So we got him to the hospital, told them he'd been mugged, and got him taken care of. It wasn't too hard to dissuade him from bringing the cops in. I got rid of Mitch.'

The music stopped and the dancer took a bow, almost falling off the stage as she did so. Martha pulled a face of disgust at the girl but said nothing. Arvo guessed the poor anaemic dancer didn't have much longer in this job.

Martha laughed.

'What?' Arvo asked.

'Just remembering. The girl, the dancer the asshole was grabbing. I think she and Mitch had a thing going. She kind of liked the attention, anyway. I think it excited her. Mitch was her hero for the night.'

So the girl had been impressed by Mitch's use of violence. Enough, Arvo wondered, to make him think, as his mind became more unbalanced, that the way to a woman's heart was to kill for her? 'Do you remember her name?' he asked.

'Candi, I think. With an "i."'

Arvo made a note of it. Hadn't Carl Buxton mentioned a Candi, too? 'Would you happen to have her address anywhere?'

Martha shook her head. 'Sorry, honey. Candi's *ancient* history. She was only with us a couple of weeks, as I remember, and we never did get around to the paperwork.'

'How did Mitch react to being fired?' Arvo asked.

'Pretty well. Admitted he got out of line. Begged for another chance, of course. Who doesn't? When he saw he wasn't going to get it, he said he'd got a better job lined up anyway and then he up and left.'

'Was there a job?'

'Search me.'

'Did he make any threats of revenge?'

'Nope.'

'And there were no unusual incidents afterwards?'

'No.'

'Do you know anything about him?' Arvo asked. 'His private life, his background? That sort of thing.'

Martha shook her head. 'Sorry. I never socialize with the hired help.'

'Do you know if he'd ever been in trouble with the police?'

'I'd say he'd be hard-pressed not to have been, wouldn't you? But I can't say for certain. He sure as hell didn't put it in his résumé.'

'What about a mental institution?'

She shook her head. 'He always seemed in control to me, even when he broke the guy's arm. Cool as anything. But I suppose there are all kinds of mental illness. He was very manipulative, but that's hardly a mental illness, is it, or most of our politicians would be in the crazy house.' She shook her head. 'Again, I can't say I know anything about it. Sorry.'

'Parents? Family?'

'No – Oh, wait a minute. One of the girls had been talking to him and she said she felt sorry for him because his parents died when he was young and he'd been raised by foster-parents. He had a brother and a sister, too, but I never saw them. Something wrong with the brother, some sort of disability.'

'A mental disability?'

'No. Physical. Blind or something. Sorry, I can't remember.'

The music blared up again as another dancer hit the stage.

'You must have had some personal details?' Arvo said. 'Maybe from his employment application?'

'Sure.'

'Do you still have it?'

'I think so. In the office.'

'May I—'

But Martha was already on her feet. 'Wait here,' she said. Then she turned and added to the bartender, 'Give him a shot of bourbon while he's waiting. On the house.'

Arvo accepted his drink, thanked the bartender and swivelled his stool to watch the show.

She was a bouncy blonde with a bright toothpaste smile, very large and impossibly firm breasts, and a perky, energetic dancing style. She certainly looked healthy enough, and Arvo found her act about as sexy as watching an aerobics class. But then, he reflected, some people found aerobics classes sexy. Hadn't most of the people who watched that '20-Minute Workout' years ago been men? It took all sorts.

Martha came back with a sheet of paper in her hand. She handed it to Arvo and he looked over the scant information. She was right; it didn't say much. It did, however, give a Social Security number, a reference address, from another bar by the looks of it, and an address and telephone number on Collingwood.

Arvo pointed to the address. 'Where is that?' he asked.

'He's not there any more,' said Martha. 'I can save you the trouble of going there. We mailed a couple of forms to him, internal revenue stuff, but they came back return to sender.'

Arvo nodded. 'Can you remember exactly when that was?'

Martha frowned. 'Not exactly, no. But I'd guess it was about six, maybe nine, months ago.'

'Where is Collingwood, anyway?' he asked.

'It's down past the end of Market Street. In the Castro.'

Arvo looked up from his notebook with wide eyes. 'The Castro? Isn't that—'

Martha waggled her left wrist. 'Sure is, honey.'

34

Sarah didn't get Arvo's message because stars simply don't get most of the messages people leave for them. Given that they are protected by a gauntlet of secretaries, bureaucrats, gofers, security guards and highly guarded phone numbers, it isn't surprising. Sometimes it seems the only people who *can* get through to them are the crazies.

So Sarah wasn't thinking about Mitch when shooting finished for the day and everyone disappeared into the night. Had she been thinking about him, it is doubtful that she would have remembered much anyway, as she had hardly noticed him; to her, he had been just another vague shape in the haze, someone to hold open a car door while she smiled, stumbled in and fell over the seat.

It was almost nine, and Stuart should be waiting for her over in his office. At night, the lot was well lit and there were enough people still coming and going, some of them security, that Sarah didn't feel especially afraid.

It had been a frustrating evening spent filming a short, simple scene over and over again until Sarah got sick to death of saying, 'Please, Mrs Sanchez, you must understand we're not here to cause you any trouble.'

She blamed herself for not concentrating hard enough, as she had told Stuart at lunch, but if truth be told, everyone was so stunned by Jack's murder that no one was firing on all cylinders. But, as Stuart had said, the series goes on, and you're either on the bus or you're off it.

Sarah sighed. Sometimes she wished she were back in rep performing old chestnuts by the likes of Noel Coward and Terence Rattigan, with the occasional Restoration comedy thrown in for good measure. There were times when she almost missed the poky digs with the peeling wallpaper, the toilet next door flushing loudly at all hours of the night, the hot water that never worked, the cold toast and runny egg for breakfast and the overcooked roast beef and soggy sprouts for dinner.

Instead, she spent her days surrounded by union technicians in fake courtrooms and precinct offices with computer-produced backdrops for views, speaking trite, witless dialogue.

Still, she told herself, the money was good, and instead of the poky digs she had the beach house. Or used to have.

As she turned a corner by a row of trailers, she heard the hum of a studio cart come up behind her and slow down. She suddenly felt exposed, found herself looking for the best direction in which to run. A group of technicians stood outside one of the sound stages having a smoke, and she knew she could make a break and dash over to them if she had to.

She tensed as the cart drew up alongside her, but it was only Geoff, one of the lighting technicians, a fellow Brit from Newcastle, slowing down to ask if she wanted a ride. Gratefully, she took him up on his offer. But even then she found herself wondering if *he* could be the one. He dropped her off at the administration block and waited outside until she had gone through the door.

She checked in with the security guard at reception, who told her nobody would get past him. Stuart wasn't back yet, so she waited in his office, watching *Murphy Brown*.

She turned the TV off when *Murphy Brown* finished at nine-thirty and looked out into the long corridor to see if Stuart were coming. Though there were still some people working, most of the office workers had gone home and the place had that eerie, deserted feel of the *Marie Celeste*. It even looked like a long deck on an ocean liner with cabin doors on either side.

She checked her watch again. Quarter to ten and still no sign of Stuart. What the hell could be keeping him?

At ten o'clock, she started pacing the office, looking out the door every few minutes. At a quarter past ten she finally saw Stuart turn into the corridor from the stairwell.

He was out of breath when he got to the office. 'Sorry I'm late,' he said. 'Hope you weren't worried.'

'What happened? Long meeting?'

'Accident on the freeway, is what. I tried to call you here, but the fucking car phone's gone kaput.'

Sarah smiled. 'Not to mind. Ready?'

'Let's go.'

They got into Stuart's Caddy out front and waved to the guard at the gate as they left the lot. Because Sarah was regarded as being safe at the studio, and her friends were in danger, Zak the bodyguard had kept an eye on Stuart during his trip to Hollywood and his meeting there. Now he would have driven on before them to check out Stuart's house.

The freeway was busy, but not unusually so, and before long they were coasting Sunset heading into Brentwood.

Flat-roofed, all white stucco, plate-glass, and sharp angles, Stuart's house was a modernist monstrosity, at least to Sarah's taste. Though she would never tell him so, she thought it looked like a dental clinic.

On a slight incline, the house was reached by a semicircular driveway that turned off a residential street, ran past the front door, then rejoined the road again.

Zak's grey Toyota was already in the carport just off the driveway. The motion-detecting lights came on as Stuart pulled to a halt outside the front door. Inside the house, some of the lamps were lit, all synchronized by a complicated system of timers to make it always seem as if there were someone at home.

Sarah turned her back on Stuart to get out of the car and immediately became aware of a sudden flurry of activity behind her. The next thing she knew, Stuart had slumped back in over the front seat, groaning.

She was on her feet by the passenger door, which she hadn't closed behind her yet, and now she saw the figure standing back in the shadows near the trunk of the car, simply beckoning for her to come, crooking his finger.

She screamed for Zak, but nobody came.

She jumped back in the car as quickly as she could, pulled Stuart all the way in and locked the doors. When she looked through the back window, the figure was still there, all in black, standing completely motionless, as if rooted to the spot, waiting for her to get her purse or something.

Sarah could feel her heart pounding so hard she thought it would burst. Christ, how she wished that she could *drive*. She had to do something; she couldn't just fall apart. Stuart was groaning beside her clutching his stomach, maybe dying, and she was sitting there like a fool waiting for the cavalry to come.

There was no cavalry. Where the hell was Zak?

And still the dark figure stood there behind the car, watching. All she could make out was that he was medium height, fairly muscular, and blond-haired. Christ, she thought, could it even *be* Zak?

The car doors were locked; the phone didn't work; the key was still in the ignition. There was only one thing she could do.

Turning sideways, she dragged Stuart over towards the passenger side. It took all her strength, but there was a lot of room to manoeuvre inside the Caddy, and she finally did it. When Stuart was half on the passenger seat and half on the floor, she climbed over the back and into the driver's seat.

Her hand slipped on the leather and when she saw the whole seat was glossy and slippery with blood, she almost lost control.

She pounded the wheel and screamed, shutting her eyes and praying all the horror would go away and she would wake up to the sun on the Pacific. But Stuart was groaning on the floor, curled in the foetal position. She had to do something *now*.

Then Sarah looked out of the window to the passenger side and saw the face of her tormentor staring back at her. She couldn't make out his features clearly because they were superimposed on her own reflection in the glass, but she could have sworn he was smiling at her. *He looked pleased with himself.*

He tapped on the window.

Sarah took a deep breath and turned the key in the ignition.

35

Arvo waited for the stoplight at Broadway and Columbus, breathing out plumes of fog and holding his jacket collar closed around his throat to keep out the chill.

There was an Italian restaurant near here, he remembered, where he had dined with Nyreen on their one and only weekend in San Francisco last March. What a weekend it had been: glorious sunshine, walking, eating, shopping, making love, a ferry ride to Sausalito and deli sandwiches and wine on the beach looking back over at the San Francisco skyline.

No, he mustn't get caught up in those memories again. While cops can enjoy beauty as much as the next person, given the right circumstances, the job often alters their perceptions, and they don't always see things the same way other people do.

Cop vision, Arvo had often thought, compares more to those heat-sensitive photographs that describe the world in reds and greens and oranges, the way he remembered seeing the city spread out on the monitor during a night ride in one of the LAPD helicopters. In vivid, shifting primary colours, they see the dark side, the predators and prey, losers, grifters, the starving and the desperate, the con men, the lost souls and the psychos.

Finally, Arvo was able to cross. He started down Columbus, passed the City Lights Bookstore and found Vesuvio's, directly across the garbage-strewn Jack Kerouac Alley.

Inside was almost as colourful as the mosaic-like

stained-glass and tile exterior, with local artworks on the walls, along with a framed set of W.C. Fields playing cards, each with a photo and a legendary saying from the old curmudgeon himself. The place was crowded and noisy, but at some of the tables, people were ignoring the clamour all around them and sitting hunched forward, hands over their ears, concentrating on chess games. Around the top was a gallery with more tables looking down on the bar's main floor. Dress styles and ages varied, Arvo noticed, but there was a general air of youth and artiness.

The small area behind the bar was cluttered, too, and most of the stools were taken. A small canvas screen hung high on the wall above the ranged bottles, and a slide show of old Victorian nudes and music-hall personalities flickered over its surface.

When he had got his glass of Anchor Steam beer, Arvo asked the woman behind the bar if she had ever heard of Mitch Cameron, and gave as good a description as he had. She said he sounded vaguely familiar but it would be better to ask Cal over there, because Cal had been around for ever and knew everyone.

Cal was a modern beatnik of about fifty, with a beard and wispy grey hair poking out of a black beret cocked at a rakish angle. He was sitting at the bar reading a book of poetry written in lower-case letters with lines of wildly differing lengths. Beside it was a notebook and a chewed yellow HB pencil stub.

When Arvo tapped him on the shoulder, he turned his head slowly. His eyes were as grey as his beard and attempted – but didn't quite manage, in Arvo's estimation – a look of infinite wisdom and compassion.

'I'm looking for someone who knows a guy called Mitch Cameron,' Arvo said, without introducing himself as a cop. 'The bartender said you know everyone.'

Cal smiled. 'Guess that's true. Mitch Cameron, you say?'

His face darkened a little. 'Sure, I know him. He hasn't been around here for a year or more.'

'Any idea where he might be?'

'No. And I can't say I care, either. I didn't really know him well. What happened was, one day he showed me his poems and asked me what I thought.'

'What *did* you think?'

'They *rhymed,* for Chrissake!'

'What did you tell him?'

'That they were full of clichés and pious platitudes masquerading as philosophy, and that he should send them to those greeting-card people. What's their name? Hallmark?'

'How did he respond?'

'Punched me in the face, picked up his folder and walked away. Why are you asking? You a cop or something?'

'Uh-huh,' said Arvo.

'I knew it. I can spot cops a mile away, man.'

Good for you, Arvo thought. 'Some people say he's a scary character.'

'Maybe they should've told me that before I said what I thought of his poetry. He damn near broke my jaw. That's scary enough for me. The man's crazy.'

'Know where he might be right now?'

'Nope. Sorry, man, I can't help you, but there's one of the chicks used to run with his crowd upstairs. Can't miss her. Ditzy looking brunette, strictly space cadet, nobody home.' He tapped his skull. It didn't echo, but Arvo got the point. 'Hangs out in the lady psychiatrists' booth.' And he turned back to his poetry book, scribbling something illegible in the margin.

Arvo hadn't a clue what Cal meant, but he made his way up to the gallery, which turned out to be less crowded than downstairs. Then he saw a little nook with a joke sign reading 'Reserved for Lady Psychiatrists' hanging over it, and two people at the table.

He walked over, told them his name and said he was look-ing for Mitch Cameron.

'Mitch?' said the woman. 'Oh, yeah. Shit, Mitch. Right. Sit down, sit down.' A long skinny arm shot out of her baggy sleeves and she gestured for him to sit. She had rings on all her long, thin fingers, including the thumbs. 'This is Brook,' she said, introducing the angst-ridden young man next to her, with his pale complexion and lock of hair falling over his eye. 'He's working on a movie screenplay and he wants me to be in it, don't you, Brook?'

Brook glared at Arvo and grunted. Wants to get laid, more like, thought Arvo. Screenplay. Jeez, some things don't change even north of Santa Barbara.

'I'm Candi,' she said. 'With an "i."'

At last, the elusive Candi. Exotic dancer and blow-jobber *par excellence*. 'Pleased to meet you,' Arvo said. 'Is there a little heart over it?'

She frowned. 'Over what?'

'The "i"?'

Candi just looked confused. Maybe she hadn't seen *LA Story*. She had long straggly brown hair that looked as if it could do with a good wash. Her face was pleasant and open, free of make-up, but it had that blurred, unfocused quality, like her eyes, and probably like her life. Drugs will do that to you. Arvo didn't know if she were drunk or stoned right now, but she was something. He hoped she was older than she looked.

'I'm trying to find Mitch,' Arvo explained slowly. Candi's eyes were on him but not quite fixed. She had a mixed drink in front of her and sucked it through the crushed ice as he talked, making a slurping sound. Brook lit a cigarette and stared at the slide show. Arvo decided there and then it would be best not to tell them he was a cop. Maybe they'd guess, like Cal, but he wouldn't put money on it. He probably looked like a tourist. Or a bookie.

'He's gone,' Candi said finally.

'Do you know where?'

'Why do you want to know?'

'He owes me some money.'

'Huh. Good luck.'

'Do you know where he's gone?'

'LA. We went down there with Gary Knox, you know, the rock star, the guy who died of an overdose last year.' She nudged Brook. 'I fucked him, you know,' she said to him. 'I fucked Gary Knox.'

'Oh yeah?' said Brook. 'What was he like?'

Candi frowned, then giggled. 'Well, would you believe it, I can't remember. Maybe I just blew him. What the hell.' She waved her arm and almost knocked over her drink.

Better work quick while she's still on her feet, Arvo thought. 'So Mitch stayed in LA?'

'What? Oh, yeah. Well, like, I had this new dancing job to come back to and all, but Mitch, he didn't have nothing. He'd gotten fired. You know why, man?' She nudged Brook.

'No. Why?' he mumbled.

'For protecting me from this drunk asshole who was, like, grabbing my tits, that's why.' She looked at Arvo, eyes burning briefly with excitement at the memory. 'Broke the guy's fucking arm, Mitch did. And his face. His nose, I mean. Got himself fired. Shit.' She giggled. 'He was my knight in shining armour.'

'So Mitch stayed in LA?'

'Uh-huh. Said it was his big chance.'

'Big chance? How?'

'Mitch wanted to be a rock star. Didn't you know that? He played guitar, wrote songs and poetry and stuff. Gary Knox said he liked them and Mitch thought maybe he'd record some. Maybe he'd even let Mitch be in his band. But he died.'

'Do you remember Gary's girlfriend at the time? Sally?'

Candi screwed up her eyes. 'I think so,' she said. 'Hey, is that the one who's on that TV cop show? I had this argument with a guy—'

'That's the one,' Arvo said.

She banged the table and made the glasses rattle. 'Whoo-ee! Holy shit! I knew I was right. That's twenty bucks Pete owes me.'

'Did you know Sally?'

'She was a cold one. Spaced out most of the time. No, we never talked. I fucked Gary, though. Did I tell you that?'

'You did,' said Arvo, smiling. 'What about Mitch? Did he like girls?'

'Pants or skirt, it didn't matter to Mitch. If it moved, he'd fuck it.' She laughed.

'He was bisexual?'

'Like a pendulum.'

'Did you notice how he got along with Sally?'

'Did he fuck her, do you mean?'

'How did he treat her?'

'He called her his Little Star. I don't think he fucked her. She was a cold one, man, did I say that already? Prob'ly like fucking an iceberg. But what would I know? I don't do girls. A girl's got to draw the line somewhere, don't you think?'

Arvo took a deep breath. He asked her if she knew what kind of car Mitch drove.

'A red one,' she said. 'Or it might have been blue. I don't know.'

Her head was starting to droop and loll onto her chest now. Brook seemed to be getting impatient beside her, Arvo thought, if indeed that was what the occasional tics and sighs coming from his general direction meant.

'Do you know where he might be living in LA, anyone he might be staying with?'

She shook her head without looking up.

'What about money? Work? He'd need a job. What kind of work does he do?'

At this she looked up. 'Security,' she said. ''S'all he can do apart from write songs. Bouncer. Bodyguard. Do you want to know the truth?' She wrinkled her nose and crooked her finger at Arvo to come closer. He did. Close enough to smell the gin on her breath. 'They sucked,' she whispered. 'His songs sucked. But don't you tell him I ever said that or he'd kill me.'

'He would?'

'Sure. I mean, I'm not his Princess, his Little Star, am I? Sure he would.' She started singing to herself, '"Twinkle, twinkle little star, how I wonder what you are . . ."'

At which point Brook put his hand on her arm and said, 'I wouldn't let him, baby. I wouldn't let anyone hurt you.' And he glared at Arvo with reinforced passion. Like hell, thought Arvo. From what he had heard, Mitch Cameron would make sushi out of someone like Brook.

There was nothing more to be learned from Candi. It was time to let the seduction run its course, if it wasn't already too late, and it was time for Arvo to head back to the hotel and check if there were any messages. Maybe he would call in Mitch Cameron's Social Security number. The DMV runs driving record checks for cops twenty-four hours a day, while you wait.

As he walked, Arvo remembered something Candi had said, and a little warning bell went off in his mind. She had said all Mitch could do was act as a bouncer or a bodyguard. Arvo had briefed Zak himself, and he remembered the compact body, the blond hair. Zak – Mitch. Surely it couldn't be . . . But if he was right, Sarah was in great danger. He pulled up his collar and hurried towards the hotel.

36

Try to stay calm, Sarah told herself. Right foot, gas; left foot, brake. At least that was how she remembered it. She pressed her right foot down. Why wasn't it moving? Then she remembered. First she had to shift the stick from *park* to *drive*.

She took her foot off the accelerator, pressed down on the brake and moved the lever. Then she stepped on the gas again.

The engine roared and the car started to shudder, but it still wasn't moving. She realized she still had the brake pressed down to the floor, so she let it go.

The car kicked up gravel and shot forward into the drive with a squeal of tyres, swerving wildly from side to side. Sarah panicked and trod hard on the brake without taking her foot off the gas. The car slewed into the shrubbery that lined the drive, hit the base of a small palm tree and skidded to a halt.

Sarah banged on the wheel and let her head drop. Tears blurred her vision. She couldn't do it; she couldn't possibly control this monster. She had felt the same way that time trying to drive out in the desert.

The engine had stalled, and all she could hear was Stuart's uneven breathing. Then she heard the noise of a car starting break the silence behind her, and she realized he was coming after her.

She didn't have any alternative now.

She started the car up again. The problem now was that she was out of the range of Stuart's motion-sensor lights, she couldn't see where she was going. Headlights. Where was the headlight control switch? It had been daylight in the desert.

There were dozens of switches and buttons on the dashboard, all with little symbols that were supposed to make them easy to use. Sarah couldn't understand a bloody thing, and she'd got the windshield wipers going and country music playing on the radio before the beams of light shot out and lit up the gravel drive and the road about fifty yards ahead.

Stuart shifted and groaned on the floor. His knees were wedged up against his chest, and his head rested between the edge of the seat and the door. He clutched his stomach with both hands, as if to keep his insides from spilling out.

'Stuart, can you talk?' Sarah asked.

'Bleeding . . . hurts . . .' was all she got out of him.

'I'm going to get us out of here,' she said. 'Just hang on.' Stuart groaned.

Sarah saw headlights in the rear-view mirror.

His headlights.

She put the car in *drive* again, eased her left foot off the brake and put her right foot on the accelerator, not too hard this time. The car coasted down the drive. At the end, Sarah turned right onto the road, but the arc of her turn was too wide.

A horn blared and two bright lights came straight at her. She held the wheel straight, and the oncoming car skidded across the road with a squeal of rubber, hit the curb and turned over.

Sarah kept her foot down.

She had no idea of how to judge the car's width and guess how much space she had around her. The Caddy was a big car, and she had always felt nervous when Stuart drove by the rows of parked vehicles in the street, sure he was so close he would hit someone getting out, or at least clip a wing mirror. There must be some secret to it. Lacking any knowledge of what it was, she decided the best she could do was stick with the car ahead and follow its tail-lights.

The windshield wiper squeaked across the dry glass every few seconds, and Garth Brooks was singing about a broken heart on the radio. Sarah loathed country and western, but she didn't dare take her eyes off the road ahead for a second and she didn't want to risk fiddling with the buttons and switches again.

A couple of oncoming cars blinded her with the dazzle of their headlights, honked their horns and veered away to the right at the last moment, when they realized she wasn't going to give way. It was a fairly narrow road by Los Angeles standards, and Sarah realized she must be hogging the centre.

The red tail-lights were still in front of her, and behind she could still see the glare of his headlights. There was a cloying, slightly metallic smell in the car now, and she realized it was Stuart's blood. Her hands felt sticky on the wheel and her jeans and T-shirt were stuck to her skin with blood and sweat.

At least Stuart was still alive, moaning on the floor beside her. The windshield wiper squeaked over the glass every second or so. Garth Brooks had given way to Tammy Wynette singing 'Stand By Your Man.'

Then she saw the intersection up ahead. Sunset. And a red light. The car in front edged as far left as he could without being on the wrong side of the road and stopped. His left-turn indicator started to flick on and off.

Sarah followed him over, took her foot off the gas and pressed down on the brake. At least she knew how to indicate a turn, and she pushed the lever by the steering-wheel. As she waited for the lights to change, she took the opportunity to press a few buttons on the dashboard and stop the windshield wiper without turning off her headlights.

But her respite lasted only a brief moment. Just when she

had succeeded in getting Tammy Wynette to give way to The Doors singing 'Love Her Madly,' a set of headlights grew bright in her rear-view mirror. *He* was still behind her.

She had no plan. She had to get Stuart to a hospital, that was clear enough, but where was the nearest one? There was a big medical centre in Santa Monica, but she didn't know how to get there. It was all she could do to stay on one winding road following the car in front, let alone negotiate right and left turns through the LA urban maze.

Before she could come up with any ideas, the light began to flash green and the car in front turned. Sarah took her foot off the brake, pushed down on the accelerator again and started to turn the wheel as she shot forward.

But she had put her foot down too hard and she didn't turn the steering-wheel far enough. Instead of gliding smoothly and effortlessly around the ninety-degree bend, she skidded too far towards the right.

The Caddy bumped over the curb. Metal scraped against the low stone wall of the house beyond the grass verge with an ear-wrenching scream, and Sarah saw sparks fly.

Instead of stopping, she kept her foot on the accelerator, and before she lost control completely she twisted the wheel sharply to the left. The back of the car clipped a signpost, then Sarah felt a bump as she passed over the curb and back onto the road again.

By now the traffic lights were favouring through traffic on Sunset, and Sarah managed to drive another two cars off the road in a blare of horns, blaze of lights and banshee screech of tortured rubber.

Christ, she thought, mouth dry, heart pounding in her throat, this was Los Angeles. She was more likely to get shot by an angry motorist than stabbed by a crazy fan. Surely a cop car would come along soon?

Now she was back on the road again, staying in the outside

lane, with tail-lights to follow, the going was a little easier. She could afford to think for a moment about what to do.

Her best bet, she reckoned, was to stay on Sunset and hope a police car came along. She kept looking around for flashing red lights, listening for sirens, but she couldn't hear any. She must have forced about five cars off the road already. Had nobody reported a crazy driver in the area yet?

She could try to drive Stuart to Cedars-Sinai. It was miles away, but all she had to do was keep going along the same road.

She thought she saw the lights of a garage at Barrington, but the traffic light was green and she was going too fast to pull over safely. Sunset wound on, all gentle curves and dips, nothing but curb, grass and houses on each side. There were no streetlights, and dark trees overhung the road.

But Sarah didn't dare risk turning off. She might get lost, get stuck on some dead-end street, and *he* would be right behind her, just waiting for her to make a fatal error.

The radio was playing the Stones singing 'Sympathy for the Devil' now, but she didn't bother trying to turn it off. In a way, any music was a comfort, a necessary link to the real world. Stuart shifted position on the floor, trying to push himself up onto the seat. He managed it about halfway, then exhausted his strength and slipped down to the floor again with a groan.

'Stuart?' Sarah asked. 'Are you all right?'

He mumbled something unintelligible and Sarah assured him again that they would soon get help.

She could smell his blood even more now it was getting warmer in the car. She didn't know how to operate the air conditioner, but at least she knew where the electronic window button was. She reached out and pressed it. The window beside her slid down slowly and silently, and a welcome gust of cool evening air blew in.

She saw lights ahead, and a red light started to blink at the back right of the car in front. Sarah was about to follow suit when she realized this must be the freeway. She knew she had to stay on the surface streets if she hoped to have any chance at all of surviving this nightmare. She couldn't drive on the freeway. They would die there for sure.

With a slight twist of the wheel, she edged over to the lane to her left. She managed to stay on Sunset and cross the bridge over the freeway, aware only in her peripheral vision of the speeding blurs of red and white light spread across the lanes below. Despite the breeze blowing in through her open window, she felt sweat bead again on her brow and start to itch behind her ears. It was worse than being under the studio lights.

As she crossed the overpass, she could see no one immediately ahead of her, and she felt frightened, alone, cut adrift. Luckily, someone exited the freeway just in front of her, heading east, so she eased her foot off the accelerator to let him in and settled down to follow. Her ankle and her neck were aching with tension. *His* headlights were still dazzling in her rear-view mirror.

Some of the curves south of Bel Air were very tight, and Sarah bit her tongue in concentration as she made them. It was still dark all around her, even as she passed the north end of the UCLA campus. No haven there. Best stay with the car ahead, which she saw as a kind of umbilical cord, her only lifeline reaching up from the bottom of a deep, dark shaft. She knew she wouldn't be able to handle both driving *and* thinking about where she was going at the same time.

Then, with a shock, she remembered that Cedars-Sinai was on *Beverly* Boulevard, not Sunset. She'd seen it on shopping trips to the Beverly Center. And she didn't know which cross-street to go down. Rising panic clutched tight at her chest and stomach. She just couldn't do it. Stuart was going to die. She would never be able to forgive herself.

Despair almost overwhelmed her. *He* was still behind her, his malevolent headlights blinding her whenever she looked in the rear-view mirror. She had no choice; she had to keep going, stay safe in the car and pray the police would stop her soon. She honked the horn loudly a few times, then kept it pressed down for a full minute, but nothing happened.

At least he hadn't tried to overtake her or run her off the road. If he had wanted to, he could have made her pull over at any time, broken the window, killed Stuart and made her go with him. He still could. Carjackings happened all the time in LA, and nobody in their right mind would stop to help.

But he hadn't. Why?

Perhaps, she thought, if he *did* try to run her off the road, he might injure her accidentally, and he didn't want to do that. It wasn't in the script. Whatever the full-range stretch of his fantasy was, he still felt the need to protect her at this point. It was *his* hallucination; nobody else could be allowed to control it. So he was running protection for her, saving her; he would bring things to an end his way, in his own time. Unless she could do something to stop him.

Suddenly, she noticed there were streetlights, and the street signs were white, with little bumps on the top. That meant she was in Beverly Hills. The road broadened here, east- and west-bound separated by a grass meridian, and the traffic started to move faster. Tall palms lined the roadside and beyond them stood the high walls of wealthy estates.

Suddenly a white stretch limo shot out of a hidden drive-way, and she couldn't swerve aside without clipping the front before the driver jammed on the brakes. It was only a glancing blow, but it shook her up and the panic sent her skidding over into the fast lane, causing another flurry of horns and squeal-ing brakes.

She righted herself and got back into the outside lane, moving slowly and carefully, ignoring the impatient drivers who honked at her from behind. Maybe hitting a limo in Beverly Hills would bring the cops down on her? She hoped so.

The radio was playing the Grateful Dead's 'Casey Jones' now. Up ahead, Sarah could see a tall glass office tower. Some of the windows were lit, but there would be no one around so late at night. There was also a large billboard advertising KOOL cigarettes. Civilization. Surely there must be cops around?

The road veered sharply to the left ahead, and as Sarah approached the corner she noticed the first flashing red light in her rear-view mirror. The limo driver, she bet, got straight onto the cops on his car phone.

She was just about to take her foot off the accelerator and put on the brake, when a bright cone of light shot down suddenly from the sky and enveloped her.

She put one hand up to shield her eyes, lost concentration and pressed the gas pedal instead of the brake. The car bounced over the curb at the corner and ran straight through the plate-glass window of the Hornburg Jaguar showroom in a shower of glass and screech of tortured metal.

Part Four

37

When Sarah opened her eyes all she could see around her was whiteness. Her mouth felt dry and her eyes prickled, as if they were full of ground glass, her lids under heavy weights. Pennies? Like they put on dead people's eyes? Maybe she was dead. Then the sounds and sights of the hospital room came into focus and someone bent over her.

'Sarah?' the voice whispered. 'Sarah?'

She groaned. 'What happened?'

'Don't you remember?'

Sarah closed her eyes again; they were so heavy. She tried. It was all very vague, but she thought she had been driving. Impossible. She couldn't drive. Something must be wrong with her mind, then. Brain damage; that was it. She was a vegetable. She tried, but she couldn't move her head. Her neck must be broken. She would be in a wheelchair for the rest of her life.

Seeing if she could move her hands, she reached out and touched skin. Hairy. A man's hand. Slowly, she opened her eyes again. It was the detective, Arvo. So she wasn't dead.

'Take it easy, Sarah,' he said.

She opened her eyes wider. They were beginning to feel better, less spiky. Arvo looked tired, his sport jacket all creased, bags under his red-rimmed eyes. 'You again,' she croaked. 'Have I really died and gone to hell?'

He smiled. 'I'm glad to see you haven't lost your sense of humour.'

She licked her lips. 'What happened?'

'You went off the road at Sunset and Cory. Want the good news first, or the bad?'

'The good.'

'You didn't hit anyone and you're not badly hurt.'

'And the bad?'

'You ran into a brand new Jag. The showroom owner's really pissed.'

'It's true, then? I *was* driving?'

'You might call it that. Others would disagree.'

'But I . . . I can't drive . . .'

'That's what the traffic cops told me.'

Slowly, her memory started coming back. 'There was a bright light, all around the car. It made me go off the road . . .'

Arvo nodded. 'Police helicopter. Thirty-point-five billion candlepower. No wonder it damn near blinded you. They'd been chasing you since about the sixth car you drove off the road. Which says a lot about the general level of driving in LA, don't you think?'

Sarah suddenly remembered something important and tried to sit up. 'Stuart? Is Stuart all right?'

She felt Arvo squeeze her hand and push her gently back down onto the pillows. 'Stu's going to be okay. He lost a lot of blood but they got him here in time. He might not be eating any burgers with the works for a while, but he'll live.'

'Thank God,' Sarah murmured. '*He* was after us. I think he stabbed Stuart. I had no choice. I didn't know any hospitals, how to get to one . . . I was scared of turning corners.'

'I know,' said Arvo. 'You did the right thing. You saved his life. Do you think you can tell me what happened?'

'I . . . I'm very thirsty . . . Do you think . . . ?'

Arvo passed her a plastic container of water with a bent straw and she sipped it greedily. When she'd finished, she gave a little burp and blushed. ''Scuse me,' she said, putting her hand to her chest. 'What about me? You said I was okay, but I feel like I've been through the wringer. I can't move my neck. Am I paralysed?'

'No. You're fine. It's mostly shock. Some minor cuts and bruises. Mild concussion. Nothing broken. They kept you in overnight for observation, that's all. You've been sedated. That's why you feel a little strange. And your neck's in a brace. Whiplash. You should have worn your seatbelt, you know.'

'Yes, well, I had other things on my mind. Does Karen know?'

'She's with Stu right now. Really, Sarah, don't worry. You both came through it okay. Would I lie to you?'

The left corner of her mouth twitched in a smile. 'You'd better not. Was I right? *Did* he stab Stuart?'

'Yes. Twice, in the stomach. Like to tell me what happened?'

Sarah collected her woolly thoughts and found that they were getting sharper. The sedative was wearing off and she was regaining her normal clarity. As best she could, she told Arvo everything, right from the start, when Stuart stumbled back into the car and she saw the man beckoning her. There was something she'd forgotten. The silver Toyota in the carport, that was it.

'Zak. Have you caught him? It *was* Zak, wasn't it?' she said. 'My so-called bodyguard.'

Arvo shook his head. 'I must admit that's what I thought, too, for a while. But no. Zak was in an auto accident on the west-bound Santa Monica Freeway earlier that evening.'

'The accident Stuart saw,' she said. 'The one that made him late. But I don't understand. It doesn't make sense. He can't have been. It was Zak's car at Stuart's. I saw it.'

'Maybe it was *like* his, but it wasn't his car.'

'Is he all right?'

'A few broken bones, but he'll live.'

'Thank God for that. I don't think I could stand another death on my conscience.'

'It's *not your fault,* Sarah. Try to remember that. Now what did the man look like? Did he look like Zak? Do you remember?'

'You haven't caught him?'

'No. He didn't bother hanging around when the cop car came after you.'

She shook her head. 'He was in the shadows, or my face was reflected over his in the window. He was dressed in black.'

'What colour was his hair?'

'Blond.'

'How tall was he?'

'Not really tall. Medium, I'd guess.'

'Fat or thin?'

'Medium, again. That's why I thought it must be Zak. I'd only seen him from a distance and they were the same size and colouring.'

'I know. Was this man muscular?'

'I don't know. I mean, he wasn't skinny or fat. It could have been muscle. I'm sorry I'm not being much help. I was so scared, so worried about Stuart, so confused.'

'It's okay. Did you recognize him?'

Sarah frowned. 'I didn't get a good look. Why? Should I?'

'Do you remember someone called Mitch? Mitchell Cameron?'

Her brow furrowed. 'The name sounds vaguely familiar.'

'From the tour with Gary. He was a kind of unofficial bodyguard, wanted to write songs for Gary, be part of the band. You met him in Vesuvio's in San Francisco. He looked after—'

'Yes,' Sarah said, her hand tightening on Arvo's. 'Yes. I think I know who you mean. I always called him "The Creep."'

'I was given to understand that *he* liked *you* very much.'

'Are you saying this Mitch is the one?'

'I don't know for sure,' Arvo said, 'but it's looking more

than likely. We know he came here to LA with the tour and we think he's still here. *Could* he have been the one?'

Sarah tried to picture the face at the car window. The problem was that she really hadn't got a good enough look, and she couldn't remember Mitch Cameron clearly. She knew the name, had a vague memory of his being around with his quiet brother, opening doors for her and such. But the truth was she had been either too stoned or too depressed to really notice anyone at that time. Sadly, she shook her head on the pillow. 'I'm sorry.' She felt something pushing at the surface of her memory, trying to get out, like a hand reaching through the darkness, clawing away the cobwebs. 'Just a minute.'

'What?'

'I've remembered something. It was my birthday. We were in San Diego, I think, and someone – maybe even Gary – hired a restaurant for a party with a cake and everything. They were all there. All stoned. I just have this mental image of someone starting to sing "Twinkle, Twinkle, Little Star" and everyone joining in. I think it was him who started it. Mitch.'

'Are you sure?'

'Yes! Yes.' She started to sit up but Arvo pushed her back gently and told her to take it easy. 'I knew I remembered it from somewhere,' she went on. 'I'm sorry, I really *wasn't* holding back before. When I first saw it written there, on the letter, it rang some sort of distant bell, but I didn't know why, or where. Now, all of a sudden, I can picture him singing it very quietly, almost under his breath, and looking at me with those eyes.' She shivered at the memory.

'Can you remember anything else about him?'

'Not really. I mean, he was a presence. He was around. He must have liked me because he was always smiling at me and calling me pet names, but he gave me the creeps.'

'Did he ever make a pass at you?'

'No. I don't think so. He never got that close, really. He was always just on the periphery, in the background. I think the closest he ever got physically was opening a car door for me.'

'When did you see him last?' Arvo asked.

'Before I went to stay with Ellie. He was . . .'

'What?'

'Nothing. Just something I thought I'd remembered, but it slipped away again.'

'You broke all contact with Gary and his entourage?'

'Yes. I never saw or talked to any of them again, and none of them ever tried to contact me.'

'Could they have found you?'

'Not easily. I was either at Ellie's or at the Shelley Clinic.'

'Did Gary know about Ellie?'

'Gary might have, yes. But Gary died.'

'No one else in the group knew you had a friend in the area called Ellie?'

'No.'

'So you disappeared into thin air.'

'Yes. And I wasn't in the public eye until the series aired in September. A year later.'

'Which is about the time you started to attract the stalker's attention.'

'But I didn't get the first letter until early December. That's over two months since the series started.'

'That makes sense. He's been trying to pluck up the courage to approach you. The first time he meets you – on the tour – you're both members of a crowd, a pretty weird crowd, and he forms some sort of attachment to you. Then you simply walk out of his life. He broods about you for a year. His attachment develops into an obsession, then suddenly there you are again, on television.

'He can't believe his good fortune. First, he has to find out where you live, then he watches you and fantasizes about you a lot. Guys like him often find anticipation even more exciting than the real thing. Sometimes anticipation is about all they can manage. And fantasizing is a major part of the obsession. At first, he's tentative. Everything's at a distance. The letters. Even the first killing. But now he's edging closer, getting braver. He's graduated to doing it right in front of you. He wants your approval.'

Sarah moved her head slowly. It made her feel dizzy. 'What will he do next?'

'I don't know. But he's getting more and more reckless.'

Sarah paused for a moment. 'Do you know,' she said, 'I had a funny thought while he was behind me in the car last night.'

'What?'

'That he was trying to protect me, not kill me.'

'I wouldn't count on that.'

'Like at the house, he just stood there and crooked his finger. He could have taken me if he'd really wanted to, but it's as if he wants me to come to him of my own free will. He seems to think if he arranges things right, that's what I'll do.'

Arvo leaned forward until his face was only inches from hers. She could see the stubble on his chin and smell mint breath freshener. 'Sarah, don't think for a minute that he won't come after you and force you to do his will. These guys, their fantasies don't work out exactly like they want and they're only too happy to give you a little help. Like I said, I think he might be unravelling, coming unstuck at the seams. He failed to kill me and he failed to kill Stu, and he won't like that.'

'Kill you? I don't understand.'

Arvo told her about the attempt to set fire to his house.

'I'm sorry,' Sarah said. 'I'm glad you weren't hurt. I wasn't trying to say I didn't think he was dangerous. I know he is. I mean, just look what he's done. Jack and all . . . It's just that . . . he could have taken me easily last night, but he didn't.'

'Then he's not reached that part in his script yet. Listen, this man is so completely self-centred that he has his own explanation for everything, and it doesn't involve any fault on his part. *He can't be put off.* If you slam the door in his face, then you're only being careful; if you insult him, it's only for show; if you shoot him, it's because you want him to enjoy the afterlife. Do you see what I'm getting at? Whatever you do to oppose him simply means you're not ready yet to recognize how much you love him. And he knows there are certain things he can do to help you come to that realization.'

'Like what?'

'Well, murder is obviously one of them. Beyond that, we don't know how far he'll go to make you see that you love him, that the two of you are meant for one another.'

Sarah swallowed. 'He's not just crazy, he's very clever, too, isn't he? Do you really think you can stop him?'

'We'll stop him.'

'How long?'

'I wish I could say. At least we've got some strong leads now. We're not just whistling in the dark any more. The more disorganized he becomes, the more he acts out of panic, then the more mistakes he's likely to make.'

'Where can I go until you find him? I can't go home and I can't go back to Stuart's.'

'I think the doctor wants to keep you here a little longer, this morning at least, just for a few more tests. You're safe here. We've got guards on the door. They'll keep the media away as well as the stalker.'

'The media? I'd forgotten about them. I suppose they know all about it now?'

'They monitor the police radios, so they know you were involved in an auto accident last night. I'm sure they're busy putting two and two together and making twenty-two. But they're the least of your worries.'

Sarah wrinkled her nose. 'Do I *have* to stay here? I hate hospitals. I can't stand the smell.'

Arvo smiled. 'I suppose I could always put you under arrest, get you a nice comfortable cell.'

'Arrest? For what?'

'You've got enough traffic violations to get you put away for quite a while.'

'Swine. What about work?'

'I don't know,' Arvo said. 'Maybe they can write a black eye, whiplash and a cut forehead into your character. It shouldn't be too difficult. Things like that do happen to cops sometimes.'

'It's not, is it? My eye? Black?'

Arvo nodded. 'Very.'

She put her hand to it. It didn't feel swollen, but it was throbbing a bit. 'You're enjoying this, aren't you?' she said.

'Not at all.' Arvo stood up.

'You don't look so hot yourself, you know.'

He ran his hand through his hair and sighed. 'I know. I didn't get much sleep. I got the first flight back from San Francisco after I got the phone call from Robbery-Homicide about what had happened to you and Stu. Look, I mean what I say, Sally. You've go to stay here for now. Don't worry. I'll be in touch soon. This afternoon. We'll work something out.'

'You called me Sally.'

'Did I? I'm getting confused. I suppose it must be because I've been talking to people who knew you as Sally. Gets to be a habit. Sorry.'

'I didn't say I minded.'

'Good.'

'Just who have you been talking to?'

'Stan Harvey, Carl Buxton, a woman called Candi. She was with Mitch when Gary picked him up in San Francisco.'

'I hope you don't believe everything you hear.'

'I'm a cop. I take most things with a large pinch of salt. There is just one more thing.'

She narrowed her eyes. 'What?'

'Maybe when all this is over you'll let me give you some driving lessons?'

'Bastard!' Sarah grasped the pillow beside her and threw it with all her might. But she couldn't move her neck, and her might wasn't up to much at the moment. Arvo dodged it easily. Then he was gone and Sarah was left alone in the stark white room with her black thoughts.

38

At eleven-thirty that morning, Arvo sat with Joe Westinghouse in a greasy spoon near Broadway and Fourth watching the seemingly endless parade of panhandlers and street people. It was probably happening in most big cities these days. Mixed in with the tall shiny office towers, the food courts, delis, pretty girls sitting by fountains, you also got the homeless and the crazy. You could always spot the crazies, he thought; they're the ones who wear woolly hats and tattered overcoats when it's eighty-five degrees and sunny out there. Maybe they have to keep their brains at a higher temperature than the rest of us.

Having eaten nothing that morning but a bag of salty pretzels on the plane, Arvo tucked into his ham and over-easy eggs with a total disregard for their cholesterol content. So, maybe he should have gone for the fresh fruit and bran special even the greasy spoons offered in LA these days. So what? He mopped up runny egg yolk with his enriched white-bread toast and enjoyed every mouthful.

Joe sat wedged in the booth opposite Arvo, shoulders taking up so much room no one could have found space next to him. He was wearing a neatly pressed brown suit, dazzling white shirt and muted tie. Arvo hadn't been home yet and was still wearing yesterday's clothes. They'd been to San Francisco and back on him, and they felt like it, too.

Joe held a sheet of paper in front of him and read as Arvo ate, pausing only to sip his coffee every now and then. He seemed able to do that without taking the toothpick out of the corner of his mouth.

'We got this from the Social Security number. Mitchell Lorne Cameron. Born January 3, 1967, Bakersfield, California.' Joe looked up and grinned. 'Well, what do you know? Looks like the little slimeball has a birthday today. I dug out the state birth records. Mother, Marta Cameron; father unknown. After that it got easier. According to the Bakersfield PD, Marta used to run with the local biker crowd, real motorcycle mamma, had a few run-ins over drugs, fights and the like, but nothing serious, no dealing or trafficking as far as they know.'

'What happened to her?'

'OD'd on heroin, July 21, 1972.' Joe sipped some more coffee. 'But not before she'd had three kids to three different fathers. Mitch was the middle one. He's got an older half-sister, called Marianne, and a younger half-brother, Mark. After Marta OD'd, a distant relative in Eureka took them all in.'

'Did you talk to this relative?'

'Nope. She's been dead five years.'

'Anything on the other two kids? They might be able to lead us to Mitch.'

'We're trying to trace them. It's early days yet.'

'Bar manager in San Francisco said something about the brother being disabled. She thought he was blind.'

'That's something we can check. Got to be registered somewhere.' Joe made a note.

'Anything else?'

'Sure. Plenty. Listen, while you've been having fun up in San Francisco watching strippers and sitting around here talking to pretty starlets, I've been on the phone, fax or computer. All morning.'

'Okay, so give me a hard time, why don't you.'

Joe grinned. 'I checked with ATF. No firearms registration.'

'Huh. Like half of LA. Doesn't mean he's not carrying, though, does it?'

Joe raised his eyebrows. 'He hasn't used a gun so far.'

'True,' said Arvo. 'But I don't think it's because he couldn't get hold of one. For some reason it's just not part of his scenario. Anything from DMV? I was going to call in from the hotel last night but I got the message about the accident first.'

'Yup. Drives a red 1990 Honda Civic. I got the number out on the street. The black-and-whites are keeping an eye open.'

'Photo?'

'Uh-huh. Driver's-licence photo. Not much good. Could probably be any blue-eyed blond kid in LA. After a while they all get to look the same to me.' Joe's eyes sparkled for a second and he flicked the toothpick towards his nose. 'The lab phoned and told me they *did* find some blond hairs at the Marillo scene. Dyed blond hairs.'

Arvo pushed his plate aside and sipped some coffee. 'It's looking good, isn't it? If only we could find the bastard. What about the address on the driver's licence?'

Joe put down his toothpick and lit a cigarette. 'Eureka. And I mean the place, not the classical allusion. The distant relative's address. It's a dead end. The people who live there now never even knew the old lady.'

'Shit.'

'My sentiments exactly.'

'What about the phone company, utilities?'

'Still checking. Nothing yet. At least not under his real name.'

'Why would he use an alias?'

'Maybe there are people he doesn't want to find him?'

'Like us?'

Joe shrugged. 'Maybe others, too. Maybe he owes money. Who knows? Anyway, all I could find was that he skipped out of San Francisco owing Ma Bell a few hundred bucks and they haven't come across his name since. Maybe that's why.'

'Can you pull the phone records?'

'Already being done.'

'Have you checked mental institutions?'

'Wondered when you'd get around to that. As a matter of fact, I didn't have to. I ran him through records. Seems he has a history of assault charges, mostly minor stuff, but about ten years ago in Stockton he went down on a felony assault charge. Bar fight.'

'What happened?'

'They sent him for psychiatric evaluation. Must've checked out okay because after that he did eighteen months in Tehachapi. Witnesses said the other guy started it. That went in his favour. Anyway, we've got his prints, for what good they'll do us.'

'Have you checked them against the Heimar and Marillo killings?'

'We got nothing from Heimar and only partials from the Marillo place. No guarantee they were the killer's, either. We ran a fingerprint check, but we couldn't come up with a positive match. The lab also found red cotton fibres, which indicated he probably wore gloves.'

'What about Stuart Kleigman's car?'

'I don't think we'll find anything there, either, but it's being done. This guy plans, Arvo, he doesn't just act on the spur of the moment.'

'But he's getting more and more careless. I don't suppose he's on parole or probation?'

'No such luck.'

'Did you check with the military?'

'Uh-huh. Drew a blank there, too.'

'What about the psychiatric evaluation? What were the conclusions?'

Joe stubbed out his cigarette in the foil ashtray. 'I've got someone digging it out for me,' he said. 'They'll fax it to us as soon as they can. I wouldn't hold out much hope, though. It'll probably just say Cameron had a short fuse and needed to learn to control his temper.'

'Probably. But you never know. Now, how do we find the son of a bitch? Anything from the IRS?'

The waitress came by with the coffee pot, and Joe pushed his cup and saucer towards her. Arvo declined. He'd already had too much coffee for one morning. Besides, it tasted like battery acid.

'You know how close-mouthed those bastards are,' said Joe, 'but I did get the date of his last return and the address it was sent from.'

'And?'

'Two years ago. An—'

'Let me guess, an address in the Castro, San Francisco?'

'You got it. Same one I got from the phone company.'

'Shit. That gets us no further. It's like he never got an address in LA at all.'

'I know. I've got a couple of guys back at Parker Center still checking around. You know, Welfare, State Licensing Board, Workmen's Comp.'

'I won't hold my breath. It looks like this one's slipped between the cracks since he left San Francisco.'

'Sure looks that way. For what it's worth, I also got a couple of guys putting more pressure on some of the agencies that sell celebrity addresses. Nothing so far, but you never know.'

'Right. And now we can try the car-rental agencies, too.'

'Why?'

'Because of what happened last night,' said Arvo. 'My guess is that Mitch has been watching Sarah's routine for a few days, just like he did when she was at the beach house. He noticed that Zak, the bodyguard, always went on ahead to check the house before Sarah and Stuart went back there from the studio. Last night, Zak rode shotgun for Stuart to a meeting in Hollywood while Sarah was safe at the studio. The stalker must have followed them and taken his chance on the way back. According to the accident report, there's at least one witness thinks someone deliberately pulled in front of Zak's car and forced him onto the hard shoulder. It's a miracle Zak wasn't killed.'

'But why check the rental outlets? We already know Cameron drives a red Honda Civic.'

'Because Sarah Broughton said she saw Zak's silver Toyota in the carport at Stu's house. Since we know it can't have been Zak's, Mitch must have gone and rented the same model, same colour.'

Joe whistled. 'Know how many car-rental agencies there are in LA? Know how many people per day rent cars?'

'We're only interested in silver Toyotas rented over the last three or four days. That should narrow things down a bit.'

'Uh-huh. Any other bright ideas?'

'One,' said Arvo. 'We know that about the only work the guy's done is security, club bouncer, and that he thinks he belongs in the rock business. Now, we can easily find out if he's working for any of the big, official security companies like Loomis or Brinks because he'd have to be bonded, right?'

'Right. We have, and he isn't.'

'Okay. So if he is working, he's probably somewhere they pay cash, no questions asked.'

'Like a bar or a nightclub?'

'Exactly. Or a strip joint. Just like he did in San Francisco.'

'Great,' said Joe. 'Only about ten thousand in the city.'

'You're right.' Arvo rubbed his eyes. 'Shit. There's got to be another way. Let's think it through. The guy comes into town with Mr Big Shot, Gary Knox, and his entourage. He must have some pretty big ideas about himself, right?'

'Uh-huh. Then the goose that lays the golden eggs OD's and the party's over.'

'Right, and the entourage is cut loose. The band members drift off into session work, retirement, or whatever. It's like the Stones without Mick.'

'The Vandellas without Martha.'

'Right. And I suppose the road crew and sound technicians find similar work with someone else.'

'And the hangers-on, the groupies?'

'They find someone else to fuck. Now, Mitch's position is ambiguous, I'd guess. Nobody liked him but Gary, or so it appeared. So no one's gonna take pity on him and give him a job. He's got no real skills or talent and probably no money, given he got fired in San Francisco and skipped out owing the phone company.'

'So?'

'So he's got a number of problems. He's already got a car. Next, he needs somewhere to live. Then he needs a job.'

'A job without too many questions asked,' Joe added. 'From what you've told me I doubt he'd get much of a reference from that broad in San Francisco.'

'You're right there. But there's something else. Mitch is a liar and a dreamer, a big talker. He thinks he's got talent, thinks he's got a future in the music business. He's also a man with a powerful will. So, do you think he's just gonna sit on his ass strumming his guitar, or work as a nightclub bouncer, till his big break comes?'

'If you're thinking—'

Arvo leaned forward and put his hands palm down on the table. 'An agent. It makes sense, Joe. Everyone in this city has an agent.'

Joe laughed. 'That's true enough. I even know a few cops have agents. Know how many of them there are?'

'I didn't say it'd be quick, just that it would be worthwhile,

maybe quicker than checking all the bars. And if we concentrate on small agents representing musical acts . . . What do
you think?'

'Could be.'

Arvo smiled. 'Unlimited resources,' he said. 'That's what
the Chief told me.'

'What now?'

'First I'm gonna go home, take a shower and change my
clothes. Then we're going to make a concentrated effort to
find Mitchell Lorne Cameron.'

'Okay, let's go.'

And they walked out into the bright noon sun.

39

At three o'clock that same afternoon, still no closer to finding Mitchell Cameron, but at least clean and wearing a fresh set of clothes, Arvo pushed a wheelchair out of Cedars-Sinai right into a throng of newspeople waiting outside.

Sarah Broughton sat in the chair. Her right eye was swathed in bandages, and she was wearing a neck-brace. She also wore dark glasses over the bandage to protect her one good eye against the bright January sun.

As soon as she hit the street, the questions began:

'Ms Broughton, can you tell us why you were driving down Sunset Boulevard yesterday evening without a licence?'

'Is there any truth in the rumour that you've been receiving death threats?'

'How will your injuries impact on Good Cop, Bad Cop?'

'Is it true that the network is thinking of axing the series?'

'Was it a publicity stunt?'

'Ms Broughton, why were you in the car with Stuart Kleigman? Why had his wife and children gone to stay with family in Santa Barbara?'

'Do these letters have anything to do with Jack Marillo's murder?'

'Ms Broughton. What's the connection between the body you found on the beach and the murder of Jack Marillo?'

'Are you being stalked, Ms Broughton?'

'Could you comment on the statement made by Luanna Costello, the famous psychic, that someone has put a curse on Good Cop, Bad Cop?'

'Is it true that the killer cut the hearts out of both victims and mailed them to you?'

And so it came from all sides – from the *Los Angeles Times* to the *National Enquirer,* from CNN to KFMB – boom microphones, mini-cassette recorders, TV cameras. Just the way it had been when she arrived at LAX after the news of Jack's murder.

Sarah kept her head down as Arvo helped her into the unmarked car, scanning the crowd and the surrounding area as he did so. He drove her the short distance round the block to Ma Maison Sofitel, the nearest hotel, on Beverly Boulevard.

Security at the beach house would be difficult to organize because the area was so open, Arvo had explained, so Sarah had agreed that even a hotel would be better than the hospital. At least it wouldn't smell of antiseptic.

Arvo accompanied Sarah up to her room, then, after checking the locks on the door and window and assuring her that she would be well guarded, he left, reminding her to lock up after him.

One of the hotel employees had picked up some books that Sarah had requested in advance and placed them on the coffee-table: Alan Bennett's *Writing Home,* the latest William Boyd paperback and a Sharon McCone mystery by Marcia Muller. Beside them lay a *New Yorker* magazine and a copy of last week's London *Sunday Times*. After all, they hadn't got Mitch Cameron yet; she might be here for a while.

Alone, Sarah set the deadbolt, put the chain on and leaned against the door to take a deep breath. Then she went into the bathroom, took the bandages off and examined her bruises for the first time. By the looks of them, her eye had a whole rainbow of colours to go through yet. Arvo was right, though; the writers could probably work her injuries into the show the way they had written in Jack's murder. Now the painkillers were wearing off, her face and head had started to ache.

Back in the room, she stood and looked out of the floor-to-ceiling window. It framed a spectacular and panoramic view from the eastern edge of the Santa Monica Mountains, on her left, through Beverly Hills to the Hollywood Hills to her right. The sky was pale blue, with a few swirls of cloud over the hills, and today there was hardly any smog to obscure the scene.

Dotted all around the ragged purple-brown horizon were clusters of buildings, signs of human habitation everywhere. To the far right, Sarah could just about make out the HOLLYWOOD sign. In the foreground were the streets of West Hollywood, mostly residential areas of small bungalows and low-rise apartment buildings, along with the trendy shopping streets like Melrose and La Brea.

As she scanned the view, inhibited by the damn neck-brace, Sarah had an odd, disembodied feeling, as if she were slipping into a dream. It was as if the hotel wasn't there, and she was suspended in mid-air over Hollywood. Her senses felt enhanced, as they had sometimes when she was stoned. But her mind was clear. She knew what was happening. Had known since she remembered Mitch calling her 'Little Star.'

Somehow, the terror of the chase or the car accident itself had jogged her memory and released a flood of information.

Sarah turned away from the window, feeling a little dizzy, and paced the room. God, she was tired; she hoped they caught the stalker soon. They were close; she could sense it in Arvo's manner, in the way he had hurried off after bringing her to the room, like a hound on the fox's scent. It was the thrill of the chase, the whiff of blood. She wanted her life back. All of it.

She helped herself to a gin and tonic from the minibar and sat down on the sofa. She didn't really want a drink, but she felt restless. It was something to do, and it might help take the edge off her nerves now the sedative had worn off. She thumbed through *The New Yorker* but couldn't seem to concentrate on anything. There was nothing on TV, either, except soap operas.

As soon as she tasted the gin, she thought of the tour. Gin and tonic had been Sarah's drink then, and the taste brought back memories. So did hotel rooms. They acted on her the way the 'madeleine' did on Proust.

Sometimes on tour, she would sit up all night with the band playing poker, smoking, drinking, maybe listening to late-night radio stations in Detroit, Chicago, Pittsburgh, New Orleans or Phoenix. She couldn't remember the places, just the one composite hotel room, the pills, the joints, the drunkenness and the hallucinatory quality of it all: someone fucking in the bathtub while one of the sound tekkies puked down the toilet; someone, maybe Gary or the lead guitarist, whatsisname, going crazy and trashing the room.

Now she had the memories back, they didn't matter. She knew now that she hadn't really lost her memory in the first place, hadn't blocked out incidents. The whole thing had been *exactly like* her memories of it. That was it. There *was* no more. The entire experience had been a blur; it *was* vague. That was exactly the quality that life had possessed above all others at that time: a kind of hallucinatory, jump-frame vagueness. What seemed blurred now *had been* blurred then. In fact, things were perhaps a little clearer *now* than they ever had been at the time.

It had been a long walk on the wild side for her – more of a stagger, really – and if she had slept with a few people she shouldn't have, so what? Chalk it up to experience. After all, she hadn't caught any diseases, and she had *come through*.

She also remembered the incident that had finally driven her to run away from the tour madness and into a different kind of madness of her own, the incident she had begun to tell Arvo about in hospital. Thank God she had stopped herself in time.

*   *   *

It had been a very hot day and the band was staying at a hotel in Anaheim. They were supposed to be playing at the stadium there the next night. Gary needed some designer-drug cocktail or other, and Mitch had found a guy who lived over in the trailer park across the road. Someone who dealt a little.

So, they had gone over. Gary, herself, Mitch and his brother. Inside, the trailer was hot and stuffy. One of the windows was open an inch, but it didn't help much. Someone had stuck yellow plastic daisy and sunflower appliqués on the walls beside the crude drawings of cocks and cunts, the kind of thing she'd once seen in a gents toilet in Bognor Regis one drunken night long ago.

Sarah was sitting in a battered armchair, she remembered, the kind with the seat so worn and low that it's difficult to get out of easily, especially if you're as spaced as she was. There was a fat woman at a table by the door silently removing her bright red nail polish, head bent so she showed at least three chins. She was wearing shorts and a black tank top that strained at its seams over her bulk. The acrid smell of acetone infused the hot, stale air.

The man from whom Gary was buying the drugs was skinny and wore only a pair of garish Hawaiian shorts. He had no hairs on his chest and a tattoo of an anchor on his upper right arm. His teeth were bad, like a speed-freak's; his long hair was greasy, and he hadn't shaved for a few days. He smoked one joint after another. The other man in the trailer looked like a biker to Sarah, with a full beard, beer gut, black T-shirt and torn, oil-stained jeans. The smell of oil and grease formed an undertone to the nail polish remover and marijuana smoke. Like the woman, he too remained silent.

The only ones doing the talking were Gary and the skinny guy. Sarah remembered wanting to leave, but she was so out of it, and so deep in the armchair, that she couldn't muster the energy.

Seven of them in there, then. And the dog. A bow-legged, mean-eyed, ugly pit-bull with a black-and-white snout. It looked like the dog equivalent of a shark, Sarah thought – single-minded, merciless, vicious – and it scared her the way it kept coming over to her and sniffing. She asked the biker to tell it to go away but he ignored her. So did the skinny guy and the fat woman too. They all snorted a sample of the designer drug. All except Sarah, who had just about had it by then, and Mitch's brother, who never touched drugs.

Everyone got more bright-eyed and excited. God knew what was in the cocktail, but they either seemed to find every word a priceless witticism or every sentence a pronouncement of the most profound importance. It was all getting to seem very silly to Sarah, who was coming down fast now, and she was trying to work up the energy to get out of the damn armchair.

But the dog wouldn't leave her alone. It kept sticking its snout in her crotch, pushing hard up against her. She kept shoving it away but it just glared at her and came back for more. She was wearing a short skirt, and the position she was stuck in, the dog could get its nose under the hem, right between her thighs and rub against her panties.

Getting scared now, she smacked it hard on the snout one time and it snarled at her. The others noticed then, distracted out of their drugged haze for a moment. Then the skinny guy pointed, said 'Look,' and they all started to laugh. Sarah couldn't see because of her position, so she twisted sideways and saw that the dog had an enormous erection.

She told them she didn't think it was funny and tried to get out of the chair again. But the dog stopped her. This time it put its forepaws up on her breasts and tried to straddle her. This brought howls of laughter from the skinny guy and the fat woman. Even the biker grinned. 'Hung like a horse, that dog,' he said.

Then, before Sarah knew what was happening, the dog was

sniffing and rubbing around her thighs with its snout, great hard-on down between its back legs, and the mingled smells of motor oil and marijuana smoke and acetone were stifling her, the heat making her skin burn and her heart pound. Christ, she was coming down so fast it was leaving skid-marks on her brain.

Someone tried to pull her out of the armchair. He got her almost all the way out, then she felt dizzy, slipped out of his grasp and slumped over to one side, hanging over the chair arm. She could feel the dog nudging her and sniffing between her legs from behind now and someone said something about doggie-style and she felt a hand pull at her panties.

She kicked back hard, hit flesh with a sharp heel and heard someone curse, then she mustered all the strength she could and got to her feet. She swayed for a moment, dots swimming in front of her eyes, and steadied herself with her hand on the wall. The room was spinning around her; everyone was looking at her like faces in a fish-eye lens.

The dog growled. Gary was holding his shin but still laughing. The fat woman near the door had put down her bottle of nail polish remover and was starting to look threatening in a blank, porcine kind of way. The dog was still worrying Sarah, barking, rubbing against her legs, licking them and jumping up to push its snout in her crotch.

Nobody moved. They were all just watching her. Sarah managed to dredge up all her reserves, and with what felt like a superhuman effort, she pushed open the door. Just before she got outside, the fat woman grabbed her roughly by the arm and tried to drag her back in.

As she struggled, she became aware of a quick movement and a slapping sound from behind her. She turned. Mitch Cameron had hit the fat woman in the face and blood poured from her piggy mouth. Her grip loosened and Sarah staggered out, crying, into the harsh daylight. Nobody else tried to stop her. She weaved her way through the trailer park, then towards the road, dodging between the lanes of honking traffic on the wide road and tottering on her high heels back to the hotel.

She looked behind once, but no one was following her. Something snapped inside her, and now there was only one thought in her mind. *Run far away from here.*

By the time she had crossed the road, she had regained enough basic control to know that the only thing she could do was take a cab to Ellie Huysman's. She knew the address by heart, even when she was stoned. Ellie would help her.

The doorman at the hotel recognized her, knew she was hooked up with money and got her a cab. It was only when she had collapsed in the back seat and given the cabby Ellie's Redondo Beach address that she realized she'd left her purse, wallet and everything else she owned either back at the trailer or in the hotel room. But by then she didn't care. There could be no going back; it was all over; she just had to get away. Ellie would pay the cabby. All Sarah wanted to do was sleep. Sleep and cry.

Sarah rubbed her eyes, as if to erase the memory, then pushed the gin and tonic aside. Why she had even poured it in the first place, she didn't know. She hadn't touched a drop of the stuff since she had walked out on Gary. Damn hotel rooms, the things they made you do, made you remember. She took a small can of ginger ale out of the fridge and sipped that to take the taste of the gin away.

An airplane left a vapour trail across the horizon above the Hollywood Hills. Closer to the hotel, a police helicopter whirred over the Blue Whale, maybe keeping an eye on her. Sarah sighed and picked up *The New Yorker* again.

Nothing to do now but wait.

40

Waiting. Waiting. Waiting.

He hadn't been able to wait outside the hospital all night – there were other things he had to do – but he was certain they wouldn't let her out until morning. He had seen the crash from a distance, and though it had wrenched his heart to watch and to think he might have been partly responsible, that there had been a misunderstanding, he could tell that she hadn't been seriously injured.

Now, in different clothes, with darker hair and driving a new rental car, he watched the chaos outside the hospital as the detective wheeled her out.

*She was **Their** prisoner now. His love was a prisoner, and there was nothing he could do. It was obvious **They** had tightened security since last night. That studio bodyguard had been pathetically easy, only too willing to jump to the bait of a macho game of freeway cat-and-mouse.*

Now, though, he was certain that the car following them was an unmarked police car, and he made sure, after he had broken from the crowd of reporters, that he stayed well behind.

Again, it turned out to be remarkably easy. His sense of luck was developing fast and strong. Instead of taking her to jail, they took her to a hotel. Well, a hotel could become a jail easily enough, couldn't it?

He knew there would be guards on her door and maybe even a bodyguard in the room with her. The thought made him shake with rage. He gripped the wheel until his knuckles turned white and told himself to be calm, calm, calm.

He wanted to kill them all and carry her high into the mountains or deep into the sea. He no longer had any fear of the unknown. The way things had been going, with the lies they had probably brainwashed her to believe about him and the shyness and awkwardness that still inhibited the way he communicated with her, he knew now that their best chance, their only chance, lay beyond the confines of the flesh. She must learn to love the unknown with him.

Soon. It would be soon. Nothing to do now but wait. Wait and think.

41

Stan Harvey's office was on the fourth floor of a low-rise stucco building on Hollywood Boulevard, just a stone's throw from the Capitol Records Tower, that bizarre construction on Vine, built to look like a stack of records. It was showing its age, Arvo thought as he parked. These days it would be built more like a stack of CDs.

Harvey himself answered Arvo's knock at the frosted-glass door and excused himself for a moment. He was on the phone, he apologized, and his secretary had left early. Wearing jeans and a black Rolling Stones T-shirt, the kind with the tongue sticking out between red lips on the back, he looked about fifty. He was mostly bald, and whatever grey hair he could muster from the sides and back was tied in a ponytail. Lord deliver us from middle-aged men with ponytails, Arvo thought. Don't they realize how ridiculous they look?

While Harvey finished his phone call, Arvo studied a signed photograph of Gary Knox among the dozens of other framed celebrity photos on the walls. He had forgotten how decadent, how aristocratically, poetically and elegantly *wrecked* Knox had looked, a sort of cross between Jim Morrison and Keith Richards, with his full lips in a pout, faintly sneering expression, five o'clock shadow and the lank brown hair perpetually falling over one eye.

The other eye, however, stared out with disconcerting clarity, as if piercing into your soul, *knowing* all your faults and secret shames. Knowing and not forgiving. Gary Knox looked merciless in his judgements.

As he looked at the image, Arvo found it impossible to picture Sarah Broughton as part of this man's life. From what he knew of her, she seemed an intelligent and sensitive woman; what on earth could she possibly have seen in him? On the other hand, Arvo knew well enough that whatever powers governed human coupling often showed a very black sense of humour indeed.

'Nasty looking piece of work, ain't he?' said Harvey, hanging up the phone and lighting a cigarette with an initialled gold lighter. Not much to look at himself, he had a scraggly grey beard and matching moustache. Where the facial hair left off, little red veins were visible under dry skin. Above the thin lips and the slightly hooked nose, his eyes seemed to weave the motifs of his hair and complexion; they were grey, streaked red with burst blood-vessels.

Harvey was yet another member of the Brit 'Mafia.' A cockney, by the sound of him. 'Siddown, siddown,' he said. Arvo sat in a black swivel chair opposite the cluttered desk. 'What can I do you for?'

'How long have you been in this business?' Arvo asked.

Harvey sucked on his cigarette. ''Ard to say, really,' he answered, blowing out smoke as he said it. 'Since the sixties, I suppose. I used to hang around the London clubs when the Stones, the Yardbirds and the rest used to play there. Christ, those were some days. You can forget Liverpool. I mean, *fuck* Liverpool, man. London was where it was at. The energy. The talent.

'I was just a snotty-nosed little kid back then, didn't know my arse from my elbow. I got into the business slowly, in a small way at first, working as a roadie for a local band, arranging a few gigs for my mates. Then, poof, all of a sudden these local bands are in demand. Record contracts materialize out of thin air. There's money in it. Well, Stan, this beats clocking on for a nine-to-fiver, I told myself, so I set up as a semi-pro. One thing led to another, and here I am.'

'When did you come over here?'

'Late sixties. Matter of fact, I came over for Woodstock – the original one – and never really went back again. Well, you know what I mean, not back to settle there, like. Business trips, of course. But LA's my home now, for my sins. England's finished. Fucked. Has been for years.'

'What exactly was your relationship with Gary Knox?'

'Purely business. I kept the bastard at arm's-length as much as I could. Between you and me, he was an evil little pillock. Talented, sure, but what a manipulative, arrogant son of a bitch. Unreliable, too.' Harvey shook his head slowly. 'You meet all kinds in this business,' he said. 'Mostly they're egotistical little pillocks without any talent, so I suppose Knox at least had one over them on that score. But the bastard cost me money.'

'How?'

'No-shows, for a start. And that notorious gig in Omaha – you must have read about it – when he staggered on stage late, tried to get the opening of the first song right for about five minutes, then swore at the audience and walked off. Stoned. Naturally, they all asked for their money back.'

'What was your job?'

'Well, basically I promoted the tour. You know, arranged the venues, the publicity, transport, accommodation and so on. When I say that, I don't mean I *did* it all myself, of course. Most of the work was delegated or contracted out to local promoters. I guess my office sort of coordinated things. I used to work with Kenny Little, Gary's manager, in London years back.'

'Did you have any contact with Gary and the band while they were on tour?'

'Too bloody much. Knox was such an obnoxious prat, I kid you not, that he'd phone me in the middle of the night to complain if the hotel had Courvoisier instead of Remy in the minibar. Which can happen a lot if you're doing places like Milwaukee and Rapid City, no matter how ritzy the hotel, believe me. I mean, you'd be lucky to even get cognac, some of those places. Don't know Remy from cough syrup.' He stabbed out his cigarette in an ashtray shaped like a gold record with curled edges. The smouldering butt fell to rest among about twenty others.

'But you didn't actually spend any time with them at the hotel or backstage?'

Harvey stared at him, open-mouthed. 'Spend time with those infantile piss-artists? You must be joking.' He pointed his thumb at his chest. 'This may be my job, but I've got a life, mate.'

'What about when they were here in LA?'

'Same thing. No, wait a minute. I did have to go down and sort something out once.'

'Sort what out?'

'I like to give local bands a chance to play as openers some-times, if they're good enough, and I'd arranged for a band I liked to open at one of Gary's LA shows. Naturally, they're all excited, so they get there early and set up their equipment. Then Gary's roadies arrive and start dismantling it all. They said there wasn't enough room on the stage for both Gary's *and* the support band's amps and speakers, and they wouldn't have time to set up for Gary between acts, so the support band would just have to fuck off.'

'Nice guys.'

Harvey smiled. 'Welcome to the music business. So, when I get there, there's almost a fight going on, and Gary's stoned already, just sort of watching and standing back. I sort it out – find a corner for the support band's gear – and leave.'

'Did you meet Sarah? Sally Bolton?'

'Oh, yeah. She was backstage, just sitting there, you know, crying her eyes out, and everyone was ignoring her. I remembered meeting her once before, in London. I asked her what was wrong.'

'What did she say?'

Harvey shook his head. 'Didn't say anything. Too stoned.'

'So what did you do?'

'I told her she'd be better off if she left the bastard, that he was a worthless son of a bitch who'd only ruin her life, if he hadn't already.'

'Did she respond?'

'Just smiled at me through the tears in that stoned kind of way. Christ, she looked so young and lost, like a kid whose favourite doll has just got broken. I told her there was a plane ticket back to England waiting for her in my office anytime she wanted to pick it up.'

'Did she?'

'No. I never saw her again. Not until she turned up on TV, anyway. Done well for herself. Good on her.'

'Did you know any of the hangers-on, any of the people they picked up on the way?' Arvo asked.

'Like flies to shit, people like that, in my experience.'

'Ever heard of a guy called Mitchell Lorne Cameron?'

Harvey frowned and lit another cigarette. Arvo was thankful that the strong urge to start smoking again that swept over him around Christmas had dissipated.

'No,' said Harvey. 'Can't say as I have. Was he a friend of Knox's?'

'In a way.'

'Never heard of him.'

'They picked him up in San Francisco, him and a couple of others. He stuck to them all the way down here and after. I guess after Knox's death he was sort of cut loose. He hadn't been popular with the other band members anyway, so there's no way they'd tolerate him, not with the boss out of the way.'

'You got this from Carl Buxton?'

'Yes. And seeing as I got his name from you, I thought I'd come back to the source.'

'Sorry you've had a wasted journey, man. But Carl's a decent enough bloke. Thinks a bit too highly of himself, but show me one rock musician who doesn't. Like I said, Carl's about the only one of them hasn't fried his brains with drugs.'

'This Cameron,' said Arvo, 'he fancied himself as a bit of a player himself. Do you know what I mean?'

Harvey nodded, eyes narrowing. 'Uh-huh.'

'Apparently, Gary Knox said he liked Cameron's poems and songs, and Cameron thought he had a chance to get into the band, or at least into the business. Anyway, we think Cameron is still somewhere in LA, and we'd really like to talk to him.'

'So exactly what is it you want from me?'

'Cameron feels he belongs in the music business. He thinks he's got talent. He's even done coffee-house appearances, that kind of thing, according to people who knew him. Maybe even played with local bands back in San Francisco. He also thinks that Gary Knox saw and recognized his talent. He feels endorsed, somehow, singled out for stardom. It wouldn't surprise me if he felt it was his job to take over from where Knox left off, so to speak, carry on the flame. What would he do?'

Harvey reached for another cigarette and lit it from the stub of his old one. At this rate, even the second-hand smoke was getting to Arvo and making him feel dizzy. 'Any number of things,' Harvey said. 'If he didn't already have contacts in the business here, most likely he'd advertise in one of the music papers and try to get together with a band. Or maybe he'd look for an ad and answer it. From what you say though, a guy

with an ego like his would have difficulty fitting in with someone else's idea of a band, especially if he fancied himself as a
great songwriter. He'd want to gather people around he could
control, you know, direct them towards expressing *his* vision.'

'Makes sense,' said Arvo. 'How long do you think it would
take him to find such a band?'

Harvey shrugged. 'It's variable. Anywhere from a week to a
lifetime.'

'What I'm thinking,' said Arvo, leaning forward, 'is that he
might be at a stage now, solo or in a band, where he has an
agent. And that agent might be able to give me his address.'

Harvey sucked on his Dunhill. 'Could be,' he said. 'Could
be. But why come to me. I mean, I'm not an agent.'

'You might be able to save us some time, is all. There's a lot
of agents in this city, but we're looking for someone who might
take on a guy at Cameron's level. In other words, local,
unproven talent. I've never heard the guy, so I don't know if
he's got it or not. I'm assuming if Knox really did think something of his music, then he's got at least enough talent to get
himself a low-level agent.'

'Hmm,' Harvey murmured. 'Could be. And you want some
names?'

'It would help. Look, Stan, we think this guy is very dangerous. The sooner we find him the better.'

Harvey laughed nervously. 'Well, make sure you don't let
him know who told you.'

'Can you help?'

'Yeah. I know a few small-time agents might just handle
someone at his level, or at least know about him.' He looked at
his watch. 'It's getting late. Want me to call now?'

'Let's give it a try. If you would.'

Harvey pulled his Rolodex towards him and flipped through
it. 'Would you do me a favour?' he asked.

'Sure,' said Arvo.

'I skipped lunch. There's a coffee shop and deli just next door does a great Reuben sandwich.'

'No problem.'

Arvo left Harvey to the phone and went to pick up the food. While he was there, he also got a corned beef sandwich for himself. When he got back to the office, Harvey looked over and gave him the thumbs down sign.

Arvo nibbled his sandwich, the first meal he'd had since his greasy-spoon breakfast, sipped hot black coffee and watched it get dark around the Capitol Record Tower.

It must have been about the fifteenth or twentieth call – Arvo had stopped counting – when, after the usual preamble, Harvey asked his question, and this time a smile started to spread over his rough features.

'You *do* know him?' he said, and stuck his thumb up. 'Sure? Yeah. Great.' He reached for his pen.

Gotcha, you bastard, thought Arvo.

42

Traffic was heavy on the Santa Monica Freeway at nine o'clock that evening as Arvo drove the unmarked police car to the address Stan Harvey had got for him. Both Joe Westinghouse and Maria Hernandez rode with him.

Yes, the agent had said, Mitchell Lorne Cameron was listed with him, though he hadn't been able to get him any work for three or four months. Problem was, Mitch was getting a bit of a reputation as an arrogant bastard, not to mention an occasionally violent one, and no one wanted to work with him. The last gig he'd played, he'd punched out the manager after accusing him of falsifying the previous night's attendance records. The kid had some talent, sure, but he lacked the social skills.

People were also sick to death of hearing him go on about how he was the true successor to Gary Knox and how close he and Gary had been.

Arvo turned with the hundreds of other red tail-lights onto the San Diego Freeway, then took Venice Boulevard west. According to the *Thomas Brothers Guide,* the street Cameron lived on was about as far away from the beach as you could get and still be in Venice: way out in the east side, close to the freeway.

At the nearest intersection, two police cruisers waited, as requested. The detectives needed back-up, but they didn't want to go in with sirens blaring and guns blazing. The cruisers would block off the street at both ends in case Cameron made a break for it. The crime-scene techs had also been alerted, and their van was on its way.

Arvo found the house without much difficulty and pulled up beside a fire hydrant out front. Number 14536 was a small bungalow in a street of similar small bungalows, not affluent, but certainly not run-down either. Typical of the LA single-family dwellings put up in the idealistic thirties, most of them had postage-stamp gardens, where some of the more house-proud owners cultivated a little lawn, a few begonias here and a few geraniums there.

After getting Cameron's address, Arvo and Joe had applied to the judge for a 'no-knock' warrant and got one, mostly because Cameron's level of danger was regarded as extremely high, and the chief was taking a direct interest in the case. A quick solution would look really good after some of the disasters that had plagued the LAPD in the past few years. So Arvo knew he had better not fuck up. If he did, then he might find himself transferred to Hollenbeck Division for a little 'Freeway Therapy.' And he didn't like the idea of driving all that way to and from Santa Monica every day. Spring Street was more than far enough, and he had almost considered moving during the months the freeway was closed after the earthquake.

'To knock or not to knock,' said Joe under his breath as they walked towards the short path leading to 14536. 'That is the question.'

As arranged, Joe went around the back of the house and Arvo and Maria took the front. The porch light was on. Arvo flipped the mailbox open. Empty. Inside, the house was dark and silent as a grave.

Maria took out her gun and stood to one side of the door. Arvo stood to the other side, stretched out his arm and knocked. More than one cop had bought it with a shotgun blast through a closed door.

Silence except for the laughter of a television sitcom audience a few houses away.

He knocked again and called out for Cameron to open up. Still silence. It was a clear, cool night, but Arvo could feel the sweat at the back of his neck moistening his collar, prickling on his brow. He wiped his forehead with his sleeve.

Curtains twitched across the street. Somewhere, a door opened and swung shut. A car with a really sick muffler passed by. Inside Cameron's house, the phone rang. The sudden, sharp sound made Arvo and Maria jump. Seven, eight, nine, ten rings and no one answered. No answering machine picked up the message.

When the ringing stopped, Arvo thought he could hear the *M*A*S*H* theme music start up from the bungalow next door.

He kicked the flimsy door and stood back. Maria went in first, crouching low, both arms fully extended, sweeping a hundred-and-eighty-degree angle. Covering her, Arvo flicked on the light switch.

They stood in a short hallway with coats hung on either side and two doors leading off. The first door led to the kitchen and the second to what seemed to be the living room. After checking the place out quickly, they went to open the back door for Joe, who said he had neither seen nor heard anything outside. Though it looked like there was no one home, they all kept their guns out until they were certain.

The living room looked ordinary enough. Cheaply furnished with a worn grey three-piece suite and a scratched coffee table, it didn't give much away. A framed poster of Gary Knox hung on the wall, full length in concert, holding a mike stand, and a red electric guitar rested against a small amplifier directly below the print. The wallpaper was peeling. The room smelled of stale smoke. An overflowing ashtray on the table explained why. Joe touched one of the butts. 'Cold,' he said.

The only other interesting thing in the room was the stereo equipment with two large speakers and compact discs piled haphazardly on the floor. Some of the small, thin discs were out of their jewel-boxes, scattered on the floor. Well, the manufacturers did say you could eat pizza off them or use them as Frisbees.

The kitchen held nothing it shouldn't; in fact, it was missing many things that *should* be there – like plates, pots and pans. Cameron mostly ate out or ordered in, by the look of things, and he favoured Mexican and Chinese, going by the empty cartons in the garbage. Next to the kitchen was a small dining area with a Formica-topped table and four matching chairs.

Another door led off the living room, this one locked. Arvo bent his head and put his ear to the wood, but no sound came from within. With Joe and Maria covering him, he kicked the door open and stood back while Joe knelt in front of him, sweeping the room with his gun. Nothing. Arvo switched on the light. The three of them stood around the entrance.

'Jesus Christ,' breathed Joe. 'A shrine. It's a fucking shrine.'

From floor to ceiling, the walls were covered with pictures of Sarah Broughton. Some looked like stills from her movies and television series, others like studio publicity shots; some were head and shoulders, others full length; in some she was clothed, in others naked. Many of the pictures looked like collages, bits and pieces of Sarah pasted together in impossible combinations.

When he was able to take his eyes off the walls, Arvo noticed the computer equipment. Maria was already checking it out and whistling between her teeth. It took up about a quarter of the whole room, set up around one of the corners. Not only was there a state-of-the-art Macintosh computer and a colour laser printer, there was also a digital camera, a 35-mm Film Scanner, a 14,400 bps modem and a double-speed CD-ROM set-up. Two VCRs and a monitor were hooked up to the computer.

On the bookshelves above stood mostly software for graphics, desktop publishing and image-enhancement. Expensive stuff for a club bouncer and wannabe rock star, Arvo thought, wondering what else Cameron might be into. Drugs? Computer theft? Or maybe he just had a lucrative sideline in desktop publishing.

Maria picked up a stack of printouts from the desk and passed them to Arvo. More pictures of Sarah. This time Cameron had been editing them, playing with the images on screen, cutting off her head and sticking it on a little girl's naked body, separating arms, legs, head and torso and mixing them up again in increasingly bizarre combinations. Maria raised her eyebrows. Arvo handed the pictures to Joe, who shook his head slowly.

'I suppose you guys see lots of this weird shit?' he said.

Maria shrugged. 'It's not uncommon.'

Joe put the printouts down and gave a little shudder. 'Give me a dead crack-dealer any day.'

Another shelf revealed three back issues of a desktop-published fanzine called, simply, SARAH. Written solely by Cameron, Arvo guessed, it featured more of the same collage-type nudes, bits of Sarah and bits of women from porno magazines. One showed what Arvo took to be a close-up of one of Sarah's eyes with a spread beaver shot superimposed.

All the text said was, *'Sarah Sally Sarah Sally Sarah Sally Sarah ...'* over and over again in a variety of fonts. Pretty unimaginative, Arvo thought. You'd think the bastard could at least have written her a poem or two. Wasn't he supposed to be creative? When Arvo put the magazine down he felt like washing his hands.

'Come and have a look at this, Arvo,' Maria said, and he walked over to join her in the other corner.

It was an altar. At least that was what it looked like to Arvo, and he had seen such things before. Cameron had erected his homage to Sarah, including his favourite framed photograph. Sarah was looking over her naked shoulder, butterfly tattoo in clear sight, directly into the camera, an enigmatic expression on her face. Cameron had surrounded the photograph with red candles, most of them half burned.

Lying on the square of black velvet beside the photograph were a wallet and a small spoon. Trophies, most likely. Carefully, holding it between his thumb and forefinger, he flipped the wallet open. John Heimar. He put it back for the crime-scene experts to deal with. There was nothing else in the room except a single bed with a red quilt and a bedside table. The sooner they got out of the place and sealed it, Arvo thought, the less likely they would be to spoil any evidence. Besides, the room was starting to give him the creeps.

Back in the living room, Joe bent over the coffee-table. Next to the ashtray stood a yogurt carton full of matchbooks. All of them were from a club called Ten Forward, on Melrose.

'What do you think?' Joe asked, holding up one of the books so Arvo and Maria could see.

'Make it so,' said Arvo.

43

La Cienega seemed to take for ever. Every light a red one. Still, Arvo told himself, Sarah Broughton was safe at the hotel, and if Cameron were working at the club, he'd be there until the early hours. There was no hurry. They certainly didn't want to announce their arrival in a blaze of lights and cacophony of sirens, any more than they had at the house. But still he felt anxious. It wouldn't be over until they had Mitchell Cameron in custody.

Between Pico and Olympic, Arvo radioed in to arrange for patrol cars to secure the area around the club, then he used the car phone to call Sarah. She sounded bored and irritable but said she was okay. Arvo told her to hang in there and keep her fingers crossed, they were getting close.

On Melrose, Arvo pulled up by the curb right outside Ten Forward, ignoring the No Parking signs. A group of kids hung around the entrance, arguing with a tall man with a shaved head and a black T-shirt who towered head and shoulders over them. The T-shirt must have been XXXL, if such a size existed, Arvo thought, and it was still tight over his biceps and pecs. *He* wouldn't have stood there arguing with the guy. But kids always do think they're immortal, and with the designer drugs they take these days, they think they're omnipotent, too.

Finally, the doorman managed to shoo the teenagers away. When he saw Arvo, Joe and Maria approach, he made a disgusted sound and said, in an unexpectedly high-pitched and raspy voice, 'Fucking kids, huh. Underage. Cops?'

'That obvious?' said Joe.

The man grinned, showing a gaping black hole in an otherwise seamless band of white where one of his upper front teeth was missing. 'I don't want no trouble,' he said.

'Hey, man, you won't get any from us,' said Joe. 'Guy named Mitchell Cameron work here?'

'Mitch Cameron? Sure.'

'He inside now?'

'Uh-huh.'

'Since when?'

'Started at nine.'

'Back entrance?'

'Uh-huh. Round the alley.'

'And no one gets past you, right?'

'You're the boss.'

'Okay. We're going in.'

The man gave a little bow and extended his arm towards the door. 'Be my guests.'

Joe said he would take the rear entrance while Arvo and Maria went into the club to smoke Cameron out. They might look a bit less like cops than he did, he added with a grin. At about six-four, wearing a dark suit, white shirt and low-key tie, he was probably right.

Arvo and Maria found themselves in the bar area. Modelled closely on the *Star Trek: The Next Generation* Ten Forward, but darker and bigger, it featured moulded plastic, futuristic tables and chairs, and even a starscape backdrop on screens that were supposed to represent the large windows of the starship. Galaxies whirled by, the stars all a little blurred. Must be travelling at warp speed, Arvo thought.

It was also a hell of a lot noisier than the TV bar. Hot, too. Kids milled around, some of them looking hardly any older than the ones the doorman had sent away, and waitresses dressed in tight-fitting Trekkie-character costumes held trays of drinks aloft. One of them looked like Deanna Troi, another like Tasha Yar. Conversation competed with loud music, all of it merging in a deafening wall of noise.

The music itself was hard to describe. Part raw rock, part disco beat, part synthesizer funk, it seemed to exist solely for the sake of the dancers, who jumped, bobbed, weaved and swayed on the vast floor under yet more swirling galaxies. Arvo noticed a few glazed eyes. Drugs. Ecstasy, probably.

The clientele was an odd mix of cyberpunk – all studded leather and torn T-shirts, shaved or spiky hair, tight black pants or leggings, with a lot of earrings and a more than average percentage of nose-rings – and an occasional computer nerd looking to get laid, badly dressed, with greasy hair, acne and glasses.

It was almost impossible to spot any single individual in such a heaving, throbbing mass of people. Arvo pushed his way to the bar and asked the bartender if he knew where Mitch Cameron was. The bartender just shook his head and went to serve a customer. Either he hadn't heard through the noise or he didn't know any Mitch Cameron. Most likely he just didn't care.

Arvo and Maria were already drawing strange looks from some of the kids, a few of whom quite wisely slunk away from them, maybe to sell their illegal substances elsewhere or flush them down the toilet. No matter what Joe had said, in this crowd they did look like cops.

Had Mitch Cameron been the same size as the man on the door, it would have been easy to spot him, but according to all Arvo's information he was of average height and rather stocky, muscular. Just because he had had a dyed blond brush-cut a year ago, it didn't mean he had one now, though dyed blond hairs had been found at the scene of Jack Marillo's murder.

Arvo and Maria stood by the bar looking over the dancers. The music changed, though not much, and the overhead galaxy started spinning the other way. Searchlights danced over the crowd. A Federation starship passed by on an over-head screen and some of the dancers stopped and cheered.

Then Arvo noticed, over to his left at the far side of the dance-floor, a couple of kids facing off. Others were moving away, clearing a space around them. They looked to be fighting over a girl who was standing with them. She seemed to be exhorting one of the kids to mop up the floor with the other, and the more she yelled – though Arvo couldn't hear what she said over the music and general din – the closer the guys came to throwing punches. Before they got that far, however, the bouncer appeared.

Arvo nudged Maria, who had been scanning the other side of the club.

'That Cameron?' Maria yelled in his ear.

'Could be. Let's go ask him.'

The bouncer was too busy keeping the two kids apart to notice Arvo and Maria heading towards him. He was about the right size, Arvo estimated, and his hair could have been blond, though it seemed to be plastered down with some kind of gel that made it look darker. He wore it combed straight back, with a greasy ponytail hanging down over his collar.

When they reached him, Maria grasped his elbow and said, 'Mitch Cameron?'

Cameron shook her hand off. 'Yeah, I'm Cameron,' he yelled without turning around. 'Just back off a minute, bitch. Can't you see I'm busy right now?'

But the tension between the two kids had dwindled away by now. They'd passed the flare-up point and hadn't caught fire. The girl looked disappointed.

Maria pulled out her wallet and flipped her badge right in front of Cameron's face. 'I think these kids can manage with-out you for a while, Mitch. Detective Maria Hernandez,

LAPD. And my colleague here, Detective Arvo Hughes. We'd like to talk to you.'

Before either Maria or Arvo could see what was coming, Cameron sucker-punched Maria and she went down on her knees with blood pouring down her chin. That drew a gasp from the crowd. Then Cameron took off over the dance-floor with the galaxies swirling over him and a couple of Romulan warships casting their shadows across his path. He cut a swathe through the dancers, pushing people aside left and right. Arvo bent to see if Maria was okay and she waved him away. He headed after Cameron.

Cameron was fast, but the crowd between him and the door was thick and it slowed him down. By the time Arvo took after him, he had already cleared a path between the dancers, some of whom were still picking themselves up off the floor looking confused. The music throbbed all around them and the lights went on spinning. Arvo could feel the sweat trickling down his forehead and neck. It was beginning to sting his eyes and he rubbed it from his eyebrows as he ran. He glanced back and saw Maria was behind him now, not more than twenty feet away. She gestured for him to keep chasing.

Cameron broke through the last cluster of dancers and skidded across the few feet of empty space to the door. He was heading for the front exit. Arvo was only about fifteen feet behind him now, Maria maybe thirty.

Cameron collided with a couple of kids walking into the club, but he regained his balance immediately and pushed the front door open. Arvo could almost reach out and grab a fist-ful of his T-shirt by now, but the heavy door swung back hard and blocked his path for a moment.

Cameron shot out into the street, right into the doorman with the shaved head. The man hardly flinched, and when Arvo and Maria came out a split-second later, panting for breath, he held Cameron up by the ponytail and said, 'Take

him, why don't you. I never did like the slimy little cocksucker.'
Cameron's mouth was bloody, and Arvo saw him spit a tooth-
fragment on the sidewalk. The bouncer shrugged, raised his
eyebrows and spread his hands, dropping Cameron at their
feet.

Joe came out of the front door, gun out. 'What the fuck's
going on?' he asked. 'Couple of kids came running out the
back door saying there was some real heavy shit going down
inside.' Arvo told him what had happened.

Maria leaned against the car holding a white handkerchief
to her mouth. It was already stained red with blood. Joe cuffed
Cameron and bundled him into the back of the car. Arvo and
Maria got in the front. Arvo put his hand on her shoulder.
'Okay?'

She nodded, took the handkerchief away and looked at it.
'I'm fine. Bastard split my lip is all. More mess than damage.'

Cameron, who sat twisted forward because of the cuffs,
said nothing as they drove to Parker Center. He just kept on
staring straight ahead at the tail-lights on Wilshire, with a
creepy smile on his face, and only God knew what he was
thinking or seeing.

44

On first impression, Arvo thought, Mitch Cameron wasn't much different from the white trash he'd arrested any number of times back in Detroit. He had the look of someone who knew how to handle being pushed around. And whatever you said or did to him, it didn't touch him emotionally because it was nothing in comparison to what he had suffered growing up.

However well he had been treated at the foster-home in Eureka, you didn't have to be told to know that Cameron had endured a deprived and abusive childhood before that. It was in his every sullen, obedient movement, the way he bent with the flow; it was in the smug, cynical smile he wore on his face. Cameron wasn't afraid. He wasn't even angry. The habit of abuse had inured him to such feelings of weakness.

No matter what indignities the system piled on him, much worse had been done. And he had done worse himself. Out on the streets, he would be every bit as cruel and vicious as whoever had abused him as a child, yet in captivity he took to the handcuffs, the punches and the shoves just as naturally and as meekly as he would take to the foot-irons and prison routine. You couldn't touch him; he could no longer feel a thing. In a way, it gave him power. And it made him a supreme manipulator.

It also made him arrogant as hell, which is how they hoped to get him to talk without a lawyer present telling him to shut up every time he opened his mouth. That and the felony rap hanging over his head for assaulting a police officer. But Arvo sensed he wasn't the type to respond to threats and plea-bargains. No, if it was going to happen, it was going to happen because Cameron wouldn't be able to contain himself, because he wouldn't be able to resist showing off.

He looked relaxed and comfortable in the moulded orange plastic chair: legs crossed, hands clasped loosely on his lap, mouth cleaned up. Too comfortable, Arvo thought.

The interview room had no windows; the walls were drab olive, not repainted in about five years; and the only furniture consisted of one table, bolted to the floor, and several chairs. The door was closed and the place was stuffy. Arvo leaned against the wall; Maria stood beside him, arms folded across her chest. Their turn would come later.

Joe started. 'Mitch,' he said. 'You don't mind if I call you Mitch, do you?'

'Call me what you want, man.'

'Do you prefer Mitchell?'

'Mitch is fine. Mind if I smoke?'

'Sorry,' said Joe. 'This building's a smoke-free environment. Want a toothpick to chew on? I find it helps.'

Cameron laughed and took a toothpick. 'Shit. The whole of California's a fucking smoke-free environment.'

'Ain't that the truth,' said Joe, with a smile. 'Never mind, you'll have plenty of time to smoke in San Quentin, Mitch.'

Cameron ignored the jibe and glanced at his watch. 'Look, boys and girls, can we cut the crapola and just get on with it, huh? When this is over, I've got to go and see if I've still got a job left after that stunt you guys pulled at the club.'

'Ever heard of a kid called John Heimar?'

'Nope.'

'He worked the Boulevard.'

'Not my scene, man.'

'You trying to tell me you're not gay, Mitch?'

Cameron leaned forward. His eyes hardened. 'If I was gay, I can't see that it would be any of your business. A little homophobic, are we, Detective? It's not politically correct, you know.' He sat back and examined his fingernails. 'Besides, an attitude like yours usually indicates latent homosexual desires, did you know that? Is that your problem, Detective? Not been sucking enough cock lately? Or been sucking too much?'

'Cut the amateur psychology, Mitch. I'm not impressed. John Heimar and what happened to him *is* my business.'

Cameron rested his hands on the table, palms down, and sat up straight, his eyes fixed on Joe. 'Okay,' he said. 'I don't know who these other two cops are, but you told me you're a big shot from Robbery-Homicide. So let me guess: this kid was robbed and killed? Right? And I'm supposed to have done it, right? But you haven't got enough evidence to charge me with it yet, so you come up with some bullshit felony rap and hope to drag a confession out of me? Am I on the right track, Detective? This is why you've probably lost me my job?'

'Where were you on the evening of December 19?'

Cameron slouched back in his chair and looked down at the table. 'How the fuck would I know? Probably at work. How do you expect me to remember that far back? Where were *you*?'

'Did you go down to Santa Monica Boulevard that evening? Did you pick up a kid called John Heimar? Did you kill him, dismember his body and bury it on the beach near Pacific Palisades?'

'No. No. And no. What *is* this?'

'Where were you over Christmas?'

He shrugged. 'At work. At home. Visiting friends.'

'What about your family?'

'I don't have any family. Well, only Mark, my brother.'

'You were with him over Christmas?'

'Some of the time. We don't see a lot of each other.'

'And the rest of the time?'

'Work doesn't stop just because it's Christmas, you know. The club's busy. People like to party.'

'What about your sister, Marianne?'

'How'd you know about her?'

'Did you see her?'

'No. She lives in Boston. Besides, we don't get on.'

'Do you own a hammer, Mitch?'

'A hammer? I guess so. In the toolbox. I don't—'

'Ever heard of Jack Marillo?'

'Yeah. The TV guy who got killed.' He laughed. 'Don't tell me, you're going to pin that one on me, too, right? Just pick on old Mitchell Cameron. This is absurd. Tell me, why would I want to kill a TV star I've never met?'

'How about last night, Mitch? Where were you then? That's a bit more recent. Maybe you can remember what you were doing then?'

'Working. At the club.'

'Ten Forward?'

'Uh-huh.'

'Sure you weren't up in Brentwood?'

'Brentwood? What the fuck would I be doing in Brentwood? Who do you think I am, man? Member of the country-club set, maybe playing a few holes of golf in Bel Air? Don't talk stupid.'

They would check his alibi, of course. But Cameron was good, Arvo thought. Even denied cigarettes, he wasn't showing any of the traditional signs of stress or of lying. Occasionally, he would probe his broken tooth with his tongue, but that was a normal enough reaction to pressure – and to a broken tooth.

He didn't sweat, fidget or chew his lips, and for the most part, his eyes remained calm and steady, fixed on Joe. They were very expressive eyes, though, Arvo noticed. Most of the time they showed only amused, cynical detachment, but they could turn hard. Arvo also thought he saw a kind of cruel hunger in them, a hunger for power over people, dominance for its own sake. A manipulator.

The absence of guilty body language proved nothing in itself. If Cameron were the man who had terrorized Sarah Broughton, killed John Heimar and Jack Marillo and stabbed Stuart Kleigman, then he could hardly be expected to react in a normal way to interrogation.

On the other hand, he was showing no outward signs of schizophrenia or manic depression. Perhaps he had learned to hide the symptoms; or perhaps his problem lay elsewhere. A serious delusional disorder might not be so obvious to an outsider. As planned, Arvo let Joe carry on asking Cameron about the murders. His turn would come soon. Cameron did seem to be getting a little confused now and then, and maybe that would give them the edge they needed to crack him. He certainly did like to talk.

'Why did you run when we came to question you?' Joe asked.

'You know why I ran. I've got a record. You guys come and roust me, you're looking for an arrest. I mean, if you look at what's happening right now, it's point proven. Pretty soon you'll have me down for every unsolved murder on your books.'

'We don't work like that, Mitch.'

'Bullshit you don't.'

'What have you got to hide, Mitch?'

'Nothing. I told you. I've got nothing to hide.'

It was there, Arvo noticed. A chink in the armour. Gone almost the moment he saw it, but there: a slight twitch, no more than a tic, at the corner of one eye. In someone as controlled as Mitchell Cameron, it was a sure sign he was lying.

Joe had noticed it, too. 'Come on, Mitch, you can't expect me to believe that old line.'

'I don't care what you believe.'

'Sure you do. You want us to believe you're innocent.'

'I *am* innocent.'

'So tell the truth.'

'I did.'

'Why did you run, Mitch?'

Arvo could see Mitch thinking, weighing up the pros and cons of making up another story.

'Why did you run, Mitch?'

'I owe some men some money, that's all.'

'Which men?'

'Just men, okay. Loan sharks. The kind who don't necessarily do things the legal way.'

'What do you owe them for?'

'Money. I borrowed some money for a new guitar.'

Joe paused, then leaned forward and spoke softly. 'But the two officers who came to talk to you at Ten Forward identified themselves as police officers, Mitch.' He turned to face Maria and pointed. Her lower lip was swollen and red. 'Yet you punched Detective Hernandez here in the face. That's a serious matter. Did you think she was lying, showing phony ID?'

Cameron shifted a little uneasily in his chair. 'Maybe. It wouldn't surprise me, man.'

'And because of that you hit a woman?'

'Can't trust nobody these days, man. Women, they can be just as mean as men.' He looked at Maria and bared his teeth in an ugly grin. 'Meaner, sometimes.'

'You can do better than that,' said Joe.

'Maybe the guys I borrowed the money from got cops in their pockets.'

'You into conspiracy theories, Mitch? Is that what you're trying to sell us? I mean, I thought you must be a few cards short of a full deck, but conspiracy theories? Come on, I still think you can do better than that.'

'Oh, yeah? What if I give you names?'

'Cops?'

'Uh-huh. Hollywood Division.'

'Then we'd check them out.'

Cameron gave him two names. Arvo didn't recognize either of them. Then Joe gave Arvo the signal to ease into his chair and take over questioning. Maria sat beside him, at a sharp angle to Cameron, so he would have to turn his head to look at her. She and Arvo had arranged a signal system for if and when he wanted her to ask the questions.

Arvo took off his jacket and hung it over the back of the chair. Then he loosened his tie.

'You knew Gary Knox, didn't you, Mitch?' Arvo began.

Cameron hardly reacted at all to the change of questioners; he merely flicked his disdainful eyes in Arvo's direction, as if he were looking at some sort of lower life-form.

'Sure I did,' he said. 'Gary and I were close. He liked my songs. If he hadn't died . . .'

'What if he hadn't died, Mitch?'

'Well, I'd probably be famous, wouldn't I? A star. He was gonna have me in his band for the next album, record some of my songs.'

'You met him in San Francisco, is that right?'

'Uh-huh.'

'In a bar.'

'Right. Look, if you know all this, why are you asking me?'

'Just want to get it straight, Mitch, that's all. Do you remember Jim Lasardi, the bass player?'

'Sure.' A guarded look had come into his eyes now, and he shifted in his chair again. He still wasn't sweating, though, and it was hot in the room.

'Do you remember an incident in Santa Barbara, where you broke Jim Lasardi's nose and hit a hotel manager?'

'Yes, I remember. Lasardi was ragging me. Had been all evening. The guy was an asshole. A has-been. He couldn't stand to see the new talent coming in. I could've had his job if Gary hadn't OD'd, you know that?'

'You play bass?'

'Sure. Bass. Lead. Rhythm. You name it.'

'But that's not the way I heard the story, Mitch. I heard that Lasardi made some joke about you writing your autobiography on the back of a postage stamp, and you sat and drank and sulked and brooded over it all night, then you hit him.'

'I told you, the man was insulting me, insulting my background and my talent.'

'What talent?'

Cameron snorted. 'What the fuck do you know about music?'

'But don't you think that's a bit strange, Mitch? A little bit odd? Sitting and brooding *all evening* over some petty remark? Isn't it a bit of an overreaction? Maybe a bit *obsessive*?'

Cameron probed his broken tooth and said nothing.

'Do that a lot, do you?' Arvo asked.

'Do what?'

'Brood. Sit and think about things, get ideas in your head. Ideas you can't seem to shake, things you just have to follow through on.'

'Are you trying to say I'm some kind of a crazy? And that's why I killed these people? Is that what you're saying?'

'Ever suffered from mental illness, Mitch? Ever been treated for schizophrenia?'

'No. What the fuck is this?'

Arvo paused to write some notes on his pad, just for effect, then raised his eyes and asked, 'Do you remember Sarah Broughton?'

'Sarah who?'

'Sarah Broughton. The actress. She was Gary's girlfriend at the time of the tour. You came down to LA with them, didn't you?'

'Yeah. Sure I remember her now. Sal. She wasn't called Sarah then. I remember Sal.'

'What was your relationship with her?'

'What do you mean? I didn't have a *relationship* with her. She was Gary's girl.'

'Were you friends?'

'Friendly. I wouldn't exactly say friends.'

'Did you hold doors open for her?'

'If I did, I was just acting like a gentleman, which is more than I—'

'Did you have pet names for her?'

'I mean, shit, is it a crime to act like a gentleman these days? What you mean, pet names?'

'Did you call her "My Lady," "Princess"?'

'Maybe I did, just for a joke. What's this—'

'"Little Star"?'

'Maybe.'

'Why?'

'Why what?'

'Why did you call her "Little Star"?'

'It's the kids' song. Don't you know it?' He sang, '"Twinkle, twinkle, little star, how I wonder what you are." Sometimes, you know, she seemed about as far away as a star.'

'So you called her "Little Star"?'

'I said *maybe* I did. Where are you going with this? I'm not admitting anything till you tell me what this is all about. First you're trying to pin murders on me, now you're talking about Sal. I don't get it. What's the connection?'

'Did you address the letters to "Little Star"?'

'What letters? What are you talking about?'

Arvo gave a discreet signal to Maria, who slipped a file from her briefcase, opened it and started to read. *'"As I labor to prove myself to you, you will remember me and you will come to me. Then, my love, will we lie together and I will bite your Nipples till the Blood and Milk flow down my chin. We will hack and eat away the Corrupting Flesh, the Rank Pollution of Tissue and Sinew, and go in Moonlight shedding our Skin and spilling our Blood on the Sand through the Mirrors of the Sea where all is Peace and Silence and no one can harm us or tear us apart ever again Forever and Forever."*

Cameron seemed confused to hear a woman's voice reading the letter. He frowned at Maria, then looked towards Arvo again.

'I'd call that rather flowery, poetic, if a little overwritten, wouldn't you?' Arvo said. 'Sort of Hallmark gothic. Sounds like just your style to me. Did you write that, Mitch?'

'Fuck, no.'

'How about this?'

Arvo looked towards Maria, who turned to the next sheet of paper and read softly, as if it were a love poem. '"*The boy wanted Death. Every night he cruised the Boulevard looking for Death, for someone who would deliver him to his Destiny. The Boulevard of Death. I put him to sleep like a kind Anesthetist before I performed my Operation. My Knives were sharp. I spent hours sharpening them. I was gentle when I bent over him. He didn't feel a thing. Please believe me.*

The disentanglement of Spirit from Flesh has a Scent and an Aura all of its own, my Love. One day I will show you, let you Smell and Taste it with me. We will disentangle our Spirits from our Gross Bodies and entwine for ever, cut away the wretched excess."'

'This is crazy,' Cameron said.

'Sounds to me like you were talking about John Heimar, the kid you picked up on Santa Monica Boulevard on December 19,' Arvo said.

'I didn't pick no kid up. And I didn't write that shit, either. It's not me, man.'

'How about this one.'

Again Maria read in her low, husky voice. '"*I surround*

myself with your Image. I stand against my wall and I project your Image onto my Skin. I feel the warmth of the Light brush over me and I think it is you gently caressing me. But you were so far from my Arms and I saw you kiss him. I watched him put his Arms around you. I couldn't bear it. You know what I can do, you have seen the Fruits of my Labors.'" As she read, the cut opened on her lower lip and a thin trickle of blood oozed down her chin. She wiped it away with a tissue.

'Real purple prose, that one,' said Arvo. 'Sound familiar?'

'What is this? This is sick, man.'

'Let's get back to Sally for a minute. You treated her well, did you?'

'I already told you. I behaved like a gentleman.'

'Why were you so good to her?'

'What do you mean?'

'Why treat her with such respect? You didn't show the same esteem for Detective Hernandez here. Anyone would think you hated women.'

Cameron glanced at Maria and said nothing.

'But you looked out for Sally, didn't you?'

'Because there wasn't anybody else to do it.' He ran his hand over his hair and wiped it on his jeans. 'She was a stranger over here. She had that English accent and all, looked lost half the time. And she was so vulnerable.'

'But she had Gary, didn't she?'

'He couldn't always be around, could he? Gary was busy. People hit on her, you know, Sal. Good-looking chick like that. People hit on her all the time.'

'And you stopped them?'

'If I could. If I was around.'

'How did she react to that?'

'To what?'

'You using your muscle to keep guys from hitting on her.'

'How would I know? She never said.'

'Was she impressed?'

'I told you, I don't know.'

'You mean she never even thanked you?'

'That's not why I did it, man.'

'What'd she do? Just ignore you?'

'Yeah. I guess. I don't know.'

'But you still protected her to the best of your ability?'

'Yes. But I didn't kill anyone for her. Is that what you're getting at. Someone says I killed someone? Is that what this is all about? Well they're a liar. They're a fucking liar.' His eyes flashed with anger and he banged his fist on the table.

'Hey,' said Arvo. 'Calm down, Mitch. Tell me, how did you feel when you found out that someone else hit on her?'

'I don't know what you mean.'

'Someone told me she was the tour mattress. Everyone fucked her. Everyone but you. She just ignored you.'

'Hey, I don't like—'

'I don't care what you don't like, Mitch. Tell me how you felt when you knew someone else had fucked her.'

'I didn't feel anything. Why would I?'

Arvo rested his hand on the table as a signal for Maria to take over. She did it smoothly. 'Did you wonder what you could do to make her like you?' she asked softly. 'Do you think women are impressed by tough guys, Mitch? Do you think they like it when people kill for them?'

He sneered at Maria. 'Women like men to fight over them, sure they do. Like those two guys in the club tonight, when you came over. You must've seen what was happening there. Fucking peacocks preening themselves. Strutting their stuff.'

'Like to see some blood flow, do they?'

'Sure they do.'

'Is that what you like, too, Mitch. See a little blood flow? Is that why you hit me?'

'Look, I already explained about that. Sorry, my mistake.'

Maria sat back and let Arvo pick up the reins again. Cameron glanced between the two of them. He was getting so he didn't know where to look. 'Gary didn't treat Sal very well, did he?' Arvo asked.

Cameron crossed his arms again. 'They weren't getting along. They were close to splitting up by then.'

'Way I heard it is he liked to humiliate her, force her to go with other guys. Even women. Do threesomes, gangbangs, that sort of thing.'

'This is bullshit, man. I don't have to listen to this.' Cameron stood up but Joe pushed him back down again. 'You're not free to go,' he said. 'Sit down.'

'Hey, that's police brutality.'

'You ain't seen nothing yet,' said Joe. 'Stay seated and answer the man's questions.'

Arvo went on. 'You admit that Gary didn't treat Sal well, and that bothered you, made you protective towards her?'

'I'm not saying anything against Gary. Look, some guys just have problems relating to women, you know. That's all.'

Arvo scratched his cheek and Maria took over again. 'What do you mean by that, Mitch?' she asked. 'Exactly what do you mean?'

He glanced at her quickly, then looked down at the table. 'Well, Gary was a genius, right? He wasn't like you and me.'

'And that gives him permission to humiliate women, does it?'

'I'm not saying that. You're twisting my words. That's just what a fucking woman *would* say.'

'What are you saying, then?' Maria pressed on. 'I'm just trying to understand where you're coming from, Mitch.'

'Just that people like Gary are different, that's all. You can't judge them by ordinary standards. Like Miles Davis. He was another genius, but I read a biography said he wasn't that much of a gentleman to the women in his life either.' He looked up at Maria again and fixed her with his eyes.

Maria didn't even blink. She just went on slowly, softly and insistently. 'So being a genius allows men to beat and degrade women. Is that what you're saying?'

'No. I'm not *saying* that. What I'm saying is that people like Gary are different, and sometimes they have, like, problems relating to women. They're a bit fucked up, that's all. Genius and madness, they're pretty closely related. I'm not saying it should be condoned or anything.'

'That's an interesting point, Mitch. How would you describe yourself: genius or madman?'

Cameron shrugged.

'Or maybe it doesn't matter. The way you just described it, they're pretty much the same, aren't they?'

'That's not what I meant. I'm no crazy.'

'Did you want to make up to Sal for the way Gary treated her?'

'I never thought about it that way. I was just being nice, you know. It's my nature.'

Arvo picked up the questioning again. 'What happened after she went away? Did you lose touch with her?'

'*Everyone* lost touch with her, man.'

'Ever try to find her?'

'No. Why would I do that?'

'Maybe you just couldn't stop thinking about her?'

'What?'

'Watch much TV, Mitch?'

'Not a lot, no.'

'We noticed you got two TVs in the house. Big screen in the living room and a smaller one in your bedroom.'

'My what?'

'Your bedroom. The room with all your computer stuff. All

the weird pictures on the wall. The room you keep locked.'
Arvo sat forward, lowered his voice and rested his hands on
the table. 'See, we know all about you, Mitch. Maybe you'd
like to talk about that now, the pictures, the little altar to Sarah
Broughton? Want to tell us about that now, Mitch?'

Cameron turned pale and his jaw dropped. 'You guys went
to my house, broke into the bedroom?'

'We had a legal search warrant.'

'And you broke into the bedroom, the room with the lock
on?'

'Yes. Like I said, we had a warrant. We had to break in.
There was nobody there to let us in.'

Cameron shook his head. 'Look,' he said, 'I don't understand any of this, and I don't care about your fucking warrant.
Is this what this is all about? All that stuff about me and Sal?'
He glanced back and forth between Arvo and Maria. 'You saw
the photos on the wall?'

'More than that,' said Arvo. 'You've got to admit, it's pretty
weird, Mitch: the altar, the fanzines, all those collages. Pretty
bizarre. Want to tell us about it?'

Cameron started to laugh.

'Want to tell us about it?' Arvo repeated.

'Sure, I'd love to tell you about it. Problem is, I don't know
much about it. I've hardly even been past the door.'

Arvo frowned. All of a sudden, he felt his heart lurch and
his mouth go dry. 'What do you mean?'

'What I say. The room's not mine, and unlike you assholes,
I respect people's privacy.' He leaned forward and rested his
hands on the table.

'Mitch, you're feeding us a line. What do we look like, Boy
Scouts? It's your house, Mitch. You rent it.'

'Sure I rent it. But I sleep on the sofa-bed in the front room.
That other room's Mark's. He lives with me. And the lease is
in his name, too. You guys should do a bit more investigating

before you come around rousting innocent people, maybe losing them their jobs.'

'Mark? Your half-brother.'

'Yeah. Mark Lister. I don't fucking believe this, man. I don't believe it. Are you trying to tell me you think Mark's been killing people because he's a fan of Sal's? No way. Sure, the kid has an active fantasy life. What's wrong with that? It's harmless enough, a few photos on the wall. All kids do that. He never had much else going for him except computers. He's a real whiz with those.' He shook his head. 'This is crazy.'

'Are you saying that you didn't rent a silver Toyota from Dollar Rentals out at LAX?'

'Sure I'm saying that. What are you talking about?'

'Because we talked to the rental company and they told us it was you, Mitch. Mitchell Lorne Cameron rented that car on January 2 and returned it January 3. You saying that's not you, Mitch? You saying you didn't rent a car just like Sarah's bodyguard's, run him off the road, then stab Stuart Kleigman out in Brentwood?'

'The fuck I didn't. Little asshole must've borrowed my driver's licence again.'

'But he's blind.'

'Who's blind?'

'Mark.'

'Like fuck he is. Listen, I'm telling you, man, I didn't rent no car. Mark doesn't have his own licence so he does that sometimes, even though I told him he could get us in trouble.'

Arvo felt it slipping away from him. Martha, back in San Francisco, had told him she thought Mitch's brother had some physical disability, but she had only guessed that it was blindness. Arvo had swallowed the assumption. 'What does Mark look like?' he asked.

'We're only half-brothers, but we both take after our mother.

And Mark sort of looks up to me and copies me, you know, like dyeing his hair blond, working out, wearing the same kind of clothes and shit. I guess we look sort of alike. Enough so he can get away with using my driver's licence. Look, this is really crazy, man. I can't believe that Mark—'

'You've been taking care of him since Eureka?'

'You know about that, too? Yeah, since then. I mean, he's a really bright kid, special schools and all that. They said he was a computer genius. He just has a problem communicating.'

'What do you mean?'

'He doesn't speak.'

'You mean he's mute?'

'I mean he doesn't speak. Hasn't for years. Give him a modem and he's off and running, but the kid never opens his mouth. Shit, Mark's just a computer nerd. That's all he does. He works out of home. Desktop publishing, customized programs for small businesses, that kind of thing. Does pretty well, too. Look, this is obviously ridiculous. Mark wouldn't hurt—'

Arvo felt a shiver run up his spine. He stood up. 'Where is he, Mitch?' he asked 'Where is Mark right now?'

'How should I know?'

Arvo could think of one place he might be.

Joe was already opening the interview-room door yelling for backup and a police helicopter. Arvo and Maria followed him as fast as they could go down to the car.

45

He parked his car by a restaurant on the Coast Highway. No point following any further and risking getting caught by the cop. He knew where they were going.

His heart leapt as he walked down to the beach. She had come home! Just for him! She had finally convinced them to let her go after all this time. Let her go and meet her destiny.

Earlier that evening, keeping watch on the hotel, he had been mystified at what was happening. First he saw the detective pull up in his tan convertible and a wave of hatred surged through his blood. He knew he should have killed him when he had a chance, lit a bigger, better fire. This was the man most responsible for keeping Sally prisoner, for trying to turn her against him. Maybe he should still kill him? But no. Concentrate on the here and now. Remember the True Purpose.

Next he had seen a black-and-white pull up and watched Sally come out with the detective and get into it.

She was going home! To him.

She had finally told them she didn't want to be a prisoner any more; she wanted to be free to come to the one who loved her. They wouldn't like it, he knew that, but they had to respect her wishes. This was America, after all, land of the free.

And she had come to the place where she knew he would find her. Their first real home together. He thought of it like that even though he hadn't even been inside the beach house.

And now, as he walked along the quiet shore towards that same house, the fine sand shifting under him, he felt a little sadness mingled with his joy. After all, he knew it was too late. Too much had happened.

Maybe the police had let her go, but they would probably start watching her; they certainly wouldn't stop looking for him. He wasn't a fool. He knew he'd broken some of their petty rules and they would punish him if they could.

If only he could make them understand about love, how it must be bought with blood, how it could only end in blood. But they would never understand the glory and the holiness of his vision. Dull, plodding, pedestrian minds.

The waves broke at the shoreline and smashed into a million pieces, each one shouting her name.

No. It was too late for earthly happiness. Could there ever be such a thing, anyway? Through his love for Sally, he had discovered that to find true happiness one had to push further and further beyond the petty human boundaries. It was the only way. Through his love for her, he had learned not to fear the unknown but to embrace it openly.

They would go beyond the mirrors of sea and everyone would remember them like the other great tragic, doomed lovers of history and myth. Like Romeo and Juliet, Anthony and Cleopatra, Abelard and Heloise, Othello and Desdemona, Tristan and Isolde. For what was love without courage and sacrifice? Without blood?

He hurried along the beach. Close ahead, she was waiting for him.

46

The patrolman who escorted Sarah home checked out the house and grounds, then got back in his black-and-white and drove away. Alone and safe in her own home at last, Sarah first phoned Cedars-Sinai again and found out that Stuart was doing fine.

Inside the house, nothing had changed. Except the half-full coffee cup she'd forgotten to wash before going to stay at Stuart's had started growing mould. The place smelled musty, too, but then it had been shut up for a few days. Sarah opened the sliding glass doors and walked out onto the deck. The gate to the beach was still closed.

Mitch Cameron, her tormentor, was in police custody, Arvo had said, and she was finally free. So why did she feel so edgy?

She was also hungry. She checked the fridge. Nothing but curdled milk, a few eggs, probably stale. Maybe she'd order in. There was the Thai place that had delivered to her before. Maybe some pad thai noodles, garlic squid and yellow chicken. That sounded good. Or burn her taste buds with chicken in red sauce.

First, though, she went into the front room, turned on the dim reading lamps and adjusted the lighting the way she liked it. She put some Chopin Nocturnes on the CD player. She wanted to create the right sort of mood for relaxation.

Then she walked around the place, looking at her paintings, adjusting them a little, running her hands over the soapstone

Inuit sculptures and the smooth planes of wood. She took some of her favourite books from the shelves, opened them, sniffed the pages, then put them back.

With the sliding glass doors open, she could smell seaweed and hear the rumbling of the waves below. It was a beautiful, clear evening, with just enough of a cool sea breeze to make her wrap a shawl around her shoulders.

She made some hot chocolate and curled her legs under her on the sofa. Glancing around the room, she thought vaguely about redecorating, now the nightmare was over, or at least buying a new painting for the wall. A Hockney would be great, but not at the prices he was fetching these days. And to think he was just a working-class lad from Bradford, not so far from Barnsley.

Sarah thought she would like to go and visit Hockney. She wondered if he would receive her. Didn't he live quite near her, in the Hollywood Hills? She had heard that he was a bit of a recluse. But surely they could talk about the old days, about growing up in Yorkshire. Maybe he'd even sell her a painting cheap. Or if he liked her, he might even *give* her one. But why stop at that: maybe he would even want to *paint* her. In the nude, beside a swimming pool, perhaps? Enough foolish fantasies, she told herself.

Her reverie drifted. She also wanted to phone Paula and persuade her to come over with the family as soon as possible, take the kids out of school for a couple of weeks, if she had to. Perhaps she was being selfish, but since her Christmas visit, circumstances aside, she realized how much she had missed her family since the rift, how much a part of her they were, squabbles, irritations and all. And she also knew just from looking at him that her father didn't have long to live.

To keep her occupied, she started making a list of things to do tomorrow:

1. Visit Stuart in hospital and talk to Karen
2. Go to studio, see what's happening
3. Call Nat in New York re Broadway deal
4. Get studio to write to David Hockney to try to arrange a meeting (maybe that will impress him!!!!)
5. Until it does, check out a few galleries
6. Pick up and answer *all* mail
7. See about taking those art classes in Santa Monica
9. Go shopping. Buy *healthy* stuff like yog—

Sarah thought she heard a sound outside on the deck. When she looked up, she saw only her own reflection in the dark glass and chastised herself for jumping at shadows. Still . . .

She walked over and pulled the doors fully open. It took her only a split-second to realize that it was no longer her reflection she was staring at.

It was *him,* the one she had seen at Stuart's house, the one Arvo said had been caught.

Sarah screamed and staggered backwards. He came in and put his hand over her mouth. His skin smelled of Pears soap. She struggled briefly but he was too strong. He pushed her gently down into the armchair and he stood over her, hands on the chair arms, closing her in.

He reached forward gently and touched her hair. She flinched. He looked at her with sadness in his eyes, and she knew that whatever it was he was seeing, it wasn't what she saw when she looked in the mirror.

She remembered him now. The silent one, always in the shadows: Mitch's brother.

'What do you want?' she asked. 'Why have you been hurting my friends? Why don't you leave me alone?'

He said nothing, just kept looking at her in that twisted, adoring way.

'Look, this is crazy,' she rushed on, trying to keep the

hysterical edge from her voice. 'I don't love you. I've never loved you. I've never even given you cause to think I loved you. *Why* are you doing this to me?'

But whatever he was hearing, it wasn't what she was saying. She wished to God he would speak. His silence and his fixed, loving eyes were making her even more scared than she had been to begin with.

Then he took her hand. She tried to resist, but he grasped her wrist tightly and pulled her up from the chair. She screamed and struggled, knocking over a small table and one of the Inuit sculptures, but he held on to her and dragged her across the floor, through the doors and over the wooden deck. She managed to make him slow down enough for her to stand up. He seemed to want her to go with him down to the beach. He had obviously climbed up the rocks beside the gate, and he wanted her to go back down with him that way.

Sarah didn't want to get dragged and bumped over the rocks, and she also realized that if she could play for time, then the police might find out they had made a mistake and come looking for her.

'Wait a minute. There's a key,' she said. 'For the gate. Let me get it.'

He thought for a moment, then nodded and held on to her as she went back inside slowly and took the key from the hook by the doors. Then they walked back out, hand in hand, down the rough-hewn stone steps.

The sky was clear and the moon bright. Sarah opened the iron gate. When they walked out onto the sand, she thought she might be able to make a break for it and run for help, maybe dash towards the first place that would give her access to the road. She didn't know what she would do when she got there. Run out and flag down a car if she could, if anyone would stop. There were lights on in some of her neighbours' houses, she noticed, and she tried shouting for help, but the combination of the sea and whatever TV programmes they were watching drowned her cries.

He didn't seem to notice her screaming, or care; he was completely intent on taking her towards the sea. She felt as if his powerful fingers were crushing her wrist. She screamed again, louder this time, hoping someone in one of the nearby houses would hear between commercials or the canned laughter and come to help her, but still nothing happened, no one came.

She tried to kick him in the shins and fell on the sand. He dragged her behind him, the same relentless pace. The more she struggled, the tighter his grip became, until she could hardly feel her hand.

God, how she wished he would speak, wished he could explain what he was doing and why, what he wanted. Never before had she felt so much in the dark, felt such a desire to *understand.*

When they reached the shoreline, he stopped, turned and faced her, now gripping both her hands in his.

'Please,' she begged above the crashing of the waves around their feet. 'Please let me go. I'll do what you want. Whatever you want. Don't hurt me.'

She could make out his expression in the moonlight, and she could see from his eyes that he was trying to tell her he didn't want to hurt her. But she also knew he was going to kill her. It might seem like something else to him, something grandiose and romantic and transcendental, but he was going to kill her. She remembered his letter: *'But you must not think I enjoy causing pain. No, that is not it at all, that is not my purpose, surely you can see? . . . My Knives were sharp. I spent hours sharpening them. I was gentle when I bent over him. He didn't feel a thing. Please believe me.'* She believed him now.

'Please,' she said, 'talk to me. Tell me what you want me to do.'

Then he put his hand over his mouth and shook his head.

My God, she realized, he *couldn't* speak. But at least he could hear her.

Pleading would do no good. Sarah tried to invoke something of Anita O'Rourke's coolness and competence. *Think*, she told herself. You're an actress, goddammit, so *act*. She couldn't tackle him herself; he was far too strong. Her best bet was still to play for time. Just stay alive.

He relaxed his grip on her right hand. Not completely at first, but enough to get the circulation flowing again. Then, when he saw she wasn't going to run away, he let go of both hands completely. He didn't seem to have a gun or anything, at least no weapon that was immediately visible.

Sarah stood before him and massaged her wrists, the water lapping around her bare feet. What could she do? Run? No, he was powerful and would soon catch her. He wanted to kill her, but how? Walking out into the sea together, or some such sentimental love-sacrifice? He wouldn't see that as *hurting* her. People said drowning in salt water was like going to sleep. But how did they know? Sarah had always wondered.

Again, she remembered the letter. He didn't like to cause pain. But he had killed Jack. Knocked him out with a hammer and stabbed him. And he had stabbed Stuart. Even so, she could already sense that he was sorry he had grasped her wrists so tightly. Could she play on his sympathy?

Between waves, she could hear loud rock music from one of the houses and cars roaring by on the Coast Highway. So near.

His eyes locked with hers and he seemed to be drinking in her presence, inhaling her nearness. She realized in that moment that no amount of pleading or playing on sympathy could delay the consummation for much longer. He had one purpose and one purpose only: their eternal union through death.

Sarah thought she could hear sirens in the distance. Were they for her? Was she hearing things?

Then he reached in his pocket and took something out. His

arm moved quickly by the side of his head. Sarah thought she saw something flash in the moonlight. Was that whirring sound coming closer really a helicopter? Was it coming to save her?

He handed her something. It felt like a mixture of hard calamari and soft tomato. She held her palm open in the moonlight and looked. It was an ear. *His* ear, cartilage and lobe. She dropped it on the wet sand, screamed and stumbled backwards. Then she saw him pointing the knife towards her.

He reached out and grabbed her wrist again, the blade in his other hand coming closer. But instead of stabbing her or cutting her, he handed the knife to her, wrapped her fingers around it and stood before her.

My God, she knew what he wanted now. He wanted her to do the same, to cement their love by parting with a limb. A token.

The sirens were getting closer. She could hear cars screech to a halt by the nearest access point. And the helicopter was flying low, shining a cone of light over the beach about a mile to the south.

Still he just stood there, hands out, waiting for her to prove her love with a token of her flesh. She felt violated by his thoughts and desires; somehow, they seemed to have insinuated themselves into her consciousness.

Again she tried to think what Anita would do, then something snapped inside her, the way it had in the trailer that day. Dammit, he wasn't Van Gogh and she wasn't Anita O'Rourke. She was Sally Bolton, fighting for her life. And she would bloody well win. After all, he had given her the means. Holding the knife out in front of her with both hands, she pushed it forward with all her strength into his stomach.

For a moment, he didn't move, then shock spread across his features and he fell to his knees, the blade sticking out of his flesh. It hadn't gone very far in, Sarah noticed, but it was far enough. She felt sick. She had never hurt anyone before, let alone stabbed them, and as soon as she had done it she felt an awful guilt start to grow inside her. She had hurt another human being, however bad, however twisted he had been. He looked so pathetic now, on his knees in the foam. Not the monster who had written those letters, stalked her, murdered John Heimar and Jack Marillo, stabbed Stuart. He couldn't be the man who had made her life hell for the past few weeks; he was just a lonely and pathetic figure, hurting, dying.

She looked around. There were cops with flashlights swarming all over the beach now, and the helicopter had landed about a hundred yards away. It was like a scene from a war, she thought, or the invasion of a small island. Men in military fatigues jumped out onto the beach, sand whipping up in the downdraught from the helicopter blades, and hurried forward, rifles in their hands. Behind her, she could hear voices barking loud orders.

She was safe now. But when she looked back at the man on his knees in the sea, she still felt that she was caught in some sort of perverse mummers' play that hadn't reached its final act yet.

He got to his feet and stood in front of her, swaying a little. He had pulled out the knife and was holding it loosely by his side, but she wasn't afraid any more. He wasn't going to try to kill her now. His great vision, his intricate web of delusions, had collapsed, shattered. She had smashed it. They weren't going anywhere together.

What did he see now, she wondered? Her betrayal or his triumph? His expression was almost unreadable – the religious ecstasy of a St Sebastian pierced by arrows, crossed with all-too-human shock and surprise. Had he really expected her to cut off an ear and hand it to him? She knew that he had.

His eyes brimmed with pain, sadness and loss. He stretched his hand out to her again and she became so mesmerized by his eyes that she found her own hand reaching out to take it. She could see blood from where he had clutched at the stomach wound, blood shining in the moonlight.

She almost put her hand in his, almost got his blood on her. Christ, now she felt that she wanted to hold him, rock him in her arms, say she was sorry she stabbed him, tell him everything was going to be all right, sing him a lullaby.

What the hell was wrong with her? This man had terrorized her, killed people in *her* name. And all she wanted to do was hold him and ease his pain, maybe let him take his illusions to the grave. Then she snapped out of the spell and snatched back her hand before it touched his.

'No!' she yelled. But she didn't know if he heard her or not. Arvo and Maria had come up behind and grabbed her by her arms. They were leading her back towards the police line. *He* was backing the other way, towards the ocean.

So many men, and they all had their guns out, pointing past Arvo, Maria and Sarah at the man. 'Jesus Christ,' Sarah heard one of the uniformed policemen say as she neared him. 'What the fuck do we do, shoot him to stop him from killing himself?'

Like Lot's wife, Sarah looked back.

She saw the knife blade flash in the moonlight before he plunged it into his abdomen, just below the stomach wound, with all his remaining strength. Then, with both hands, he dragged it slowly up as far as his breastbone.

She was only about twenty feet away from him, and the moonlight and flashlights gave his eyes an eerie glow, like an animal's eyes caught in the headlights.

All the time he was pulling the knife through his flesh, he was looking at Sarah, and at the last moment, as something dark and glistening slid out of his stomach into the moonlit water like a grotesque parody of birth, he opened his mouth and emitted a long, high-pitched wail and fell to his knees. It was the only sound she had ever heard him utter and it sounded like 'Sally.' Then the light in his eyes went out like a spent candle, a strong wave knocked him over, and the water covered him.

47

Chicken pieces sizzled as they hit the hot grill and released the mingled smells of cumin, coriander, garlic and ginger. Fat and marinade dribbled onto the coals, hissed and turned to smoke. Above, a few milky swirls of cloud decorated the pale blue sky. Seabirds wheeled and squealed over the rippled blue water, which winked with diamonds of sun. Breakers crashed in a chaos of foam on the beach. Like the postcards said, it was 'Just another day in paradise.'

It was only two weeks after that terrifying night on the same beach, and even now Sarah found it hard to look out there in the moonlight, especially when she was alone.

But she wasn't alone now. As soon as Sarah had given her a brief account of what had happened, Paula had taken the kids out of school and brought them *and* her father over to visit.

They had been here a week now and were taking off to see the Grand Canyon for a few days before coming back to LA then heading home. Paula had some idea that the air in Arizona would be beneficial for their father's health. Sarah doubted it. Her father was probably past that kind of help; besides, from what she had read, the air in Arizona was getting just as bad as it was in Los Angeles, thanks to all the Angelenos and their automobiles moving out there. But she didn't say anything; she didn't want to discourage Paula, especially when she seemed to be on a rare optimistic streak.

Paula had seemed like a woman with a mission the moment she arrived. Gently, she had assumed command, given Sarah space to heal and talk when she wanted to talk. She had already rented a car and taken the kids to Disneyland and all the way to Sea World in San Diego. She seemed to have taken to driving on the wrong side of the road, even on the freeways, like a fish to water.

Sarah was amazed at the transformation in her sister. The last time she had seen Paula, at Christmas, she had been bitter, mean and unadventurous. Also, like a lot of Brits, she hadn't had a good word to say for Americans or anything American.

Still, it was a good thing that Paula had determined to be so independent over here, because Sarah had been so busy on the series most days that she hadn't been able to spend as much time with her family as she would have liked. She had fixed up a visit to the studio, of course, and the kids had loved that. Paula had been impressed, too, Sarah could tell. In fact, she could also tell that Paula liked it here.

Visitors often did, Sarah knew, maybe because they only saw the paradise and not the inferno, just as she had for so long. And, of course, Brits loved the weather. Especially in January. As it turned out, they were in the fourth day of a heatwave – the high 80s – after a week of heavy rains had washed half of Malibu onto the Coast Highway. Paula hadn't even complained about the rain.

If her father had still been well he would probably have been spending his time in the King's Head in Santa Monica, Sarah thought, drinking Boddington's pub ale. Maybe he would even join the cricket club. He had been a fair pace bowler in his day. Still, he had seen the stars on Hollywood Boulevard, and that had brought a smile to his face and a tear to Sarah's eye.

Wearing cut-off denim shorts and a white *Good Cop, Bad Cop* T-shirt, Sarah turned the chicken pieces, basting them with tandoori sauce as she did so. A big pot of rice was cooking on the kitchen stove, in chicken stock with turmeric and salt, and Paula was back there in the kitchen, mixing up a salad.

The children were playing on the beach, throwing pebbles, running at the waves and back, as if being chased by them, squealing with delight. A few yards further down, a man stood up to his thighs in water, holding a fishing rod. Optimist, Sarah thought. And to think what had happened on that same beach only a couple of weeks ago. Sarah gave a little shudder. She looked at her watch. He should be here by now. She realized she was anxious to hear what had happened.

Her father sat in his wheelchair at the other end of the deck, wrapped in a light blanket, staring out to sea. He looked lost in his own sense of impending death. Though it had exhausted him, he had made the journey to what must have seemed like the other side of the earth, and Sarah knew he had forgiven her. She loved him and wished there were something she could do other than watch him die, but she knew there wasn't. All the doctors in California couldn't cure what he had.

The doorbell rang.

'I'll get it,' Paula yelled from the kitchen.

'Okay,' Sarah shouted back.

A moment later, Paula walked through to the deck with Arvo in tow.

'Look what I found on the doorstep,' she said. 'Is he yours?'

Sarah blushed and thumped her sister on the arm. 'Paula!' She turned to Arvo. 'Please forgive my sister,' she said. 'She never did learn any manners.' Then she introduced him to her father, who nodded and shook hands. The children stayed on the beach. They had already eaten hot dogs for lunch, having fallen immediately in love with real American junk food, and they were easy to keep an eye on down there. They knew not to go out into the sea, and even if they hadn't been told, the size of the waves would have given them ample warning of the danger.

'You can put those beers in there, if you like,' Sarah said to Arvo, pointing to the cooler. Arvo did so, detaching a can for himself first. 'Anyone else want one?' he asked.

'Can't stand that weak American stuff,' said Paula. 'Tastes like gnat's piss.'

Sarah smiled. Ah, good old Paula, back on form now she's got a new audience.

'I suppose it's too cold for you,' Arvo said. 'Don't you English like your beer warm?'

'Get away with you,' she said, laughing. 'Do you know, you sound just like one of those blokes on telly.'

'Which one?'

'Americans. On telly, back home.'

'Oh, I see. Well, I *am* an American, I guess. You sure you won't have a cold beer?'

Paula gave a coy smile. 'Oh, go on then. You've twisted my arm.' He passed her a can of Michelob.

Paula actually looked quite attractive, Sarah thought, without condescension. It wasn't that she had changed her style much: Frederick's of Hollywood might have beckoned, but Paula was a Bullock's girl at heart. Still, she had a good enough body to look good in her jeans and Disneyland T-shirt, and she had picked up a tan very quickly. But it went deeper than that, Sarah thought. Paula was more relaxed, she was actually *enjoying* herself, and the frown and worry lines that had seemed so deeply etched in her face had faded.

'Want one?' Arvo asked Sarah.

'No, I mustn't,' she said. 'I've got a Diet Coke on the go somewhere. I hope you like Indian food.' She turned the chicken pieces again.

'If it tastes as good as it smells,' he said, 'I can't see any problems there.'

'Sit down.'

'Sure I can't do anything?'

'No. Everything's under control. Paula's making a salad, aren't you, dear?'

Paula stuck her tongue out and went back inside.

Arvo sat and put his feet up on the low wooden railing of the deck. He cradled the can of Michelob with both hands on his lap. He was wearing white cotton slacks, sandals and a dark green golf shirt with a tiny knight on horseback embroidered on the breast pocket.

'You a copper, then?' Arthur Bolton wheezed.

'Yes,' Arvo answered. 'A detective.'

'Never did like coppers. Never friends of the working man, they weren't. And certainly no friends of the miners.' Then he went back to staring out to sea. Sarah looked at Arvo and winked, giving a 'What can I do with him?' shrug. Arvo shook his head and smiled.

Soon the food was ready and they all sat around the wooden picnic bench to eat. Sarah helped herself to a glass of chilled white wine. Arvo and Paula stuck with beer. Arthur Bolton tried a Michelob but didn't drink much of it.

'It's okay to talk about it,' Sarah said to Arvo. 'You know, about what happened. I've told them just about everything. But there's still a lot I don't know.'

Arvo nodded and tasted some chicken. 'Delicious,' he said. 'How's Stuart?'

'He's at home. I think he's still on fluids. The knife did some intestinal damage. The doctor says it'll be a while before he's up to par. It'll certainly be a while before he's up to Indian food. Can you imagine Stuart having to change his diet?' Sarah took a mouthful of rice and smiled at Arvo. 'What did you find out?' she asked.

'Quite a lot, really. Mitchell Cameron was pretty keen to talk after he found out Mark was dead. I believe he really did care for his kid brother, in an odd sort of way.'

'Why did he run away from you?'

Arvo shrugged. 'It's habitual with some people. Mitch is a small-time felon. When he left San Francisco, he owed a lot of people money, people who wouldn't go that easy on him if they found him. He also owed the phone company and utilities. That's why he put them all in Mark's name here in LA. Mark *Lister*. Which is also why we couldn't track him through phone or utility records. Anyway, Mitch had been into dealing drugs with a couple of crooked cops from Hollywood Division. They'd arrest someone, take their stash as evidence, then it'd find its way back onto the street again via Mitch and his club connections. Trouble was, he'd been robbing them blind, and he thought they'd finally found out and sent someone over to get him. These people break limbs and shoot kneecaps. That's why he ran.'

'And meanwhile, Mark had come out here?'

'That's right. He must've thought he'd died and gone to heaven when he saw you come home. We screwed up. I'm sorry.'

Sarah said nothing. She was remembering her confrontation with Mark on the beach. Heaven? She doubted it. 'Why?' she asked. 'What made him do what he did?'

Arvo took a sip of beer before answering. 'You'd have to ask a psychiatrist that,' he said. 'And I doubt if even they would be able to give you the full answer. I don't know. His family background was one factor. His mother was a real piece of work.'

'How?'

'She hung around with a rough crowd, bikers mostly. Liked to live fast and dangerous. She died of a drug overdose.'

'What happened to the children?'

'Fostered. Best thing that could have happened to them. They got fed, schooled, well taken care of.'

'Then why did they turn out the way they did?' Sarah asked.

'Again, we don't know,' said Arvo. 'Maybe it was just too late. They'd suffered abuse and neglect when they were kids, in their most formative years. The sister turned out best of the three. Lives in Boston, got a good job with a publishing company. She wants nothing to do with her half-siblings. And who can blame her? When you get right down to it, Mitch is just another asshole with an attitude, a petty criminal. Only Mark was genuinely sick and nobody really knew because he didn't talk.' Arvo took another sip of beer to cool the heat of the spices and went on. 'Mitch told me a story which might explain part of what happened, though I don't think we'll ever be able to explain it all.

'Apparently, when Mark was a kid he was on a picnic with his mother and the bikers, so the story goes. They were on a remote beach, somewhere in Mexico. A fight broke out between his father and one of the other bikers. A fight over his mother. Apparently this guy had been sniffing around her for some time. Anyway, she egged them on and the other biker killed Mark's father. Stabbed him.'

'While he was watching?' Sarah said in disbelief.

'It gets worse.' Arvo cast a glance at Paula and Arthur Bolton.

'It's all right,' Sarah said. 'Go on.'

'As soon as he'd killed Mark's father he and the mother . . . well . . . they did it, made out, right there in the sand. He was still covered in the father's blood. Everyone cheered them on. Mark hasn't spoken a word since. Mark's father was the only one Marta Cameron had actually married. That's why he has his father's name: Lister.'

Sarah paled and pushed her plate aside. 'My God.'

'I'm sorry,' said Arvo. 'You asked.'

'Please, it's all right. What did they do with the body?'

'Cut it up and buried it under the sand.'

Sarah had a sudden image of the body she had found on the beach what seemed like decades ago. *Let's bury Daddy in the sand.* 'How did Mitch know this?' she asked.

'He says one of the bikers who was there told him when he was older. Apparently this was one guy who didn't cheer them on but didn't do anything to stop what was happening either. Mitch wasn't there himself that day. He was in school. But remember, Mitch is a compulsive liar. It could be just a story he made up to try and give his half-brother an excuse for his behaviour.'

'Except that it makes so much sense.'

'Yes. Do you want me to go on?' he asked.

'Yes. please. I just feel as if a cloud passed over the sun, that's all.' Sarah looked down to see the children still playing on the shore.

'Mark was mentally ill, but because he didn't speak and his brother protected him, he slipped through the cracks. At school he was bright and well behaved. And a loner. They say it's the squeaky wheel that gets the grease. Mark Lister never made a sound. How could anybody *know* what was going on in his mind?'

'But surely Mitch should have known? They did live in the same house, didn't they?'

'Yes. But, remember, I said Mitch protected Mark. Mostly that just meant giving him a home, a roof over his head, taking him out occasionally. The big difference between them was that Mitch was active, outgoing, and Mark wasn't very sociable. He preferred to be left alone with his computer and fantasies most of the time. They also kept very different hours. Mitch worked most of the evening and night in clubs and slept during the day, when Mark did most of his computer work. They hardly saw each other. And Mitch said he didn't pry into Mark's everyday life, let alone into his deepest fantasies.

'He hadn't actually been inside Mark's room and seen the shrine and all the computer collages. He didn't know about the letters. And he certainly hadn't seen John Heimar's wallet and Jack's coke spoon, trophies on the altar. He'd stood on the threshold, yes, and he'd seen the photos. But like he said, what's so unusual about that? Plenty of teenagers cover their walls with posters and photos of rock stars and movie stars. Mark was his little brother and he wasn't that long out of his teens. Besides, he was different, he was gifted, a computer genius.' He glanced at Paula, then back at Sarah. 'Would you believe your sister was a stalker and a murderess if you saw a few pictures on her walls?'

'He's right, you know, love,' Paula said. 'A person overlooks a lot of things in a brother or sister. We make excuses for our own, maybe when we should be helping.'

'I suppose so,' Sarah said. 'How did he find me?'

'We think he got your address through a computer bulletin-board. It makes sense. He didn't speak, so he couldn't go around asking. And a bulletin-board would be more discreet, too.'

Sarah cleared the plates and passed out more beer, then she helped herself to another glass of wine. The way things were going, she felt she needed it. The hell with the diet. She'd start her new regimen tomorrow.

They all drifted away from the table and sat in the lounge chairs, listening to the waves and looking out at the diamonds dancing in the sea.

Love. Love. Love. Sarah would never, so long as she lived, understand love. She loved her family, no matter what. They were kin and blood, and she was happy they were with her now. In his way, she supposed Mitch Cameron had also loved his disturbed, silent half-brother, Mark, too.

And she had loved Gary, yet she had watched that love die the way a patient, anaesthetized but still conscious, might watch a surgeon cut out a malignant tumour. They say that happens sometimes, that you wake up during an operation and feel it, but you're still paralysed by the anaesthetic and you can't communicate your pain. That was what happened. And she had walked away. Since then, family aside, she hadn't been capable of loving anyone. Maybe that, too, would change.

And unknown to her, someone had been standing in the wings taking it all in, twisting and colouring it all until it took on the form he wanted and needed for his own obsession. And in his own way, this someone had loved her. Mark Lister had loved her so much that he had killed for her. Now he had died for her, too.

No, she would never understand love.

She felt someone nudge her. It was Paula. 'Sorry, I was miles away.'

'He's going now,' she said, nodding towards Arvo.

Sarah stood up. 'Oh, must you?'

'I've got a few things to do.'

'Okay. Let me see you out.'

'No need,' Arvo said.

Sarah stood awkwardly. 'Well, then . . .' she said. She might never have another reason to see this man again. She didn't even know if she wanted to. She liked him now, but the thought of a relationship, even a date, terrified her.

And she had a feeling that he might be involved with Maria. She didn't know why, it was just something she had sensed when she saw them together, something in the way they related to one another.

On the other hand, Sarah did feel *something* between herself and Arvo, some kind of spark, and after everything that had happened, she didn't feel she could bear it if he just walked away, right out of her life for ever.

Christ, she was shifting from one foot to another like a silly teenager. She could feel Paula mentally urging her to say something.

But Arvo spoke first. 'What next?' he asked.

'Work,' she said, feeling silly as soon as the word was out. 'I mean, I've got a lot of work to catch up on, what with Jack's replacement and all. We're really behind. The public can only stand reruns for so long.'

'Right,' he said. 'Well, good luck.' He stuck out his hand, and they shook.

Arvo began to walk through the sliding glass doors towards his car. Paula nudged Sarah and pointed after him. 'Go on,' she mouthed.

Then, like that policeman on television, the one with the rumpled raincoat, Arvo popped his head back through the doors. 'Just one more thing before I go,' he said.

'Yes?'

'Do you think I could give you that driving lesson some-time? And maybe afterwards we could go to dinner?'

Sarah found herself smiling. 'Yes,' she said. 'Yes, to both. I'd like that.'

'Have you got a friend?' Paula yelled after him as he left, then collapsed giggling on her lounge chair.

The children came running up the steps, smelling of the salt water and making wet footprints on the wooden deck. Sarah could still smell traces of the Indian spices from the meal. She took another sip of wine.

There was a lot to take in, yes, and a lot of personal demons to grapple with. But today the sun was shining, the waves were crashing on the beach, her family was with her, she still had her job, Stuart was recovering, and a handsome man was going to give her a driving lesson. On the whole, she thought, allowing herself a private smile, things weren't looking too bad right now. Things weren't looking too bad at all.

ACKNOWLEDGEMENTS

I would like to thank Lieutenant John Lane and other members of the Threat Management Unit of the LAPD for being so generous with their time and expertise; also, thanks to Detective Dennis Payne of the Robbery-Homicide Department, LAPD.

Special thanks are due to Patricia McFall, Michael Connelly and Richard and Barbara Matthews for reading and commenting on earlier drafts of the manuscript, and to Linda Grant for her help with the San Francisco chapters.

So many people extended their kindness and hospitality on my visits to Los Angeles; in addition to the above I would especially like to thank Wendi Matthews for the studio tour, Karen and Eric Ende for their support, and Timothy Appleby and Sheila Whyte for the Laguna Canyon drive.

Any errors are entirely my own and were made purely in the interests of dramatic fiction.

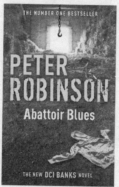

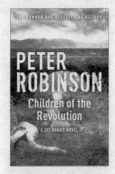

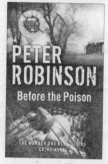
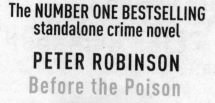

Do you wish this wasn't the end?

Join us at www.hodder.co.uk, or follow us on
Twitter @hodderbooks to be a part of our community
of people who love the very best in books and reading.

Whether you want to discover more about a book
or an author, watch trailers and interviews, have the
chance to win early limited editions, or simply browse
our expert readers' selection of the very best books,
we think you'll find what you're looking for.

And if you don't,
that's the place to tell us what's missing.

We love what we do, and we'd love you to be part of it.

www.hodder.co.uk

 @hodderbooks

 HodderBooks

HodderBooks

AS A DETECTIVE IN THE LAPD THREAT MANAGEMENT UNIT,

Arvo Hughes has dealt with every kind of stalker there is – and in 1990s Hollywood, he's not short of work.

Tasked with finding out who has been sending unsettling anonymous letters to beautiful TV star Sarah Broughton, Arvo expects this case to be nothing out of the ordinary – until the actress discovers a strangely mutilated body left in the sand outside her beach house.

Certain that Sarah's stalker must have met her before, Arvo realises his only chance to catch the killer before he gets closer to Sarah is to delve into her past. But nothing is straightforward in this case, and the squeaky-clean star seems to be keeping all memories of a shady history locked away . . .

'Classic Robinson: labyrinthine plot merged with deft characterisation' *OBSERVER*

'Gut wrenching plotting . . . top-notch police procedure' JEFFERY DEAVER

Fiction £7.99
Ebook and Audiobook available

ISBN 978-1-473-62682-9

9 781473 626829

H hodder.co.uk
inspectorbanks.com

🐦 @HodderBooks

f /hodderbooks
/PeterRobinsonAuthor

Peter Robinson is the author
of the bestselling DCI Banks
crime novels, now a major
TV series starring Stephen
Tompkinson. *No Cure for Love*
was originally published in
1995, and is now available
in the UK for the first time.